# A PRIEST'S AFFAIR

# A PRIEST'S AFFAIR

*By*

Neville Symington

Free Association Books

**FA**<sup>B</sup>

Published in the United Kingdom 2004
by Free Association Books
57 Warren Street W1T 5NR

© 2004 Neville Symington

*British Library Cataloguing in Publication Data*
A catalogue record for this book is available from the British Library

Produced by Bookchase (UK) Ltd
Printed and bound in the EU

ISBN    1  853437  64  6
D. L.: SE-4002-2004 in Spain

# Table of contents

# CHAPTER ONE

He was sitting on his settee saying Vespers when it happened. Nothing like it had ever occurred before. He was mouthing the words just as usual when he looked up and paused for a moment at the end of the psalm. He felt something like a jet of water springing up from his stomach and bubbling over in the region of his chest and at the same moment he felt God as someone on his level whom he could take or leave, say *'Hello'* or *'Good-bye'* to. He could speak to him as to a friend. Instead of being an automaton that just 'did' what he was told he felt he could freely choose to do what he wanted and that God could do the same. He felt that he and God were like two partners in a ballet, freely swinging to the melody of the music whereas before God had been like Mao-Tse-Tung at a mass-rally; a tyrant, like Suleiman the Magnificent, giving fierce commands to which he bowed his head in craven obedience.

Fr. Stonewell put down his breviary and walked to the window. There was old Mrs. O'Brien, stick in hand, making her way over the zebra crossing, past the statue of Gladstone, towards the Church. She looked as he had seen her on numerous occasions but now she looked forbidding and Fr. Stonewell felt irritated by her. There she was, walking bolt upright under a heavy matting of crisp white hair. She came with righteous loyalty to the Holy Eucharist every day and was always first at the communion rail. She was entitled to her special place in the front pew. Her numerous prayers had surely earned her that right? She was someone that Fr. Stonewell and his parish priest, Fr. Smithes, could always rely upon. She was absolutely faithful and came to Mass every day and on Sundays she came twice. Fr. Stonewell had had a patronizing affection for this loyal soul but now, as he looked at her walking imperiously across the road, seeming to expect that everyone should know her parochial importance, he felt furious and wondered why he was wasting his time ministering to this sanctimonious old bag but he was only aware of it fleetingly; it soon went below the surface though still governing his emotional attitudes. Soon his extraordinary feeling about God and himself came back and absorbed all his perceptions. He paced up and down the room. He leapt in the air and yelled to himself, *'I have choice.'* Suddenly he understood what freedom meant. He did not <u>have</u> to say his office; he did not <u>have</u> to pray, he did not <u>have</u> to say the rosary. He did not <u>have</u> to say Mass. God was a person who invited him to converse in a friendly manner with him whenever he wanted to respond to the invitation. It was a free invitation not a command. Fr. Stonewell could not believe it. He remembered now with a new vividness Fr. Conan peering through black rimmed spectacles and telling them all in the lecture hall that it was a mortal sin if they omitted any one of the nine hours of the daily office. He had not been ordained long; the ordination's holy oil had hardly evaporated from the backs of his hands. He had been saying the priestly office, the prayer of the Church, every day unquestioningly since he had become a subdeacon two years before. It had often been difficult to fit all the nine hours of the office within the time span of a day but the Church, to ensure that the law was kept, allowed certain hours of the office to be said the evening before and the deadline of midnight was extended until midday of the following day. Making the most of these licences, Fr. Stonewell had never failed to say the day's office since the day he knelt in the College Chapel and received the subdiaconate at the hands of the bishop. He said the office systematically and without question; it was a privilege to abide by the Church's sacred charge to all her priests to offer praise to God on behalf of all the people of the Church and behind the Church's regulations was a God whose all-embracing power was total. He thought that he worshipped a God of love but at this moment, on that fateful Thursday afternoon in early September he knew with vivid certainty that he had been possessed by a tyrant God but no longer, he told himself with emphasis. This God had been banished from his seat in the heavens or so Fr. Stonewell believed. It was strange because he thought that he had put away the tyrant God and exchanged him for a God of Love while in the seminary but his emotions had been deceived by the excitement of words. What happened to him now on this Thursday afternoon was the real thing. It was a revolution at the heart of the earth.

Fr. Stonewell had been brought up within the bosom of a large Catholic family and the truths of the Church were something which he had never questioned. When he was being instructed for his first communion at the age of eight by an Irish nun she had told him that to receive communion in a state of grace he must be free of mortal sin and she had frightened him by saying that it was a mortal sin if he went to communion after eating something and that, on the morning that he was going to communion, he would have to fast from food and drink from midnight. He had received his first communion and his second in his parish Church with all his family amidst the smiles of numerous relatives and other devout Catholics. Then his third communion was due to be on Easter Sunday but when he woke in the morning he forgot all about holy communion when he noticed by his bed some chocolate buttons left by the beneficent Easter Bunny and before he had thought further he had eaten a couple. Then he remembered and put his hand over his mouth aghast. His mother would be angry anyway because he was not supposed to eat sweets or chocolate until after lunch so, frightened and worried, he went to communion and on his way back from Church while all the family was talking cheerfully he returned home knowing that he had committed a sin of the most grievous kind. He would put it right however, he said to himself, by going to confession. However when he went to the Church the following Friday to make his confession the priest patted him on the shoulder saying, 'Now what little sins have you committed since your first confession' and Anthony, now a sinner as bad as the worst murderer, dared not shock gentle Fr. Donnellan and so he left the confessional not only with mortal sin on his soul but having committed sacrilege as well. The Church taught that if you went to confession with a mortal sin on your soul and did not confess it to the priest, it was treating the Church's holy sacrament with the worst contempt so if he died now he knew that the devil would take him straight into the jaws of hell. So Anthony Stonewell, to all the world a pious lad, was growing at this early age into a hardened sinner. It was only four years later at school that he dared to tell a priest in confession of his monstrous crime. The priest just simply said, *"You were to frightened to tell, were you?"*and when Anthony nodded, the priest murmured the words of absolution over him. A huge weight fell off his shoulders but strangely he felt empty inside, no doubt because he had no one to share his forgiveness with but he felt so bad and now so relieved to have been rescued from the eternal fires of damnation that he went into the school chapel and on his knees told God how sorry he was and promised with all the seriousness of a public vow that when he grew into a man he would offer himself heart and soul to God as a priest. He was now a sacrificial victim; this was his destiny and he grabbed onto it in a passionate embrace. It was like Luther who offered himself in sacrifice to God after having narrowly escaped death in a thunderstorm but this was worse, hell being eternal torment whereas a thunderstorm is a passing physical danger.

When he reached manhood; in fact on his twenty-first birthday he remembered his vow. He thought he could dismiss it but that night, after a party celebrating his birthday, he remembered his vow. He heard a voice saying,

*"If you break a promise to God, he will cast you into hell,"* and he tossed and turned all night but, as dawn broke, he heard a cock crowing in the yard outside. He immediately thought of St. Peter who had denied all knowledge of Jesus. Like Peter he wept for his disloyalty and in that moment swore an oath that he would obey God and become a priest. So it was, that four months later he found himself robed in a cassock together with a flock of fellow students at Newman College which was the seminary for the diocesan priests of London and the south of England.

He still believed in a tyrant God when he arrived at the seminary – a huge rambling set of buildings straddling the brow of a low-lying hill in the green meadows of Hertfordshire. He arrived in the last months of the Pontificate of Pius XII in a taxi crammed with four other students nervously joking as it made its way up the A10 and then, shortly before reaching the little village of Puckeridge it swung left through large iron gates and up the drive to an ugly red-brick portico. It was a mild September evening and, after hauling out his suitcase, he and the others were met and ushered into the cold stoney precincts of what was to become, except for short excursions away in the holidays, his home for the next six years. And it was here that a mighty intellectual change was wrought in him. The staff of the college was divided into two distinct camps: those who believed that God was a fiercesome autocrat who demanded obedience above all else and those who taught and believed that God's essential substance was Love. This difference was typified in the doctrine of the Redemption from Sin as taught by Fr. Conan who was the Professor of Moral Theology as opposed to a salvation wrought by a God of love as taught by Fr. Darrell who was the Professor of Dogmatic Theology.

For the first two or three months Anthony stayed tightly clasping onto the simple but fiercesome faith that he had been brought up in until he bumped into his two friends Stephen Warrior and Joe Feeney who were leaning up against the style that led from the College lawn into a field beyond that housed some sombre cows and sheep. As Anthony approached Stephen was talking,

*"Fr. Conan believes that God is like one of those twisted Irish nuns who is mortally wounded at hearing someone use bad language …"* Stephen, with his red curly hair and freckled face, was laughing as he spoke and, at the same time, putting his hands to his chest imitating a shock-faced nun. Stephen looked up at Anthony and peered intently at his pointed nose, fair hair and light blue eyes.

*"Now, don't be so fast to make it an Irish nun …"* smiled Joe *"an English one will do the trick just as well."*

Stephen gave Joe a friendly punch in the tummy but then went on unperturbed,

*"Fr. Conan believes in a God that has been so wounded by Adam's wretched little sin."* and here Stephen stopped and raised his right hand in an accusing gesture to imitate an imperious headmaster ticking off a naughty little boy *"…so now Adam, said God, you've been very naughty stealing that apple and I'm very disappointed in you. After all I had done for you. I am very hurt…"* and now Stephen crossed his hands over his breast with his two hands reaching his upper arms, *"and nothing you can do can ever make it better…"* and Stephen, imitating the offended God, cupped his hands and made as if to cry into them.

*"What about all his rage and fury to be sure?"* asked Joe Feeney in his inimitable Irish voice.

*"Well, I suppose offended people soon take revenge,"* and both looked at Anthony and he was as surprised as they were. Suddenly spirited words had taken possession of this timid mouse and where had they come from? He was not excited by his sudden outburst but rather frightened of what had taken possession of him. But before he knew where he was Stephen clapped him on the shoulder,

*"Well done,"* said Stephen bowing, *"our resident psychologist to the rescue!"*

*"That's it then we have an angry savage God taking revenge for having hurt him. That's Fr. Conan's God."*

*"Not only Fr. Conan's,"* said Anthony.

*"Every Catholic in Ireland believes just that,"* said Joe Feeney.

*"Let me finish, now let me finish,"* said Stephen. Stephen was shorter in height than Anthony but about the same age but Joe was at least ten years older than the two of them. Looking around at one who was taller and the other who was older Stephen became more than ever determined to finish his colloquy on Fr. Conan's philosophy of man's Redemption.

*"Nanny Conan's view is that God was **so** offended that he now turned savage"* turning as he said this and raised his eyebrows at Anthony in a smile of congratulation, *"and said 'You silly puny man can never mend my poor broken heart.'"* and Stephen acted the jilted lover and flung himself on the ground weeping, quickly jumping up again and laughingly said, *"so God said – 'only a member of my own family who knows my heart and shares my wonderful power can put all the pieces of my heart together again. I will send my Son, only my Son, my dearly beloved Son, can make things better for me'"* Stephen stopped, panted and said, *"God I must have a fag"* and he took out a packet of Gauloises, lit up and blew some smoke in the air. Anthony was just about to speak when Stephen stretched out his hand,

*"Now psychologist, just let me finish. The worst of the whole thing is that then we still are loaded with all the same business – 'Every time you sin,' says Nanny Conan, 'you give a pain to poor Jesus in his Agony in Gethsemane, makes his road to Calvary even more painful. It's dreadful, instead of having a God of majesty who loves us out of bursting generosity we have this miserable offended self-centred God that we all have to beat our breasts about … that is the God that Nanny Conan tries to inculcate into us'."*

Until then Anthony had drunk in all that Fr. Conan taught as a good little 'divine' should and it was not difficult because it was just as he had been taught since he was a small child. It was exactly what Mother Traynor, the Dorothean nun, had taught him when he was preparing for his First Communion at the age of eight. The students at Newman College were called 'divines'. This very word instilled even more indelibly into Anthony's heart the seriousness of his high calling. What Fr. Conan had to say about birth control was the same as what he had heard at school in his classes of religious instruction except more detailed. How long Anthony would have gone on believing all this had he not met Clarence Cider is uncertain but the combination of Fr. Darrell's lectures and his friendship with Clarence, Joe, Stephen, Rudolph, Jamie and Sean wrought a change in him; a ray of light touched the surface of his soul.

What Stephen Warrior had said that day had already touched something in him but Stephen was something of a joker and although he knew he was serious yet he kept what he said in the outer perimeter of his heart, not letting it take possession within. The change occurred at a lecture being given by Fr. Darrell which shocked him out of his servitude to a tyrant God. He was sitting listening as Sidney Darrell, in his blunt Bristol accent, began putting a series of challenging questions before the divines who were sitting in docile homage before him: *Was God really offended by Adam's sin?* asked Fr. Darrell looking challengingly at the rows of passive faces in front of him. He stroked the fingers of his right hand through his mouse-coloured hair, turning his head with its sharply pointed nose to right and to left. *What sort of God is it who can be so hurt?* he asked roughly and as he did so looked piercingly at row after row of dazed young men. There they all were in their black cassocks bending over their tired exercise books. He looked annoyed as he saw them all slavishly writing away. *What sort of God is it,* he said, *who is so wounded by an insult? Is God like some offended hostess at a party where a guest has criticized her cooking? Is this the sort of God we believe in?* He glared even more violently at his impassive audience. *Don't we admire someone who can triumph over such an insult? Can we really believe that the Infinite One who stretched out the Heavens and the Earth was personally wounded by one of his creatures? That he went crying like a hurt child demanding that he receive an apology? Is this the God we believe in? Can we really bend in worship to such a God?* At this point Sidney Darrell, whom the divines called 'Sid' for short, was almost shouting and the tones of his Bristol accent echoed off the back wall of the lecture hall. *God is a God of magnificent love, of power and fantastic goodness. He had no need to create the world. It is a mystery that man cannot fathom, that his Love was so enormous that he poured it out into a new creation – not only the world, this planet, but the sun, the stars and the whole immensity of the universe? This is the God who has made us and has come down to us in the form of his Son, Jesus Christ, so that we can all share the marvels of his eternal life.* As Fr. Darrell spoke this, his voice trembled for a moment and almost trilled like a soprano on top note and then he looked nervously ahead of him and, as if ashamed of having allowed emotion to interfere with a theological discourse, he quickly returned to the measured tones of the theological scientist. Anthony had heard Stephen say this very thing a few days before but, then, he had been able to half-dismiss it but now it was being pronounced in the Cardinal Bourne Lecture Hall by England's leading theologian. He could push it away no longer. Then, almost as suddenly as his impulse to become a priest had taken hold of him he was now convinced that all he had believed about God being a God of fearful justice was heresy and a rage took hold of him as he remembered the way he had been tortured by these false teachings. As soon as this lecture was over he went to his room that looked out upon the stone statue of Cardinal Newman. His room was small and sparsely furnished: an iron bedstead, a simple pine table for a desk and a chest of drawers. Above the chest of drawers he had placed a print of Salvador Dali's *Christ of St. John of the Cross* he looked round the room and then went to the window so he could look at the Newman statue unencumbered. He looked at it lovingly. He believed that Sidney Darrell shared John Henry Newman's largeness of vision. He looked once more at the statue against its background of three plain trees swaying in the wind. He turned back to his room and he cast his leather-bound volume of *The Imitation of Christ* into his waste-paper basket on a violent impulse saying, as he did so *The Die is Cast* there was no turning back now. He became convinced that all this sentimental piety in which he had been so faithfully reared was a fearful heresy. He had a small relic of St. Thérèse of Lisieux in the top draw of his chest of drawers. He opened it quickly, took out the relic and cast that into the waste-paper basket also. He became intellectually convinced that all these relics and sentimental piety was part of this fawning over a self-pitying God. This conviction became even more passionate after a long talk with Clarence Cider and then by the members of the Doktor Klub which Clarence had founded.

Anthony now had this verse of Isaiah written on a card above his desk:

"Let him turn back to Yahweh who will take pity on him,
to our God who is rich in forgiving;
for my thoughts are not your thoughts,
my ways not your ways – it is Yahweh who speaks.
Yes, the heavens are as high above earth
as my ways are above your ways,
my thoughts above your thoughts."[1]

So this person who could so easily be offended could not be God but rather, as Fr. Darrell had suggested, some human imposter pretending to be God and, what is more, a being of intense sensitivity. This is the way Anthony still thought as the seminary turned him out into the world on the Church's pastoral mission five and a half years later. Anthony had utterly repudiated the idea of God as a self-centred, self-conscious, moaner filled with self-pity. He had become the champion of a triumphant God of Love; a God who saw a damaged mankind who could not help himself out of his predicament and so had entered the world to

---

[1] Isaiah Ch. 55. vv.7–9.

bind up the wounds of erring men and women and bring them into fellowship and happiness with the Eternal God who was full of light and joy. A God who can be hurt needs lawyers to protect him against man's myriad trespasses and Anthony had come to see the Church as littered with laws to protect an anthropomorphic God. *Love God and do what you will*, St. Augustine had said and this became Anthony's inner motto. It was shared by his friends, Clarence Cider, Joe Feeney, Stephen Warrior, Rudolph Novak, Jamie McLeod and Sean Casey who were all ordained with him at the same time and on the same day by the same Cardinal in Westminster Cathedral. They were a small platoon in attack, an advance guard, that would each take their target parish by storm.

Every day at College when Fr. Conan had got up into his rostrum to instruct his students in the principles of moral theology the subject was sin and, for some reason, the most sinful of all sins were sexual. Sex within marriage was allowed but this was an especial concession granted by the Church to frail man but the better path was complete abstinence such as all Catholic priests had opted to follow. Masturbation was always sinful, Fr. Conan used to say, looking round as he said it to see if he could see any shameful faces. But it was not just masturbation but even a sexual thought was gravely sinful:

> *"You have learnt how it was said: **You must not**
> **commit adultery**. But I say to you: if a man looks
> at a woman lustfully, he has already committed
> adultery with her in his heart."*[2]

So any thought or feeling that had the slightest sexual taint was massively offensive to God. Slowly, as Anthony changed the direction of his belief from a severe punishing God to a God of Love so slowly his attitude to the sinfulness of sexual misdemeanours changed. Perhaps sex was not so bad after all, he thought. *Even for a priest*, he heard inside him. Was it God or was it the devil?

Anthony met Clarence properly a few months after arriving at the seminary. He had seen him in that smokey Common Room. It was the room that all the divines hastened into as soon as lunch and supper were over. As soon as they were in this room out came a hundred packets of fags and, as cigarette after cigarette were lit up, so this long rectangular room with a billiard table at one end and a piano at the other and the

---

[2] Matthew Ch. 5 v. 27.

walls surrounded with fabric chairs in steel frames and, like so many rooms in institutional buildings, was painted to shoulder height in dark green and then in a pasty cream up to the ceiling. It was designed this way to save money because the dark green did not show the dirty marks so easily. The bursar of the College had done his sums. It was here in this smoke-filled room that Anthony first caught sight of Clarence. Anthony was tall with blond hair and a slightly stooping back. Clarence seemed at least a foot shorter but, in reality, was just six inches shorter. He wore un-rimmed glasses and had thin black hair. He was at least fifteen years older than Anthony. They had just begun to talk when two other divines inter-rupted and Clarence quickly sidled away. So Anthony had not engaged in any serious conversation until a sunny cold afternoon in early December when Clarence appeared at some distance out of the south doorway of the college. Anthony had just decided to go and have a close look at the Pugin Chapel from the outside when Clarence came out of the doorway, looked up towards the sun and then round at the grassy meadow before beginning to walk slowly in Anthony's direction. At that moment Anthony was walking slowly past the Newman statue which looked so much bigger from this vantage point than from his bedroom window. Unlike the one outside the Brompton Oratory in Knightsbridge which depicted the famous convert as a decrepit old man this statue, carved by Eric Gill, portrayed him as a good looking young man, perhaps still in his Oxford days before that signal day in 1845 when Dominic Barberi received him into the Roman Catholic Church. Newman in the nine-teenth century and Ronnie Knox in the twentieth were the Catholic Church's great triumphs in England. They were surely proof that Catholi-cism was the true faith and the Anglican Church in fatal error.

Anthony liked the look of Clarence and had a very definite feeling that he was about to begin a deep friendship. He had no idea why he should be gripped by such an idea but his conviction of it grew as Clarence walked slowly but definitively towards him. As Anthony saw him approaching he slowed down so Clarence could join him. He was dressed in a perfectly tailored cassock. Anthony still felt strangely proud of himself dressed, as he was, in his own cassock since arriving at College four months before. Shortly before arriving at the seminary he had been to visit a cousin who was a nun and she had told him that he would feel quite different once he had donned his cassock and she was right. He had stepped into it the morning after arriving at the College and the moment he had done so, it gave him a strong sense of brotherhood with the other divines and, at the same time, increased his feeling of alienation from the world. He also felt womanish in it. As he put it over his head for the first time he felt all virulent potency drain away from him. A few days after arriving at the college, he had gone out in his dog collar to the local village and was shocked to find that shopkeepers looked at him differently. He remembered going into a chemist shop to buy a toothbrush and the man behind the counter hushed the girl who was talking to him and spoke in a tone which was more deferential than before. *What can I get you, Reverend,* he asked as he hushed at the woman at his side. A man of God had entered his premises and demanded a higher level of conversation. At the beginning Anthony did not like this feeling of being other but, as the weeks went by, he began to get used to it until he no longer noticed it. Later he felt tortured by being so distanced from the common man and came to wear his dog-collar as little as possible. By then he passionately wanted to drive a bridge across the chasm that separated him from others. It became part of his mission to bring the Church and common man into closer connexion with one another. But, at this early time in the seminary, he was still proud to be dressed in priestly garb. So, as Clarence approached him, he preened himself in his new cassock, feeling pleasure in his new estate. When Anthony first arrived at the seminary he believed he should love all his hundred fellow divines equally because this is what God had commanded. He must not show any preference for one over another – that would be sinful, he thought. Although he was still six years from his objective he was beginning to feel a priest already and fancied himself as one of the holiest of the divines. He believed he was a saint. In the evenings he prayed for long hours before the Blessed Sacrament and was shocked to see the priests of the staff disappearing out of the chapel as soon as Compline had been sung in the evening. He prided himself on being holier than them. He kept the rules, was meticulous about sexual thoughts, said the rosary devoutly. He believed that he had already achieved a high level of sanctity and that one day he would be canonized. To be holy was the goal not only of all his religious activities at Newman College but of his whole life. He had only been in the college six weeks when he felt certain that upon his death this would be quickly recognized. There would be a storm of devotion to him like that which had descended upon St. Thérèse of Lisieux so soon after her death. He, like her, would be shrouded in a storm of glory. But he would leave it in his will that no relics were to be inherited by his devoted followers.

He looked up and as Clarence was upon him he put out his hand,

*"I'm Clarence Cider,"* he said through pursed lips. *"I've seen you but have not met you properly yet – only once for a moment in that smoke factory in there,"* gesturing his hand impudently towards that part of the building where the Common Room was situated. He stood quite erect and, looking at Anthony, he spoke a little like a radio announcer as if he were addressing more people than just Anthony.

*"Yes hello, I'm Anthony Stonewell,"* he said a little stiffly and a bit unsure of himself, *"I was just about to walk around the chapel and have a closer look at it from the outside. Join me?".*

*"Yes, but I want to ask you what you thought of Sid Darrell's lecture today?"* asked Clarence.

He had clearly approached Anthony with the express purpose of exacting from him his opinion on this precise matter. Anthony was a bit disconcerted. He was used to some preamble prior to serious discussion. He could see though that this was not Clarence's style.

*"You mean the one on Christ, Our Saviour, the Great Sacrament, as he called it?"*

*"Yes, I thought it was terrific,"* said Anthony, *"I had never realized before that Christ was present throughout the life and activities of the Church …"*

*"And not only the Church,"* snapped Clarence rapidly, *"Sid was saying that Christ is present in the whole of humanity and that the visible Church's role is to give witness to that."*

*"You mean that Christ is present even **outside** the Church?"* asked Anthony with trembling diffidence. Clarence looked very severe and Anthony felt nervous.

*"Yes, of course he is. How **could** you think he wasn't?"* said Clarence with avid petulance. *"Christ redeemed the whole of mankind both those who were born before his time and those beyond the bounds of the visible Church. What did you believe that only those belonging to the Church can be saved? That outside the Church there is no salvation."* Clarence trembled as he spoke these last two sentences because the sentiments behind them were greater than his small frame could manage. His body literally shook under a concentrated emotion.

*"Well, that is what I've always been taught,"* said Anthony nervously. *"So how are people saved? I thought that was the whole point of being in the Church."*

*"My heavens,"* said Clarence, *"what arrogant selfishness – that you belong to the Church, that you are a Catholic just so that beautiful you can be saved. My heavens, how shocking. You can't really believe that?"*

It had never struck Anthony like that before and yet, as Clarence said this with such precision, it struck him as shocking. He looked up and then away for a moment. One of the cows was lowing. Anthony looked up and there were some dark clouds massing towards them. He had heard a farmer friend say that when the cattle are lowing it is a sign that a storm is approaching. He looked back at Clarence. His lips were quivering slightly.

"I thought," said Anthony, *"that only those who are baptized can be saved."*

"That's true," said Clarence with lips open only to the extent of a thin slit, *"Yes but baptizm is internal. It can occur when water is poured over someone's head but also be by desire or by fire."*

*"By desire?"* exclaimed Anthony skeptically. *"What **do** you mean?"* It was his turn to become emphatic. He felt that all his certainties were about to collapse and his very bodily frame was extremely fragile. He looked away for a moment. The plain trees were now swishing in the wind. He could see a few other divines walking down the drive towards the little sub-post-office at the large iron gates of the College. He looked at the sky again and thought it would soon rain.

*"It's the inner desire to be loving that joins us to Jesus, that baptizes us into Christ,"* said Clarence trenchantly. *"Pouring water over someone's head does nothing without any inner desire. It's the inner desire that makes baptizm what it is."*

*"If that's the case,"* asked Anthony doubtfully. He looked at Clarence with pursed lips and almost wanted to stop the conversation but took courage and continued, *"then what is the point of the actual sacrament of baptizm where the priest pours water over the baby's head."*

*"You see,"* said Clarence assuming a didactic tone, *"the sacrament is the outer confirmation of the inner state of affairs. The Church declares 'This is the person saved through God's love in Christ Jesus'."*

*"But then,"* asked Anthony, *"how do we know that the person baptized with water does have a loving heart?"*

*"It is,"* said Clarence, *"the Church's declaration that this is the person's new nature, his new birth. It is then the person's job to find that nature in himself and to live it. The outer ritual of baptism does not mean anything unless it is accompanied by an inner conversion of the heart and that goes for all the sacraments. The way people believe that they are forgiven in the confessional just because the priest mumbles a few words over them is a scandal. Non-Catholics are quite right to be scornful of such a procedure."*

Anthony mumbled under his breath. This was a revolutionary way of seeing things. Clarence was substituting love and commitment for magic but Anthony had been schooled in magic. Magic had been the religious coinage of his upbringing. He could feel the building toppling and he was terrified by it. He looked at the statue of Newman who said that if you disbelieve one brick of the edifice then the whole thing crumbles. He felt a constriction in his throat. For a moment he thought he was going to choke. As he tried to steady himself, he felt a little tremor of excitement, a seed of life springing up among the ruins. He remembered once walking into an old ruined building and out through a crack in the floor was sprouting a daffodil in full bloom. This memory came unexpectedly into his mind and he felt a thrill of excitement rushing through him. Then he pondered. There was something else he wanted to ask but he had lost his train of thought for a moment. Then suddenly it came to him,

*"Well what about baptism by fire?"* asked Anthony. He remembered in a religious instruction class at school the priest saying that there could be baptism by fire.

*"It's desire that is the heart of baptizm but, apart from water being poured, the other sign is martyrdom. If someone dies for the sake of Christ, joined in his sufferings then he is together with Jesus in his Passion and enters into His glory in heaven."*

*"Baptizm by fire,"* repeated Anthony. He rolled the words around in a large cavity in his head and they echoed round the walls of it and then he asked, *"what if someone is already baptized with water, has then sinned, sinned mortally but then goes through a martyrdom without going to confession and dies?"*

*"That desire to enter into the sufferings of Christ and then doing so dissolves all sin. It is the perfect consummation to life."*

The two men stood there in silence; Anthony contemplating what he had just heard and Clarence watching his new convert piercingly through his glasses. Clarence watched Anthony. His eyes glinted. Clarence could see him flinging himself onto the flames like a widow committing *suttee* in India. As the silence began to become awkward Clarence said decidedly,

*"It makes complete nonsense of Old Nanny Conan's moral casuistry."* Clarence spat with contempt as he spoke the word *Nanny*.

*"I don't see the connection,"* said Anthony. He felt an urge to get away. He looked again at the clouds. They had stopped but Anthony started walking again towards the Pugin Chapel which was only fifty yards away.

*"Well, "said Clarence," Sid Darrell's lecture placed all our morality as a free response to God and leaves our own free choice as the centre of morality. It means ultimately that it is up to the individual whether he practises birth control or not, for instance."*

*"But surely birth control is selfish."* said Anthony nervously. Clarence had spoken in an abrupt way that took Anthony aback.

*"How do you **mean**?"* snapped Clarence angrily.

*"Well it is generous hearted to have children and not to lead a selfish life where you want to indulge your own self-interest first."*

*"That's the complacent talk of a celibate priest,"* chimed Clarence, *"What about the young Irish couple living in two rooms in Finsbury Park who have three children already, would you call them selfish if they decided to have no more?"*

*"But the Pope says it's wrong",* said Anthony, feeling that he was talking to a traitor.

*"I know he does but Popes have often been wrong in history and have revised their opinions and birth control does not involve papal infallibility anyway. But I could not care a fig for all that legal stuff. I am saying that ultimately an individual is left by himself before God and he must choose. Come on, let's walk on to the chapel."* Clarence patted his cassock and with his left hand steered Anthony in the direction of the Pugin chapel, *"It's too cold to stand on a December day."*

*"Once you've said that, then you can ditch the Pope, bishops, priests and the whole lot. If it is just between yourself and God and if that is what you believe then you are a Protestant,"* thought Anthony but did not dare to voice it. He began to feel worried because he had heard one or two divines saying that Clarence had been an Anglican monk before being converted to the Catholic Church. He began to wonder if he wasn't still a Protestant at heart – a wolf in sheep's clothing. Perhaps his conversion to Catholicism was all a sham. He looked at Clarence and suddenly saw him at the side of Luther. Luther, as depicted in Lucas Cranach's painting of him came up before his eyes and there beside the reformer he saw Clarence at his side, holding his hand.

*"You need teaching <u>and</u> guidance,"* said Clarence, *"but what I am saying is that <u>in the last resort</u> what determines your choices lies with you and your conscience."*

*"That's really Protestant teaching,"* said Anthony, summoning his courage.

*"Oh, no it's not,"* said Clarence, *"it is part of Catholic teaching that the individual's guide is his own conscience and that he must follow it even if it*

*leads him into error."* Then Clarence turned toward the statue of Newman and round the foot of it was a little knot of divines, their cassocks blowing in the wind. *He,* said Clarence gesturing towards the statue, *said that if he had to choose between his conscience and a dictate by the Pope he would go with his conscience.*

*"Where does he say that?"* barked Anthony resentfully.

*"Oh, I can find it for you if you want but I assure you that it is true and Thomas Aquinas also said that the ultimate guide in moral matters is the individual's own conscience. Although this college is dedicated to Cardinal Newman and we all bow our heads to him yet as soon as anyone dares to relay what Newman actually taught and believed everyone gets in a flutter like chickens when a fox has got into the chicken run. Whenever I pass Newman's statue I salute him inwardly and remind myself that conscience is primary."* Clarence spoke with all the authority of the Pope himself.

*"What's the place of the teaching Church?"* asked Anthony, feeling sure he was being led into heresy. He thought of his father who had taught him so firmly the rightness of the Catholic Church and how lucky we were to have an infallible guide whereas the Protestants were left straying in the wilderness. Now here was a Catholic spitting on all that he had believed and loved. He thought of his father whom he loved above all men and now here was Clarence trying to lead him away from his dearest parent. It was only later that he realized with some horror that Nanny Conan's belief was his father's also.

*"Our consciences are very obscured and it is often difficult to reach a decision in complex matters. The role of the hierarchy is to offer guidance but it abuses its role when it becomes a dictator. The heart of morality is that the individual makes a choice and does not know whether what he has chosen is right or not. He bows his head humbly before God, leaving him to judge. To believe that I am definitely right and that others are wrong is the most shocking arrogance."* As Clarence said these last words he threw his right arm out and downwards like a conductor with his baton and then looked at Anthony defiantly, daring him to oppose what he had just said.

*"What about all the teaching of the Councils through the ages on doctrinal matters?"* asked Anthony clinging desperately to his point of view but feeling it crumbling beneath his feet. He looked round despairingly at the statue of Newman as if that saintly cardinal would come to his rescue.

*"That is different from morality. Here the Church is stating her faith in the facts of our Redemption, that God, the Second Person of the Trinity, has entered our world in the figure of Christ Jesus and all that flows from that amazing*

*fact."* As Clarence said this Anthony began to experience something of Clarence's passion and sincerity and no longer felt him trying to undermine his faith which was so precious to him. At the same time he felt a certain relief. Although he did not know it, there was something cloying and imprisoning about the dogmatisms to which he had clung so tenaciously since his earliest years. He felt his intellect being liberated and joining forces with an emotional current that was charging deep inside him. He looked at Clarence's blood-drained face staring in front of him pale and ghost-like. Anthony could see that he had suffered and his own youth and innocence suddenly made him shy. Clarence's whole being was in his vocation; he had been at it for years. Anthony had only just started.

*"To come back to Sid Darrell's lecture,"* said Clarence, *"his point is that Christ has entered human history and become part of the human condition and that we have an encounter with him in the sacraments and that all our behaviour is a response to that free encounter; so morality is nothing to do with being told what to do but rather responding with love to love, man's love to God's love which has reached out to us."* This time Clarence spoke in a tone which was a little more tender. He brushed from his cassock a leaf that had fallen on it and looked up and smiled.

*"But couldn't that way of looking at things allow someone to indulge anything and so someone could say he could do no better; I mean people might just say 'God loves us' and just lie back and sin to their heart's content,"* said Anthony feebly trying a last-ditch attempt to safeguard his dearest loyalties. He looked around, hoping almost, that someone would come and rescue him but that knot of divines by the statue were at least a hundred yard away by now as they were reaching the chapel and those other divines he had seen were still pounding up and down the main drive and obviously had no plan to come in their direction.

*"It's a narrow path between two extremes – on the one side imagining an ideal that you have to reach and the other just settling for where you are but the worst sin of all is to* <u>know</u> *you are right. Remember the parable of the Pharisee and the Publican. The Pharisee* <u>knew</u> *he had found favour in the sight of God whereas the Publican just begged for God's mercy on him, a sinner. And Jesus said that it was the Publican that had found salvation and not the Pharisee."* Clarence spoke again decidedly and, as Anthony looked at him, he could see his eyes looking at him through his unrimmed spectacles.

*"But you do have to reach the ideal,"* said Anthony, *"that is what holiness means. It is our attempt to reach perfection with God's help."* He was

now in utter dismay. Striving hard for perfection was what had driven him to be God's priest. He remembered how difficult it had been to confess his dreadful childhood sacrilege. Speaking his mind in the face of disapproval was intensely difficult. He had to strive, pray and devote all his energies to overcoming this difficulty. Now something completely different was hitting him in the face, like snow in a tempest.

*"Holiness is the acceptance of yourself as you are, warts and all. Know thyself is the prescription for holiness. It's the basis of human wisdom too, for that matter. The ideal, whatever it is, can never be reached. That's just a figment of imagination. Phew,"* said Clarence gesturing his right hand outwards, *"it's just a fantastic soap bubble and it's time we blew it away,"* and turning to Anthony he looked him full in the face and a warm smile suddenly flooded his features. Then he went on,

*"The sacraments are declarations of who we are, what our nature is; that we, together with the whole of humanity, have been redeemed in Christ. Holiness is finding that in ourselves; holiness is living that inner search – finding the seed of redemption in us and through recognition of it letting it grow inside us. It has nothing to do with striving for some imaginary ideal out there …"* and as he said this he swept his right hand out across the green fields of Hertfordshire.

Anthony looked back at Clarence. As he looked at him he saw that he had quite an old face with very little colour in his skin. His black hair was thinning and his unrimmed spectacles framed sad but penetrating eyes. Anthony had a sense that he had battled with these matters in his Anglican monastery and a momentary realization that it had probably been with great difficulty that he had left that comfortable haven for the rough waters of the Catholic Church. A sense that he was not trying to betray the faith but was embracing it more deeply began to take hold of Anthony and at that moment he conceived a warm love for Clarence that always stayed with him.

***"Love of ourselves with all our nastiness is the foundation stone of holiness,"*** went on Clarence pronouncing every word with precision. He might have been giving a discourse at a retreat for a hundred nuns and then he went on, *"when I was in the Anglican monastery I was given a long manuscript to type and I had to produce three copies of it, so used two carbon sheets. I had been typing for hours on end for three days when the paper went in crooked into the machine and I took it out and tried to make it right it but it went wrong again, going in crooked and then I took it out and by mistake started typing on the back of a sheet which I had* *already typed on. I got so furious that I tore up that sheet and all the others which I had typed and all that I had left in front of me were torn shreds of paper. I looked at them in dismay and then tip-toed to my spiritual director's cell and I told him bit by bit, in terrible fear, what had happened. When I told him how I'd got so furious that I tore up all the sheets of paper in a rage my spiritual director sank back in his chair and said, 'Oh, how marvellous'."*

Anthony laughed – that story appealed to him a lot, it touched something human in him and it confirmed his feeling of love and he had a further burst of affection for Clarence. It went against all that he'd thought but a deeper instinct told him that Clarence was right.

*"What about that bit in the Sermon on the Mount when Jesus says, 'Be ye perfect as your Heavenly Father is perfect'?"* asked Anthony not so much now in antagonistic defence of his position but in the spirit of genuine enquiry. He felt now that Clarence would have thought about it. He knew also, like most Anglican priests and monks, that he would know his scriptures really well.

*"In Luke's Gospel it says, 'Be ye merciful as your heavenly Father is merciful,'"* said Clarence factually.

*"But those are two different statements,"* said Anthony puzzled.

*"No they are probably not – they are just different interpretations of the one statement by the two Evangelists."*

*"Surely they just reported objective facts? They put down in words what Jesus had said surely?"* asked Anthony almost speechless with dismay.

*"They certainly didn't. They frequently report the same events with different slants and Luke includes things which suits his viewpoint and leaves out others that don't and Matthew does the same and so do Mark and John. That is why in the early Church the Evangelists played a much greater part in the affective life of the people and they are nearly always represented in early Christian art under their different symbolic forms. If the artist had left one of them out a whole lot of devoted Lucans, or Johannines, or Marcians or Matthewines would have caused a rumpus,"* said Clarence emphasizing the word 'rumpus' by raising his voice an octave higher.

*"You make everything sound very fluid and it makes me nervous",* said Anthony and at that moment the bell went for Vespers. Anthony had forgotten the time. It was a Saturday and he looked at his watch. He had five minutes within which to be in the College Chapel with his cotta and biretta on so he started to run but as he looked back he noticed that Clarence was walking and taking his time.

Then Clarence nudged him and said,

*"You should join the Doktor Klub,"*

*"What is the Doktor Klub?"* asked Anthony quizzically.

*"It is a group of five of us who meet on Thursday evenings and we discuss the Church but particularly Fr. Darrell's lectures and we don't stop until we all know clearly what he has been talking about and, if we do not understand something, one of us goes representing the group to ask Fr. Darrell to help us. We approach it from the point of view of catechumens who are learning about Christ and the Gospel as something new."*

*"What **are** catechumens?"* asked Anthony doubtfully.

"You *must* join," said Clarence. Then the two took their places in the College Chapel and in a few moments were chanting psalms together with a hundred of their brethren.

*  *  *

That evening later after supper and when Compline had been sung Anthony knelt for longer than he had ever done before. He felt his faith beginning to rock. He had never doubted the Catholic faith for a moment but Clarence had started something rumbling inside him. But at the same time he felt a warm glow of confidence springing up inside him and when he went up to his bedroom he felt a convert to a new faith, as if he had been a pagan until that date. Just before he went to sleep he found, to his surprise, that *'baptizm by fire'* kept coming back into his mind. Something about it fascinated him. He was magnetized by the words. He kept thinking of what Clarence had said: that all sins dissolved in a martyrdom when the person was joined to Christ in his Passion. Pictures of early Christians being mauled by lions in the Roman amphitheatre floated through him like dreams. To throw himself into the jaws of death had a sudden appeal. He would go straight to God. He felt excited by the idea. *'But it couldn't happen to me in a London parish'* he said to himself but, even as he had finished saying this to himself he retorted *'Perhaps it could; perhaps I could make it so'*. It took some time for the excitement to quieten down until finally his brain faded into sleep.

The next day Fr. Conan accosted him in the Common Room after lunch and invited him to walk down the College drive with him to the post-office which had been fashioned out of an old gatehouse. They had just begun walking when a divine called out from an upstairs window telling Fr. Conan he was wanted on the telephone. He hurried in and, hardly had he done so, when Stephen Warrior and Jamie McCleod were at his side,

*"You want to be very careful with Nanny Conan,"* said Stephen.

*"Why? and by the way why is he called Nanny?"* asked Anthony.

*"Oh, I can tell you why,"* chirped Jamie, *"have you ever noticed his hair?"*

*"Not especially,"* replied Anthony.

*"Well if you look you will see that his hair is always fluffy,"* said Jamie. *"Well he believes that hair is best washed in rainwater so you see that wooden barrel over there ..."* and Jamie pointed to a little fenced in group of meteorological instruments and on their nearside Anthony could see a small wooden barrel,

*"Yes, I can see it,"* said Anthony.

*"Well, that belongs to Nanny Conan. Twice a week on Tuesday and Saturday evenings you will see him go down with a large glass jug and he collects rainwater and washes his hair with it the next morning. That is why we all call him 'Nanny'."*

*"Well, it's quite quaint really,"* said Anthony.

*"You want to be very careful of him,"* said Stephen, *"I'm telling you. He's always looking out for gossip. He's our KGB man from the diocesan curia. He goes every week to the curial officials at Archbishop's House and passes on any information which he thinks will ingratiate him with the powers that be."* Stephen stopped for a moment and looked round to see if anyone was listening. *"You watch him in the Common Room, when he is talking to one person he is always looking this way and that to see what else is going on. He's an ignorant bastard too. He was having a conversation the other day with Rudolph who mentioned Etienne Gilson and he had never heard of him. He never thinks, he's like a ventriloquist's dummy to the Pope. I can tell you be very careful of Nanny Conan. All the priests on the staff know that he is a very vengeful man."* At this moment Jamie went *"Ugh, ugh"*, Stephen looked round and saw that Nanny Conan was just two yards away.

*"Are you and Jamie coming for a walk too?"* said Fr. Conan looking at Stephen but Stephen quickly replied,

*"No, no. We were just keeping Anthony company while he was waiting for you, Father ..."* and Stephen and Jamie moved off in a leisurely manner, sloping back towards the Common Room. So Anthony found himself walking down the tarmac drive with Nanny Conan. They talked for a while about the local dental services and then as they turned back up the drive and were walking up hill to the College and as they did so the conversation had slipped with the force of inexorable fate to the subject of pain and from

there by a slippery descent to the theme of punishment and then before Anthony could stop it the two men were talking about capital punishment.

Anthony hated capital punishment. As a sixteen-year-old he had read the biography of Gladys Aylward who, shortly after arriving in China, walked out into the market place and saw a man's head chopped off before her eyes with a sword in an official execution. He was almost sick when he read this and forever after thought capital punishment was abhorrent. He did not need Clarence or any of his new friends to convince him that capital punishment was a wickedness. So now he bridled as he heard Fr. Conan saying that capital punishment was morally good because the Church had declared it to be so. This declaration coming so soon after Stephen's warning of a moment ago and also following the conversation the previous evening with Clarence that it roused Anthony to defend his neophyte faith.

*"I don't see **how** killing a human being can be reconciled with the teachings of Jesus,"* said Anthony with firm timidity.

*"St. Thomas Aquinas said that when a human being has committed a serious crime he has made himself lower than the beasts and therefore the State has a right to kill the person just as it has a right to kill an animal. The person has lost his rights as a human citizen,"* said Fr. Conan in a tone that was reminiscent of a well trained altar boy chanting the correct response and as he spoke his furry head was bobbing up and down.

*"I still don't think it's right,"* stammered Anthony, *"it seems to me more in tune with God's mercy to grant someone his life and offer him the chance to reform."*

*"But you're wrong..."* said Nanny Conan and he started panting like a dog after a run. For a moment Anthony thought he was going to have a fit. *"I tell you it's wrong to hold that view. It is against the teachings of the Church. Wait here a moment..."* he scurried off with a very slight limp that made him a little lob-sided.

They had reached the building just by the library. Fr. Conan scuttled indoors and came out in less than two minutes brandishing a book with all the encyclicals of Pope Pius XII and hastened to read out a passage where the Pope said that Catholics were not to question the right of governments to punish a criminal with death.

*"But what's his reason for saying that?"* asked Anthony exasperated.

*"You have no right to enquire into that. I'm telling you that it's the teaching of the Church and I can't have given you clearer proof..."* he was exhaling heavily and his nostrils were flaring and enlarging with each breath.

Anthony felt enraged as he heard Fr. Conan cleaving to this papal dictum with unthinking dogmatism. He clenched his teeth in smouldering resentment. Luckily Fr. Conan rushed back with his precious book to return it to the library and when he re-emerged had decided to change the subject. He began talking about the new post-mistress who had arrived the day before. Anthony sighed inwardly with relief but remained exasperated. As Fr. Conan muttered on about the postal services Anthony slowly calmed down. The conversation turned to the English postal system and how much better it was than that of Spain or Italy and, sheltered by such harmless topics, the rest of the walk down to the post-office and back again passed without any further emotional outburst. So Anthony learned the art of steering conversations with Nanny along the harmless pathways of trivial subjects.

When Anthony first arrived at Newman College he thought that all priests were holy. Coming to know Nanny Conan slowly disabused him of this fact but he still thought that Nanny Conan was the unfortunate exception but it was Rudolph Novak who cleansed his mind forever of this belief that priests were holy, holier than other people. Rudolph had been to a Catholic school run by Jesuits and then gone to a Trappist monastery in southern Germany where he was in the novitiate for two years and then as a monk for a further two. He had gone to Germany because his grandfather had been pure German and the language was often spoken in his family. When he felt the call from God he knew he wanted to go to a monastery in Germany. He wanted to be one with the German people and make reparation for the Nazi war crimes. So in all he spent an intense four years as an apprentice monk before finally deciding to leave the monastery. He felt decisively called to serve God in the world but as a priest and, at the same time, he felt pulled back to England. So he went to the Vicar General of the Westminster Diocese who recommended that he spend two years in the world first so he went into the army. This brought him into touch with the world in a raw and unedited fashion. That sojourn in the world had been over for two years and he had now been for three years at Newman College. Rudolph told him that when he had been in the Trappist monastery he had asked the Abbot on one occasion whether he thought there could ever be a priest in hell. *'What?'* asked the Abbot in genuine surprise, *'Are you asking if there are any priests in Hell? I tell you, Rudolph, the place is paved with them.'* He had many conversations with Rudolph who told him that when he was in the army he had known a lance-corporal who was *'a bloody saint',* as Rudolph put it, and much more so than any of the monks in the Trappist monastery. All this was a shock to Anthony and in those first few weeks he had to assimilate the fact that priests suffered all the mean sinfulness as the rest of mankind.

These varied conversations, first with Clarence, that conspiratorial briefing from Stephen and Jamie and then that near-row with Fr. Conan which confirmed so exactly what Stephen had just told him put Anthony into a whirl. Now his talk with Rudolph just tipped all the fruit out of the wheelbarrow. He had dived into a pond with white skin and now come out gleaming yellow. He was only nineteen. He had never knowingly questioned the Church. He had been as dogmatic as Fr. Conan but never so limited. Even as a small boy he had had a questioning mind and ever since reading that biography of Gladys Aylward he had been passionately antipathetic to any law which gave the State permission to kill a human being but he had not realized that to support this intuition he had to argue his position logically and coherently and that this required him to be clear about what was Catholic faith as opposed to custom, however revered the latter might be. He had not realized when he had come to abhor capital punishment so vehemently that this was contrary to Catholic moral teaching. He had a vague idea that the Church endorsed it just as it supported the 'Just War' but it had not occurred to him that to follow through on this view and that, as he did so, other moral positions that the Church held would also come tumbling down in the wake of this first burst of steam in his engine. It was only after this conversation with Fr. Conan that he became determined to use his mind to the fullest extent possible and this outlook had massive support from Sidney Darrell and, as he was soon to learn, also from his colleagues in the Doktor Klub. He was determined however with unwavering obstinacy to become a priest. He believed passionately that he had received the Call from God but he felt rocked to and fro like a flimsy boat in a storm but a passionate determination decided him that the boat would not pitch him into the sea. He would ride on in it until the bishop had laid his hands on his head and made him a priest. He would allow nothing to stand in his way. Anthony was an obstinate man.

He had just started to doubt some of the Church's teaching but then this incipient misgiving plunged him into an unnerving crisis but one that was much more fundamental. Two days later, as he was staring at a book in the library, he began to doubt the existence of God. He looked at the book in front of him whose title was '**The Choice of God**' written by Hubert van Zeller and the word '**God**' began to steer off the cover and come through his eyes and into his brain. He didn't know whether he believed it or not. A sudden horror confronted him. That simple belief, a seemingly small psychological fact determined the foundation on which his whole life was grounded. If he didn't believe in God he would have to walk down the drive of Newman College in lay clothes and return home in disgrace like the Winslow Boy expelled from Osborne. For three whole days his world seemed to totter. He went to Mass each morning, he went to chapel at other times and knelt looking at the altar but he could not pray. He did not know what to do. He looked at his fellow divines going about their business. He could not, would not, talk about the thoughts that were torturing his soul. After all, what could he say? He felt like shouting out in the middle of the chapel that God did not exist. He was in a state of reeling confusion. He looked at all the other divines and the priests in chapel; they all looked peaceful, intent on their prayers and Anthony felt he was completely outside the quiet certainties of his fellows. He was a leper banished from the city walls. He could not sleep at night and he did not know to whom he could turn until on the third day of this torture he suddenly thought he would go and talk to Fr. Salter.

Fr. Salter was a quiet man from the north country who taught Philosophy at the College. Like many people from the north he had a solidity about him that Anthony trusted. He gave a lecture every weekday morning with the exception of Wednesdays. Since arriving at the College Anthony had devoured his lectures hungrily. He was inspired not so much by what Fr. Salter said as the place that his lectures came from. They did not come from books but from his own heart. He never had a note in front of him and he spoke from his own worked-out experience. Anthony had, on a couple of occasions, seen him from his bedroom window pacing up and down the drive, to and from the Newman Statue, in a walk that denoted to Anthony the exaltation of a new discovery; that something which he had pondered over and questioned had suddenly become startlingly clear. When Anthony listened to him in the lecture theatre he knew he was not just regurgitating Philosophy but was personally grappling with intellectual and emotional problems which he was working out in the Philosophical medium, just as a painter might work it out in the artistic one. His lectures were the fruit of those inner labours. Anthony trusted his integrity more than any other member of the staff. He felt in his present crisis that if anyone were able to help him it would be Fr. Salter. Anthony had faith in his inner sincerity and another quality which was even more important. It was simplicity. Fr. Salter was essentially a simple man. He had a passionate love of Philosophy but it was not born of any élite sophistication but rather his inquiring down-to-earth mind wrestled with the most elementary facts of human living. When he lectured he was trying to answer and grasp hold of the facts of our everyday world. 'What do we mean when we speak of a "place"?' 'What is meant by "relationship"?' Then he would worry away at the question, would elaborate to the divines in front of him the answers of philosophers, ancient and modern, and would voice his own dissatisfaction with this or that philosopher. Finally he would reach a formulation that came closest to what he believed to be right. It might take one lecture or five. He did not worry how long it took. He was oblivious of schedules. He did not let go of his subject until he had satisfied himself that he had answered the question in way that was convincing to his own mind and experience. He was a craftsman and was only satisfied with a piece of work which he had completed with all the excellence of which he was capable. Anthony always knew intuitively the difference between someone who was teaching what he had ingested without any personal assimilation from someone who had taken it in after a personal struggle in which there was much thought and personal conviction. How Anthony knew the difference between these two modes he was unable to say but it had been deeply in him since his earliest days. He had probably imbibed it with his mother's milk. So, in this moment of crisis, he knew intuitively that the person to turn was Fr. Salter. So, on the fourth day of turmoil, he waited until after Compline and then went up to Fr. Salter's room and knocked on the door.

He heard *'Come in'* from the other side of the door and he pushed his way in bashfully.

*"Can I speak to you about something personal?"* asked Anthony.

*"Yes, of course, laddie, go ahead. I'm not sure, mind you that I will be able to help but I'll try…"* and as he said this a mournful grin played around his lips. He was a tall man with fair hair. He had a protruding nose which made him slightly ugly, a diminished version of Cyrano de Bergerac but he had an extremely sensitive mouth. His head seemed to combine a rough peasant-like quality in the upper part of his face and a delicacy of sentiment about his mouth and chin in the lower part. These opposite

qualities that showed in his face came together in his down-to-earth but sensitive character.

*"Well, Father, I've been having terrible doubts,"* said Anthony nervously.

*"They're not forbidden, you know,"* said Fr. Salter with a wise and friendly smile.

*"These are not just little doubts,"* said Anthony, *"but big ones – fundamental ones."*

*"If they weren't big ones they'd be scruples not doubts,"* said Fr. Salter. Fr. Salter had taught logic and although he scorned its usefulness yet his mind had not been unaffected by his two years of learning logic in Rome twenty-five years before.

*"It's not just one of the Church's doctrines that I'm doubting but the existence of God Himself,"* said Anthony, trembling as he spoke. He had felt a terrible fear as he spoke the words *of God Himself.*

*"Tell more more,"* said Fr. Salter in a tone that denoted not only concern but scientific interest at the same time. Anthony looked at him as he dangled one leg over the side of his chair, his cassock thrown onto a stool by his side, and his thin torso covered only by an open white shirt. His dog-collar had been tossed onto his desk.

Anthony told him how he had been brought up a strict Catholic and how he'd never doubted the Catholic faith and that it was only in the last few days that his head was swimming with doubts about the very basis of everything and at the head of it all the existence of God himself.

*"Well, let's say you found that you don't believe in God what then?"* asked Fr. Salter in a blunt tone that projected out into the room his warm Yorkshire accent. Anthony found his tone enormously comforting.

Anthony was completely taken aback. He had assumed that this outcome would be the very worst of disasters. He was left silent by the implication in Fr. Salter's tone that it would not be the end of the world. Before he had found words with which to reply Fr. Salter went on,

*"There are many atheists who live good lives and find favour in the sight of God. There was a time when we believed that it was only those in the Catholic Church who could be saved and then we grudgingly deigned to include Christians of other faiths but now we recognize that Jesus came to save all men and that someone is a Christian not by the title of an external ritual which has incorporated him into the Church but by virtue of his inner desires and attitudes. This is something which the Church has always taught but not really taken to heart. Even at school when you were learning the catechism you were taught that people could receive baptism by desire. Think of all the pagans*

*who were born before Christ ever came into the world and all the savages in distant parts of the world before they had been discovered by missionaries."* He paused and said *"Do you mind if I smoke?"*

*"Of course not,"* said Anthony. Fr. Salter lit up a cigarette and then surprisingly stubbed it out, *"the bloody thing is stale. I'll do without. Look where was I? Oh yes. All of these were saved through baptism by desire – that is if their inner attitude was a generous and open-hearted one and informed by love then they had found favour in God's sight. The same is true to-day of the millions who do not belong to the Church and even are bitterly against it. It is the inner attitude of heart that brings someone to God. The Gospels are full of it once you think of it: the Samaritan who found favour in the sight of God rather than the priest and the levite; all those who had done something for 'the least of mine' If, after this inner turmoil of yours, you end up by not believing in God you will have to tread a different path; you will have to leave this college and things will be difficult for you but it will be a challenge. You will have to find your way in the world on your own and without all the help which we priests have."*

Anthony was dumbfounded but felt a great weight lifted from him. He looked at Fr. Salter quite astounded but also with a warmth in his heart that brought him near to tears.

*"Thank you, Father,"* he stammered.

*"There's nothing to thank me for, laddie. If you want to talk again just knock at my door. I'm glad this is happening to you. A lot of us priests get the idea that we are better than others. We need something to bring us down to earth. A monk I know went to give a retreat to the clergy in one of the dioceses and the bishop of the diocese came to the retreat as well. One day during the retreat he went to talk to the monk about one of his priests who had got involved with a woman and she had become pregnant. Then the bishop said to the monk 'But I can't understand how this could happen to someone who is a priest' and the monk said to the bishop, 'You mean to tell me that you can't understand how it can happen to a priest?' The monk then said to him that if he did not understand, then God would have to teach him because he would be no good as a bishop unless he did understand. And I tell you, laddie, that a year later the bishop came to the monk and told him that God **had** taught him."* As he said this a hint of an ironical smile played momentarily around his lips.

*"I knew that bishop and he was a far better pastor to all his priests after that than he had been before."*

*"Thanks,"* said Anthony nervously, *"you have really taught me something."*

*"OK, laddie, go to bed and have a good night's sleep."* Anthony was in tears as he left Fr. Salter's room. He went to bed just as Fr. Salter had suggested. He slept that night with a tide of relief so great that he had not experienced since when he was a boy and had finally confessed his dreadful sacrilege.

This encounter with Fr. Salter was what finally changed Anthony from being a robot Catholic into a revolutionary. He was intellectually convinced by a new understanding that put the intentions of the heart at the centre of the Christian endeavour. This latter conclusion however came from Sid Darrell and his friends in the Doktor Klub. There was a difference however between Fr. Salter and Sid Darrell. The latter hated the priggish Catholics but Fr. Salter did not; his heart was compassionate towards all. There was something of Fr. Salter's attitude in Anthony also but it became fatefully smothered under a zeal born not of love but of hatred.

\*   \*   \*

Anthony thought deeply about his encounter with Fr. Salter. This meeting with this wise philosopher had touched his heart in a way that was not true of Sid Darrell. Sid Darrell, unlike Fr. Salter, was intellectually incisive with a wide vision but he did not find a response in Anthony's deeper emotions. He wanted to discuss it but who with? He went through his friends, Clarence, Rudolph, Jamie, Stephen and Joe. As Joe came into his mind he felt a cool flow inside him as if he had just drunk a glass of cool water. And then a strange thing happened. Just as he had had this thought Joe Feeney appeared at his door. Anthony was in his room idling through the pages of *The Introduction to the Devout Life* by St. Frances of Sales with the door of his room half open and he heard a noise, looked up and there was Joe.

*"What a coincidence; I was just thinking about you,"* said Anthony.

*"Yes, I know I'm an apparition,"* laughed Joe, *"you think of me and I appear. You'd better feel me to see if I'm real."* Anthony leapt up and clapped his hand on Joe's shoulder.

*"Blessed is he who has not seen yet believed …"* said Joe.

*"You're not Jesus yet,"* laughed Anthony. The quickness of Joe's Irish wit brought a spark to life into Anthony.

*"Now what do you think,"* asked Anthony, *"is the difference between Fr. Salter and Sid Darrell."*

*"Well,"* said Joe, *"Fr. Salter is about 6ft.3in. and Sid Darrell is about 5ft.10in.; old George Salter has fair hair …"*

*"Oh shut up,"* smiled Anthony, *"you know what I mean."* Joe laughed and his eyes twinkled.

*"Look the reason I was asking is that I know all of us think the world of Sid Darrell but there is something about George Salter that seems more genuine, reaches deeper in me. I sometimes think that Sid is all intellect; I cannot find his heart. When George speaks I feel that it is coming from his essence."* Anthony tossed his book onto the desk; Joe was still standing, *"Sit down."* Joe looked at his watch. It was early afternoon and it was a Wednesday. There was nothing official for a couple of hours.

*"Well I suppose I may as well make myself comfortable. I had been going to go for a run but a talk will exercise my mind instead."*

*"Well what do you think?"*

*"Sid Darrell is immersed in books. He is a scholar. They say Newman used to study for fourteen hours a day. Sid is about the same. I don't know if you know he gets up at five every morning and studies for an hour, then he goes down to chapel and meditates, says Mass, has breakfast and goes and studies for another hour, comes and gives us his dogma lecture and then returns and studies for another couple of hours before lunch so that already is four hours of study."* As Joe was talking Anthony was clocking up the hours on his fingers like a child with an abacus. *"Then he allows himself half an hour's recreation before going back to his desk and he studies non-stop from two in the afternoon until half-past seven."* Anthony continued clocking up the hours and had reached his tenth finger. *"Then he has supper, smokes a pipe and is always back at his desk straight after Compline and he does not go to bed until mid-night."*

*"So that's about another three hours,"* said Anthony, *"making it about thirteen hours of study a day. Fantastic."*

*"And,"* said Joe, *"they say that in the holidays he goes to his mother's house near Bristol and he told Stephen once that after he has said Mass and his mother has given him breakfast he 'gets down to some real work', as he put it. When Stephen asked him what that meant he said he put on his slippers and stayed studying without any interruptions until mid-night."*

*"But that's inhuman,"* said Anthony without thought.

*"Well, it's because he studies and studies like a worker ant that he is able to give us such good lectures."*

*"Yes, but there's something missing …"* Anthony pondered, tapped his fingers on his desk. Joe was sitting on his bed and tapping his right foot on

the wooden floor. " … *is it **him**. I mean when George Salter is lecturing I feel it is what **he** really thinks himself. He had worked it out, it is consonant with his inner soul. When Sid lectures I feel he is giving what is intellectually correct, sometimes even brilliant but thought out by a brain dissociated from the heart."*

*"But he's passionate,"* said Joe, slightly puzzled.

*"Yes, but in a passion someone is taken up into the excitement of another but they lose their own soul,"* Anthony felt surprised that he had said this and did not even know where it had come from, as if inspired by an unknown presence within. Encouraged by what was coming out of him he went on, *"but with George I feel that his own soul has never been lost; it is in command, digesting what it meets and rejecting what is out of tune with his own essence."*

*"But does it make a difference?"* asked Joe, looking at Anthony with something like incomprehension.

*"Well it makes a difference to **me**,"* said Anthony, *"when I listen to George Salter I become myself; when I listen to Sid Darrell I lose myself. When I listen to George I am happy but sober; when I listen to Sid I am excited but drunk."*

At that moment someone knocked on the door. Anthony opened it. He was wanted on the telephone.

*"Ah well you go I think I'll go and have my run after all,"* said Joe and they each went off in opposite directions.

The College was split into two camps that Anthony, having definitely decided that Sid Darrell's attitude was more consonant with his own than that of Nanny Conan, he was swept into this new adventurous spirit that was blowing through the College. He felt uplifted but what happened to him was the very thing that he had been intimating had happened to Sid Darrell. Anthony felt so revolted by Nanny Conan's attitude that he began to be in raptures at the brilliance of Sid Darrell's lectures and his conversations with Clarence and Rudolph together with his uncomfortable encounter with Fr. Conan finally slammed the door upon his own unthinking acceptance of traditional modes of Catholic thinking. *'I have been given a mind for questioning,'* he told himself and from that day he developed a hatred of blind obedience for its own sake. But his own soul which had found such a deep resonance with what he had found in George Salter was lost forever. He became the lost sheep amidst a hundred others. Fr. Salter belonged to neither camp. He was his own man but Anthony, though he would have liked to have the resilience to manage such unfettered possession of himself yet he lacked the resources which that would have required.

Two days later he went to his first meeting of the Doktor Klub. He walked into Clarence Cider's room with diffidence and there he saw sitting round a square bridge table Stephen Warrior, Joe Feeney, Jamie McLeod and Rudolph Novak. He had not been into Clarence's room before. It was slightly larger than his and instead of looking out at the Pugin chapel and the statue of Newman it looked across at St. Irenaeus, the place where students went who had been accepted to train for the priesthood but who knew no Latin. St. Irenaeus was a Latin crammer and it was run by a fierce Jesuit whose name appropriately was Fr. Savage. His window looked out upon this luckless academy. Anthony turned and his eyes were immediately captured by a woven purple counterpane that had a white St. Andrew's Cross woven into it. It gave the room colour and modernity. Anthony stared at it:

*"Yes, I got it at Taizé,"* said Clarence. *"That's a Protestant ecumenical centre in south east France,"* seeing Anthony's blank face.

*"It's near Cluny,"* said Jamie. Anthony looked around and saw a thin steel crucifix hanging above Clarence's table. The room was stark but with an ascetic beauty. There was a wide open space on the desk and there was not a book out of place.

*"Well, welcome to the Doktor Klub,"* said Clarence staring fixedly at Anthony.

*"I did not know about this Club,"* said Anthony shyly, *"when did it start?"*

*"Only three months ago,"* said Stephen.

*"What made you start it?"* asked Anthony.

*"Well about three months ago,"* said Stephen, *"we came out of a lecture that Fr. Darrell had been giving and he kept referring to the **kerygma** – do you remember?"* Anthony nodded, *"and we were talking among ourselves afterwards and not one of us knew what it meant so we decided we would meet once a week and discuss its meaning and then we decided to meet each week to review other things we had not understood. To begin with none of us had a clue what Fr. Darrell was talking about but we all knew he was onto something that was mind-breaking and we really wanted to grasp the heart of what he was saying. Although we've only been meeting for three months we have already learned a great deal. For myself I can say that I am not the same person."*

*"And since we've started,"* said Jamie beaming happily, *"we need each other's support. It's difficult for all of us, changing careers, we suddenly find ourselves in a different world."* Anthony looked at Jamie and felt that he could be comforted by Jamie although he felt a bit disdainful towards his idea of support. Jamie was friendly and beamed a smile at him.

*"Why what career were you in before?"*

*"I was at medical school training to be a doctor ..."* said Jamie.

*"And?"* said Anthony raising an eyebrow.

*"I was at a physiology lecture when the lecturer said that the mind and all things spiritual were just myths of a bygone age and that all spiritual and mental things were produced by the brain just as saliva is produced by salivary glands."*

*"Is that what convinced you to change from being a doctor to being a priest?"*

*"I suddenly had a strong feeling that I wanted the soul. I went to bed that night and thought I wanted to be a doctor of the soul and then I realized that that meant being a priest; that priests are doctors of the soul."*

Anthony looked at him. He had a mellow round face and dark brown hair verging on black and he was the same age as Anthony. They were sitting next to each other and had this little exchange between themselves. There was a silence and, with some embarrassment, they both looked up and saw Clarence looking irritatedly at them both for this interruption. He continued:

*"So,"* Clarence was saying, *"we began to grasp what was meant by kerygma and then we moved on to other topics."*

*"Well **kerygma** means the central core of Christian doctrine doesn't it?"* said Anthony with a superior air.

*"So what **is** that? You **tell** us."* barked Clarence who sat staring indignantly at him. Anthony looked round and Stephen was sitting forward drumming the first two fingers of his right hand on the table and running his left hand through his curly red hair and Joe Feeney was smiling at him trying to melt his discomfort while Jamie was lolling back but looking to one side.

*"Well,"* stammered Anthony, *"it's the announcement that God, a God of Love, has come among men in Christ Jesus and that we are all part of Him."*

*"Well done,"* said Joe softly tapping the table, *"to be sure that's a fine answer now."* Joe's melodious Irish brogue would have charmed a bird out of a tree. He was in fact very musical and played the piano beautifully and whenever he spoke it was like hearing leprechauns chanting in the woods.

*"But how does that affect the way we live our lives?"* asked Clarence sharply sensing that Anthony was just repeating a formula.

*"Well,"* said Anthony tentatively, *"it means that we all have a message of love to which we need to bear witness."*

*"Yes, but **how** is that different from the way Fr. Conan bears witness? He bears witness to the Church's teaching? In fact with apostolic zeal,"* said Clarence.

*"In an objectionable way, you mean,"* chirped in Stephen sharply.

*"Oh, no he doesn't,"* said Anthony gathering momentum, *"he just repeats what the Pope says in his Encyclicals. That's nothing to do with the message of Christ Jesus and there is no apostolic zeal; there is no inner spirit informing what he says; he just repeats dry formulae."*

*"But you're just repeating what Fr. Darrell has said, like Nanny Conan repeats what the Pope says,"* said Rudolph with a contorted grimace. Anthony looked at Rudolph's angular face, dark hair and sharp nose. His face was quivering.

*"Jesus set up the Church with Peter as the founder. Peter was the first Pope and all the Popes down through history owe their existence to Jesus. They speak for God in the world to-day,"* said Clarence in a solemn tone.

Anthony looked at him. He looked entirely serious and yet he was sure he could not be:

*"You don't believe that,"* said Anthony.

*"How do you know I don't?"* asked Clarence.

*"Well I've heard you speaking about the Spirit of Christ living more in the hearts of the laity than in the Church hierarchy so what you've just said doesn't square with that,"* said Anthony warily and looking around at the others. He was relieved to see Jamie wink at him.

*"But you have not said anything that shows **me** that the kerygma is anything different from what I've just said."*

Anthony sat down and pondered. He felt himself trembling inside and his confidence draining away.

*"Well,"* said Joe in his musical voice and taking pity on Anthony under this close questioning, *"it's the difference, you see, between being in love with a woman with all the passion of it throbbing through your breast and listening to a sermon on marriage by a desiccated celibate priest,"* and he laughed and Jamie laughed and Stephen roared but Clarence remained serious only letting the slightest smile cross his lips.

*"That's a good parallel,"* said Clarence, *"because the difference lies not in statements but a living spirit. At Pentecost the apostles were filled with a thrill of excitement and it was not words but a passion and love beating through their breasts. They knew the love of God as a living experience. It is just as Joe said, the difference between being in love and hearing someone talking about it."* Clarence's voice became quite shrill and it was the first time that Anthony noticed a thrill shimmer through him.

*"So that's the **kerygma**?"* asked Anthony.

*"Now he's got it,"* said Clarence slapping a book on the edge of the table with his ends of his fingers. This made Anthony look at the book. He picked it up and turned it over *'Le Milieu Divin'* by Teilhard de Chardin.

*"Is this new?"* asked Anthony, *"I've read, or at least tried to read,* **The Phenomenon of Man**, *but I had not heard of this,"* turning the book over in his hands.

*"It is* **the** *spirituality for our world to-day,"* said Clarence. Until this point Rudolph had been looking down at the ground with a tense expression on his face and had said nothing but now he spoke and out of the side of his mouth and rapidly:

*"You all know I was in a Trappist Monastery and many of the monks believed that they were holier than any outside of its sacred precincts. Then the Abbot read Teilhard de Chardin's writings on the spiritual life and as he read it he realized that there were many people living lives in a bloody turbulent world outside his small monastery that were much holier than the monks and he began to say this in his discourses and the monks were furious. Some of them began to write him poison pen letters. Teilhard de Chardin's writings implied just this and it was the reason why the official Church did not allow them to be published but they were circulated secretly on roneoed sheets together with some of Henri de Lubac's writings ..."*

What Rudolph was saying was not very different from what Fr. Salter had said to him but it was in a different tone, it carried a different message. Fr. Salter was not in a passionate rebellion against the Church, against the hierarchy. Fr. Salter had reached some deeper truth within himself and did not need to be in rebellion. He cradled within him a deep truth that he had personally assimilated.

*"Why what was wrong with Teilhard de Chardin's writings?"* asked Anthony nervously.

*"Bloody nothing,"* said Rudolph, *"but ever since the Modernist crisis at the beginning of the century the Holy Office has stamped on anything that had the slightest hint of contemporary thought creeping into Catholic writing. Anything that suggested that the official legalism of the Church was wrong was immediately stamped upon. George Tyrrell was excommunicated but he bloody well shouldn't have been. It was just stuffed up prejudice. I go every April and pay tribute to him at his grave at Storrington in Sussex. Tyrrell was a saint not a heretic. Loisy was the same."*

*"But how could the Church be so wrong?"* asked Anthony with rising doubt in his voice.

Speaking rapidly and still out of the side of his mouth Rudolph said,

*"The Church is a human institution and gets trapped into bloody dried up conservatism. The Church has no special protection against corruption and distortion of the truth."*

*"But why does that happpen? and what about Christ's guarantee to be with the Church and to guide it with His Spirit?"* asked Anthony.

*"The Church can go centuries before it gets corrected. The Church often has got it wrong and then eventually everyone senses that things are wrong and a Council is summoned and then the Church corrects errors it has fallen into. It's just arrogant to think the Church is not human like every other institution. Just like Jesus was divine and human as well, so the Church is the same. It sure is I can tell you,"* answered Rudolph with irritation. Anthony felt too frightened inside of himself to question any further. Rudolph's snappish manner silenced a timid child inside him. He was relieved when Clarence, undeterred by Rudolph's peremptory closure, kept open the enquiry, by trying to answer his question,

*"The Truth is something invisible that statements point towards. We are sustained by throwing ourselves into its arms ..."*

*"Yes,"* said Joe, *"like a father now who tosses his baby to his wife. He **knows** she will catch it but how does he know? Instead its like tossing himself knowing he will be caught ..."*

*"And,"* said Clarence, *"the alternative is to stay clinging and not daring to fling forwards. Flinging forwards feels dangerous but actually what is dangerous is not to do so but to stay clinging. The clinging comes from fear and behind it is an invisible God who hates. The same statement in words is radically different according to whether you are using them to fling yourself forwards or clinging with fear."*

*"You mean,"* asked Anthony suddenly feeling excited, *"that each edict from the Church is a thrust forward towards something else so that it is only ever a partial statement, not the whole truth ..."*

*"Yes, exactly,"* said Stephen, *"and you see that is the battle that is going on in the Council at the moment. At the First Vatican Council Papal Infallibility was pronounced but that was just a first thrust. It was only partially true and people like Cardinal Koenig, Frings, Alfrink and Suenans know that and are saying that it now needs filling out and correcting by saying that the Pope is not infallible on his own but only when he is holding hands with all the bishops of the Church. You see he cannot have the truth just as a lone individual. It makes complete nonsense to think like that. It is like taking a line of Scripture and turning it into a truth out of context. This idea of the*

*Pope being right on his own is just as bad as the Protestant idea of a line of Scripture being the truth without any community to support it."*

Stephen Warrior had red curly hair and of medium height. He had been an Anglican and while doing his National Service had met the army chaplain who was a Jesuit. One leave, instead of going home to stay with his parents, who lived near Birmingham, he went instead with Fr. Whitstable, the Jesuit, to a little parish he had helped to found in Stornoway on the Isle of Lewis. Stephen was so moved by the priest's warm hearted humanity and a quiet courage that at the end of the two week's leave he decided to become a Catholic and then when he was demobilized from the army he decided to become a priest. Stephen threw himself into projects with atomic energy. He always spoke with passion, slight exaggeration and humour.

*"And you see,"* said Joe in a now impassioned Irish tone with all casual indolence evaporated, *"the conservatives like Ottaviani don't understand that; not at all they don't. To be sure they are cling like bats on a cellar ceiling to just one formulation at Vatican One; as if that was the truth, the whole truth and nothing but the truth, to be sure. They think if they leave go of it the baby will tumble into an abyss."*

*"Yes,"* said Stephen, *"they're just blinkered idiots. They can't see anything outside of their own one-track minds. When old Ottaviani goes to a restaurant he has to ask for the menu in Latin or else he doesn't know what he's eating."*

They all laughed.

*"Ottaviani is represented here at College by Fr. Conan and Suenens, Alfrink and others are represented by Sidney Darrell,"* said Jamie.

*"The Church is split in two,"* said Clarence, *"right from the highest level in the Vatican to the divisions here in College to the priests and lay people at parish level. I can tell you that when we get out into the parishes the battle will be far worse than anything here. The parish priests are all cast in the mode of Ottaviani."*

*"There are a few exceptions like Fr. Victor Stilton on the Isle of Dogs in the East End,"* said Jamie.

*"Well it's more than ninety per cent,"* said Clarence grimly.

*"Yes, we're really up against it,"* said Jamie, *"and we need each other if we are to survive and carry the message and not go under. We need each other very badly; that is why the Doktor Klub is a support for all of us."* As he spoke Anthony looked round. Rudolph was looking ahead like a sea-captain on his bridge, severe and humourless. Stephen was leaning back sweeping his right hand through his curly red hair and Joe was

nodding his head and Jamie, who had just spoken, was looking uncertainly from one to the other, his eyes flickering.

The six of them then got into a red-hot discussion about the spirituality of Teilhard de Chardin and how it was capable of bringing Christians into sympathetic connection with Science. Joe Feeney had made Evolution his special area of study and told the others about the discoveries of Louis and Mary Leakey of the fossils of *homo sapiens* in the Olduvai Gorge in Tanzania which were being dated at about a million and a half years ago. He raised the issue of whether the human race had emerged from just one original pair or several – monogenism or polygenism.

*"But doesn't it matter which is the truth?"* said Anthony looking at Joe.

*"Not at all it doesn't. I doubt it very much whether scientists will ever know whether hominization burst forth at one spot of the planet or several."*

*"'Hominization'…?"* queried Jamie.

*"It's that moment of transition from apes to man,"* said Joe.

*"Did that moment require a special intervention from God?"* asked Anthony.

*"No, definitely not,"* said Clarence barging in, *"once you say that you keep having to bring God into every development that occurred on earth – from non-life to life, from unicellular organisms to jelly-fish, jelly-fish to fish, fish to reptiles, reptiles to mammals, mammals to primates, primates to man,"* he was looking straight ahead, his eyes expressionless.

*"But,"* said Anthony, *"you are giving each of those transitions equal value. From non-life to life and from primates to man are bigger jumps than the others."*

*"Well,"* said Joe, *"they are not so big as we've always thought. Crick and Watson with their discovery of the DNA have shown that the distance from non-life to life is not as great as we thought and the big apes can be taught language. Apes have minds and, if we could see it properly, there's been some mind stuff from the beginning of creation."*

*"What an amazing idea!"* said Stephen throwing out his two hands with his palms sending out invisible rays of certitude into the group.

*"Well,"* said Joe, *"it's much more glory to God to see the planet from the very beginning having in it the potential for everything that has developed out of it. That in the acorn you have the leaves, the trunk and the branches and that in the earth's beginning you have life-stuff and mind-stuff there. If, to be sure, God has to bow down and tinker with the machine the whole time then he hasn't made a very good job of it, to be sure he hasn't."* Joe was sitting back speaking in a somewhat dreamy way but what he had just been

saying excited Anthony. The wonder of God, the wonder of life, the wonder of the world sent a thrill right down into his loins.

Clarence, speaking somewhat like a barrister defending his client, the Sacred Scripture, interrupted Anthony's moment of reverie and said, *"We have no idea whether humans emerged from one pair or from many. The Bible gives us no scientific message about that. We know that* <u>homo erectus</u> *developed out of an ape that preceded it and that from* <u>homo erectus</u> *came Neanderthal Man and Homo Sapiens. The priestly author of the chapter in Genesis on creation was teaching that all men and women the world over come from God and that is true. He does so by using a mythological image ..."*

*"But he did not know it was a myth,"* said Rudolph sharply, *"he bloody well thought the world was like that. He did not know anything about evolution."*

*"But it's still a myth,"* said Joe, *"even though he did not know it was a myth. There is a religious truth and a scientific truth. The priestly author's science was mythological but the truth enshrined within it was religious and as true to-day as it was then: that the whole of mankind came from God and the rest of the planet as well* **and***,"* Joe stopped to lay special emphasis and looked around at them all and repeated, *"**and** that it was all good. That the world is basically good and we need this message to-day as much as then, more than then, to be sure."*

*"But it's not bloody well good,"* snapped Rudolph, *"what about Hitler and the holocaust. Go and tell the Jews that that was good."*

*"There was a good being attempted even there,"* said Joe.

*"What **do** you mean?"* snarled Rudolph.

*"There was an attempt to purify,"* said Joe who was not deflected by Rudolph's acrid manner, *"to clear up corruption. But Hitler was like one of the Baal worshippers that the prophets were chastising, to be sure ..."*

*"Explain,"* asked Anthony fascinated.

*"Well,"* said Joe, *"the prophets were saying that neither good nor evil must be represented in blocks of wood. In other words, now, good and evil are always spiritual, mental if you like, but as soon as you point to a wooden statue and say it is evil or you point to the Jews or the gypsies or the blacks or whoever and say they are evil then you have slipped into pagan worship, the worship of Baal. Jeremiah would have recognized straight away, he would, that Hitler was erecting a wooden statue ..."*

*"What was the real evil then that Hitler should have been trying to cleanse?"* asked Jamie looking troubled.

*"Probably it was the demoralized state that the German people had been plunged into after Versailles and the hyperinflation in 1923. What needed purifying was their humiliation. What Hitler did was to put up a wooden statue and say that was the cause of Germany's distress. The wooden statue was the Jews. It's much easier to eliminate the Jews that do the slow work of re-building a nation's confidence, dissolving its humiliation."* Anthony again looked at Joe amazed. Behind that slow languid posture of Joe's was an amazing insight into human affairs.

*"You should explain that to people,"* said Anthony, *"it is an approach which is so much more positive ..."*

*"You see,"* said Clarence, *"the Biblical author if he had been living in Hitler's time or if someone had really understood the spiritual message of Genesis then Chamberlain and Churchill could have been brought together into a united vision."*

*"What **do** you mean, that's rubbish,"* barked Rudolph. Clarence opened his mouth to speak but Joe put up his hand in the 'halt' mode and Clarence swallowed his words and waited for Joe to speak,

*"What he means,"* said Joe, *"is that Chamberlain kept pretending to himself that Hitler was good at heart. Churchill said he was evil. Churchill knew the determined passion of the man. Churchill knew too the humiliating terms that the allies had imposed on Germany. It was good to try to give Germany back her confidence. That was a good goal, to be sure it was but to set up the Jews as a visible totem-pole was just like the Baal worshippers of ancient times thinking they could wipe out evil by destroying a statue."* Joe stopped speaking and there was a silence. Joe had that agility of mind that was able to transpose essential elements from one historical period to another. He encompassed within his vision the whole wide canvas of human history. Clarence lit a cigarette and after blowing a smokey ring to the ceiling he returned to the defence of his client,

*"The first eleven chapters of Genesis are mythological. We only touch history in the eleventh chapter with the advent of Abraham."* He looked at his watch and said,

*"It's time for us to stop."* He looked around and amidst some inconsequential murmurings the five of them loped out of Clarence's room.

\*   \*   \*

Anthony now went faithfully every week to the Doktor Klub and as he did so he became more and more deeply swept up with enthusiasm into the new and violent ferment in the Church. When a further three months had passed he had changed from being a conservative pious Catholic into a radical reformer. The Doktor Klub of which he was a zealous member were all in rebellion against conservativism and tradition. He was a true believer of the new gospel and yet, unbeknown to him, he was still ruled by a severe God of Justice; it was only that he had moved from his seat in the heavens to become incarnate in the conservative prelates in the Church. He thought he had made a great decision, that he had embraced the spirit of renewal in the Church. He believed in it passionately and had no doubt that it was a deep personal faith within him but in fact he had just attached himself to the Darrell camp with all the fearful clinging with which Fr. Conan at College and Cardinal Ottaviani in the Vatican in turn clung to their conservative totem-poles. He was just coming out of his room shortly after lunch one day and he ran into Sid Darrell walking past on his way to the staff Common Room which was just past some glass doors to the right of his room. He was trilling the middle finger of his right hand along the wall.

"*I liked your lecture this morning,*" said Anthony. Sid Darrell looked up, wakened out of some problem he was musing over.

"*Well what was it you particularly liked?*" asked Fr. Darrell stressing the syllable *tic* in the word *particularly* with his voice reaching a crescendo in the word *liked*.

"*I had always believed that God had been hurt by Adam's sin but after listening to your lecture I know that must be nonsense.*" Anthony stood nervously with both his hands fumbling in his cassock pockets.

"*With that view there is no mystery. The ineffability of God's love is cancelled out – instead you've just got God repaying a debt to God. It makes God not a God of Love but a sort of lawyer God who demands redress for an insult ...*" Again he spoke the word *redress* with a voice that swooped down on the last syllable.

"*Why on earth has nearly all Catholic education got it wrong?*" asked Anthony looking shyly at Sid.

"*In all religions there is a tendency for the mystery to degenerate into super-stition. It's easier for the mind. The mind,*" and here Sid stopped and then he tapped his head for emphasis and repeated himself, "*the mind has to stretch itself to encompass mystery ...*" and as he said *stretch itself* he moved his two hands away from each other to convey the idea of the mind expanding, "*–and it's an effort.*"

Sid looked at his watch and said,

*"Heavens I must go. I promised to meet Louis Weber in the Common Room at a quarter to three and it is now ten to. Keep studying every day, Anthony,"* and with that he strode off quickly taking long paces.

Anthony turned back into his room. *"I hate those old superstitious conservatives"* he said to himself. He now supported the change in the liturgy from Latin to English with all the passion of a Savanorola. The difference between him and Savanorola however was that, by what seemed a miracle of concordance, the Vatican Council going on in Rome was endorsing the views of Fr. Darrell and that band of his fanatic disciples in the Doktor Klub. When Anthony met Fr. Conan he spoke politely to him and veered the conversation off any area which he felt was likely to lead to friction. In this way he travelled a diplomatic passageway through his six years at Newman College but what he did not know was that radical and liberal though he was intellectually, yet in a hidden reservoir in his soul he remained emotionally a slave to a fierce Old Testament God. All his radical conviction was impelled onwards by the zeal of revolutionary words – **kerygma, commitment, history of salvation, the Good News, the apostolic mission.** However he did not copy like a parrot for he had a good understanding of the spirit of the people whom he read and listened to. He reflected inwardly on the sense of what they were trying to convey and of all the divines at Newman College he was the best at giving an exposition of what the German theologian, Karl Rahner, taught about sacramental life or what the Abbot Odo Casel from the monastery of Maria Laach believed to be the centre of the Paschal Event of Easter. He understood them intellectually; he even understood something about the emotions which moved their minds but there was something inner which remained as it always had been, inert and paralyzed with terror. He had taken on board something that belonged to others, what they believed was something which he felt in sympathy with and yet it was not his. Where was his own soul? It was as though he had scooped up all these teachings of the new liberal theologians in order to batter a stupid faithful Catholic of the old school into submission. He did not know it but he was a more fervent missionary to himself than ever St. Paul had been to the gentiles. He could not bear automatism or robotic learning and he preached against it with a fervour born of intense hatred. He believed incorrectly that he had rid himself forever of this savage God that he hated so vehemently.

# CHAPTER TWO

There was a consonance between Anthony's "conversion" and a huge revolution that was going on in the Catholic Church. Anthony arrived at Newman College on 22nd September 1958. Just two and a half weeks later after bicycling to visit a lady who was a polio victim and was in an iron-lung in a little clinic just outside of Much Hadham, he was putting his bicycle away in a little shed put aside for that purpose when Stephen came panting towards him,

*"Got some news. The Pope has died."* Stephen and Anthony walked excitedly towards the main gate of the College and there a group of divines were all talking and wondering who the next Pope would be.

*"It'll be Montini,"* said Clarence. At that moment Fr. Conan came past. He had overheard Clarence saying it would be Montini.

*"No, it can't be Montini,"* said Nanny Conan nodding his head, *"the Pope has to be elected from one of the Cardinals and Montini is not a cardinal."* As soon as he had said this he hurried with his shoulders hunched but looking this way and that, out of the window onto the grass quadrangle before climbing the stone steps that led up to his bedroom. The residential part of the College had been built in square formation surrounding a grass quadrangle. On the ground floor there was a wide stone-flagged passage like a monastic cloister that enclosed the courtyard. Upstairs on the first floor were the rooms of the staff and the divines. Half the rooms looked out into the quadrangle, the other half looked outwards north, south, east and west. This day when a Pope had died Nanny Conan had no time for casual gossip. He had more urgent business to attend to.

*"Nonsense,"* said Clarence as soon as Nanny was out of earshot, *"anyone can be elected Pope. It does not have to be a cardinal, it doesn't even have to be a bishop, doesn't even have to be a priest in fact."*

*"I know I know,"* said Stephen impatiently, *"but unfortunately just this once Nanny is probably right. I don't think they will elect a Pope from someone who is not a cardinal. So that rules out Montini."*

So for the next nineteen days there was a hubub of excitement with bets and guesses going this way and that but not one either of the divines or the priests on the staff of Newman College guessed that the new incumbent to the Papacy would be Roncalli. Although he was the Patriarch of Venice he was seventy-seven and been considered completely out of the running. He was the one hundred to one outsider. As soon as he had been elected Clarence declared,

*"He's just a stop-gap. Nothing will happen for the next four to five years."*

Clarence echoed what most people thought but he and they were wrong. No one expected much to happen from this ageing Pope but the cynical prophets in the Curia and conservative circles in the Church generally were shocked to discover that there was a revolutionary handgrenade tucked away in the ample bosom of this magnanimous Pope. He had not been pope for three months when he told his Secretary of State, Cardinal Tardini, that he would summon an Ecumenical Council of all the bishops of the whole Church and a month later made a public announcement at the Church of St. Paul's Without the Walls in the presence of eighteen cardinals.

Anthony had been at Newman College four years when the Council opened on 11th October 1962. By this time Anthony had been converted from a watery church goer into a fiery evangelist preaching the new gospel of **commitment, relevance** and **apostolic mission** that was enflaming the hearts of hundreds of Catholics in what became known as the **aggiornamento** in the Church. He did not just believe but *knew* that the liturgy should be in English, that the Bible not only should be but was the spiritual foundation for all Catholics and that God was a God of Love who, out of infinite compassion for mankind, had entered the human condition in order to transform it and heal man of his alienation from himself and God. Anyone who thought otherwise was a traitor to the cause. Nanny Conan was no longer just wrong or misguided but rather was like a cancer to be rooted out with divine fervour. Anthony not only believed but knew that the Mass should be celebrated in English but he, in a cynical apathy, did not think that the Ecumenical Council would change a custom that had enshrined the Mass in Latin for fifteen hundred years. He turned cynically to Clarence while they were watching on television that vast procession of bishops in all their finery entering in solemn procession into St. Peter's on that propitious Thursday morning in October 1962 and said,

*"Little hope of those pompous codgers changing anything."*

*"Yes, they'll repeat the same old platitudes and all will go on as before,"* said Clarence. But when within three months these aged prelates had

declared loud and clear that the Mass, which had been celebrated in Latin for fifteen hundred years, would now for evermore be celebrated in English. Anthony, Clarence, Rudolph, Jamie, Joe and Stephen were ecstatic. Before this they had some lingering doubts about the rightness of their views. Now a divine light had swept all doubt from their souls. A more censorious and self-righteous band of young men had not stepped onto the stage of history since Lenin and his Bolshevik comrades had taken Russia by storm in 1917. Anthony even looked different. Whereas until then his blue eyes had a dreamy look beneath his fair hair as the world drifted past him; now they jabbed out into the world like daggers at anyone who dared to contradict him. Their blueness had turned to purple as some blood red passion surged into his ocular nerves. Little did those bishops in Rome know the fires they had lit inside of this little band of zealots in distant Newman College.

That concordance between this group of radicals at Newman College and the highest dignitaries of the Church turned, like a chemical catalyst, all doubt into certainty and then certainty to dogmatism and dogmatism to fanaticism. Anthony did not know that he was a fanatic with a fiercesome Old Testament God installed in his own breast proclaiming with vehemence that the old conservative codgers were in the wrong. The head of the English hierarchy had gone out to Rome expecting that all the holy practices of the Church would be re-affirmed with pontifical solemnity. He was shocked when, on the opening day of the Council, Cardinal Liénart proposed that the members of the various commissions, the members of which had all been schooled by the Roman Curia should be supplanted by bishops from countries worldwide and that his proposal was overwhelmingly supported. As the Council opened on this rebellious note Anthony, Clarence and a small group of 'radicals' were overjoyed.

*"They should all be excommunicated these Catholics who won't obey the Council,"* declared Clarence. It was a cold February day in 1963. He was standing between Newman College and St. Irenaeus on a small grass triangle holding court with Anthony and Joe listening to him, pinned to the ground as if mesmerized by the charism of their leader.

*"Yes, they should be hanged, drawn and quartered,"* chimed Anthony.

*"Ah well,"* said Joe, *"I'd just give them a big penance – make them wash the feet of all the bishops who have voted for reform."* Joe Feeny with his bald domed head capping a round Friar Tuck face always had a smile of humour. The human scene with conservatives and radicals waving

their fists at each other was always on the inner stage of his mind. On judgment day the sinner would be forgiven. Anthony and Clarence would banish him to hell.

Fr. Darrell was now on fire. All that he had worked for had come to pass with the speed of lightning. Now, instead of starting a lecture with a turgid account of the Mediaeval attitude to the Eucharist, he would start with the latest news from the Council and, as ancient Catholic practice after ancient Catholic practice came tumbling down from their august positions to lie forever moribund like broken cars in a breaker's yard, so his faithful band of apostolic disciples were clapping the hands of their minds like workers at a Trades Union Congress. When the news came through that the Council had voted that the whole liturgy be henceforward in the vernacular Anthony, Clarence and all the members of the Doktor Klub now knew that the Holy Spirit was undoubtedly with them. Fr. Conan and his little clique of conservatives were like the fallen tyrants of a right wing dictatorship and they looked with hypervigilance this way and that to see what radical's missile might be coming in their direction. At the same time these conservatives dug their heels in and were determined to crush this new spirit of zeal in the Church. They could not change what the Vatican Council had promulgated but they would do all in their power to dilute its spirit so that, at parish level, nothing would change the venerable structures.

In the midst of all this something happened inside of Anthony personally that strengthened even more his missionary passion. Suddenly one day, on his way to breakfast after Mass in the Pugin chapel, he saw the three great movements of renewal in the Church – the Liturgy, the Bible and Catechetics – as a unity. The central fire which animated them all suddenly burned itself into Anthony's heart and mind. He stood rigid on the stone corridor as if transfixed by a paralyzing dart. He turned and went back to the chapel. He knelt down and stared at the brass crucifix above the tabernacle. As he knelt and prayed so the whole History of the World seemed to unfold from the time of Abraham onwards and he saw himself, the Church and the whole world within the Church in one great River of Time. At the centre of this unified vision was the mystery of God's love embracing the whole of mankind. Like a hologram the whole was in the part and the part was in the whole. His conversion was now complete. He rose and returned to the refectory where semi-cooked bacon, and greasy fried eggs and soggy toast were hardly noticed as his heart and mind were on fire with a new passion.

Anthony argued passionately for the vernacular liturgy and now he had utter contempt for those old fogeys who insisted on preserving the Latin Mass, saying as they did so, that Latin preserved the 'mystery' Anthony was scornful in the extreme.

*"Nanny Conan and his mob don't know what mystery means,"* said Anthony to Clarence. They were sitting in the Common Room after lunch on Sunday. As it was a fine day most of the divines had walked outside into the cool but bright air, but these two were sitting at the far end of this low-ceilinged room with just four divines at the far end playing billiards.

*"No they think it means that they know everything and that it's their job to keep it hidden from the laity,"* Clarence tapped the ash off his cigarette into the chrome free-standing ash-tray that stood like a wooden soldier with an upturned helmet just in front of him.

Anthony thought for a moment, *"It's transcendence that's missing,"* he said, *"The mystery lies in the amazing fact of God's love for mankind. There was no necessity for God to love mankind; there was no necessity for God to create; there could be no necessity in God."* He stopped. He'd been looking with those piercing purple eyes at a large tawdry photograph of the basilica at Fàtima in Portugal. He turned intently towards Clarence and went on, *"the conservatives think that God is contained in the Church like a rabbit in a cage. They possess him. He belongs to them. The mystery means to keep what they possess hidden. They are completely ignorant of God who transcends all that we know and understand ..."*

*"Yes, they are atheists in sheep's clothing. And sheep they are. They just follow what they have been told. One sheep crosses the road and all the rest follow,"* said Clarence.

*"What it means,"* said Anthony passing his right hand through his flopping fair hair on the right side of his head, *"is that Nanny Conan and all those old conservatives have no idea that human minds are limited in their comprehension of the world, the universe and God. They believe that they know it all but if they keep everything in Latin then they will know it but their poor starving flock will be in humble submission to the clergy."* As he said this Anthony looked at Clarence with fire darting out of his purple eyes. He looked at his watch. It was nearing half-past two. Anthony had a class of young children to teach down in the local village of Standridge at three o'clock.

*"I have to go,"* said Anthony, *"I have my class down in the village."* They parted; Clarence to the library and Anthony to his bicycle which would take him down to the village just in time to teach the children.

*   *   *

So Anthony studied the Bible even more fervently, the Fathers of the Church and the more enlightened ways in which to teach God's great message of love. He took weekly the French magazine *Fetes et Saisons* which was full of ideas of how to teach the Christian message using the natural symbols of light, darkness, water and the earth to convey even to the simplest folk the message of God's love. He studied St. Paul's letters and the Gospel of St. John with special fervour. He particularly focussed on those books on Scripture written by Anglican theologians and he frowned with acrimony upon all those who looked with censure upon them. Now he argued that scriptural studies by Anglicans were likely to be even better than those of Catholics because they had been so steeped in biblical studies ever since the time of the Reformation. Everything that was against Catholic parochialism had his most fervent support.

He read of a conference which had taken place in Strasbourg between Catholic theologians and atheist intellectuals. The difference between them, he both read and believed, was far less than would have been expected. In fact their core beliefs were the same whereas the differences were due to the social structures in which the two species of intellectuals had been reared and educated. As he read this he also read more deeply into the nature of the Church and became convinced that there were numerous people in the *Invisible Church* that seemed on the face of it most unlikely to be members of it. As he read his mind went back to that disturbing interview that he had had with Fr. Salter. All his sympathies now were with those who were outside the Church. The *Visible Church* was composed of devout Catholics who went to Mass every Sunday, took the sacraments and said their prayers daily.

*"They are so proud of themselves,"* said Anthony to Stephen one day after a particularly complacent lecture from Nanny Conan, *"just like the Pharisee who turned with scorn upon the humble publican."* Stephen was striding out of the lecture hall with all the intensity of a fox terrier who had smelt a rabbit in the bracken.

*"It's not worth paying any attention to Nanny. We all know he's a narrow-minded prig. It's not worth wasting any energy on him."* Anthony nodded.

*"The Invisible Church, the publicans of to-day are the Protestants, Jews and Hindus but not only them but the Communists, Atheists and Agnostics too. If we follow what Jesus said then all of these are looked on with more favour by God than all those pious Catholics who come to confession and communion every week."* As Anthony said the words 'all those pious Catholics' a tremor of hateful emotion made his teeth chatter. Stephen looked at him, patted him on the back,

*"We'll change them, we'll change them when we get out on our parishes,"* said Stephen.

*"You're an optimist,"* said Anthony, *"but what do you think our job is if we believe that the Protestants, Atheists, Communists and all are already members of the Church. There is no need to go converting anyone."* Stephen looked at him slightly taken aback. This thought had passed through his mind but he just wanted to get on with things.

*"The life of a priest is action. I don't worry too much about these academic questions,"* said Stephen a bit querulously. He sometimes tired of Anthony's endless questioning, *"our job is to love, spread love to Catholics, Protestants, Atheists, the lot. It's up to God to reap a harvest from our work. We just have to get on with it."*

But Anthony could not stop questioning. He read, discussed and thought. Sometimes he stayed up studying in his room until one or two in the morning. It was against the College rules but this did not deter him. He was working now for his future mission in the Church. So what was the Church's mission, he asked himself? It was to bear witness to man's destiny, to reveal the gracious origin of all good deeds of men and women of good will in the world. He came to despise what had been his own narrow-minded and arrogant attitude: that Catholics possessed the truth and were therefore superior to the rest of mankind.

He made the relationship of the Catholic Church to the other Christian Churches a subject of special study. He became convinced that much of Luther's critique of the Church was fully justified. He believed that indulgences and much of the devotion to Mary and the saints was superstitious and often indistinguishable from idolatry. One day in the middle of the night he crept down to the Common Room and removed the photograph of the basilica at Fàtima. He took it up to his room and hid it under his mattress until he saw two days later the big rubbish truck parked outside the back door of St. Irenaeus. He sidled past and threw the photograph, frame and all, into the truck. It was soon mangled to bits. The Protestant distrust of the Catholic Church's excessive devotion to Mary was, he believed, fully justified. He did not go so far as to think that **all** representation of Mary and the saints should be smashed but he felt proud that he had removed from sight that offensive photograph of that modern basilica. He felt sure that Luther would be approving from his seat in heaven. Iconoclasts have sprung up sporadically from earliest times in the History of the Church. The headless statues in the niches of cathedrals all over England are there to remind us. Anthony and his friends could boast an august genealogy of forebears.

This iconoclastic passion drove him into furious study. Inspired by Sid Darrell and pushed from within by a fiery spirit he travelled through all the contentious topics of Catholic belief. Like Luther he had ditched devotion to Mary and the saints and he now with almost fastidious deliberation took delight in toppling one Catholic icon after another. He demoted Francis Xavier from his status as canonized saint and replaced him with Matteo Ricci, his uncanonized hero. Francis Xavier had demolished Hindu temples in Goa whereas Matteo Ricci had bowed his head in reverence to them.

Anthony was walking down to the village of Standridge with Sean Casey. He was talking as fast as a steam train as they walked over the hill from Newman College. They were of equal height, equal enthusiasm and equal energy. They were talking furiously, oblivious of the countryside through which they walked.

*"Francis Xavier was a proud ecclesiastic,"* said Anthony, *"what arrogance to assume that everything in Hinduism was false."*

*"To be sure I don't know too much about him,"* replied Sean tugging at his brown protruding hair. Sean was from Cork and spoke in an Irish accent but it was very different from Joe Feeney's. Whereas Joe's was melodious, almost musical, Sean's was rough and rasping.

*"He knew he was right and everyone else was wrong. Have you heard of Matteo Ricci ?"*

*"No I can't say I have now – no to be sure I haven't now,"* he turned and looked at Anthony and shook his head. Sean looked Anthony straight in the face. They were both the same height: just over six foot but whereas Sean had a dark complexion with oily hair, Anthony's face was pale white and his hair was like lightly browned toast; and his eyes were blue and his nose was short and, in profile, was at the same perpendicular axis as his chin. His mouth, when he was not talking, was firmly closed. His lips were broad. So he replied to Sean:

*"His attitude was one of reverend humility towards Buddhism in China. This was in the seventeenth century."* Anthony stopped and looked at Sean.

*"Shall I give you a brief run down?"*

*"Yes, tell me for sure. I'm fierce ignorant you know, Anthony. I only learn as much as I can pray about,"* said Sean sniffing and rocking back his head, *"you see I read the Gospels again and again and the psalms. As long as I have enough to feed my prayer life then that is enough for me. But tell me about ... Mat Richy ... what do you call 'im now ?"*

*"Matteo Ricci,"* said Anthony pronouncing the Italian name syllable by syllable.

*"Matteo Ricci,"* repeated Sean, tapping his forehead at the same time.

*"Well,"* said Anthony, *"Matteo Ricci donned Buddhist robes and learned all he could of Buddhism through practising it as closely as he could and learning the language and, after nine years, he introduced some concepts from Christianity which he believed would enrich the Buddhist way of thinking but without in any way destroying his hosts' religion. He devised a liturgy in the Chinese language but back in Rome the Curial bureaucrats said it was heresy to change the liturgy in any way. It must be in Latin, they said, and not be changed one bit from how it was celebrated in every Italian church in Rome."*

*"Gosh,"* said Sean, *"to think that they stopped the Word of God reaching all those Chinese."*

*"And they did the same with another one called Roberto de Nobili who went out to India and learned all about Hindu mysticism. He had the humility to learn from that great old religious tradition. They did exactly the same in Rome with him,"* said Anthony turning to Sean and fixing his eyes upon him. They were just reaching the ford at the edge of the village.

*"Look at that beautiful clear water,"* said Sean, *"it reminds me of a little brook near my home in Cork."* He paused for a moment, *"You know what,"* he said, *"I'm going to bring our kids down here and show them this clear pure water and explain to them how the early Christians went right down into clear pure water like this so they would come out pure of heart like the water. They'll understand, to be sure, if they don't just hear but see."* Anthony turned and looked at him. He was staring at the water as in a trance. Anthony did not want to interrupt him. There was a purity in his face, a simplicity that made him feel that he himself was too intellectual.

When soon after this Pope John released his Encyclical *Pacem in Terris* and that the example, and the only example, that the Pope gave of a missionary that he commended was Matteo Ricci Anthony's heart surged with delight. He now had Papal authority for his certainty.

In June 1963 just a year before Anthony was to be ordained Good Pope John died and the whole world felt a personal loss. His love and warmth, and simple peasant piety had reached out to the whole world.

Anthony, together with many of the other 'divines' wept when the news crept through the corridors of the College that he had died. The world had lost one of those rare souls who cut through all the claptrap and who had achieved simplicity and goodness such as had not been seen on the papal throne for centuries. He sighed with relief when Montini was elected Pope and soon declared that he would carry through the Ecumenical Council started by his predecessor but, as Anthony looked at pictures of the new Pope with those dark burning eyes a fear descended upon him and he felt that all would not go well for the Church or for himself. It was a passing feeling but the loss of Pope John weighed heavily upon him. He sighed with nostalgia as for a lost friend.

There was one other inexorable topic that Anthony was determined to tackle. Nanny Conan had taught them all that contraception was wrong because Pope Pius XI had declared it to be wrong. If Nanny Conan said it was wrong Anthony was sure that the truth was the opposite. So he read all the latest ethical reflections on the subject by moral theologians influenced by the *aggiornamento*. Finally he read a book called *Contraception and Holiness* written by a series of radicals and was convinced that the Church's position was wrong. The belief that the sexual act had to occur *naturally* without any human intervention to prevent conception assumed that it was wrong for human beings to extend or amplify their animal capabilities through the intelligent use of tools. Why couldn't a couple plan the births of their children through the use of mechanical or pharmacological means for preventing conception ? The Church's answer was that it was against the *natural law* and this was interpreted as meaning that nothing must be done to interfere with the performance of the sexual act; that 'natural' meant that the act must be performed as two animals might perform it – in other words without the use of human invention, that the semen from the male must be allowed to travel up the vaginal canal and be deposited in the womb of the woman without any interference and *natural law* was interpreted in this sense. As Anthony read and studied he became not just an opponent of the Church's official position but positively believed that contraception was a good thing.

*"The natural law is nothing more than the voice of conscience,"* said Anthony who was talking to Sean again. They were on their way back from Standridge. Sean had done what he said he was going to do. He had led his six little eight- to ten-year-old pupils out of the little

classroom and, in a little crocodile behind him, to the crystal clear water of the stream. There he had sat by the water, flipping his hand in and out of it, letting it trickle back into the stream and there playing joyfully with it told the children the meaning of baptism. Anthony, watching him, with an entranced group of children looking up at him, imagined that at any moment the heavens would open and a dove would come out of the skies and settle upon this new Baptist. After they had delivered the children back to the classroom where their parents were waiting for them, the two divines, dressed in the priestly suits started the walk back to Newman College. They were silent for a while. Something of beauty had occurred. But it was Anthony, his heart filled with apostolic zest for his new-found belief in the wonders of contraception, who broke the silence.

*"The natural law written in men's hearts, as St. Paul in his letter to the Romans made clear, was the voice of conscience and not behaviour uninfluenced by human intelligence and technology."* said Anthony repeating himself. Sean was still thinking about his pupils, the beauty of the occasion still in his mind. When Anthony had started he was only half with him and had murmured, asking him to explain what he meant.

*"The sexual act is not primarily to beget children and only secondarily to promote love between the man and woman,"* insisted Anthony with ruthless determination. He was going to make Sean listen, even if he didn't want to listen, *"the goal of the act depends upon the intention of the couple not on the technology of how they do it,"* said Anthony angrily. The two men like black bishops on a chessboard were coming over the horizon and one was throwing his right hand down towards the earth and the other turned his head like an electric impulse to the downward stroke of other's hand. The final word of the dictator's speech had been spoken. The two men walked in silence now for a few minutes.

*"Umph,"* said Sean, *"well we've done the Lord's work this afternoon,"* and this should have closed the conversation but Anthony was not to be stopped until he had finished.

Sean was not a member of the Doktor Klub but had an almost sensual love for the liturgy and all its symbolism. He loved teaching children and had a special gift for conveying to them the Christian doctrines as they unfolded themselves in the events as recorded in the Bible. He taught children about the call of Abraham, the Exodus and the early psalms as sung by King David. When Sean taught them, while using visual aids, of his own imaginative construction the children in the class in front of him would have their eyes glued with fascination. He was able to make the Biblical stories come alive as if they had happened yesterday. Sean wanted passionately to bring knowledge of it to the Catholic world but he remained intellectually somewhat conservative in ethical matters. Newman College had come back into sight and, almost like a theatrical cue, it started Anthony back onto his topic of artificial contraception declaring to Sean that it was morally good but Sean asked nervously,

*"But what about papal infallibility now? The Pope himself, Pius XI it was, declared that it was immoral and against the teaching of the Church – that's what I've always been taught,"* and he looked at Anthony and then went on, *"and it was spoken by the Pope to all the Church and that makes it infallible or my name's not Sean, to be sure."*

Anthony took up the cudgels:

*"The Church is at the moment following the teaching of Pius XI in his Encyclical Casti Connubii. That is not infallible. It is not of the same nature as the Pope's definition of the Assumption of Our Lady into heaven. It is not a point of Christian doctrine but rather a decree to Catholics to obey the Pope in a particular matter. Popes have made other such decrees which are no longer followed."*

*"Like what Anthony? What are you talking about now?"* asked Sean in his harsh Irish tone.

*"For instance Pope Pius IX in his Encyclical Quanta Cura in the last century condemned as evil the right of every person to religious liberty but it is not asserted now; in fact the Church has taken the opposite position."*

*"Well I don't know about all this history but I know what I've always been taught,"* said Sean angrily. He felt his simple faith being undermined. He did not like all this high-brow intellectualism. They had now crossed the main road and were climbing up the hill towards the College. Sean went on:

*"What you're saying Anthony can't be. I've never heard that before. Come to Ireland and see if you ever hear that."* Sean was eyeing Anthony with the same suspicion with which Anthony himself had eyed Clarence Cider not so many months before. Anthony was unperturbed and continued in the same vein,

*"At that time,"* and here Anthony's voice assumed a superior air, *"when an extreme rationalism following the French Revolution was proclaiming that people were not subject to any authoritative guidance and could go in whatever direction suited them best, the Pope was making a*

*declaration against this."* Anthony seemed to be speaking almost deliberately in a dry academic mode but it was because he had only read all this the day before so he was repeating what he had read like a parrot. He had not taken in what he had read, he had not questioned the writer in his mind but was speaking like a BBC announcer on the radio. He went on, *"His statements were in a particular historical context and not very well formulated. It is the same with Casti Connubii, it set out to combat the idea of 'Open Marriage' proposed by Bertrand Russell and similar types of position but it is a muddled document. The Pope never explains why the sexual act must not be performed using contraceptive devices ..."*

*"Well sure it's obvious,"* said Sean, *"because he condemns married couples limiting their children."*

*"Oh no he doesn't,"* said Anthony with growing passion, *"because he allows couples to limit the number of children by using the rhythm method."*

*"By gorrah, you're right to be sure. Yes, to be sure you're right there Anthony,"* said Sean startling himself, *"but then why does he forbid contraception by using artificial means?"*

*"You see,"* said Anthony who was now full of glee. At last Sean had seen. He felt his heart leap within him and he warmed to his subject. He'd become the professor with a new pupil, *"he is not logical because even,"* and here as he said the word 'even' he stopped and slapped the branch of an overhanging tree, *"the rhythm method relies on instruments of measurement. What the Pope is condemning is the couple preventing the advent of children while having sex. If the sexual act is performed it must be done in such a way that it is capable of causing pregnancy. If one asks why he took this line it is because he thought of natural law in animal terms rather than as the law that is written into the human heart; conscience in other words."*

*"So you mean for sure,"* said Sean bluntly, *"that the bloody Pope just doesn't like married couples having sex."* This took Anthony by surprise. This blunt Irishman with his peasant instincts got to the heart of it straight away.

*"Contraception allows people to have sex without the danger of the woman falling pregnant. It is bound to increase promiscuous sex and obviously randy married couples could have sex day and night, using contraceptive devices and not have children. The Pope was trying to remind Catholics that sex is for begetting children. With contraceptive devices people might forget that but like most laws and decrees the first formulations are inadequate; they need refining and stating with more precision but, because*

*of the conservatism of the Roman Curia that never wants change, Pius XI's decree has been carved in stone when it should have been written on a printator…"*

*"What's a printator now ?"* asked Sean glancing at Anthony warily.

*"Oh you know those things we all had as children – where you write on a framed pad and then you can delete it by pulling it through an erasing tab at the top."*

*"Oh is that what you call them? At school back in Cork I had one and I always called it a mystical writing pad."*

*"Oh well,"* smiled Anthony, *"you would give it a holy name in Ireland."*

*"We all called it 'mystical' because the writing was there one minute and had gone the next – like an apparition of the Virgin at Knock,"* roared Sean. They were just approaching the northern driveway to the College. They entered what was almost a tunnel of horse chestnut trees.

*"I get what you are on about. The bloody Pope don't want married people to have sex just because he can't 'ave it."* It was Anthony's turn to be shocked. It was so obvious as almost to be obscene. When the Irish were converted out of their superstition they became more revolutionary than any other race on earth.

*"What **Casti Connubii** leaves out is the primacy of love. True love that is overflowing will lead in the direction of children …"* said Anthony.

*"Now you are talking sense,"* said Sean feeling happier, *"of course if there's love it will flow out into children. The Pope's just …"* Sean paused looking for a punchy word *"a sex kill-joy."* Anthony looked at him. He couldn't believe that Sean had so suddenly thrown over all his pious Popish veneration. No wonder, he thought, that the Irish had converted with passion so many souls across the seas and that when they abandoned Christianity they embraced Communism with equal fervour. What would the Trade Union Movement be without those Irish firebrands of the Great Dock Strike. He could see Sean muttering and foam coming out of his mouth. Now was the moment to strike,

*"Why don't you join the Doktor Klub?"* asked Anthony.

*"I love the Bible, the liturgy and teaching children,"* said Sean, *"but I would be no good with your bunch at all. I'm not intelligent like all of you now. I've always thought that all of you are heading to become theologians, professors in Colleges. That's not for the likes of me. I'm just going to be a simple priest on the parish now."*

*"Oh no, you've got us wrong there. We are all heading for parishes. Our whole orientation is pastoral, like Pope John in fact."*

Anthony paused. He could see Clarence Cider in the distance coming up the eastern drive towards the College. The sight of Clarence encouraged him to persuade Sean:

*"Why don't you come to a meeting and see? In fact next Thursday Clarence Cider is opening the discussion on how we are to understand the Real Presence of Jesus in the Eucharist ..."*

*"By gorrah,"* spluttered Sean *"You've just turned me against the Pope. What are you going to do now? Stop me believing in the Real Presence? Next you'll persuade me that God himself does not exist."* Anthony just looked at him coyly raising his eyebrows:

*"OK,"* he said, *"I will."*

Sean was Anthony's first convert just as he had been Clarence's. Sean became a devoted member of the Doktor Klub. He was not interested like Anthony in intellectual argument but he was caught by the enthusiasm of the group and he loved being part of it and he added fire to it. Anthony felt proud that he had been responsible for making Sean a member but it did more than that. Making a convert made him more zealous than ever before. He was now a confirmed missionary, just as iconoclastic as Francis Xavier.

It was a Saturday and half an hour later Anthony was in his pew with ninety-nine fellow divines. They were all dressed in their cassocks but the dismal blackness was relieved by the white cottas that were obligatory for Vespers on a Saturday afternoon. The pews were in choral formation as in the choir of Kings College Chapel in Cambridge and like the choirs in all the cathedrals and abbeys throughout Europe. The schola, a small group of divines with musical talent, stood forth in the aisle and started chanting and in a few moments a surge of music went up from fifty throats on one side: *Beatus vir qui timet Dominum: in mandatis ejus volet nimis* and then it was the turn of Anthony's side: *Potens in terra erit semen ejus: generatio rectorum benedicetur.* As he was stopping for breath so he looked across and could see Sean with his *Liber Usualis* held high in front of him and his eyes glued to the next set of words which flew out of his mouth: *Gloria et divitiae in domo ejus: et justitia ejus manet in saeculum saeculi.* He watched Sean who was utterly enwrapped in the limpid tone of the plain chant. Anthony then lost himself also in the next verse: *Exortum est in tenebris lumen rectis: misericors, et miserator, et justus.* At that moment he felt himself merged as into one being with all the divines and the priests on the staff. For a moment a surge of love pulsed through him and there was no difference between Fr. Conan and

Fr. Darrell. His own separateness and that of all the others in that chapel had unified like so many individual ingots in a furnace. He, Sean, Clarence, Fr. Darrell, Fr. Conan, Fr. Salter and the hundred bodies that made up the community of Newman College were merged into a single hymn of praise to the Almighty.

There they all were in their black cassocks cloaked in snow-white surplices and all them with four cornered birettas upon their heads. At the conclusion of each psalm as the schola intoned the doxology: *Gloria Patri et Filio et Spiritui Sancto* so in military unison all the clerics removed their birettas and bowed their heads only to replace them as *Amen* was intoned at the end. So in thronging unison and in the most evocative plain chant those hundred clerics, priests and divines, threw themselves with plaintive melancholy into the songs of David until all five had ascended to the thrones of the most high and finally as the organ stopped and the music died away then the centennial shapelessness sank back into each individual mould. As they all processed in columns out of the chapel and down the stone flagged corridor towards the refectory a glum mood descended. As they reached the quadrangle whose west side gave way onto the refectory there were wooden benches painted grey and each divine pulled his cotta off and laid it together with biretta upon the bench. To an outsider each cotta and biretta looked identical but they were quite individual to each priest and divine. No one ever made the mistake of picking up the wrong ones when the meal was over.

In the refectory were ten oblong tables made of eucalyptus wood which after every meal was washed down with soap and water by a band of industrious Italian maids so the tables, even when adorned with citrus fruit in a bowl in the middle and steaming pasta at the servers' end, stank of carbolic soap. Nine tables were in three parallel rows and at the far west end on a raised platform was one longer table set at right angles to the rest. At the centre sat the President of the College and surrounding him were all the priests. On the President's right was Fr. Salter. He was the Deputy President and then arrayed around the table in no formal order were the other priests responsible for teaching. There was Rodney Edwards who taught Scripture, Aelred Vincent who taught Church History, Robin Underhill who lectured in Canon Law and then Sidney Darrell and Nanny Conan, and finally sitting timidly at the far north end of the table was Francis Benson, the spiritual director. It was to him that the divines went to confession each week. It was he who gave a spiritual homily every Monday night in the College Chapel.

Everyone was standing behind their chairs. No one moved until everyone was in place. Then at the table nearest the door a divine started to intone the grace in a sonorous Latin. The grace was intoned backwards and forwards between the one and the many until after a genuflection and a thunderous *Amen* there was a tremendous clatter of chairs and a moment later everyone was sitting. At a lectern next to the top table a divine started to read the *Martyrologium Romanum* for that Saturday. Each day charted the fearful tortures undergone by the early Christian martyrs and when the full catalogue of blood, swords, beheadings and dismemberments had been read with Latin relish the reader ended with the words: *Et alibi aliorum plurimorum sanctorum martyrum et confessorum atque sanctarum virginum* to which a whole hundered voices thundered in blessed relief: *Deo Gratias.* The President rang a little bell and then, and only then, were the priests and divines allowed to speak but, the martyrology having taken about quarter of an hour to read, all the meal had been consumed. Conversation slows a meal remarkably. So another ten minutes passed and the President rang his bell again and all clattered noisily to their feet for another grace of thanksgiving.

Their religious duties were not at an end. There was still the rosary to be said and the day's work to be ended with Compline. So priests and divines trooped out of the refectory in pairs and in a long crocodile each one said the rosary with a partner. Anthony found himself next to Peter Cradle and together they recited the five joyful mysteries of the Rosary: first it was Peter's turn to start the first ten Hail Marys of the first mystery: the Annunciation; then it was Anthony's turn to start with the Visitation. Anthony was shocked at the speed with which Peter had raced through the first ten Hail Marys so he deliberately went slowly but he dared not go too slowly. Peter had set the pace and he felt to go too slowly would nettle Peter. The divines all knew that Anthony was a member of the Doktor Klub and he wanted to avoid giving the impression of a pious superiority so he said the Hail Marys quicker than he wanted to say them but slower than Peter had recited them. He had hardly finished that decade when Peter started on the third joyful mystery: the Birth of the Infant Jesus in Bethlehem and he raced through those ten Hail Marys even more quickly and there was a note of exasperation in his voice. Anthony felt annoyed but at the same time intimidated. After announcing the mystery of the Shepherds visiting the

Baby Jesus in Bethlehem he started slowly with the Our Father. He heard Peter sigh and he looked sideways and his companion was grimacing. Feeling even more driven into a corner he quickened his pace with his last ten Hail Marys. He finished more slowly with *Glory be to the Father and to the Son, and to the Holy Ghost as it was in the "Beginning is now and ever shall be world without end ..."* He did not have time to say '*Amen*' before Peter raced through the last decade of the Rosary. He did not even announce which mystery it was. As he was finishing he fumbled in his right hand pocket and had withdrawn a packet of Players cigarettes. He steered Anthony into the Common Room. As he got in he looked over and saw that Joseph Gorce and Raymond Cluedo were already there with their cigarettes lit,

"*Damn,*" said Peter, "*I usually get in before them.*" Anthony felt uncomfortable. He wanted to move away but felt it would offend Peter if he did so.

"*Half an hour for smoking after supper is not enough,*" said Peter.

"*Oh, it's long enough for me,*" said Anthony.

"*Oh well, you don't smoke.*"

"*I used to,*" said Anthony feebly.

"*I bet the Doktor Klub made you give it up,*" cajoled Peter. Just as he was about to reply Joseph and Raymond thrust themselves towards them.

"*So you were Mister Slow to-night eh !*" said Joseph smirking, "*we beat you to it.*" Peter made a sideways glance in the direction of Anthony.

"*Oh so you slowed him up, did you Anthony?*" said Joseph.

"*Keep up the good work,*" said Raymond, "*we have a bet on it you know.*"

"*What, what ...*" Anthony spoke awkwardly, he rubbed the index finger of his right hand along the inside of his clerical collar, "*... a bet?*"

"*Yes, a bet,*" said Raymond, tapping his cigarette on the soldier ashtray at his side, "*the first one to light up in the Common Room after the Rosary is owed a cigarette by the others.*"

"*Who by?*" asked Anthony feeling a sinking feeling in the pit of his stomach,

"*Oh any of the rest of the four of us,*" said Raymond. Anthony looked awkward and confused.

"*Well I can see three of you here but who's the fourth?*" The three looked shiftily at each other.

"*Come on tell me,*" said Anthony feeling excluded from a secret.

"*Promise you won't tell?*"

*"No course I won't,"* said Anthony without thinking. He saw them looking at each other.

*"Fr. Robin,"* said Peter. Anthony whistled. It had never occurred to him that one of the priests on the staff would be part of this 'First to Finish the Rosary game' Anthony knew that Robin Underhill who taught Canon Law was one of the conservatives and he had often seen him walking with Raymond and Joseph but he was shocked that he was in on this cynical game.

*"Now, don't you go telling any of your Doktor Klub members,"* said Raymond menacingly. Anthony looked down at his crinkly hair. He was about four inches shorter than himself. He had a way of standing that suggested that he was leaning against a parapet without such an object being present. Anthony felt awkward and, he was just mumbling something when Fr. Robin came up. He was extremely small, with dark hair and a very soft Irish voice. He was speaking as he joined the group and Anthony had to lean over towards him in order to hear what he was saying,

*"Hello, Father,"* said Joseph, *"so where were you to-night ? I didn't see you at supper."*

*"No, I had to go down to the village. Poor old Mrs. Graham is sick and dying and I had to go down now to give her the Last Sacraments."*

*"Did she die?"* asked Anthony,

*"No, Anthony, she's not dead yet but by the morning she will be, to be sure. She was only just breathing as I was giving her the sacraments. Can you give me a fag?"* he looked up like an imploring child.

*"Here,"* said Raymond. He whipped out a packet of Woodbines from the right pocket of his cassock, pulled back the flap of the lid and offered what was left of the box to Fr. Underhill.

*"Ah, thank you Raymond. I'll pay you back…"* then he paused, looking nervously up at Anthony.

*"It's alright, Father,"* said Peter, *"We've told Anthony the book we keep."*

Fr. Robin looked nervously at Anthony then looked back at Raymond and said,

*"Well, you know you owe me one so we're quits,"* winking at Raymond. Then there was a moment's silence as the four of them blew their smoke up to the ceiling. Anthony thrust his hands into his cassock pockets. He stood awkwardly. Then he saw Jamie across near the billiard table.

*"Excuse me,"* he said, *"I can see Jamie McCleod. I have something to tell him."* Without waiting for any response he stepped briskly out of the

gambler's circle and crossed the five metres of floor space, pushing between two groups of divines and sighed with relief as he reached Jamie McCleod. As he reached him he waved his hand which was paralled to the ground up and down in front of his face as if to blow away a stink in front of his nose.

*"What too smokey for you?"* smiled Jamie.

*"No I've just been with Peter, Joseph, Raymond and Fr. Robin and I am trying to blow their conversation away."* As soon as he had said it he began to regret it. Jamie would ask him what their conversation was about but luckily he just said,

*"Don't tell me, Anthony, I can imagine. Telling you about the way they lay bets as to who finishes the Rosary first."*

*"How did you know?"* asked Anthony.

*"Everyone knows. They are always first into the Common Room. They even bet on the fastest Rosary. A packet of cigarettes if someone can do it in less than four minutes."*

*"Four minutes,"* gasped Anthony.

*"Yes, four minutes. I think Raymond claims to have done it in three and a half minutes."* Jamie saw that Anthony's mouth was opening in astonishment, *"Don't be too shocked. Back in Ireland many of the priests say the Rosary as quick as that."*

*"What's the point of saying it at all?"* asked Anthony.

*"It's to fulfil their obligation,"* said Jamie, *"that's just the way they are."*

Half an hour had hardly passed when a loud bell was clanged up and down the corridor outside of the Common Room. Cigarettes were reluctantly extinguished and, divines and priests moved back not into the Pugin Chapel but instead a small and again low-ceilinged building known as the St. Francis de Sales sanctuary. Compline was spoken not sung and, as it only consisted of three short psalms, this office was prayed and finished in less than ten minutes. Anthony however always stayed praying long after the office had been finished. He prayed to God to make him a holy loving priest. Especially on this Saturday he thanked God for having made him the agent for the conversion of Sean to a new commitment to Him. He thanked God for calling him to holiness. Only half and hour later when only one divine was left in the sanctuary besides himself did he get up from his pew, genuflect and, as he left the chapel, take holy water from the stoop at the back. He walked out slowly and a few paces after leaving the sanctuary he turned left up the stone stairs and the corridor was empty as he made his way to his room.

He looked at his watch. It was twenty to ten. He turned the lamp on above his desk and settled down to read further Louis Bouyer's *The Meaning of Sacred Scripture*. But he couldn't read because his thoughts kept being interrupted by the smokers' betting ring. He could not understand why they wanted to be priests. He would thrust the thought aside and then return to the book but the gamblers' talk kept cutting into his concentration. He struggled on for an hour until sleep beckoned. He took off his cassock and hung it up on a peg in the middle of his door. He took off his shirt, trousers and finally his underpants. For a moment he stood naked in the middle of his room. As he stood there quite bare he felt his being become paper thin. He quickly reached for his pyjamas which were under his pillow. They were light brown. His mother had made them for him. As he knelt down by his bed to say his prayers he felt comforted by the feeling of those pyjamas upon his skin.

*   *   *

Anthony arrived with Sean at Clarence Cider's room on Thursday afternoon. Clarence was sitting upright and gazing straight ahead through his un-rimmed spectacles. The room looked even starker than when last he'd seen it. The steel crucifix above his table looked cold in its unsparing isolation. Clarence hardly glanced up as Anthony came in with Sean but nodded as the two of them sat down. In a few moments Rudolph Novak came in and then Joe Feeney, followed by Jamie McCleod and Stephen Warrior. There was an air of expectancy because they all knew that Clarence had something radical to say about the Real Presence of Jesus Christ in the Eucharist. When they were all seated Clarence looked sharply from left to right and then tapped the table with a pencil which he was holding in his right hand. His lips were quivering as he began to speak.

*"We all know,"* said Clarence, *"that Jesus is present in the Church. He is present because we all believe that he rose from the dead after having been crucified and continues to live to this day. When he rose from the dead his body was spiritual. It did not have mass or extension and, as Fr. Salter would tell us, mass and extension are what defines a material body so Christ's body was not material. He was able to pass through doors so his body could not be material."* He stopped and tapped his pencil. He was sitting at the edge of his table-cum-desk. Sean was sitting erect with his back to the window on an iron-framed chair. Jamie was sitting on a yellow cushion on the floor with his back semi-against the wall. He was the only one in the

room who looked restful and unconcerned with what was about to be said. Rudolph in contrast was looking with intense grimness down at his shoes which were black and unpolished. Joe Feeney was sitting facing Clarence on the opposite side of the table looking with a knitted concern on his brows at the Taizé counterpane. Stephen was sitting on the bed itself and running his finger impatiently along the white of the St. Andrew's Cross that edged the purple weave. Clarence looked around before he went on, *"What the apostles were witnessing was a spiritual presence and it is this presence that lives on. Because Christ is a spiritual presence he is able to inhabit a material body. He can take up his abode in any material thing. The place where he dwells is in all of us. He dwells in all those who open their hearts to him. He takes up his abode in us …"*

*"But what about the Eucharist?"* asked Sean nervously.

*"Just as the spiritual body of Christ was able to pass through doors and inhabit us he is also able to inhabit a piece of bread,"* said Clarence decisively.

*"You see,"* said Stephen chipping in with his sensuous voice and shaking his curly red haired head, *"Christ was only seen after his Resurrection because the apostles believed in him. If there had been some pagan by-standers they would not have seen Jesus at all. It is belief that opens the eyes and 'makes' Christ present."*

*"But,"* said Sean aghast, *"do you mean to say that in the Blessed Sacrament Jesus is only present to believers?"*

*"Yes,"* said Rudolph with incisive certainty, *"St. Thomas Aquinas said that if a mouse ate the consecrated host it would only be eating bread. It is the belief of the worshippers that turns it into Christ."*

*"But,"* asked Jamie dreamily, *"why is it Body and Blood? Those sound material enough."*

*"It's because,"* said Clarence, *"that the Mass is a memorial of the Last Supper but it is a living memorial through faith. Christ is present spiritually whole and entire in both the bread and the wine. It's a spiritual presence in both."*

*"I always thought of His Presence in a more real way,"* said Sean.

*"It is entirely real,"* said Clarence.

*"But,"* said Sean, *"every year we say a public prayer because someone threw a consecrated host into that pond out there in the meadow,"* and as he said this he turned round and pointed out the window.

*"That's not because Jesus in the host was damaged but because the man who did it was sneering at God. Like someone deliberately shitting on the sanctuary of a church,"* said Clarence.

*"Each of us is present here in our bodies but a person can be present through the telephone or through the written word. Christ is present through the medium of belief both in us and in the Eucharist,"* said Rudolph.

*"So you mean a living person can be inhabited by the spirit of a dead person?"* asked Anthony incredulously.

*"Yes, certainly,"* said Rudolph, *"just read Homer and you will see how they all believed that the spirits of their fathers who had died were still living and protecting them.*

Stephen Warrior laughed and said,

*"When you die Anthony you'll come and inhabit me,"*

*"And that can happen,"* said Clarence seriously, *"through the power of Christ."*

*"It happens through belief,"* said Rudolph, *"I knew a woman once whose husband died and she believed that he was present in her and people even noticed that her movements became similar to his but they were robotic, not natural. It happens quite a lot. The difference between that and Christ's presence is that with the latter it is natural."*

*"It sounds all very fine,"* said Sean, *"but there is something I don't know what it is but, to be sure, it's not right. I know that for sure."*

Anthony strained forward, looked at Sean and then back at Rudolph. He was fascinated by what Rudolph had said. The idea that the spirit of someone could take up habitation in another. In fact Anthony's mind went on thinking about it and he only heard the rest of the conversation going on as a background noise. When the meeting came to a close he was still thinking about it. *'So a dead person can inhabit the body and soul of a living person',* he said to himself. Usually when the Doktor Klub meeting finished he would stay and chat to Clarence or Stephen especially but sometimes to Joe Feeney but this time he walked off meditatively to his own room. There was something about the soul of a dead person inhabiting a living one that kept circling around in his mind.

\* \* \*

So this small platoon of dedicated zealots finally left Newman College to be ordained after having been at the College for nearly six years. They were the new apostles and they were going to preach their message to the whole world but first they would convert their parish priests and parishioners. They were full of confidence. The spirit of God was with them, or so they believed.

# CHAPTER THREE

So on Trinity Sunday in 1966 he and all his friends, these blood brothers of the Doktor Klub, were ordained as priests in Westminster Cathedral. As soon as the ordination had happened and they had had a celebratory drink with Cardinal Molony the young priests dispersed each to their own families at a variety of different venues. Anthony gave his priest's new blessing to his mother and father. This was a moment of embarrassment and tender feeling. His father knelt down devoutly and made the sign of the Cross as Anthony laid his newly anointed hands upon him and then he did the same for his mother. His mother looked up at him rather shyly. She looked momentarily into his eyes; she seemed to see something unspoken between them. Was this really his vocation? Anthony had never doubted it but in this micro-second as their eyes met he wondered if this whole ceremonial was a sham. It was the most fleeting thought, not even a thought but rather a subliminal flash as his eyes met hers.

The transition from being a pious divine at Newman College to being an ordained priest was as different as the butterfly is from the caterpillar. At his first Mass celebrated at his parish in Brighton Catholics all called him 'Father'. Each time someone called him this, he felt awkward. He did not feel comfortable in this new role. He had been ordained a priest but he did not feel a priest. These Catholics flocking around calling him 'Father' expected him to act as a traditional Conservative Catholic. He was asked to bless medals, offer prayers to Our Lady of Lourdes and grant indulgences which were now all practices in which Anthony no longer believed. As the pious Catholics surrounded their new priest he felt a fraud.

Shortly after ordination Anthony received a note from the Vicar General of the Diocese instructing him to take up his first post as a curate in the parish of Bow in the East End of London. Stephen Warrior had been posted to the next door parish in the borough of Poplar. Clarence Cider was sent to Kentish Town, Joe Feeney to Camden Town, Jamie McLeod to Mile End which was just west of Anthony's parish, Rudolph Novak went to Edmonton and Sean Casey was sent to the town of Hertford. Anthony arrived with enthusiasm at his new parish but what Anthony was experiencing now so shortly after ordination was something quite new. A person, a new life, was bursting out of its crysalls and it was very alarming and the young priest had no idea where it was going to take him but he felt in his bones he was just beginning a new and frightening journey. All his enthusiasm, passion and intellectual conviction nourished and developed through years of study, listening to lectures and discussions in the Doktor Klub was the froth on a tankard of Guinness. What he was drinking now was the substance of life itself. What had gone before was a filtered abstraction from life that evaded the terror of life itself. It was the difference between reading a manual on how to fly a plane and flying a real plane in reality.

Anthony's response to this experience on that Thursday afternoon so soon after arriving at his parish when he felt God now as a friend rather than a lordly emperor was to throw himself even more fervently into his priestly missionary task. He had convinced himself that the message of Jesus Christ, the Saviour of Mankind, was not understood by the people of the parish and least of all by Fr. Smithes, the parish priest. He believed, like many of the worker priests of France had believed, that he was a missionary in a pagan country and though like most European nations it called itself Christian yet it was only so in name. The Christianity which people professed was just a veneer. One holiday when Anthony was still studying for the priesthood he had gone with Clarence to Pontigny in France which was the headquarters of the worker priest movement. He had met there an elderly French priest called Pierre Michau whose role was to try to inculcate Christian values among businessmen.

> "Many businessmen," he had said, "lead very good family lives; they are faithful to their wives, bring up their children well but when it comes to business they are ruthless savages. They cheat, do down a friend, think nothing of lying to get a contract, pretend that their products are good. They lead two lives informed by quite contrary values."

Fr. Michau spent his time visiting big businesses in France to try and sow the seed of Christian charity into the heart of industry. Anthony was determined to do the same. He would bring the Christian faith to the people of Bow in London's East End. He would do what Fr. Michau was doing in France. He knew that God had chosen him for this task. He must also act quickly, he thought cynically, before he was moved onto another parish. He had forgotten that Fr. Michau had told him that he thought it would take a hundred years to bring about some change. Anthony was going to produce visible results and people would see that he was the agent who had brought them about. On arriving at the parish he had accommodated himself initially to Fr. Smithes's leisurely pace and old-fashioned ways of doing things but now, in the grip of an inner zest, he threw himself into his new missionary work with a zeal which surprised everyone and very soon brought him acclaim, even from high places.

What he did not know was that he had been terrified of that new emotional experience that had hit him on that Thursday afternoon in early September. He had only been in his parish for three months. Although it came to him as a great relief, it also terrified him. In fact his missionary zeal was propelled by a stampede to evade a panic generated by his frightening vision. When he had had those doubts about God's existence when first at Newman College he was free to leave in the way that Fr. Salter had suggested should the doubts resolve into a certain atheism but it put him into a panic that he should be visited by a radical emotional upheaval once he had been ordained a priest. He had vowed himself to the perpetual service of God in the priesthood. He had given his blessing to all his family who had surrounded him with love and devotion. What on earth would Fr. Salter say now? And why had this emotional upheaval hit him so soon <u>after</u> ordination rather than before? The experience was enormously liberating but, at the same time, terrifying. He fled from it and it was significant that the hero of his mind was no longer Fr. Salter but instead Sidney Darrell.

He rushed round the parish on his bicycle and gathered as many of the married couples who were practising Catholics as he could and formed them into groups of missionary couples. He formed six of these groups. He was going to spearhead a revolution in the Christian life of the parish. He took the Gospels to heart and based his missionary enterprise upon passionate expositions of the sayings of Jesus. He would then make sure that a meeting never broke up without each married couple individually and jointly having agreed to action which was the natural outcome of what they had read and studied together. These couples became caught up in the fervour of Anthony's enthusiasm. One of the groups which met on a council estate near Bow Road decided to find out all the lonely old people living in their area. One of the group, Teresa, then visited regularly an old ninety-year-old woman and after a while she said to Fr. Stonewell,

*"I enjoy visiting old Mrs. Camphor now so I suppose it's not a good work any more"*. Anthony took up her remark with excitement and tried to explain that the good and the pleasurable should coincide and that the idea that what was good was only ever discovered in a moral imperative which went contrary to natural sympathies was a false spirituality.

*"But what about the saints who whipped themselves?"* asked Teresa.

*"That false kind of asceticism came into the Church through the influence of the Albigensian heresy in the twelfth century. Although the Church condemned it, yet it left its foul-smell upon it; it was a betrayal of the original Christian vision whose whole stress was on the centrality of love."* Teresa did not understand any of this history but as she looked at Anthony she felt captivated by his spirit.

*"There must be a lot of people who have got it wrong,"* said Teresa, puzzled rather than doubting the authenticity of Anthony's impassioned certainty ...

*"You are right, there are,"* said Anthony, stamping his foot as he said the word 'are'. They were standing at the side of Devons Road just outside Teresa's flat where their meeting had taken place. On both sides of Devons Road were council flats which had all been built during the Labour Government that had come to power at the end of the war. Teresa and Vince lived however in a council flat which had been more recently built. The building looked less tattered and worn. Teresa and Anthony were walking back up this road which sliced this large housing estate in two. He was returning to his presbytery and she was going to catch the bus down to Stratford to visit her mother.

*"And when did we begin to get things back into perspective?"* asked Teresa just as they were passing the little turning that led to the primary school. Anthony explained vehemently that it was only within the last few years with the renewal of interest in the Bible in the Church and in the Liturgy and in Catechetics that the Church was getting back to how Christ had meant it to be. He did not notice Teresa looking at him nervously. He knew his message was right. The message, like some feared bandit, had kidnapped his mind so totally that he did not notice his disciples' responses. People were either on his side or against him. Once they were on his side there was no light and shade. They were his undoubting devotees. Back at the presbytery he knew he was bringing the Christian message to the people of Bow. It was the first time they had heard the message. He was their apostle. He was satisfied as he said Compline that night and a thrill of pleasure travelled around his frontal lobes.

The couples in this Family Gospels Movement were excited and enlivened by their meetings and from the activities which developed out of them and they talked incessantly about Fr. Stonewell whenever they met. In the many years of their lives as parishioners of Catholic parishes they had never come across anything like this. They had participated in the Legion of Mary and helped to run jumble sales but this was different. It was clear to them that Fr. Stonewell was breathing a new message and life into them. Previous priests and Fr. Smithes had taken it for granted that they all knew the faith; Anthony started from the premiss that they did not know anything about God or Christianity. They were ignorant pagans but hypocritical ones because they believed they were devout Christians but Anthony was going to disabuse them with all the fervour in his thumping breast. He was going to breathe into them a new spirit, a life from God himself. Teresa realized one day that she had never really believed at all but had treated the Church as a club for decent people to pay their respects to God like feudal peasants paying homage to the Lord of the Manor. As her excitement rose so Anthony's fervour reached a new intensity. People felt excited, though at the same time they felt uneasy. Why, they wondered, if all what Fr. Stonewell said were true had they not heard about it before? However the Church was changing in symphony with Anthony's pastoral methods. The Mass had been celebrated for sixteen hundred years in Latin and suddenly the Church declared that it was to be offered in the national language of each country. If the Church could have been wrong for so long then perhaps Fr. Stonewell was right.

One evening Teresa was sitting at home after supper while her husband had gone out to the local Trades Union Meeting. She was sitting with one leg up on an imitation leather settee turning the pages of *The Universe* with idle attention. Their flat was compact and neat. It was on the ground floor and luckily those who lived in the flat above them were an elderly couple so the flat was also quiet. It faced away from Devons Road so it did not catch the noise of traffic. Teresa and Vince had lived there for six years and they had become fond of it. The lounge suite was finished in white imitation leather. The window looked out onto a playing area and there was an acacia tree framed in the left hand side of the window. Teresa's pride was a small grandfather clock which she had bought in the City. She worked in an insurance office at Tower Hill. One day she had gone out at lunchtime and seen in a funny old furniture shop a small grandfather clock. It cost £38. In great excitement she had bought it, took it back to the office and dragged it home with her in the tube that evening. She had rung Vince who met her at Bow Road Station and helped her to carry it back to their flat. She installed it between the settee and the window. It struck the hours and the half-hours. It however annoyed Vince so she turned off the strike mechanism when he was at home.

There was a knock on the door. She threw down her Catholic newspaper, jumped up niftily and ran to the door. It was her friend, Anna. She liked Anna. Anna was not married and was the daughter of young Bob. Teresa's husband, Vince, was a docker and his mate Bob was a stevedore. Bob and his wife, Julie, were devout Catholics and Anna, just nineteen, had a job as a secretary in the City, like Teresa. Teresa who was in her early thirties had helped Anna find her job and gave her friendly advice. Teresa was infertile; she had decided not to adopt but had gathered around her some young teen-agers who turned to her as a surrogate aunt. She was pleased to see Anna at her door but guessed that she was in some trouble. Teresa already knew that she had a boyfriend who had been married before so the Church would not allow her to marry. She was prohibited by the Church from marrying a divorcee. Anna had come to Teresa for help. She was desperate. There was nothing to be done but she always felt better when she had spoken with Teresa.

*"The only thing to do,"* said Anna, *"is to marry in a register Office but it will break my father's heart."*

*"How about going and speaking to the priest?"* asked Teresa.

*"Well I know what the priests will say. They will say that I'll have to give him up and I'm not prepared to."*

*"Go and speak to Fr. Stonewell,"* said Teresa without a moment's hesitation. As Teresa said this she said,

*"Have a cuppa?"*

*"Yeah, please,"* said Anna. Teresa went and plugged in the kettle. The tiny kitchen was open to the sitting-room via a hob on which the kettle sat. Teresa, her face though slightly thinner, was not unlike the portrait of St. Teresa of Avila, the saint after whom she had been named. Her maternal grandmother had been Spanish and was born in Avila. She had the same curved nose, lively expression and a certain sad wisdom in her eyes. She returned to her seat on the settee. Anna was sitting on its matching chair. They looked at each other and smiled.

*"Is he that new young priest?"* asked Anna. Anna and her parents lived in Wapping and attended the Church in Commercial Road. Old Fr. Dunstan had been parish priest there for thirty-two years.

*"Yes, do talk to him,"* said Teresa enthusiastically, *"he's as different from Fr. Dunstan as fish from tomato."*

*"But what could Fr. Stonewell say?"* asked Anna.

*"Wait a minute,"* said Teresa as she fished for two Lipton tea-bags and took two fawn mugs from out under the hob.

*"Two sugars or one?"* asked Teresa.

*"Three if you please,"* smiled Anna.

*"Cor, you'll be drinking treacle."*

*"Yes, that's what me Mum always says. Says I'll become a piece of Brighton Rock, she does."* They both laughed. Anna had dark hair cut short, an untidy brown skirt, a fluffy yellow blouse and eyes that laughed as she spoke.

*"Serious, though,"* said Anna, *"what could Fr. Stonewell do. All them priests are under orders, aren't they ?'*

*"Not Fr. Stonewell,"* laughed Teresa.

*"How's he different then?"*

*"E's 'uman,"* said Teresa, *"that's what 'e is. And my he's got it up there,"* she said tapping her forehead.

Two days later Anna was knocking on the presbytery door. She was surprised to find a priest who was so young. He looked really handsome, she thought. He moved in a sprightly manner. Going first he led her past the dining-room and kitchen doors on the right and he threw open a dark stained heavy door. The room was dull grey. There was an old wooden table that was on a slant and a few old wooden chairs around it. It was obviously a room for meetings. On the wall was a photograph of Pope Pius XII. Anthony had wanted to replace it with a photograph of Pope John XXIII but Fr. Smithes had said with a hurt smile that he had a special love for Pius XII so the photograph had remained. Anthony beckoned Anna into a chair with a engaging smile.

*"What can I do for you?"* he asked in his impeccable King's English.

*"Probably nothin', Father, but Teresa Nixon tells me I should come and see yer', so 'ere I am."*

*"So, what's the problem?"* asked Anthony, leaning forward towards her with an eager stare.

*"Well, it's like this, Father, about a year ago I took up with Alan, me boyfriend, and we've been going steady for about nine months and now we want to get married ..."* she hesitated.

*"And ...?"*

*"Well, you see Father, Alan's been married before."*

*"Is he a Catholic?"*

*"Yes, he is, Father, but he's not been practising."*

*"Was his first marriage in the Church?"*

 *"Yes, Father."*

*"Why did it break up?"*

*"Well, I don't really know, Father, he don't talk about it."*

*"Well, find out about it. We need to know whether you can be married in Church to him or not."*

*"What if I can't, Father?"*

*"If I tell you that you can't be married to him in Church what will you do?"*

*"Well, to be honest, Fa'ver, I'm goin' on thirty and I think I would marry 'im."*

*"Ok, I've got the picture. Go and find out from Alan all about his first marriage. Get him to come and talk to me if that would help and then come back and see me."* Anthony was quite crisp and businesslike. He liked to get the legal situation clear.

Three days later Alan called to see Fr. Stonewell and in that interview he confessed that he had not been married in the Church but that in fact his wife had been divorced and the whole thing was a disaster and only lasted a few months. After a short discussion it was clear that Alan was free to marry in the Catholic Church because his previous marriage was invalid in the Church's eyes. The Church did not recognize a marriage when one of the partners was a divorcee. Anna came back to see Anthony at the week-end and he explained the situation to her clearly and briskly. She was over the moon and rushed back to tell her friend, Teresa. In a short time Anthony got the reputation for being a whizz-kid who could sort out all these awkward legal tangles that were a source of so much distress to devout Catholics. When Teresa spoke to him and said how grateful she was to him on behalf of Anna he said,

*"People manufacture problems that are not really there."*

Teresa repeated this to all the other married couples in her group and soon his saying had spread around the parish and beyond the boundaries of the parish. It became known that if a Catholic had some awkward situation then Fr. Stonewell was the person to see. Catholics were coming to see him even from distant parishes. The more they came the busier did Anthony become.

One day Matthew Flaherty from the Wapping parish came to see him. He confided that he was homosexual. He told Fr. Stonewell that he had been practising as a Catholic for some years but then about eighteen months before he had taken up a permanent relationship with a man and he knew that there was no point in going to confession because he was not going to give up the sexual side of his relationship.

*"Do you love him?"* asked Anthony.

*"Well I loves 'im as much as many married people loves each other,"* he said resentfully.

*"Do you think that God condemns you?"*

*"Well I know the Pope does, Fa'ver …."*

*"We know what the Pope says but what do you think?"*

*"Well, I don't think it's really wrong, Father. I did not choose to be 'omosexual-like, I just turned out that way. I tried it with women and all that but it was just no good, Fa'ver, me whole nature is the other way."*

*"If that's what you think you must back what you think and decide for yourself that it's not a sin."* said Anthony.

*"What shall I say in Confession then, Fa'ver?"*

*"Confession is for sins,"* said Anthony curtly, *"if it's not a sin then there's nothing to confess."*

*"But you mean I say nothin' about it when I goes ter confession?"*

*"Confession is for sin,"* repeated Anthony decisively, *"Sin is when you offend God in your heart knowingly. If you feel that you are on terms of friendship with God then there is nothing to confess. If you treat your partner unlovingly then confess that."*

Matthew felt a great weight lifted off his shoulders and soon the word went round among homosexuals that Fr. Stonewell was a sympathetic priest and he soon found his confessional full of homosexuals and other people with sexual difficulties. His name spread and he found that he was being asked to preach and lecture to many different lay groups. Fr. Stonewell always accepted these invitations so consequently his week became more and more full up and he began to be sought after by many people in the Church who were looking for someone understanding and open to the modern world and its problems.

\* \* \*

He had only just established the Family Gospels Movement when he started a branch of the Young Christian Workers (YCW). At Newman College he had already involved himself in this movement which had been started in Belgium by Joseph Cardijn and it was closely involved with the Workers' Priest Movement in France. He went to visit Fr. Victor in Millwall. He had run YCW groups for years and Fr. Victor had been a hero to the members of the Doktor Klub since he had first joined it at Newman College. He had seen him at a deanery meeting but not to speak to. Anthony decided he would just go and visit Fr. Victor unannounced. It was a Wednesday morning. He had already done the rounds of the wards in St. Andrew's Hospital and, having finished just after ten in the morning, he mounted his large framed police bicycle and pedalled down through Poplar onto East India Dock Road which encircled the Isle of Dogs peninsula until he reached the Catholic Church. Fr. Victor was a legend, not only in the East End of London, but throughout the clergy and laity in London. He had introduced the liturgy in English a year before it had been approved by Rome.

*"It's always better to be ahead of the Pope,"* he said with a jocular laugh, *"then there's no danger of being behind the times."* Anthony had seen him once or twice at clergy meetings but had not encountered him face-to-face. He cycled up to the door and propped his bicycle against a circular iron railing that connected the door of the presbytery with the wall of the entrance. He knocked. He put his head towards the door and listened. He knew that Fr. Victor had no housekeeper. He waited and then he heard heavy foot-steps and, in a flash, Fr. Victor swept the door open.

*"Hello, come in. A priest at the door eh! I must have committed a sin to draw a priest to my door,"* he said with his eyes twinkling. He stood about five foot ten inches with white hair clipped short and an oblong face. He stood in black baggy trousers and a heavy black tweed coat. He led the way through to a bare wooden table that was in a room whose window looked out on the cranes in the midst of flats in a housing estate.

*"You're looking at those cranes, eh?"* Anthony nodded and Fr. Victor continued, *"If you look on the right you will see a dirty British coaster. There's a canal that comes right between the blocks of flats."* Anthony stretched his neck at the side of the window and, sure enough, he could see the black funnel of a small steamship.

*"Have a coffee, a black coffee. Nothing better in the middle of the morning, keeps the spirit awake in the body."* Fr. Victor poured a thick black liquid from a large brass pot that had been sitting on his ancient stove since morning. Anthony sipped it. It was burnt and tasted foul but he did not mind. He watched Fr. Victor gulp down a large cup in three huge mouthfuls.

*"Well, it's nice to have a visit from a priest. Some of you young priests seem to listen to me now. For years all my contemporaries have dismissed me as*

a madman. I've been telling them that our only job is to establish a relation-ship between ourselves and God and that all those rosary beeds, plaster stat-ues and holy water are a lot of nonsense. They're alright for Italian widows but no good for dockers, stevedores and lightermen." He was tapping his fin-gers on the table and looking keenly at Anthony and paused.

"I want to start a group of Young Christian Workers in my parish, Father."

"Hurrah," shouted Fr. Victor and he clapped his hands together so a loud echo reverberated from one wall to the other, "hurrah; the East End has got a priest at last instead of one of those functionaries lighting candles and collecting money." Anthony smiled shyly.

"I've come to get your advice. How do I get it started?" Fr. Victor paused for a moment,

"I've got just the person for you. Young Terry Hughes. He was in my group but he went away, was co-opted to unload a huge ship that had come into Tilbury and when he returned he went back to live with his Mum and Dad and that's just near to you. He was going to come back here but I'll tell him to help you get a group started. Then we'll have two groups in the East End. Things are looking up. He'll help you get the YCW started." Fr. Victor got up, pulled out a draw from the side of the table and grubbed through several papers and then,

"Here it is. Here's his address…" and he turned the paper towards Anthony. "Look take a pen and copy this and I will keep this one for myself." Anthony took out a pen and copied the name, address and telephone number. Then the two men sat back. One in his late sixties, full of life and energy and the other in his late twenties full of hope and expectancy but already on the verge of despair.

"Get hold of Terry," said Fr. Victor, "and he will get some of his mates. They won't all be Catholics mind. They'll be rough but if they see you're ded-icated they'll follow you to the gallows. The spirit of Christ is natural to them. No need to do a lot of explaining. Just sit round with them, take a Gospel pas-sage and they will bring it to life. It'll be like the first time you've heard the Gospel when they just react to it. Jesus draws people to him just by the sim-plicity and truth of what he says. All they need to see is that you have your heart in it and St. Paul himself will not have had more devoted followers. I can tell you," Fr. Victor stopped and looked intently at Anthony, "it has been humbling for me to be with these young lads and lasses having the courage to say a prayer in a factory when someone is injured. People around them laugh to start with but inside them their hearts are stirred. They have the love of Christ in their hearts and their courage is an inspiration to us priests. There's no difficulty for me to pray here in the Church but just think of *the courage it needs for a young seventeen-year old to kneel down and say a prayer in the docks with everyone laughing at him."*

The two priests sat and talked earnestly. Although Fr. Victor was quite different to Fr. Salter, far more humorous and out-going and powerfully expressive, yet he had that same quality which was golden for Anthony. He spoke from the heart; he spoke directly what he thought; it was him speaking and not a tape-recorder repeating what had been programmed into it. He not only spoke from the heart but he had that same non-sectarian attitude of heart. An atheist could be holy, a young factory worker could be holy, a communist could be close to Jesus. There was something deeper in human beings than political associations or cultural groupings. Something deep within Anthony resonated with this. It was this that sprang up on that day when suddenly the world changed on that memorable Thursday. But it was a delicate flower always in danger of being swept away by mob-zeal.

Anthony rode away with a thrilling tremor in his chest. He cycled back up through Poplar, Bow Common and finally back to Bow Road and his presbytery. That very evening he was knocking on the flat of Terry Hughes. He lived in his parents' home in a block of flats on the other side of St. Andrew's Hospital. It was an older, slightly dilapidated block. It had been built just before the war. A sensitive face met him at the door. He was standing in blue sports shorts, a striped football jumper and stockinged feet.

"Hello, Father," he said shyly.

*"I've come after speaking to Fr. Victor,"* said Anthony looking at Terry's tousled fair hair. As soon as he mentioned 'Fr. Victor' Terry's eyes lit up. Anthony, a cinder inside him, caught between the sparkling eyes of Fr. Victor and Terry, set a petrol bomb alight inside him. He did not sit down, he just poured fourth, there in the passageway with Terry blinking at him, his desire to start a YCW Gospels Group. Terry's eyes glistened in response.

"Super, Father," he said, *"I'll get Tommy, Spark and Lilian and I know Lilian will bring her friend, Josie. With me that will make six of us."* In no time a deal had been struck.

*"Can we meet at the presbytery, Father?"*

*"Of course."*

*"Which evening is best for you?"*

*"What about Monday?"*

*"That's a good night for all of us."*

Ten days later Anthony was waiting in the interview room in the presbytery. He had put seven chairs around the bare wooden table. He had bought seven copies of J.B. Phillips' *New Testament* in modern English and put them in front of each chair. He sat on one of the chairs; he looked at his watch. It was ten to seven. They were due at seven. He wrung his hands. He was nervous. After that excited interchange with Terry when the deal had been struck he felt that a lot would be expected of him. He might despise old Mrs. O'Brien but he knew that she would be loyal and faithful just because he was a Catholic priest but with this young group it was different. He had to prove himself. The status of priesthood was not enough. It was who he was as a person which would determine the success of the group. He stood up, paced up and down, looked around the room. The walls were a darkening yellow and the paint was pealing. There were two old cupboards against two of the walls and the window was high up and a single globe hung from the centre without a shade. There had been a photograph of St. Bernadette of Lourdes but Anthony had removed it and also a fading picture of St. Francis of Assisi receiving the stigmata on Mount Averno. There were just two objects on the walls: one was a baroque figure of the Crucified Christ which had been re-nailed to a simple modern wooden Cross and a picture of Matteo Ricci in sanyasi robes and painted in Chinese style in the sixteenth century. Anthony had put them both there not long before. He looked at his watch. It was just three minutes before seven. He sat down and opened the New Testament in front of his seat. He looked again at the passage which he had chosen for discussion. He put his finger on it and was just starting to re-read it when the door-bell rang. He jumped up and hurried to the door. He opened it and there was an expectant pack of youngsters,

*"Evening, Father."*

*"Come in; come in,"* said Anthony. He hardly saw the individual identities of the little gang as they walked in, looking to right and left. They were all dressed in dark clothes except Terry who was in light fawn trousers and a matching shirt.

*"Take seats, any chairs you want."* A moment's giggling and shuffling and then all were seated. Anthony took the chair at right angles to those on the two sides. Terry sat on his far right and, as he smiled, he said,

*"Introduce yourselves."*

*"OK, I'm Anthony."*

*"Yes, Father,"* they all chorused.

*"I'm Tommy,"* and Anthony saw on his far left, opposite Terry, a boy with a wide open face and semi-fair hair with a relaxed smile. He wore a dark wool jacket and corduroy trousers. He reminded Anthony slightly of Joe Feeney. He had that same casual relaxed attitude. Then on his right were the two girls, sitting next to each other as if for protection.

*"I'm Lilian,"* said the one furthest from Anthony and next to Terry. She had dark hair and bright blue eyes and wore a rain jacket, a tweed blouse and blue trousers. Anthony smiled at her and then looked to her left and next to him,

*"And I'm Pauline,"* she was wearing a dark blue anorak with a purple skirt and a purple blouse of brushed cotton. Anthony smiled at her and then turned to his left. He knew this must be Spark. He had dark hair, a pointed nose and looked keenly at Anthony with his dark brown eyes.

*"Well, Fa'ver, I'm Spark. I'm Terry's mate and 'e tol' me that ye was a friend 'er Fr. Victor. I ain't got much time for priests an' all that but any friend of Fr. Victor's is me friend."* Then he turned to the girl right next to him on his left and raised his eyebrows at her inviting her to introduce herself:

*"I'm Josie,"* she said, *" and it's me that's brought Pauline,"* she said nodding across the table at her friend. Josie was blond and wore red trousers with a jacket to match. She smiled warmly at Anthony. He knew it was now his moment to speak.

Then there was a pause. All looked at Anthony. He felt awkward as all eyes were pinned on him. Now was his moment. No Church pulpit had ever aroused in him such anguish.

*"When Jesus died,"* started Anthony, *" his disciples and apostles were in despair. Their hopes had been right up there,"* and Anthony pointed with his right hand up to the ceiling, *" they were full of dedication and enthusiasm and then, in less than three days their leader had been executed like a common criminal,"* he nodded to crucifix on the wall. The three who were opposite it looked at the forlorn figure nailed to the Cross, the other three turned round and looked at it. There was a momentary pause, then the three that had their backs to it, spun back round again quite suddenly. They all glued their eyes upon Anthony.

*"Jesus came to show a new path for mankind, for every one of us, but it was more than that. The twelve apostles were in despair and then suddenly, fifty days after Jesus had been battered to death for all Jerusalem to see, His Spirit gripped hold of the twelve and they were all filled with his energy and life."* As Anthony spoke he felt enthusiasm draining out of him. He was

drumming up a message that he did not believe deep in his heart. He dared not stop. He kept going with even greater determination.

*"So he's in all of us. What we have now to do is to live him."* He stopped momentarily and all eyes were on him again. He knew he had to continue. He felt he was walking to the gallows.

*"So what I want us all to do here is to take a small passage from the Gospel and discuss it."* At this moment Anthony turned to his copy of the New Testament and he had in it a bookmark – the ordination card of Stephen Warrior. He looked up and said, " *I'm going to read to you a short passage from St. Luke's Gospel:*

> *"And what is the point of calling me, 'Lord, Lord', without doing what I tell you to do ? Let me show you what the man who comes to me, hears what I have to say, and puts it into practice, is really like. He is like a man building a house, who dug down to rock-bottom and laid the foundation of his house upon it. Then when the flood came and the flood-water swept down upon that house, it could not shift it because it was properly built. But the man who hears me and does nothing about it is like a man who built his house with its foundations upon soft earth. When the flood-water swept down upon it, it collapsed and the whole house crashed down in ruins."*

*"Now what I would like us to do first is to just look at the passage and **See** what it means. Let us just start with that. What do you think the passage actually means, Terry?"* Anthony looked at him on his far right,

*"Well, Father, I think it means that words have to be taken in deep down not just heard and head nodded and sayin' 'OK' let's move to the next point."*

*"Could you think of an example?"* asked Anthony.

*"Yes, well Father, there's a young stevedore that belongs to one of e churches and he's always preachin' love of neighbour an' all that but the last week me mate Rob was knocked unconscious when a crate tipped and hit 'im on the 'ead and one of the ol' dockers who's always swearin' and cursin', 'Cursin' Tom' we call 'im – it was 'im that ran to me mate, nursed 'im in 'is arms and carried 'im all 'e way to the 'ospital on 'is shoulders. E young stevedore was there and did nothin'. Well the ol' docker's words were not good but 'e acted like a real Christ follower. I should think 'e 'ad taken in 'e words of Jesus, Father; well 'e was putting 'em into practice anyway."* Terry spoke quite slowly, leaning back in his chair. He might have been conducting a seminar at a university.

*"Fav'er when you reads out that there bit abaht digging down ter rock-bottom it makes me think of me Mum,"* said Josie, turning and looking at

Anthony, *" she always says that yer niver knows somethin' until yer dream abaht it. The other night I 'ad a dream and in it I saw me Mum's sister bein' it by a car an' she fell in 'e road and I rushed up but when I got there she was dead an' I woke cryin'. Now that was wot 'appened like ten month back. She was 'it by car and died a couple 'er days later. When I tol' me Mum she said ter me, 'that's e way, Josie, now yer knows it, an' its funny, Fa'ver, she used them very words. She says ter me 'Now yer know rock-bottom in yer soul that dear Doris is dead'.*

"Yes," said Anthony excitedly, *"and it's only when it's deep down that you practice it just like Cursing Tom did. So that what it means – something can be deep down or just on the surface and it's only when it's deep down that the person lives it."* Anthony spoke this with all the energy of a whistling curlew. As he spoke it he thought of that moment when he suddenly realized that God was a friend he could talk with. It was like Josie's dream, he thought. He sat back for a moment and there was a peace in the room.

*"So do you think that is what Jesus meant? He was inviting us to take what he said deep down into our souls?"*

"Yes, Fa'ver," said Spark, *"that's wot 'e means alright. It's no bloody good 'avin' it 'ere,"* he said leaning forward and tapping the right temple of his forehead, *"if it's not 'ere first,"* thumping his chest with his closed fist. *"That's 'e bloody trouble with all 'em churchgoers it's just all 'ere,"* he tapped the right temple of his head again.

"OK," said Anthony closing this phase of discussion, *"so we all know what Jesus meant."* He stopped and looked at Lilian and Pauline on his right and then Tommy on his left, *"do you agree ?"*

*"Oh yes, Fa'ver"* chirped the three who had not spoken.

*"OK, we've done the first part of our job. We've SEEN what Jesus meant. Now we come to the difficult bit: we have to work out how we put this into effect in our lives. We call this section JUDGE. Now is there some way in which this is not being done that we can start doing? Like Terry you mentioned Cursing Tom carrying your mate, Rob, when he was knocked unconscious ... by the way was he alright?"* Anthony asked suddenly.

"Oh, yes, Father," said Terry, *"'e jus' 'ad concussion. They keeps 'im in over night at e 'ospital and he spent e nex' day at 'ome wi' 'is Mum and 'e was back at work two days later."*

"Oh good, I'm glad," said Anthony.

"I tells yer wot, Fa'ver," said Pauline, *"all of us 'ere, except Terry and Spark, work in the big flour mill down Coventry Cross at bottom of Devons Road.*

*Don't know if yer remember, Fa'ver, there was an explosion in th' mill two month back. Four people were badly injured an' they ain't been properly compensated."*

"No, that's right," said Lilian, "we all know it but we ain't done nothin' abaht it."

Anthony looked at Tommy, *"What do you think, Tommy?"*

*"Yer, I agrees with th' girls. I don't think it's right, Fa'ver. All of us getting our pay as ever an' them four blokes on jus' 'arf pay, like."*

*"What can be done?"* asked Anthony.

*"I could go an' speak to Mr. Cozens,"* said Pauline.

*"Who's 'e?"* asked Spark.

*"E's th' manager of the Mill,"* said Pauline.

*"Is 'e the one responsible for workers' pay?"* asked Terry.

*"Well e's responsible ter Mr. Silver, 'e's th' General Manager of 'e whole kaboodle. It's up ter Mr. Cozens ter speak on be'alf of all 'e workers in the mill,"* said Pauline.

*"What's yer needs ter do,"* said Spark, *"is ter tell ol' Cozens that yer goin' to speak ter ol' Silver and that if yer doesn't get satisfaction then yer goin' to th' Union. That'll get Cozens goin', for sure."*

*"Yeah, that's a great idea there Spark,"* said Pauline, *"could all four of us go ter speak ter Mr. Cozens?"* she looked at Josie across from her and then at Lilian on her right and, only after she had eyed both of them did she look across to Tommy.

*"I'll come wi' yer,"* said Josie looking straight at her.

*"An' so will I,"* said Lilian.

"I'll come," said Tommy in a deep voice.

*"What about me and Spark?"* asked Terry.

*"Well we'll 'ave ter do somethin' down the docks,"* said Spark.

"I know," said Terry, *"we could go an' ask the PLA, that th' Port o' London Authority, Father, to set up a First Aid Centre. What 'appened to Rob las' week is always 'appenin'. We need a little centre with a nurse."*

*"Cor, what a super idea, Terry,"* said Spark, *"bloody marvellous. Why didn't we think of it before? Cor, Fa'ver, if Jesus can get those three men at the Mill their full pay an' we can get a First Aid Centre then Jesus is a powerful bloke."*

*"So that's your action,"* said Anthony, *"you four,"* he pointed with conscious deliberation first at Pauline, then at Tommy and then at Lilian and finally Josie, *"you four will go and speak to Mr. Cozens and tell him you want to see those three injured men on full pay and you, Terry, and Spark,"* and again he pointed with his right hand to Terry on his far right and then

Spark on his near left, *"you will go to the officials of the Port of London Authority and ask for a First Aid Centre to be installed in the docks."* He looked at them all holding his eyelids back, staring intently, *"Agreed?"*

"Yeah, we'll do it, Fa'ver," said Pauline.

"We sure will," said Spark nodding at Terry.

"OK," said Anthony, *"that's our Gospel Enquiry finished. There is an action for everyone and we all know what it is."*

"It sounds simple, don't it Fa'ver," said Josie, "but it's 'ard."

"Very hard," agreed Anthony, *"OK, the meeting's ended. Anyone like a beer?"*

"Wouldn't mind, Fa'ver," said Spark and Anthony went and fetched a large drum of bitter and with a tap drew off seven glasses of refreshing light brown liquid. They sat and drank and chatted for a quarter of an hour and then they departed, but not before all had agreed to return the following Monday.

So the meetings continued Monday by Monday with a dedicated faithfulness that was greater than the Sunday observance.

\* \* \*

Anthony was pleased with himself. People were seeking him out. The faithful felt that he thought about things and did not just give a pat answer and he also found that priests who were his contemporaries consulted him on matters of moral theology and canon law. He felt he was now truly one with Jesus. He was soon elected onto the council of priests who helped the Cardinal to run the diocese. One day at a meeting of the clergy he heard someone say that within ten years Anthony Stonewell would be a bishop. Anthony glowed with pleasure but despite all this informal acclaim he had one great difficulty and that was his relations with Fr. Smithes, his parish priest.

Fr. Smithes was a man of about fifty. He was kind and gentle and he never heard anyone say an unkind word against him. Frequently people said that he was 'holy'. This used to annoy Fr. Stonewell who thought people should be saying it of himself. No one ever said that Anthony was holy, only that he was understanding and full of energy and different from the previous generation of priests. Fr. Smithes was gently and quietly obedient to his superiors and his pastoral aim was to bring people back to the Church if they had lapsed and to the sacraments if they had ceased attending them. When he saw a parishioner who had not been practising his faith return one Sunday to Mass he beamed with a quiet joy. When Anthony saw this he became bitter inside. The best people, Fr. Smithes kept repeating, were those who came to communion every week. When Anthony attempted to say that what counted was a person's love towards his neighbour not whether he came to Church or not Fr. Smithes always answered that it was coming to the sacraments that enabled the good parishioner to be loving towards his neighbour. Anthony's words tumbled like waves against the cliffs of Dover and he also was equally impervious to words of Fr. Smithes. Fr. Smithes visited all the Catholics in his parish. He had the electoral list in his office and he systematically visited all the Catholics street by street.

> *"It is visiting the Catholics year in, year out that will bring them back to Church,"*

said Fr. Smithes. His persistence in going around the parish with single-minded devotion to the cause of rounding the lost sheep back into that stone pen every Sunday infuriated Anthony. What was Fr. Smithes doing and how could he think what he was doing was worthwhile, he kept asking himself. Anthony knew he was on a higher plane; he was concerned about his parishioners' inner state, their relationship with God. Attending Church, he kept repeating to himself is no guarantee that someone is in communion with God. He remembered his own sacrilegious communions as a child only too well.

> *"If they come to Church on Sunday they will hear the Word of God, go to the sacraments and be in a state of grace,"*

said Fr. Smithes again and again. Slowly but surely Fr. Smithes began to wear the young priest down. The zeal which had filled him like wine in a huge wooden vat slowly drained away until it was nearly empty.

On Saturday evenings the two priests heard confessions; Anthony in the confessional at the right side of the Church and George in the one on the left. Anthony kept the light on in his confessional so that the penitents could see him and he could see them. On the other hand George kept his confessional in darkness. Those who preferred anonymity went to George; those disciples of Anthony who were imbued with his stress on the human relationship went into Anthony's confessional. It might be thought that those with the worst sins would go to George and those with sins that were more venial to Anthony but it did not work out that way but in fact but quite the opposite. The queue at Anthony's confessional became longer and longer as homosexuals, those 'living in sin' and priests in difficulty began to hear of his 'understanding' approach whereas the pious parishioners like Mrs. O'Brien confessed to Fr. Smithes. Fr. Conan had taught the students at Newman College to give traditional penances – a Hail Mary for a small sin or a decade of the rosary for larger ones. George always gave to his penitents penances of this kind whereas Anthony, who knew better, enlightened by the New Theology, would give as a penance a reparative act towards the person the penitent had sinned against. When someone confessed to being uncharitable towards a friend Anthony would give as a penance an act of kindness towards the offended person or if a lie had been told then the penance might be to tell the person the truth within a few days. Lapsed Catholics and those who had strayed from the Church liked this approach whereas good practising Catholics were disturbed by it and preferred Fr. Smithes's traditional penances. They also warmed to George's gentle kindness. When confessions were over George would invite Anthony into the dining-room where he had assembled some bottles of alcohol in the form of whisky, wine and Dubonnet. It was George's opportunity to erode Anthony's enthusiastic practices under the soothing influence of his mellifluous voice oiled with alcohol.

*"I wouldn't turn the light on in your confessional, you know,"* said George quietly, *"the parishioners prefer the dark. They prefer not to be seen. Although I know we usually know who they are they prefer to think that we don't."*
Anthony felt awkward. George spoke so kindly but if he let a remark like that pass and say nothing he would go up to bed later feeling defeated and hopeless. He believed strongly that it was better to have the light on. He and all the members of the Doktor Klub had discussed it. The more human the encounter the better it was, they all believed. So he replied,

*"If we do know who they are then I prefer to be honest about it. I think the people who come to see me quite like it."*

*"I have been hearing confessions for over twenty years now and I don't think you are right. There may be one or two young people who don't mind but the faithful Catholics of the parish will not like it. They may come once or twice but you will find over time that people will keep away from your confessional."*

*"You see,"* George went on, *"good Catholics have been taught to be ashamed of their sins so they prefer to confess them in the dark."*

*"Strange to say,"* said Anthony infuriated by George's complacency, *"I think people who are more guilty and feel estranged from the Church, like homosexuals, for instance, rather like the opportunity to see the priest, to*

*speak to him, to think of him as a friend in the way that sinners found Jesus to be a friend and I think the light helps them."*

"Oh," said George, *"you don't get homosexuals here in the East End of London. All the homosexuals gather in clubs and similar meeting places in the West End and if they go to confession at all they go to Churches like St. James's in Spanish Place."*

Anthony sighed. He did not know what to say. That very evening three homosexuals had been to his confessional and sought guidance. He could not say that. Anthony knew why George had this perspective. A little while back he had been speaking to a woman at the hospital who had told him that she had recently had an abortion. He knew that she often spoke to George so he had asked her if she had told Fr. Smithes. She smiled at him awkwardly and said, *'I couldn't tell Fr. Smithes, he's so good I felt I would shock him.'* Anthony was sure it was the same kind of thinking that steered homosexuals and those estranged from the Church to his confessional rather than George's. So what could he say? He also thought it would be breaking the seal of the confessional to tell him that three homosexuals had confessed to him only a short while before. So he just said weakly,

*"I think you do get them in the East End as well. It's just a stereotype that they congregate more in the West End."* Anthony knew these were wasted words.

*"I think you'll find I'm right. I was brought up in the East End of London and I know the kind of Catholics living here quite well."*

The two men lapsed into silence. George felt that Anthony suffered from the worst of all sins: pride whereas he knew that he himself was humble. There was nothing worse than a proud priest. Anthony was so sure of himself. George poured him another whisky. He remembered young Fr. Conlan in his north London parish. He had been wild and cocky to begin with but George had slowly calmed him down and nothing helped more than a few drinks on a Saturday evening. So George sat back comfortably in his chair and said,

*"It's on Saturday nights that married couples have a 'go',"* said George with a knowing smile, *"when after a few drinks they get into bed the husband says, 'Come on, let's have a go.'"*

Anthony was paralysed again. George did not know any more than he did how married couples went about engaging in the sexual act. Just as George hated the cockiness of his young curate so Anthony could not bear George's complacent 'knowingness'. He did not say anything and George went on,

*"When I was first ordained I used to think that the vocation of marriage was much more enjoyable than our choice of celibacy but I know differently now. We have chosen the better part, you know Anthony; marriage is a much harder life and then all the hardships of bringing up children and having to earn enough money to manage. The small excitement of sex is not much to give up for what we have. Our lives are much easier."*

Anthony could hardly believe his ears. Was he really pleased to have chosen the easier path and was he satisfied with it? Was this his motive for choosing the priesthood, or at least living in it now? Anthony felt George slowly trying to undermine his youthful idealism. In this Anthony was wrong. George was simply declaring his own belief; it never occurred to him that it shocked his young curate. For George the priesthood was a way of life and, as the years had worn on, he came to believe that it was a better way of life than that of marriage. The fact that he thought it less penitential than married life only made him pleased that he had chosen to be a priest. This shocked Anthony because embracing the Christian life of a priest meant for him embracing the Cross, embracing sacrifice; the thought that a priest could be pleased at being a priest because it meant less sacrifice, less of the Cross, was an affront to Anthony. From this moment he looked down on George, despised him and hated him.

*"I always thank God that he chose me for this special vocation. We are so lucky,"* went on George.

*"I thought our vocation was supposed to be harder, more difficult and that our joy was in embracing the hardship, carrying the Cross with joy, like the early Christians."*

*"I know you will have been taught things like that by Fr. Darrell but we who have been on the parishes and not cooped up in academic institutions know better. You speak to any of the wise old parish priests and they will tell you the same. God has chosen an easier path for us."*

*"It's not what Fr. Victor thinks down in Millwall,"* said Anthony.

*"Well Fr. Victor is a bit balmy, you know,"* said George.

*"I think he is a very fine priest,"* said Anthony outraged.

*"He has put off a lot of good faithful Catholics ..."*

*"You know young Ricky Pont?"* asked Anthony seething now inside himself.

*"Oh you mean Emily's son?"* asked George.

*"Yes, that's it. Well he went to Mass at Millwall a few weeks back and through listening to Fr. Victor's sermon he decided to go and spend his*

*annual holiday working in a home for the incurably sick rather than go off with his mates to Southend."*

*"Yes, but these enthusiasms soon die down. You'll learn, Anthony, and you will find out that Fr. Victor is not so good as all that. I met several good Catholics whom he has upset."*

*"They probably needed upsetting,"* said Anthony surging with exasperated fury and spitting out the words.

*"I must go to bed now,"* said Anthony and he walked out banging the door, leaving George to drink another whisky. Anthony lay in bed without sleeping for two hours. He tossed and turned. What could he do with such ruthless kindness, such brutal gentleness, such complacent humility? He could not even talk to his friends about it. When he spoke with Clarence or Stephen about it they just said *'Well tell him your own point of view'. 'I do'* Anthony had replied with exasperation. *'Well that's all you need to do,"* said Clarence but Anthony knew it was hopeless. He was up against an enemy far more intransigent than the fiercest autocrat. A bloody minded tyrant would be far easier to manage.

It never once occurred to Anthony that his parish priest was lonely and longed for some company on a Saturday night. At the same time George could not allow this thought to himself. He believed he was doing it for Anthony's good, to tame his enthusiasm, to soften his pride. He did not know that the motive behind it was to alleviate his own loneliness; that he himself had been more idealistic when first ordained but was inwardly a disappointed man. In this the two men were similar: neither of them knew their own emotional needs nor were they in touch with their own selves. Anthony had begun to be when he had that awakening experience when first on the parish. It was this that drove him whereas George had sunk into a state of chronic despair. In each case however, but in different ways, their belief system smothered the possibility of knowing the person inside themselves.

It was a long time before Anthony went to sleep and when he woke it was into a misty dim Sunday morning.

*       *       *

As he was getting dressed that morning, Anthony decided firmly that he would not drink with George after confession on Saturday nights. So what could he do instead? He had recently met Andrea and Tony, a young married couple, who lived in a flat in Tredegar Square. Andrea was a graduate in English and Tony was at art school. He had been an electrical engineer and had now decided to take up art so Andrea was working helping her father in a picture-framing business on the edge of Roman Road in the borough of Bow but close to the boundary with Bethnal Green. Her father had been a docker and her mother died suddenly of a heart attack five years earlier. Her father had an uneducated but robust love of art. In their small council flat there were several photographs of Michaelangelo's *David* from different angles and he had encouraged Andrea to *'eddicate 'erself'* as he put it. Under her father's inspiration she went to night school at Birkbeck and took a degree in English which she had just finished and was looking for a teaching job. Andrea and her father were lapsed Catholics but Andrea's father had seen Anthony in the street one day and stopped to speak to him.

*"You must visit me daughter, Andrea. She needs a bit of eddication comin' into the 'ome. I can see you're a man of learning, Fav'er, and it'll do 'er good to see there's some in the Church as 'ave got minds still."*
Anthony laughed.

*"I mean it,"* he said, *"cor, Fav'er, you don't know we've 'ad some rough uns down 'ere. You should 'ave met old Canon Circle at Lime Street. I can tell yer, Fav'er, you'd never know e'd seen a book."*
Anthony warmed to him and said,

*"Well, I'd like to meet your daughter, Andrea, but I'd like to visit you first."*
*"You come whenever yer like, Fav'er, the door is always open to yer."*

A few days later Anthony visited Frank Jenkins. He was in the same large housing estate as Vince and Teresa but in one of the older buildings that had three floors. His flat was No. 35 of Bradley House. He knocked on the door. It opened,

*"Come in, Fav'er."* said Frank in excited exclamation. He pulled Anthony by his right hand and said, *"I'll puts you 'ere on this chair. You're tired? Cuppa tea?"* Anthony nodded and the cup was there within seconds:

*"'ere, 'ave a drop of Scotch in it, just a drop – it's a wonder when you're tired."* He stood over Anthony and looked down on him, a flat crown at the top of his head and his two cheekbones coming straight down. His face would have been square but for a chin that made the bottom of his face circular. Anthony looked at him:

*"Well 'ow is it, eh?"* as Frank watched Anthony sipping the hot and potent brew,

*"Really good,"* said Anthony feeling a burning sensation travelling rapidly down his chest. Frank was still standing over him but as he

got an answer from the young priest, he withdrew onto an armchair opposite. Then Anthony looked round and was surprised to see a group of photographs of Michaelangelo's *David*. Frank saw Anthony looking at them,

*"That's the greatest art on earth…"*

*"Have you seen it?"*

*"Me, cor, no, Fav'er, I've never been out o' London much less England and as for foreign parts they might be on the moon. I doesn't need to see the statue itself. I can see it all 'ere. What's the use of cameras if they can't bring things of beauty into people's 'omes eh?"*

Anthony was about to speak but Frank went on,

*"That's the greatest piece of art on earth. Michaelangelo was only sixteen when 'e done that. Fantastic. No, I doesn't need to see it. I got them photos from all angles so they've put the statue in there,"* he said tapping his forehead with his right hand. It was a surprise to Anthony that a Cockney docker would have this interest.

*"I knows what's you're thinking. You're thinking 'ow's he, just an old docker, interested in art. 'ow's he come by eddication?"*

*"That's what you were thinking, wasn't it, Fav'er – now don't say 'No' 'cos I could see it in yer eyes?"*

Anthony smiled ruefully.

*"I'm afraid I was."*

*"Well, I'll tell you. Eddication comes from 'ere,"* he said pointing to his head, *"and you don't 'ave to go to Oxford for that."*

*"But how did you become interested?"* asked Anthony.

*"I know beauty that's why. When I finished school and was startin' in the docks me Mum took me to the art gallery in Trafalgar Square. She said to me 'Before you fill yer mind with all that filth they talk in them docks I want to show yer beauty' and she did, God bless 'er and it always stayed in me brain."* He tapped his head again.

*"E' first ten years I was in the docks I went every Saturday afternoon back to that gallery and then when me Mum died I went every Sunday afternoon. Most folk visit their Mum's grave Sunday afternoon but I says to me'sel that me Mum would 'ave preferred me to visit that gallery so that's what I did and I still does."*

*"Have you visited any other galleries?"*

*"Listen to 'im. What would I want to visit others for? Don't yer think there's enough paintings in that them gallery? 'ave you been there, Fav'er?"*

Anthony nodded. *"You don't need to see gallery after gallery – one's enough for me. I only ever looks at one painting when I goes. I've got about a dozen in 'ere,"* he said tapping his head again, *"and I could draw 'em for yer ..."*

*"...and I tells yer, Fav'er, there's more good religion in some of 'em pictures than in all yer sermons, Masses and what-not. Seurat's The Bathers – marvellous. Me 'eart goes to God when I sees that picture."*

Anthony was so wholeheartedly in agreement with this man's religious sentiments that he was dumbfounded. Here was someone in relation to God. Anthony felt humble in his presence and that it would be an insult to suggest that 'coming to Church' would be something better for him. His job as a priest was to bring people to God but this man was there already, in fact well ahead of him. He sat in a bemused miasma, almost paralysed with accord. It united this man to him in that profound internal experience that had brought him into free responsive friendship with God when he first arrived in the parish. He felt so much closer to Frank Jenkins now than to anyone, even his friends in the Doktor Klub. The additional factor that he experienced now was profound admiration. Here was a man whose religious devotion would go unrecognized because it did not conform to any ecclesiastical norms but, more than that, something had stirred in his soul that took him out of the normal thoroughfare of what was conventional for a docker's out-of-work past-time in London's East End. Here was a man in whose presence Anthony wanted to kneel, at the shrine of 'The Unknown Saint' as people honour the grave of 'The Unknown Soldier' at Westminster Abbey on Armistice Day.

*"What led you to take up picture-framing?"* asked Anthony.

*"Well, Fav'er ...look I'd like to call yer by yer real name – look, no disrepect mind but I likes to keep reverence for God 'imself and I'll give yer respect mind, and if you ever 'ear me sayin' somethin' disrespectful just 'it me over 'e head ..."*

*"My name is Anthony."*

*"Ah, that's a good name. Yer Mum must 'ave been a sensible woman. Well, Anthony, it's like this. When me ol' woman died ..."*

*"Your wife, you mean? When was that?"* asked Anthony.

*"Five years back. Well it just broke me up, Anthony, broke me up it did. We'd been married thirty year and, she was full of stupidity and nonsense but, I can tell yer, I loved 'er much more than the day I married 'er. Then she got the cancer, didn't she, and it broke me up. I 'ad ter go up me brother's place in West 'am and he and 'is ol woman looked after me. Almost six months I stayed with 'em and after that I couldn'a go back in them docks no more. I'd 'ad it. So, I says to mesel' 'I know – I'll take up picture-framing.' At least*

*I could frame e prints of them marvellous paintings and some'ow, can't explain, I knew me ol' woman would be wi' me in that."*

*"And I know you have children because you told me about Andrea …"*

*"Listen to 'im. Of course I got children. I'm not a bloody priest, yer know."*

*"How many?"* laughed Anthony.

*"Two daughters I 'ave. One's good and e other's bad."*

*"How do you mean?"*

*"'ow do I bloody well know. All them psychologists and social workers runnin' round the place these days pretend to know why one turns out good and the other bad but they don't blinkin' well know any more than I do or you do. Only God knows and 'e don't tell us."*

*"Where are they?"*

*"Andrea, she's me luv, she lives down Tredegar Square, with 'er 'ubby. She's just finished 'er degree in English, English Literature at Birkbeck and 'er 'usband, Tony's at art school at Camberwell. He was an electrical engineer but 'e wanted to take up art and I says to Andrea 'We'll put in a few more hours doin' the framing and that'll pay for 'im to go to art school'. It's no bloody good working at somethin' when yer 'eart's not in it, even if the pay is good. It ain't money, yer know, that brings 'appiness. I'll give yer their address, it'll do you good to visit 'em. You need some spirit put in yer – what's they doin' to yer up in dat ol priest's house, eh?"*

Anthony smiled but just said:

*"Thank you very much. I'd love to visit them."*

*"Well 'ere – ere's their address: 46 Tredegar Square – up on 'e top floor, they are. Just ring e bell downstairs and up yer go."*

*"And your bad daughter?"* asked Anthony.

*"She went and married a doctor. Nothin' wrong wi' that mind but she took up all 'em airs and graces. Was ashamed that 'er Mum and Dad lived in a council flat in dockland. Started pretendin' 'er parents lived in bloody Kensington. Kensington – can yer imagine that? Could yer see me in bloody Kensington? Well, could yer?,"* his eyes and forward thrust of his square head demanded a response from Anthony.

*"No I couldn't,"* said Anthony obediently.

*"I'd die asphyxiated with all 'em la-di-da poshness. Well she started pre-tendin' 'er parents lived in bloody Kensington then when 'er in-laws wanted to meet 'er Mum and Dad she suddenly said they 'ad both died in a car accident. A plant only flowers if water flows up from the roots. It's no bloody good if yer cuts off yer own roots. An I 'ope you're not offended by what I say about Kens-ington. You might 'ave been born and brought up there and I don't mind that*

*as long as yer don't pretend you was born in West 'am. Health is knowin' yer own roots. Well, anyway Stephanie, that's 'er name, married this 'ere doctor and lives now in Tunbridge Wells. I ain't seen 'er for eight years. It broke me ol' woman's 'eart it did. So, she went to the bad but why – heaven knows. No one knows. It's the way it is. The sun shines on the just and unjust, that's what the Bible says an' it's true."*

*"So I knows yer come from posh parts but I 'opes yer don't try ter teach us 'ere East Enders all that posh kinder religion. We're workin' class and we need a workin'-class religion."*

Anthony breathed a sigh of relief and told Frank about the YCW group that he ran.

*"How many of 'em come to the meeting?"*

*"Eight come each week – every Monday night. They come straight after work on Monday and the meeting starts late afternoon and stretches into the night."*

*"Every Monday eh? An what's yer do in them meetings?"*

*"We study the gospels, the words of Jesus and then try to live them."*

*"And I suppose they all goes to Church?"*

*"No, most of them don't. In fact two of them aren't Catholics at all."*

*"Well that sounds like the real thing. You keep that up Fa'ver – that'll do more good than all them posh Sunday fashion parade goin' to Mass."*

*"Well, Anthony, I 'ave to go ter collect me shoes that's being mended. But remember go visit Andrea and Tony. It'll do yer good."*

So that is how Anthony came to visit Andrea and Tony. The more tense the situation became between himself and Fr. Smithes the more often he visited them. So on this Sunday after he had celebrated three Masses in the morning, preaching at each one of them, he turned back to the presbytery to lunch with George. He always produced a bottle of wine at lunch on Sunday. Anthony walked into the long dark room and saw George already sitting at the head of the table. The room was about thirty feet long with a refectory table about twelve feet in length. At the near end was a heavy old bronze type-writer surrounded by papers. The walls were papered in heavy red-and-black brocade and staring vacantly into space were two framed prints: one of the Sacred Heart of Jesus and the other of the Immaculate Heart of Mary. Anthony's heart sank as he saw George sitting with a newly opened bottle of wine and two plates with roast beef and Yorkshire pudding already in their two places.

*"Ethel has got us some good roast beef to-day with Yorkshire pudding."* In any other circumstances or company Anthony would have relished

such a meal but a biblical passage from the Book of Proverbs kept running through his mind:

> *Better is a dinner of herbs where love is*
> *Than a fatted ox and hatred with it.*[1]

They were about to eat the 'fatted ox' and another biblical line came to his mind:

> *His speech was smoother than butter,*
> *Yet war was in his heart;*
> *His words were softer than oil,*
> *Yet they were drawn swords.*[2]

George's words were smoother than butter or softer than oil but there was hatred between them but one that could not be prised open and seen.

"*I saw that old McCarthy was back in Church. He has been lapsed for years and I noticed to-day that he came up to the Communion Rail.*"

"*Yes,*" replied Anthony sullenly, "*I hope it indicates a change of attitude in him.*"

"*How do you mean?*" asked George sharply.

"*Well, when his next door neighbour, old Tom Cunningham, was dying he never once visited him or offered his wife a helping hand.*"

"*Tom Cunningham never came to Mass.*"

Anthony could not reply. He had tried every angle. It was a hopeless project. He slumped into silence and said no more. Not a word was spoken between them until the end of the meal. When they had both finished a dish of rice pudding Anthony got up and said,

"*I'm going out for a walk.*"

"*Shall I come with you?*" asked George.

"*No, I think I'll say a bit of Office at the same time.*"

"*Oh, yes, I understand,*" said George.

Anthony went to his room and put his breviary into his shoulder bag and walked out of the presbytery. He had no more duties that Sunday so he decided to call in on Andrea and Tony. He walked down Bow Road first crossing over Fairfield Road. He glanced down it and could see in the distance on the right the Bryant and Mays match factory. It was the

---

[1] Proverbs Ch. 15 v.17.

[2] Psalm 55 v.21.

"Matchgirls' Strike" at this factory in 1887, followed by the Great Dock Strike the following year that was such a landmark in the establishment of the Trade Union Movement and the beginning of fairer hours and pay for the working-class. Anthony was pleased that this piece of history was in his parish and only a four minute walk from the presbytery. He felt a bond of sympathy with these early Trade Union missionaries who had fought for their rights against conservatism and prejudice. He walked on along the north side of Bow Road and soon passed the small terraced house that had been the home of George Lansbury, leader of the Labour Party between the wars. Another three minutes and he had reached Tredegar Square. Andrea and Tony lived in No. 46 on the top floor. A clever developer had bought the house and converted it into three flats. Andrea and Tony owned this flat, paying mortgage instead of rent like Andrea's father. It was a fawn brick building with a purple door. The purple door had been Tony's idea and the other tenants had agreed. He had painted it himself and installed on it a beautiful brass door knocker. It was rarely used except occasionally by those who visited the owners of the ground floor flat. The bell was on the left hand side with the name 'Foral' written above it in ink. Anthony rang the door-bell and Andrea came down and let him in. She was on her own. Tony had gone to visit his mother in Forest Gate.

*"I know who you are: you're Fr. Stonewell. Heavens, you look worn out,"* said Andrea suddenly as she looked at Anthony and then cupped a hand over her mouth and said hurriedly, *"Oh pardon. Don't mind me, Father. I knew you would be coming. My father told me that you'd said you'd come and he told me that you weren't the sort to say a thing and not do it. Sorry about sayin' you looked worn out."*

"It's quite alright," said Anthony with a laugh, "because *I am,*" and he sighed.

*"Have you been saying Masses all morning, Father?"*

*"Yes, I've said three this morning."*

*"I suppose that is wearing,"* said Andrea without conviction. There was a pause. Anthony had never said anything about his difficulties with Fr. Smithes but he decided to give some indication.

*"Yes, I find it a bit claustrophobic in the presbytery too."*

*"You mean just you and Fr. Smithes?"*

*"Yes,"* said Anthony, *"there's a lack of life. We shouldn't be locked up in that dark old presbytery but in a building with light and colour with people flowing in and out."*

*"Suppose it must be a bit dull,"* said Andrea, *"is there anything we can do to help?"*

Anthony thought this was his opportunity and decided to take it.

*"What I find particularly difficult is Saturday evenings. We hear confessions and then there is a long evening ..."*

*"Why don't you come round here on Saturday evenings. We don't go out like most others; we are either here on our own or one or two people come round."* Andrea spoke without an East End accent. She was a solid sort of being. She stood with her feet parallel and about a foot apart. She looked somewhat like Frank, the same flat top to her head but the proportions were all smaller. She had hair that was transitional between brown and auburn and she kept it clipped so it did not fall lower than her ears. Her skirt was brown and her khadi type of blouse was a mottled brown also. She had that same uncompromising manner as her father but her demeanour was about two octaves lower so much so that Anthony could hardly believe she was Frank's daughter. She spoke in an accent which was almost King's English. He would not have known that she was an East Ender, a cockney.

*"Well, that would be super,"* said Anthony brightening. They both sat down in wooden chairs opposite each other. There were newspapers scattered on the floor between them.

*"So, you've just finished English at Birkbeck, eh?"*

*"My father told you."* Anthony nodded.

*"Yes, I just finished the middle of this year. It was hard work but I loved it."*

*"What author did you like best?"*

*"Oh Hardy's my favourite. I could read him again and again ..."*

*"Which of his novels do you like best?"*

*"I love **Tess of the d'Urbervilles** best"*

*"You must like sad endings,"* said Anthony with a hint of a question mark in his voice.

*"Yes, I do. Those books which end 'they lived happily ever after' turn me sick. Life just isn't like that but not many authors dare to say things as they are but when they do they find that their books go down really well."*

*"Yes I like Wuthering Heights too and that ends with all the main characters dead and the book ends in the graveyard."*

*"Yes, well, there you are and that is one of the most read novels in all English Literature and you know where Emily Bronte makes Heathcliff dig up the body of Catherine ..."*

*"Yes, I know."*

*"Well, Emily's sister, Charlotte, tried to make her remove that bit. She said it would shock people too much but Emily wouldn't remove it. Good on her, I always say. Sad endings are true to life. After all every life ends in death anyway, doesn't it?*

*"It certainly does. The end of all is death.* There was a silence. After a while they started talking again but soon Anthony looked at his watch,

*"Heavens, I must be going back. Fr. Smithes is saying the late afternoon Mass and I need to be at the back of the Church to talk to people."*

So from then on when confessions were over on a Saturday night Anthony went out immediately. Fr. Smithes was disappointed. He had designated those Saturday evenings to the task of taming his fiery young curate. He also wondered where he was going each Saturday night. He knew that one of the worst things that could happen for a priest was to start befriending parishioners. It was bad for the priest and bad for the parishioners. But George just sighed and slumped every Saturday night in front of his television and then would doze off to sleep and, waking past midnight, would stagger up the stairs and fall into bed.

\*   \*   \*

Fr. Smithes's programme of rounding up the Catholics into that stone pen, as Anthony contemptuously called the Church, each Sunday extended also to other Catholic institutions. He wanted Catholics to belong to Catholic youth clubs, to belong to Catholic guilds, to educate their children in Catholic schools. Anthony hated this policy of protection. His mission was to send out his apostles into the world. He kept quoting that saying of Jesus from the Sermon on the Mount:

> *"You are the salt of the earth; but if salt has lost its taste, how*
> *shall its saltness be restored ? It is no longer good for anything*
> *except to be thrown out and trodden under foot by men.*
> *"You are the light of the world. A city set on a hill cannot be*
> *hid. Nor do men light a lamp and put it under a bushel, but on a*
> *stand, and it gives light to all in the house. Let your light so shine*
> *before men, that they may see your good works and give glory to*
> *your Father who is in heaven."*[3]

He quoted it to himself but it informed much of what he did. Christians imprisoned in Catholic schools or Catholic youth clubs were a

---

[3] Matthew Ch. 5 vv. 13–16.

lamp under a bushel. Anthony's Family Gospels Group and YCW followed the dictum of Jesus: letting their light shine before men. The Vatican Council had consecrated the phrase *the apostolate of the laity*. It was the inner spirit that mattered not external observance. He hated Fr. Smithes's desire to protect all his little Catholics from the influence of the wicked world. Teilhard the Chardin had dedicated his book on spirituality *Le Milieu Divin* '**To Those Who Love the World**' and this was Anthony's theme song. He wanted his Catholics to go out into the world and change it and not be frightened of it. He did not realize that he was in a panic-stricken stampede himself. The more he tried to put his point of view to Fr. Smithes the more his parish priest became entrenched in his conservative and dogmatic point of view. Soon there were two dogmatists at silent and resentful war with each other. After months of having breakfast, lunch and dinner together nearly every day, Anthony slowly despaired of ever getting anywhere with such a dispiriting old priest as his superior. It did not occur to him that he was just as intransigent as Fr. Smithes, just as certain that he was right as Fr. Smithes was.

It was a Saturday evening in late August. Anthony had now been just over fifteen months in the parish. Following his resolution he had been to visit Andrea and Tony but he did not stay for very long, just long enough to be sure that Fr. Smithes would have left the dining-room with its bottles and retired to his study and be slumping in front of the television. He had to say the early Mass the following morning. Although it was still August and not quite September it was a cold night; he wore an overcoat and a black Russian hat. That hat had become a familiar sight around the streets of Bow in the winter months but it was unusual for it to appear so early in the year. There was a chill wind but no clouds. He looked up and could see the Plough up in the sky. He walked back along the well-trod pavement and in twelve minutes he was back in the presbytery. As he opened the door with his Yale key he heard moans coming from upstairs. He leapt up the stairs two at a time. He stood outside George's sitting-room; there was silence then suddenly there was an unearthly groan. Anthony did not wait to knock but abruptly opened the door. George was lying back in his armchair, head collapsed like a rag doll over the right hand arm. The groans continued and clearly George was unaware of Anthony's presence. Anthony thought quickly. He knew that Ron Dawson just down Fairfield Road ran a taxi. Ron was not a Catholic but his wife was and he had given Anthony a lift in his taxi when, on his day off, he went into central London. The telephone was there on George's desk. He picked it up while the groans continued.

"*Hello, who's that?*"

"*It's me, Fr. Stonewell, is that you,Ron?*"

"*Yes, Fa'ver, what's up?*"

"*Look Ron, could you come around in your taxi immediately. I think Fr. Smithes has had a heart attack. I need to take him to hospital.*"

Anthony ran up the stairs to the top floor and went, for the first time, into George's bedroom. He could not find a case so he took his own suitcase and packed into it George's pyjamas, slippers and dressing-gown. Then he went into the bathroom and collected his toothbrush, toothpaste, face flannel and razor, shaving-brush, stick of shaving cream and brush and comb. He had just put them all into a case when the door-bell rang. He ran downstairs and there, even on this cold night, was Ron with just open shirt and cardigan with tight fitting grey trousers. He was stolid and short in height and stood there as if he had such calls every night of the week.

"*I'll help you down wi' 'im,*" and the two men were in a moment in George's room. Now his eyes were open, mumbled something incoherently, and Ron got him under his legs and Anthony laid George's head against his chest with his arms under George's armpits and the two men carried their burden down the stairs, out of the front door, through the rock garden and, with a flick of one hand, Ron opened the door of the taxi.

"*You get in and I'll lean 'im against yer,*" said Ron.

Anthony did exactly as he was told. Then he remembered George's things which were in his case.

"*Could you hold him for a second, Ron, while I run and get his case with his things.*" While Ron was holding George Anthony went in a flash and collected the case, made sure he had his keys and was quickly back to relieve Ron. George was no longer moaning. He seemed relieved that he was being taken care of.

"*Where shall I take 'im?*"

"*Well, St. Andrew's Hospital,*" muttered Anthony.

"*I think Fa'ver, it'd be better ter go to the London 'Ospital. It won't take more than seven minutes at this time 'er night and they 'ave all the facilities for 'eart attacks, strokes and the lot. I know 'em there.*"

"*OK,*" said Anthony, "*I've got him well nursed so take us as fast as you can.*"

Ron jumped into his driver's seat and in a moment, using all the cab's superb lock to its best ability, he was driving back down Bow Road. Anthony looked down at the sighing body slumped across his lap. George looked up. Both men were comforted by the sound of the steady-throated purr of the London cab.

"*Where are we going?*" he whispered.

"*To hospital.*" said Anthony.

George murmured but Anthony could not hear what he said.

Twenty minutes later George was in bed in the emergency ward at the London Hospital. There must have been thirty beds in the ward, each pushed back against a frame that had names and a clipboard with medical details. Anthony looked down the ward. It was now midnight. Most of the occupants of the beds were asleep. There were a string of glowing green night-lights down the centre ceiling. Two nurses were rustling curtains around George's bed and two young doctors were attending him. Anthony, once he saw that George was well in the care of the hospital staff, tip-toed back to the end of the entrance to the ward. He sat on a grey plastic chair and waited. He wrung his hands, got up, walked up and down and sat down again. He was anxiously waiting to hear the verdict from one of the doctors. At last the elder of the two doctors, tall, fair haired and in white coat with stethoscope dangling from the right hand pocket, came out and found him at that moment pacing up and down.

"*Well, what's wrong with him?*" asked Anthony with his head thrust forward, looking intently at the young doctor.

"*He's in a bad way, Reverend, but I don't think he's had a heart attack. I think it's a severe attack of hepatitis. We'll monitor him closely and you can ring in the morning and find out.*"

"*Thank you, doctor.*"

Anthony went back into the ward. A nurse was drawing a curtain around George's bed. Anthony bent over him to say good-night. George was wide awake now,

"*Would you hear my confession, Father, before you go?*" croaked George.

"*Yes, of course,*" said Anthony though feeling acutely embarrassed.

The young priest bent over his parish priest. George's lips were quivering as he made his confession. Anthony asked him quietly to say one *Our Father* for his penance, if he felt able. George nodded and Anthony raised his right hand, made the sign of the Cross over him and said the words of absolution "***I absolve you of your sins in the Name of the Father, and of*** *the Son and of the Holy Ghost. Amen.*" George gripped his hand and said with tears in his eyes,

"*Thank you, Anthony, thank you. I will pray for you.*"

Anthony turned and then turned back and had one last look at his parish priest. He had sunk back onto the pillows and his eyes were closed. Anthony turned and went resolutely back to the front entrance where Ron was faithfully waiting for him. He climbed back into the cab and sat on the back seat. Ron got in and pulled back the glass partition that separated the cab-driver from his passenger. The car purred into life and, in a few seconds, driver and priest were nosing their way back into the Commercial Road.

"*Now it's your turn to look after the parish, Fa'ver,*" said Ron, "*ye'll 'ave ter make all the decisions. 'til now ye've 'ad some'un to guide yer, now it's all up ter you.*"

"You're right," said Anthony feebly. He looked out the window. The cab was just passing the large Catholic Church in Commercial Road. The only other traffic was an old Hillman about a hundred and fifty yards away on the other side of the road coming towards them. There was a quiet peacefulness in the middle of the night. Apart from that single old Hillman there was just one pedestrian also on the other side of the road – a tall man walking purposefully westwards. Anthony wondered where he had been but imagined that he was heading for home.

"*Hope's yer don't mind me saying, Fa'ver ...*"

"No, it's alright; go on," said Anthony, now glad to listen to Ron.

"*It'll be up ter you. Yer might do 'e right thing; yer might do e wrong thing, but it'll be up ter you from now on. Ye'll 'ave to take the gears into yer own 'ands.*"

As Ron said this Anthony felt a surge of excitement. Now he could really fashion the parish into a compact cluster of dedicated Christians. Ron was speaking again,

"*You may worry that yer're doin' e wrong thing but ye've js got ter do it. Like a pilot in a plane goin' solo for 'e first time. 'arry, me brother-in-law, learned to fly like and 'e tells me e first time e instructor got out and left 'im all on 'is own. Terrified he was, 'e tol' me. If 'e crashed it, then 'e knew 'e 'ad no one else to blame but 'iself. That's 'ow it is fer you, now, Fa'ver. Ye've got to take the controls an' fly the plane yerself. It's up ter you now. If you makes a muck of it then ...*" at that moment Ron swung the cab round out of Burdett Road and into Mile End Road. Two minutes later the cab was standing with its motor still running outside the presbytery.

*"What do I owe you, Ron?"* asked Anthony fishing for a wallet in his right hand pocket.

*"You owe's me nothin' but a prayer, Fa'ver. Yer know I'm not a Catholic but pay me with a prayer."*

*"Oh, oh, thank you so much, Ron."*

Ron clapped him on the back,

*"Remember, yer on yer own now, Fa'ver."*

\* \* \*

Anthony slept a mere three hours. When he woke it was just after five in the morning. It was Sunday and his first Mass was at seven. Then he had two more but George had been going to say the Masses later in the morning and the one in the evening. Anthony rose and had a shower, went downstairs and made himself a cup of tea. He looked around the kitchen. It was a dismal scene. The butter dish had a cigarette stubbed out in it. Unwashed dishes stood on the little oblong table covered with a mottled white and red plastic covering. George had put away the bottles from next door, probably intending to return to the kitchen, but then was taken by his violent attack. The housekeeper was on her annual holiday back with her family just outside of Leeds in Yorkshire. Anthony looked at his watch. It was twenty past five. He filled the sink with hot water and squeezed washing up liquid into the sink as the tap hissed. Frothy bubbles filled it. The sight of all the dirty plates and the cigarette stubbed out in the butter dish turned Anthony's heart from compassion to scorn. He threw all the dishes, knives and bowls into the sink. In ten minutes he had washed and dried the lot. He looked round with a feeling of satisfaction. Was it too early to ring Clarence? he asked himself. Clarence had moved from his parish at Kentish Town to lecture in Scripture at a new catechetical college called *The Risen Christ* in Notting Hill Gate. He had no obligatory Masses to say on a Sunday. Anthony thought it better to wait awhile so he went into the Church, turned on the lights and lit the candles on the altar and then walked to the back of the Church and unbolted the door. The Church had been built in 1928 and its outer walls were of stone and it was in the neo-Gothic style with the two sides of the sloping wooden roof inside meeting at an angle of 45 degrees. Anthony, having done all that was needed in preparation for parishioners to enter the Church an hour later he slipped into a pew and knelt. He looked at the large crucifix that hung above the tabernacle. The head of Jesus was downcast like in the Crucifixion by Velazquez.

Anthony said a prayer for George but as soon as he had done so he remembered the cigarette in the butter dish and ground his teeth. He wondered whether he would die. He looked at his watch. It was now just past six o'clock. He rang Clarence who answered immediately. Yes, he could come. Anthony sighed with relief.

By eleven in the morning Anthony had said three Masses and Clarence had just arrived in time to offer the remaining Masses of the day. He had rung the hospital and discovered that George had a serious attack of hepatitis. He would need to stay in the London Hospital for a week and George had already arranged that he would then go to St. John & St. Elizabeth's Hospital in St. John's Wood which was nursed by Catholic nuns. The doctor had advised him that he would need intensive nursing there for a further three weeks and that then he should go to convalesce for a month. When Anthony realized that George would be away for at least two months he whooped with joy. Now, with Clarence's support at week-ends, he would take this opportunity to make the parish into a vital Christian community. When he heard the news he went into the Church and knelt down and said a prayer to St. Paul:

*"St. Paul make this parish of Bow into a new Corinth,"* said with fervour.

In his enthusiasm he began to discourage all those who were, in his opinion, only nominal Christians. He would, he told himself, slowly change the parish community into a fiery young squad of Christian apostles. He would bring about a transformation and turn a rabble of nominal Catholics into a passionate small group of dedicated Christians and if they would not be converted he would dismiss them. He would close the door upon all those who came to Church just for christenings and weddings. After all Jesus had overturned the tables of the money-changers and driven them out of the Temple and this same spirit of Jesus was now in him and he would overturn the rituals of all complacent Churchgoers too. He also intended to act speedily and make the most of this time of grace while George Smithes was away.

That Sunday night he spent the whole night, until two in the morning in fact, talking and planning with Clarence. His oblong room was about twenty-two feet long and ten feet wide. The west side of the room boasted a suite with a sofa and two armchairs. He had bought the suite soon after he arrived from an old junk furniture shop in Bow Common Lane and just near the primary school in Rainhill Way was a small factory workshop that made sacking. Anthony had bought this rough fabric and one of the nurses from St. Andrew's Hospital had tailored it to cover perfectly his three pieces of furniture. This part of the room was divided by an island book-case which had been made for him by Andy, a West Indian carpenter. On the other side of this was his desk and a filing cabinet. When he had first arrived the room had a broken down settee and a desk and the walls were dark grey. Now the room's walls were shining white and on the wall he had a large colour print of Velazquez's *Crucifixion*. At the side of the book-case was a dark stained wooden lectern which had also been made by Andy. He had this made because he noticed that if he sat down to read in early afternoon he started to dose so now he put his book onto the lectern and stood up to read. This warded off the impulse to sleep, like a man determined to keep going when tempted to lie down in the snow. The room had a light pile carpet. Anthony was proud of his creation.

Anthony was sprawling on the sofa while Clarence was sitting up straight-backed on the chair with its back to the windows. The lights, turned to the floor, gave the room a restful glow.

*"Now, you've got no excuses,"* said Clarence. The two had already been talking for three hours, *"God has sent this disease to Fr. Smithes like he sent the plagues to the Pharaoh and like Moses you will have to take advantage of it and lead the people out of bondage."* Clarence looked characteristically straight ahead through his glasses that had no rims. There was a packet of Players cigarettes on the right arm of his chair. In a measured way he took out the packet and removed a cigarette, tapped it on a book that was on the other arm. He lit it, blew smoke in a cool ring upwards to the ceiling,

*"So there it is,"* he said, *"God has laid it straight into your lap."* Anthony thought of Ron in the taxi the night before. All the decisions were now his, Ron had said but Clarence's words now momentarily frightened him.

*"Yes,"* he mumbled. Clarence looked at him,

*"Start acting straight away. No more words, just act,"* barked Clarence.

*"I will,"* said Anthony, *"I will, I definitely will."*

*"That's good,"* said Clarence, *"I'll be back next Sunday and you can report on progress."*

*"There'll be progress I promise."*

*"You know,"* said Clarence, *"I have been giving a young woman instruction to become a Catholic and suddenly she said to me last week, 'You know what, Father, I think I believe already. I believe God knows my actions. I already think they come from God.' Then I listened to her and she was a better Christian than me. She told me that a year back she was walking back to her flat near Portobello Road and there was an old homeless*

woman sitting on the pavement. The woman asked her for something to buy some food. '**Do you have no home?**' she asked her, '**No, I'm 'omeless'** so, Father, she said to me '**I took her home with me and she is still with me at home. Cathy her name is.**' When I heard that I said to her that she did not need any more instruction. I took her straight into the little chapel and received her into the Church." Clarence tapped the tobacco from his cigarette with his right index finger into a small pottery ash-tray. Anthony looked moved by what Clarence had said,

"It's like the wedding feast where Jesus that those who were invited were not worthy. Remember Jesus said **Go therefore into the thoroughfares and invite to the marriage feast as many as you can find**. All the nominal Catholics have lost their right to the marriage feast. That woman I received was out in the thoroughfare. Now you can go and do that. Clear away all the Pharisees and hypocrites and bring people like that woman into the Church. Then we will have the Church that Christ meant us to have." Clarence stopped and stubbed out his cigarette decisively. Anthony looked at his watch.

"We must go to bed." As he spoke Clarence leapt up. The two priests went to their respective bedrooms and both were soon asleep.

The next day Clarence had left the presbytery when half an hour later the door-bell rang. Anthony went to the door. There was standing a young girl with straight black hair, dark eyes and a sky blue skirt.

"Me name's Pat Malloy," she said on the door-step, "and I've come to arrange me wedding."

"Come in," and he led her into a small cubby-hole interview room at the back of the Church on the left. Normally he took people through into the larger interview room but her manner irritated him; he took her into the dark unwelcoming room. She sat down and repeated, even before Anthony had sat down,

"I've cum ter arrange me wedding,"

"Do you believe in God?" asked Anthony. She looked insulted and then said,

"What's that got to do with it?" she asked petulantly.

"Well this is God's Church," replied Anthony, "and it's for people who believe in God."

"Well, that's not me business. I'm 'ere to arrange me wedding. I want it ter be the second Saturday in November."

"We'll have to see first whether it's right for you to have a wedding in this Church."

"What de yer mean? I lives in this parish in Usher Road, just off Roman Road and I knows this is the parish Church 'cos me gran said it was."

"Church weddings are for those who have love in their heart and believe in God."

"Well I knows nothin' about that. I'm pregnant and me Dad tol' me ter get married quick. Tol' me to make sure I married in a Catholic Church to make it all look right wi' e' neighbours."

"We don't conduct weddings here to make things look good on the outside," said Anthony standing on his dignity. The young girl pouted and said abruptly,

"Alright then I'll go to the Registry Office."

"I think that's a good idea," said Anthony. The interview had begun and finished all within five minutes. The young girl, short in height with a dark pony tail, pranced out without saying a word. Anthony returned to the presbytery. His purging of the parish had begun. He was making a clean sweep with a harsh bristled broom.

Anthony felt pleased with himself that he had had the courage of his convictions and refused the sacrament to someone who only wanted the wedding in the Church because it looked nice. The sacraments were the expression of an inner commitment to Christ, he repeated to himself. There was no commitment there, he told himself; it was all for show. He remembered Sid Darrell emphasizing in one of his lectures that the sacraments were all an outward sign of an inner commitment. Only those committed to Christ deserved the privilege of the sacraments and Anthony was not going to give them to those who openly had no intention of following the way of Christ but only wanted a wedding in Church for show. While Fr. Smithes had been present a gentler kinder side of him was stimulated into life but with his parish priest gone all the enthusiasm of the determined fanatic, fanned by Clarence's fiery ardour, gripped hold of him. He was going to make his parish like one of the early Christian communities that St. Paul had founded. He rang up Clarence and told him what he had done. He had just walked into the catechetical college,

"That's it, that's the way. Slowly it will sink in and we'll clear all these parishes of the Pharisees and hypocrites." This cheered him on, like an athlete gathering strength from the shouting crowds. Very soon his parish would be the new Corinth, he, the new St. Paul, and when he died he would be raised to sainthood. He went away from the telephone with his breast beating with enthusiasm.

It was just a day after he had turned Patricia Malloy away from the presbytery that he went to the door to find himself confronted with a fierce panting Irishman. Mr. Malloy put his boot in the door and said,

*"Are you the priest by the name of Fr. Stonewell?"*

*"Yes, that's me,"* seeing that trouble was coming.

*"So yer won't marry me daughter in the Church, eh?"*

*"You're Mr. Malloy, I take it?"*

*"You are right there".*

*"Would you like to come in?"*

*"I'm not puttin' one door in this devil's den til yer tel me that ye'll do me daughter's marriage."*

*"Do you believe in God?"* asked Anthony.

*"What's that bloody well got to do with it, eh?"* At this Mr. Malloy slammed his fist upon the door-frame and there was a resounding thud and the door shuddered.

*"The Church is for people who believe in God, who love God."*

*"I can tell yer, fuckin' reverend, I'll bring a curse er' God upon you and all you bloody priests unless yer say right now that ye'll marry me daughter in this Church."*

*"No not if you don't believe in God, and love God. If you don't, this is the wrong place for you and your daughter too."* Mr. Malloy lurched momentarily towards Anthony and he crashed his right hand against the door-frame again,

*"Call yerself a priest of God, eh? Puttin' me daughter to shame in front of all her mates eh? And yer call yerself a priest of God."* He moved his head towards Anthony menacingly, *"I tell yer, Father, you won't 'ear 'e end of this. All me family and me cousins livin' up Roman Road way will come to this parish no more."* His eyes glared hatred and he crashed his hand on the door-frame once more and spat across the threshold and turned away and as he walked he shouted and swore. Anthony soon knew that Mr. Malloy had been active because he knew some of his relatives in Usher and Armagh Road and though they usually came to Church on Sunday not one of them was there the following Sunday.

This did not deter Anthony. This was now a sign that the new Christian community was in the process of formation. Not a week went by when Anthony did not refuse to baptise a baby because the parents weren't living a Christian life but wanted it 'cos it looks right', refuse a Church wedding to lapsed Catholics and soon he was beginning to say in his sermons that coming to Church on a Sunday had no value in the sight of God unless the person was coming because he wanted to worship God in his heart. He even gave the instance of Frank Jenkins although not by name. He told of someone who was moved in his heart towards God by going and seeing a painting every week in the National Gallery and that this was more pleasing to God than those who came to Church on Sunday but with no movement of the heart within them. He said that if someone came to Church out of fear of Hell or what the neighbours might say he would do better to stay at home. Anthony had a way of speaking very directly from the pulpit so that people felt personally spoken to. In a short time everyone in the parish was talking about Fr. Stonewell's sermons. People had not heard a priest say the things he was saying. Anthony himself felt encouraged when one day in the confessional a young Irish lad said to him after having made his confession,

*"I thought I'd tell yer, Father, that I'get a great deal like from yer sermons on Sunday. Yer might think that they fall on deaf 'ears but they really mean somethin' to me."*

Anthony had not been sure. In his more sober moments he wondered whether he was right to be saying the things he was but when he heard this he became convinced that he was right and it intensified his conviction that forming this new vibrant Christian group was God's will. The numbers of those coming to Church on a Sunday dropped dramatically. He knew that sooner or later, either when Fr. Smithes returned or another member of the clergy received a complaint from one of his offended parishioners, there would be trouble but it did not worry him because he was sure he was in the right and he got a hundred per cent backing from his friend, Clarence Cider and every time he was praised it increased his conviction that he was in the right but he was convinced he was right when he received condemnation also. After all, he told himself, Jesus met with plenty of opposition. It was proof to him that he was at one with Jesus. He was Jesus' beloved disciple, the new St. John.

This dogmatic certainty received even greater endorsement from the fact that all the declarations of the Vatican Council were now being implemented in the parishes and it was the young newly ordained priests like Anthony who knew and understood the new liturgy and the doctrine that underpinned it. Just as in the last decade of the twentieth century it is the young who understand computers so in the Catholic Church in the 1960s it was the young priests who understood the new liturgy. It was a shock to conservative old priests like Fr. Smithes who had

had to turn to Anthony to help him with the celebration of the Mass in English and in the parish Church the altar was turned round to face the people. Anthony was delighted but poor old Fr. Smithes felt awkward and even somewhat ashamed. He did not like being so exposed. Suddenly everything, including himself and his own private priesthood, which had been shrouded in mystery was revealed to the people. Fr. Smithes had loved the hidden mysteriousness of his life as a priest. With his back to the congregation he could keep hidden his own thoughts but now with everyone looking straight at him, scrutinizing him he had no hidden place to run to. Anthony, on the other hand, wallowed in this new exposure. He had nothing to hide. He ran Bible classes in the Church hall and large audiences came to hear him. All the readings that had been hidden away in Latin were there for everyone to see. Unlike Fr. Smithes he loved facing the people, having his light on in the confessional. All that had been hidden was now in the open. He condemned the use of the iconastisis in the liturgies of the East. For years Catholics had been told that the Bible was the preserve of Protestants and here suddenly not only Anthony but the whole Vatican Council and the Pope himself were proclaiming that reading and understanding the Bible was at the centre of spiritual life for a Catholic. The idea that the Church had been wrong for centuries was deeply shocking for Fr. Smithes but Anthony was delighted that all that had been murky and concealed was now open for inspection and all the declarations from the Vatican Council told him he was right.

So while Fr. Smithes was ill in hospital Clarence came every Saturday evening to help him hear confessions and then stayed overnight and said some of the Masses for him on Sunday. After confessions were over on the Saturday evening they would go together first and visit Andrea and Tony and stay and sip some wine for an hour and then return together to the presbytery and they sat up until the early hours discussing Anthony's missionary effort and Anthony was helped a great deal by Clarence's superior knowledge of the New Testament and the workings of the Church in the first three centuries of its existence. Clarence convinced Anthony that the stir which his sermons were having was a sure sign that he was preaching the *kerygma* – the Good News of Jesus Christ – the heart of the Christian message was reaching the people just as it had in those days of wonder after Pentecost.

*"What's the purpose of a Church if people are saved whether it's there or not?"* asked Anthony. They had just returned from Tony and Andrea's.

It was the second Saturday in September. George Smithes was now in St. John and St. Elizabeth's Hospital in St. John's Wood. He would be there another two weeks and then he had been ordered to convalesce for a further two months. Clarence was sitting in his accustomed posture in the hessian-backed armchair and Anthony was lolling on the sofa. Anthony was fingering a glass of red wine. Clarence was carefully lighting another cigarette.

*"It's to give witness to others of God's love in the world."*

*"You mean that there are no signs of it without the Church?"* asked Anthony doubtfully.

*"Don't be ridiculous,"* said Clarence stressing the syllable 'dic' in 'ridiculous', *"of course whenever someone acts lovingly there is God in the world."*

*"You mean our job is to point to it whether it is in the Church or outside of it?"*

*"Of course. Our job is to point to it wherever it is just like Jesus pointed to the Good Samaritan."* Clarence got up, *"I'm just going to the loo."* He left his cigarette burning in the ash-tray. Anthony watched the smoke drifting towards him. He liked the smell of cigarettes but rarely smoked them. He let his mind drift with the smoke.

*"Our job,"* said Clarence, *"is to gather those who act lovingly into a communal group so that they can be an effective force in the world."*

*"That communal group **is** the Church,"* said Anthony with excitement, *"that's what I am trying to do at the moment but I have to get rid of the hypocrites who fill our Churches. But…"* Anthony paused, he was not quite sure what he was trying to say. He took another sip of wine, *"look but how do you gather people into a group? Take Andrea's father, for instance, Frank Jenkins. He's warm hearted, believes in God, actually speaks about the way beautiful paintings raise his heart to God yet he wouldn't dream of coming near this community that comes to the Church every Sunday."*

*"Well, of course, he's right too,"* said Clarence,*" he'd find himself among hypocrites. What good would it do him?"*

*"Yes, then what's the solution?"* replied Anthony, *"Here we are with a whole lot of churchgoers with no love of God in their hearts and people outside like Frank Jenkins who don't want to come and join them."*

*"Then it's **your** job to clear out the Scribes and Pharisees so that the likes of Frank Jenkins can come in. That's your job. Then you will have a community bearing witness – then you have Jesus present in the world to-day, visible for people to see."*

"*Heavens,*" said Anthony, "*St. Paul had an easier job – he could start from scratch.*"

"*No one ever starts from scratch,*" said Clarence, "*St Paul started with the Jewish communities and when they would not accept the message he went to the Gentiles. You have to do the same. If they won't listen in this stone Church you have here then you go out into the hedgerows and gather together those with love in their hearts.*"

"*And abandon the churchgoers?*"

"*Yes, abandon them if they won't listen to the message.*"

"*I suppose it's a bit like Matteo Ricci in China in the sixteenth century. He found the truth within Buddhism and within Confucianism and then added aspects of Jesus' message where he thought it was necessary.*"

"*Yes, I like that story about Matteo Ricci when he went and washed and bound the sores of a leper outside the one of the cities in China and then a whole group of those who followed Confucius who saw what he was doing said, 'if this is what Christianity teaches it must be the true religion.'*"

"*I had forgotten that …*" said Anthony and his voice drifted off. Clarence looked at him. A strange expression passed over Anthony's face.

"*I must give myself in sacrifice …*" his voice trailed off again then "*I must give myself in sacrifice …*" Clarence looked at him. Anthony seemed to be in a trance and he went on, "*…it's me that God wants in sacrifice. That's what a priest is – he offers sacrifice and is the victim at the same time …*" Clarence wondered for a moment where Anthony was. He seemed to have entered some strange realm and seemed to be a hundred miles away.

"*Well, you've got a job to do,*" said Clarence abruptly, trying to bring Anthony down to earth again, "*you're not in China. You're here in the East End of London and you have a job – it's to fashion the new Christian community.*" Anthony shook his head suddenly and seemed to come out of the trance.

"*I've got to do what Tolstoy did – renounce superstition. The churchgoers are just pagans in disguise. That's what I meant about it being more difficult than what St. Paul had to do. I have to strip off the disguise.*"

"*Yes, that's more like it.*" said Clarence.

"*It's not as easy as you seem to think,*" said Anthony.

"*Who said it's easy?*" asked Clarence "*I kept telling you at Newman that it would be very difficult.*" Clarence got up and poured himself a glass of wine also.

"It's all very easy for the bishops in the Council to pronounce how it has to be but …here at grassroots …"

"Exactly," said Clarence, "it's here that the job has to be done. You've started and with George Smithes away for another three months you can really get going."

"The churchgoers are like the worshippers of Baal in Ancient Israel," chirped in Anthony,

"The worshippers of Baal were not people going off and worshipping a pagan God but worshipping what they thought was the real God but by making images of them they were in fact worshipping something false. That is what the prophets were clamouring about You're in exactly the same position. When your faithful churchgoers think that by taking a white wafer into their mouths they are now filled with God then they are exactly the same as those ancient worshippers of Baal. It's the belief that I am in favour with God by bowing down to an external ritual. It's the golden calf all over again."

"The other day," said Anthony, "I was giving out Communion and a host dropped out of the ciborium onto the floor. I just quickly stooped down, picked it up and put it back into the ciborium. Then, you know what happened?" Anthony looked at Clarence who stood up and brushed himself.

"Tell me."

"Well, later that morning poor old Mrs. O'Flaherty came to the presbytery door and as soon as I opened it she burst into floods of tears. I said to her **'Come in dear what's wrong'** I thought her husband had suddenly died or something and apparently she was just at the Communion Rail at the place when I dropped the host and she felt that she had made Jesus fall …"

"That's exactly it," said Clarence decisively, "it's the belief that God inhabits a stone statue, a wooden totem-pole or a bread wafer. It's all the same. It's Baal worship instead of the worship of Yahweh."

"Oh, ho, ho, ho," laughed Clarence after a pause. "Just scatter holy water over the churchgoers, lock them all in so they can't get out, tell them they have to stay all day in the Church for their sins and then sail out into the parish to your Frank Jenkinses."

"Oh, you're drunk," laughed Anthony.

"I may be but **in vino veritas**," he laughed, "but as soon as you think you have captured God here on earth and tied him down in a physical place or object that can be identified then it is Baal not Yahweh you are worshipping."

"What about all the holy places throughout Christendom?"

"They're an affront to true belief," said Clarence, "I've been to Jerusalem and where they show you a footprint that is supposed to be the last place

*Jesus trod before he ascended to heaven and you see people kissing the foot-print ... it's just what Jeremiah screaming about. Once you locate God in a place you have all the modern evils on your door-step."*

*"What do you mean?"* asked Anthony puzzled but intrigued.

*"Nationalism is nothing more than a group believing that they and no others have got the possession of God."*

*"Heavens, that is a thought. I suppose that's right. And I suppose we in the Church do the same as soon as we believe we have possession of the eternal God."*

*"Exactly. The great danger with the sacraments is that we can easily slip into that arrogant belief."*

*"It's the same with confession I suppose ..."* said Anthony. He got up and poured a little more red wine into Clarence's glass and then his own.

*"Of course it is. Just because you mutter a few words it does not mean anything. It does not indicate any change of heart."* Clarence helped himself to another glass of wine.

*"Our job is to move the heart. It is my heart that I must give in sacrifice ..."* and Clarence saw that Anthony was drifting again into that strange trance-like state.

*"I'm going to bed,"* said Clarence and he leapt up, gulped the remainder of his wine.

*"Me too."*

Before getting into bed Anthony tried to pray for Fr. Smithes, for his return to health but he could not stop himself hoping he would die. As soon as he had had the thought he felt a pang of guilt. He thought again of offering himself in sacrifice like a burnt offering to God.

\*   \*   \*

The effect of these intense discussions with Clarence was to make Anthony even more passionate in his dedication to creating Christ's community out of his East End parish. It was not long before he had the youth of the parish, not only the YCW group, reading bits of the gospels. He showed them that they were protecting themselves by belonging to a Catholic youth club and in a short time he had closed the youth club and he had encouraged, almost dragooned all its Catholic members to join other youth clubs and Anthony fired them with the belief that they were the light of the world and that they had to let their light shine before men. In his four gospel groups for married couples, Anthony welcomed non-Catholics to join them. When these did not want to become

Catholics in any formal sense Anthony was not worried, in fact he almost discouraged them from doing so. He thought their missionary fervour would be tempered if they came into contact with the complacent churchgoers. They were, he impressed upon them, part of the Christian community in virtue of their love and desire to be loving towards their neighbours. So Anthony joined forces with some of the Anglican and Methodist priests and ministers. This was real Ecumenism, thought Anthony: here at the grassroots level among young adolescents and in young married couples the real work of unity was being forged and not at the Lambeth Conference or in formal meetings between the Pope and the Archbishop of Canterbury. It was not long before he had two Anglican priests, and a Methodist minister and a Congregationalist minister joining together with him in forming joint gospel groups.

His fervour and enthusiasm became a source of admiration to many. He was up at half-past five every morning and prayed for an hour before he said Mass at seven in the morning. As soon as that was over he gobbled a breakfast and then pedalled on his bicycle as fast as he could go, down to the hospital where he visited not only the Catholics but all the sick people who welcomed his ministrations. One day he was going into the hospital when a nurse who knew him well came running up to him and told him that Mr. Jewson had just died – very suddenly of a heart attack. Mrs. Jewson was just returning home, having identified the body. Now Anthony knew Mrs. Jewson quite well because she had once come to ask him to say a Mass for her father who was ill and lived in the north of England. She had told Anthony on that occasion that she and her husband were loners and, being from the north of England, had never managed to make many friends in this locality which was new and alien for them. She had told him that all her relatives and her husband's family lived in Yorkshire and that they always went there for their annual holiday. He had seen her outside of Church on a certain number of occasions and waved to her cheerily in the street. She was a woman of about fifty-one and her husband was a few years older and they were childless. Anthony could see that each one's life was involved in devotion to each other. When Anthony heard of Mr. Jewson's death he rushed off on his bicycle to see Mrs. Jewson who had just arrived back in her flat. She was a brave woman but Anthony could see that she was glad to see him and talk to someone and have some company in her distress. He sat with her for an hour and tried to console her. After an hour he left her, having agreed to return the next day to arrange the funeral. As he went home on his bicycle he thought of Matteo Ricci washing the sores of the lepers. He would form a group of caring people who, like Matteo Ricci and his disciples, would go and bind up the wounds of those who had just lost a spouse and had no one to comfort them.

So he quickly organized a rota of ten people who gave their telephone numbers and who were all willing to go either to the hospital or the home of someone who had just lost a husband or wife. Over the following year about once a month on average one member of the rota was roused and went quickly to the aid of the bereaved person. These widowers or widows were overwhelmed by this concern and love and when they heard that the impetus for this human kindness had come from Fr. Stonewell more than one decided to embrace the faith of this missionary priest. These converts, Anthony told Clarence on one occasion, were true Christians not just slavish churchgoers. The hospital authorities, although appreciative of Fr. Stonewell's efforts, yet resented his interference especially as he went out of his way to indicate that he thought this was a service which the hospital itself should provide. Fr. Stonewell was someone who was becoming very uncomfortable to live with – his apostolic zeal which was excellent and praiseworthy in themselves were nearly always tinged with moral censure towards those who did not participate in his efforts. When Anthony heard someone saying that he was becoming awkward he was sure that Jesus had not been an easy person to live with either. This encouraged him because he saw it as an additional sign of his at-one-ment with Jesus. As he pedalled furiously on his bicycle with his head thrust forward and his sharp nose pointing in front of him and his bearing demonstrating his singleness of purpose, parishioners felt excited but also afraid. The old faithful churchgoers muttered among themselves and Fr. Smithes had been away for only three weeks when they were longing fervently for his return.

After he had said Mass and been to the hospital he went to the secondary school where he was chaplain and went into one of the classes on each occasion. Here were his young apostles and he went out of his way to try and show them what Christianity was. When one of the boys said he was shy of going to confession and told him privately that he masturbated but was nervous of telling the priest in confession,

*"But you've told me just now,"* said Anthony.

*"Oh yes, but that's different,"* said the boy. He looked up at Anthony with his blue eyes and blond hair.

*"But how is it different, Pat? I'm a priest and you've just told it to me."*

*"But there's no confessional here,"* said Pat.

*"In the early Church there were no confessionals,"* said Anthony, *"they were only brought in by a chap called Charles Borromeo in the sixteenth century in Italy because he thought it gave priests protection from seductive women. Confession is telling to a priest things you've done that your are sorry about. Then if the priest is understanding you feel forgiveness and that helps you not to sin again."*

*"I've never 'eard it explained like that before,"* said Pat.

*"A lot of mystique gets built around many of the Church's rituals. Well now, Pat, do you want to confess your masturbation?"*

*"Yes, I'll go to confession, Father."*

*"But you just have; I'll give you absolution. Just genuflect on one knee."*

And there in the corner of the playground without anyone noticing Fr. Stonewell gave him absolution. Pat rushed around to all his mates in the school and told them what had happened. From then onwards he heard confessions in the school in an empty classroom during the morning break.

*"I often feel funny going into Church and waiting there in the queue for confession with all 'em old ladies, Fav,"* said Tony Caddy.

*"Well you don't ever have to – you can ask a priest to hear your confession anytime. It's no big deal."*

Clarence and Anthony called this 'demythologizing' the Church's rituals. *Demythologizing* was another buzzword of this new sect of enthusiasts. Anthony scorned those who wanted to keep everything cloaked in mystery. He did not realize that people felt safer to keep God in a safe place, in a closet that did not interfere unduly in the conduct of their lives. Anthony thought of Jesus eating and drinking with the publicans and how the Pharisees condemned him for doing so. When the conservative Catholics condemned him he knew he was walking in the shoes of his Master. His Master had been crucified and put to death. He had sacrificed himself. To be crucified, to die condemned and despised would be a supreme triumph, he thought.

Anthony believed that the centre of mystery lay in God's love and not in wooden confessionals or the Latin language and that this love was transmitted through the human-ness of the priest and of Christians towards one another. So Anthony swept away everything that smacked of sanctimonious observance and replaced it with what he came to call *Riccian* humanity, after Matteo Ricci, Anthony was sure that God's spirit was in him and not in Fr. Smithes. Anthony did not stop to ask himself why all these complex customs had grown up as Matteo Ricci would certainly have done. He just swept them away as Francis Xavier swept away the pagan temples. He was just as much an iconoclast as those he condemned.

\*    \*    \*

Joanna Murphy, known always as Joe Murphy, had lived all her life in the parish. She was quietly spoken and walked always unobtrusively but with a slight forwards stoop. Her hair had a hint of red in it and her face was almost snow white. She nearly always wore a little blue cap-like hat. Her eyes were blue and sadly gentle. Her husband was killed in the war and her only son died of polio at the age of six, three years after the war had finished. Her grief was so intense that she could never speak about it. Only her oldest friends knew of that immense sorrow that reigned quietly at the centre of her. His name had been Patrick and she could never hear a child called by the name without having to look the other way and search for a handkerchief. On 17th March, St. Patrick's Day, she would go to the grave of her dear boy and put upon it a bouquet of flowers and kneel and pray for a long time. When Patrick had died, a kind old Irish priest, Fr. Fitzpatrick who was at the time parish priest at Mile End, had performed the funeral and done all he could to comfort her. Once a week after Sunday Mass she went down to the cemetery at St. Patrick's, Leytonstone, and put flowers on the little grave of her son. She had a medal blessed by the Pope which Fr. Fitzpatrick had given her and each week she would put it on the grave and say a prayer. She came to believe that the medal had special powers. When she was ill she used to hold it while saying a decade of the rosary and whenever a friend of hers was ill she would touch her with it and pray. Several times people had got better after Joe Murphy had put her medal onto the skin of a sick person and said a decade of the rosary. She had a quality about her that gave people confidence that her presence would bring them health. She had a quietness about her that radiated a deep peace. She never spoke a bitter word about anyone. After her dear son had died she had for two years collapsed into drink and debt, sleeping with different men and cursed God and one night she nearly threw away the papal medal that Fr. Fitzpatrick had given her but something stopped her. That 'something', whatever it was, grew stronger and three months later she repented of the way she had been and she sought out Fr. Fitzpatrick who was now in a parish in north London and went to confession to him.

He forgave her not just as God's representative but with his own heart as well. He did not condemn her a bit. It was from that time that the papal medal became especially precious for Joe Murphy. It became for her the symbolic expression of Fr. Fitzpatrick's humane forgiveness and comfort which he had offered her at the time of her dear son's death and also of his sympathy during her 'bad time', as friends used to call it. She was not superstitious because she did not believe that the medal had power to save her from God's wrath; she knew that the medal was a symbol of life and hope and also of God's loving kindness, shown to her through the person and humanity of Fr. Fitzpatrick.

One evening, just as he was going to bed, the telephone rang and one of the sisters on duty at the hospital rang to say that there was a Catholic from the parish, dangerously ill, called Mrs. O'Shaughnessy. Anthony rushed to his office and got his little leather sick-call set and then went into the Church to the tabernacle to put a sacred host into his pyx which he put into its little jacket which he hung round his neck. He bicycled down to the hospital as quickly as he could. Mrs. O'Shaughnessy was quite bright when he arrived, though she was breathing heavily with severe bronchial pneumonia.

*"I get it every year at about this time, Father,"* she spoke the words in a rapid Irish accent. Anthony looked at her breathing heavily. Her hair was white with yellow streaks running from her forehead down on the right hand side and she had a moustache of hairs around her upper lip. She looked up sharply at Fr. Stonewell. She was one of the parishioners who did not like his sermons. She looked up at Anthony while clinging tightly to her rosary in her right hand.

*"I've brought you Holy Communion, Mrs. O'Shaughnessy,"*

*"Oh praise be to God, Father."*

*"And I've brought you the Sacrament of the Sick"*

*"What's that, Father, I've never heard of that."*

*"It used to be called Extreme Unction."*

*"Ah glory be to God can't all them bishops, Pope and all, stop changin' everything. It's been called Extreme Unction ever since I was a toddler and that's what I'm goin' to call it and what's more, Father, I don't want it. It's for the dyin' and I'm not dyin' yet, I'll tell yer."*

*"Well you never know,"* said Anthony harshly.

*"Ah to be sure, I'm not dyin' yet, Father."*

*"But anyway,"* said Anthony, *"it's called the Sacrament of the Sick now because it's not only for those who are dying but those who are sick too – so you*

should have it. The Church wants people who are sick to have it; it can give people the grace to get better."

"I know yer the priest, Father, but I'm tellin' yer. That sacrament, Extreme Unction, is for the dyin'. I remember Fr. Donnellan in me 'ome in Donegal tellin' us that in catechism class. I can see 'im sayin' it as if 'e were standin' there now, God bless him." She stopped and looked defiantly at Anthony and then she seeing him staring at her with a pathetic expression on his face she said, "Oh well, if it can help me to get better then I'll 'ave it. Can't do me any 'arm, I suppose. What with that and Joe Murphy coming around to-morrow with 'er medal I shall be as fit as a fiddle." At the mention of a medal Anthony stiffened.

"What's this about Joe Murphy's medal?" asked Anthony roughly.

"Oh, haven't you 'eard of Joe Murphy's miracle medal, Father?" she heaved herself up on the pillows and stared at him, "what's you been in this parish for … a year it must be and you 'aven't 'eard of Joe Murphy's miracle medal? To be sure I know Fr. Smithes knows about it. Joe Murphy's a saint she is and when she prays with 'er miracle medal she cures people just like Jesus did. She's cured lots of us who's been ill. It's a Pope's medal she's 'ad, well Father, from long back, and when one of us who lives near 'er is ill she comes and puts it in our 'and and says a decade of the rosary. I've had Joe Murphy's medal five or six times and it'll cure me if nothin' else does. Anyway she's comin' to-morrow so what with yer new sacrament and 'er medal I'll be as right as rain. As sure as St. Patrick lives in 'eaven I'll be as fit as a young chicken."

"But that's wrong," said Anthony with harsh fierceness, "it's just superstition; it's an insult to have that after having the Church's sacraments to-day." At this Mrs. O'Shaughnessy's Irish temper flared up. She pushed herself even more upright, threw down her rosary onto the bedclothes and waved her right hand and glared fiercely at Anthony.

"Don't you say a thing against Joe Murphy. I'm tellin'you, she's an 'oly woman and when she prays to Jesus, Mary and Joseph the sick get better."

"That's nothing to do with the religion of Jesus Christ. Jesus Christ instituted the seven sacraments to carry the grace of Jesus into people's hearts and all these medals, scapulas and bottles of holy water are just superstition," said Anthony with churlish pomposity.

"How dare you say such a thing, Father," saliva was frothing through her lips, "it's a medal a priest gave her and it was specially blessed by the Pope 'imself."

"I don't care who it was blessed by and I'm not giving you sacraments if you are going to have some pagan religious practice the next day."

*"Well, I'm not havin' yer new-fangled sacrament either, Father,"* said Mrs. O'Shaughnessy through tight but determined lips.

*"Are you sure you know what you are saying?"* asked Fr. Stonewell.

*"I am as sure as I know I'm talking to a priest of God but I'm not havin' any sacrament from the 'ands of a priest who says I can't 'ave Joe Murphy's medal and calls it superstition. Superstition indeed. Wish Fr. Smithes were 'ere. He's like dear ol' Fr. Donnellan back in Donegal, God bless 'im. He knows what's holy and good, for sure he does."* Anthony saw the fury in her eyes and her cheeks had flushed bright red. At the mention of Fr. Smithes anger surged up in him. He turned on his heels to leave the ward. Just as he was reaching the corridor outside the Sister came up to him and said,

*"Did Mrs. O'Shaughnessy take the sacraments, Father?"*

*"No, she didn't."*

*"Shall I ring you if she get worse."*

*"Yes,"* said Anthony curtly and he strode heavy footedly out of the hospital.

As he was riding back to the presbytery he wondered if he had acted rightly but he reassured himself with the thought that everything which he had learned in theology and especially in the Scriptures taught him that to put trust in idols whether they be the statues of a false religion or Catholic medals made no difference. He remembered what Clarence had said about the worship of Baal. The love of God manifested itself to man through Christ and via Christ through the sacraments. Putting faith in anything else whether it be a holy rock that has to be touched or the Sacred Doorway at Santiago de Compostela that has to be entered seven times in a Holy Year to get a plenary indulgence is superstition and idolatry. Touching Joe Murphy's medal was in this category, said Anthony to himself. Anthony Stonewell was certain. He knew his Biblical Theology. He would not give Mrs. O'Shaughnessy the sacraments until she had promised to have nothing more to do with Joe Murphy's medal. He did not have to make any such promise to himself however because just as he was putting his light out beside his bed the telephone rang. It was the sister of the ward he had just visited,

*"Mrs. O'Shaughnessy has just died, Father."*

*"What?"* said Anthony confused, *"How did it happen?"*

*"Well she seemed alright, Father, but then just about ten minutes ago she sat up for a moment asking faintly for a glass of water and she seemed very upset and kept muttering something about 'how dare he abuse Joe Murphy's medal' I didn't know what she was talking about. Anyway I went to get 'er a*

*glass of water but by the time I'd come back she'd gone, Father. It often hap-pens like that with these cases, Father."*

There was silence. Anthony Stonewell did not know what to say; he was in shock.

*"Wouldn't she take the sacraments, Father? I always thought she was a practising Catholic."*

*"No, she wouldn't take them,"* said Fr. Stonewell.

*"Ah well, you did the best yer could, Father,"* said the sister.

*"Thank you for letting me know,"* said Anthony tonelessly and he put down the receiver.

He could not sleep. He paced up and down. Had he acted rightly or not? Ten minutes before he had convinced himself that he had but now that Mrs. O'Shaughnessy had died a surge of nausea arose in him. He felt angry with her. 'Why did she bloody well die on me?' he said to himself and he almost felt she'd done it to revenge herself on him. He wanted to ring Clarence to speak to him but it was half-past one in the morning and he would be asleep. He walked down into the Church and paced around it but as he looked up at the tabernacle with the sanctuary candle burning it felt oppressive. He looked at the statues and he shook his fist at an ugly plaster statue of St. Gemma Galgani that a pious Italian parish-ioner had recently donated to the Church and which Fr. Smithes had insisted on having set up on a little pedestal just to the right of the altar.

*'There won't be room to get into the pews soon for the number of statues',* he said to himself angrily. He could find no peace in the Church. It was not a friendly home for him so he went out of its front door and walked into the dank night air. There was the faintest drizzle but he did not bother to get himself a raincoat. He should have locked the front door of the Church but he did not bother. He walked aimlessly at first but then took up a direction towards the river and the docks. The sight of river, he thought, might soothe him. He could not pray, he could not think, he just walked and as he walked it began to rain more heavily but he did not mind. He got wetter and wetter until he could feel trickles of water running from his shoulder blades down towards his tummy. He could feel the cold droplets trickling down his chest. He kept on walking. There was no one about. He had not seen anyone and he was glad. He could not have borne a cheery 'Good-night, Father' wet though he was and although he knew he should, in good sense, return to the presbytery, get dry and warm and try to sleep yet he was determined to reach the river. He needed to <u>see</u> the river. He did not know why. He just felt he <u>must</u> see

it so he walked on. He had been walking for about three quarters of an hour and he had reached the junction where Commercial Road and East India Dock Road meet and he turned down the road which he knew would bring him to a little park on the side of the Isle of Dogs and which looked across the river towards the lower part of Greenwich. He looked at his watch, it was twenty five past two. He would reach the park in just under ten minutes.

He felt a great relief as his eyes eventually clasped their gaze on the river. The Thames was a slow sluggish river which seemed to absorb all the muck and filth of London and still travel onwards doggedly towards the sea. Anthony felt a mysterious correspondence between the state of his soul and the state of this languid river. A contract was forged between their animate and inanimate spirits. Anthony took away some of the river's languid muckiness and who's to say it didn't flow more lightly? Anthony went away feeling mucky and heavy but less anguished and, as he looked back, he seemed to see more ripples on its surface.

He had not stayed long at the river and, after trudging heavily through measured raindrops he arrived back at the presbytery just before quarter past three. He threw off his sopping clothes and ran a hot bath. After sitting in it for ten minutes he dried himself and got into bed and was asleep within minutes. He must have had a nightmare because he woke sweating at one moment with the ephemeral image of huge flying foxes swooping around him as he was trying to say Mass. When he woke he remembered it and it made him think of St. Teresa of Avila who, while attending Mass, saw devils pulling at the vestments of the priest and knew he must be in mortal sin and begged him to go to confession. But Anthony Stonewell was not haunted for very long. After Mass when the housekeeper, who had arrived from her little flat over the hall at the back of the Church, had given him bacon and eggs and brought in a copy of the Guardian which he read while drinking a large cup of coffee he began to feel better. He even began to wonder what he should do about Joe Murphy. He could not let her go on performing her private rites in competition with the Church. He decided that later in the day he would call to see her.

It was just after three o'clock in the afternoon that Fr. Stonewell knocked at Joe Murphy's door – No. 10 Addington Road, a small two-storeyed terraced house. He did not know her well but she was definitely one of Fr. Smithes's admirers. He had just lumped her together with a number of others who attended the early Mass on Sunday, came to communion every Sunday and usually on weekdays too and he had seen her praying in front of two statues of dubious merit. He had also seen her talking in confidential tones to Mrs. O'Brien. In his Saturday night diatribe with Clarence Cider he had immediately designated this group of parishioners the 'Worshippers of Baal' among whom he included Fr. Smithes. They had now all become idolaters in his eyes and now, with Clarence's help, had a well worked out system of theology to prove it. He himself and most of his parishioners in the gospel groups were worshippers of the True God. The 'Baal Worshippers' were always polite to him but they did not go to confession to him and generally avoided contact with him. They felt that he was contemptuous of their simple worship and in these feelings they were completely right. That he was right and they were wrong had all the certainty of infallible truth. No pope had ever been more certain of himself than Anthony. Any possibility that he was not completely in the right was not a thought that ever crossed his mind or, if it did, it was only momentary and was quickly banished under a fresh impetus of missionary enthusiasm. When he had been walking in the pouring rain down to the Isle of Dogs in the middle of the night some uncertainty had assailed him but now that he had thrust it aside his certitude was even more dogmatic then it had been before. He stood for a moment in front of the door then he rang the little electric bell that was on the left hand side of the brown wooden door.

*"Oh hello, Father, please come in."* Joe Murphy turned around and led him into the little parlour. There was a square table and a set of purple covered chairs that surrounded it. The bow window looked out onto the street that Anthony had so recently been standing in. The lace curtains were thick and there was a large aspidistra in a pot in the middle of the table. Although it was early afternoon not very much light penetrated. Anthony glanced around the walls and saw a print of St. Thérèse of Lisieux holding some arum lilies in her right hand. On the side of the room farthest from the window was an upright piano with some music in its stand. The carpet was also a deep purple so the room, except for the table which was close to the window, was dark and somewhat mysterious. *"Can I make you a cup of tea?"* she asked looking at him timidly as he sat down at the table on one of the chairs.

*"No thank you, Mrs. Murphy, I just called in for a chat,"* he said in a moderate tone.

This was a rather modified statement of what he had intended. She had about her a peace that softened his mood. Anthony had once or twice met people from whom he had caught a sense of holiness; a sense that they had found some peace between themselves and God. He was not exactly aware of this feeling when he met Mrs. Murphy but he did realize that he was being gentler than he had intended. Her simple manner somewhat disarmed him and he found that he did not know quite where to start but she helped him,

*"Oh dear I was sorry to hear about Mrs. O'Shaughnessy. She was such a good soul but I'm sure the Lord will look after her now. I had been going to visit her to-day and let her hold my medal and say a decade of the rosary with her."*

*"That's what I came to speak to you about, Mrs. Murphy,"* said Anthony quickly, afraid that he might lose his missionary intent if he let her go on much longer.

*"Yes, Father, you've probably heard that I often go and pray with the sick. I have a special feeling for sick people."* She looked kindly at him.

*"But you shouldn't give them that medal to hold. Some people think it's magic – that if they touch your medal they will be cured."* A startled look came into Joe Murphy's eyes. She looked down at the ocre apron around her waste. She had been baking some scones when Anthony had rung at the door. She quickly took off her apron and sat down at the table at right angles to Fr. Stonewell.

*"Oh, Father, I'd never thought of it like that. It's praying with them that helps and they know that the medal is precious to me and when they hold it, it sort of makes the sick one and me'self feel close. I know it sounds kind of funny, Father, but I don't think there's any 'arm done by it."*

*"I can't let you go on using that medal. People may want the medal instead of the sacraments."*

*"Oh dear Lord,"* cried Joe Murphy, *"don't tell me that's what happened to poor Moira O'Shaughnessy?"*

*"Yes, I'm afraid it was,"* and Anthony looked down and away. He remembered his long wet walk of the previous night.

*"If that's the case, Father, I'll give you the medal but please keep it in a safe place."*

Joe Murphy went to the drawer beside her bed and out of a little box she drew her precious medal and handed it to Fr. Stonewell. A tear welled up in her right eye which Anthony did not notice. He pocketed it casually and said she was right to follow the Church and put the sacraments first. Fr. Stonewell strode out feeling he had won a battle for the kingdom of Christ. As Joe Murphy closed the door she burst into tears and took up a photograph of her dear little boy and kissed it. Then, still crying, she put it away carefully.

# CHAPTER FOUR

Two days after Anthony had pocketed Joe Murphy's medal Fr. Smithes returned from hospital, having been away for four months. He felt grateful to Anthony for having looked after his parish while he had been away and he knew that all had been run efficiently but he knew that his curate was proud at heart and, though in the kindest way, he was determined to return his parish back into the happy family which it had been before he went to hospital. He would not do it quickly but step by step he would undo the work of Anthony's frenetic activity. Fr. Smithes had seen priests like Anthony before. They create an impressive display of pastoral activity but they cannot sustain it. They are like the seed which has been sown on stoney ground.

Fr. Smithes was just fifty years old and he had been a priest for twenty-four years. He had spent all that time as a curate in one parish near Finsbury Park. He had been brought up in East Ham and came of devout Catholic parents. From an early age he had wanted to be a priest and as soon as he had finished his secondary schooling he applied to the Archbishop and, after a cursory interview, was accepted and sent off to the English College in Lisbon. Most students for the priesthood went to one of the seminaries in England but there were still three colleges, dating from recusancy days that were on the continent: in Rome, Valladolid and Lisbon. George Smithes had gone to Lisbon where he stayed for the whole six years of his training. He underwent a severe régime there where dogmatic and moral theology were drilled into the students. He did not understand very much of it and what he did he felt had very little relevance to life on the parish. He had come to know his parish in East Ham very well as a little boy. He had become an altar boy at the age of six, helped the parish priest run the youth club and went to Mass faithfully every day and never a day had gone by without him going to communion. He went to confession once a week or once a fortnight. He said his prayers morning and evening with feeling. His father had died when he was aged only four. He had died of cancer, leaving two boys, George and Tony, to be brought up by his widow who was helped by her sister. Their mother struggled hard to make ends meet and did her best to ensure as good an education for her boys as possible. She worked as Manageress of a laundry and by what she earned from this and by dint of doing some private laundering for a small nursing home, she just managed to make ends meet. Her younger son did quite well and, when he had finished schooling, started to work as a clerk in one of the branches of St. Martin's Bank in Aldgate but he had only been there two years when the war broke out and he was called up and soldiered for most of the war in North Africa and Italy. George was ordained a priest in Lisbon in 1943 and came back to England in a Portuguese ship which narrowly escaped being torpedoed by a German U-boat patrolling the Bay of Biscay. Although Portuguese shipping was neutral the commander of the submarine had suspected that this ship was carrying wolfram to the Allies. George Smithes and six of his new ordained colleagues had had to disembark in Dublin from where they found their way to England. George was sent straight away to Finsbury Park by Cardinal Hinsley who was then Archbishop of the Westminster diocese. There was one of the canons of the diocese running the parish but he was prematurely old and in a short time George Smithes was taking care of most of the parish.

He thought of the parish priest as a kind of friendly mother and he believed that if people would come to the sacraments they would grow in the grace of God. In each year he visited every Catholic in the parish, the practising and the lapsed. He would always take with him a pocketful of sweets, ready for the children. He loved children and they loved him. To see him in the playground of the primary school during break would soften the hardest heart. The children climbed over him, pulled his hair, tugged at his dog-collar and yet their respect for him as a Catholic priest was never for a moment in doubt. When he visited a Catholic household it was only a matter of minutes before the children would be sitting on his lap and asking him to tell them a story. Parents tried to pull their children away; "Leave Father alone," they would say but he smiled at the parents so disarmingly that they gave up any further attempt to discipline their children in his presence. He had seen the children grow up, he had heard their first confessions, given them their first communion, been in attendance when the bishop came to confirm them. He had seen some of them come to the altar for marriage and then baptized their first children. The Catholics of the parish were his family. He loved them just like a biological father loved his children and puts them first; in just such a way Fr. Smithes also loved his large family. He was not unfriendly toward those outside the family but he was not concerned about them. He would wave to them and wish them well but all his time was devoted to his own large family and, for the most part, they loved him and he loved them. He was happy and the old canon had great affection for him.

When, after twenty-three years as a curate in Finsbury Park, Fr. Smithes was assigned his own parish in the East End of London he was delighted. He had come from that part of London and he felt he understood it. He was not fifty and he thought to himself that he would happily live out the last twenty-five years of his active life, God willing, as parish priest in the little Church in Bow. He arrived and, as yet, had no curate but was promised one as soon as the new batch was ordained at Westminster Cathedral. He looked forward with pleasure to receiving a new priest and helping him to find his feet and have a good start to his priestly life. Fr. Smithes loved being a priest and felt so deeply happy that he had chosen this, the very best of vocations. He knew it was the highest vocation on earth and he thanked Our Lady every day after Mass that she had asked her Son our Lord to give him that special grace to become and remain a priest. He had difficulties as a priest. Loneliness was his greatest cross. He was such a naturally affectionate man that when the day's work had been done and he was on his own, as he often was, in a large high-ceilinged Victorian presbytery he felt empty and with no energy. He would slump in front of the television and would often just go off to sleep and would wake up at two in the morning. He would then get up and get into his pyjamas and put himself to bed. The next morning he would be up early and the energy seemed to return to him. It was the evenings that he found so hard. On a Saturday night after hearing confessions and locking up the Church he would sometimes have a couple of whiskies but he was never drunk. Sometimes a priest from the next parish would come around and have a couple of drinks with him on a Saturday evening after confessions but, although he was a man whom children loved and most parishioners trusted, he lacked a certain boisterous masculinity that always left him slightly on the edge of the group of Catholic clergy. 'Good old George,' they would say but when they wanted to let their hair down and have a bit of a night out, George was not the natural person they turned to.

He was a very kind man, he was a very good man but he had not ever felt strong passion, either ecstatic joy or deep grief or violent anger. He was a child within and had not grown sufficiently in emotional resourcefulness to experience emotions of great intensity. He had not ever had serious doubts about the existence of God; he had not been racked with sexual temptation; he had never hated or loved passionately. He was devoid of zeal. He loved calmly, he had trust, he had affection. He was drawn to the more gently piety of St. Francis of Sales than the violent passions of a St. John of the Cross or a St. Teresa of Avila. One of the first conversations he had had with Anthony Stonewell had been about the merits and demerits of the two St. Teresas. George was devoted to St. Thérèse of Lisieux. St. Thérèse loved her family and she said she could never be like the saints who cut themselves off from their families in order to seek God. She had not believed that the Christian has to do great acts. *'If you pick up a pin with love, you can save soul,'* she said in her autobiography. *'Do not climb up into the mountains to find God but go down into the valley and God will come and find you there.'* Fr. Smithes had modelled himself on St. Thérèse and he shied away from the excesses of St. Teresa of Avila and he did not like Bernini's statue of her in Rome. Anthony Stonewell, on the other hand, admired St. Teresa of Avila. He thrived on her excesses and it rung a concordant bell with the passionate stirrings of his own heart. George became quite fearful when he first heard Anthony ardently praising St. Teresa of Avila and when Anthony told him that he'd been on a special pilgrimage there and had walked barefoot from the Convento de la Encarnacion outside the walls of Avila to the Convento de San José in the middle of the town and had then fasted for three days following the example of the great St. Teresa, George realized that he was likely to have a difficult time with his new curate.

"*But don't you admire St. Teresa of Avila?*" asked Anthony exasperated at George's mild tolerance and, he felt, slight condescension toward the great Spanish mystic.

"*I think she was great for her time,*" said George, " *but I think St. Thérèse of Lisieux is more relevant for our times. It is not chance that she was canonized so shortly after her death and that she has been particularly held up as a model for present day Catholics by Pius X, Benedict XIV, Pius XI and Pius XII.*"

"*But don't you admire St. Teresa of Avila who, at the age of fifty, when the Carmelite Order in Spain was lax and corrupt, went out with three other nuns and founded the Convent of St. Joseph against great fury and anger from the nuns of her own order and also of the townsfolk. Don't you admire someone that can brave the insults and contempt for the sake of what she believed to be the will of God for her?"*

*"I am sure that the Church needed that in the Spain of her day but to-day the Church does not need reform as it did then. The Popes were corrupt in the time of St. Teresa but now they are not. The Church is not a great temporal power as it was then. The Church doesn't need reforming. All we need is to do what the Church requires of us and to do it with love and humility."* That was shortly after Anthony had arrived in the parish and before his great moment of enlightenment. They were sitting in George's study-cum-sitting-room. They were each in low slung chairs. It was early afternoon on a Sunday. The morning masses had been said, lunch had been eaten and the two priests were relaxing. George's desk to the right of the two chairs was piled with papers and books. Opposite it was the television set with another easy chair in front of it and, just on the other side of it, was a pre-dieu and in front of it was a plaster statue of Our Lady of Lourdes.

*"But how do you know that everything that the Church requires of us is right? After all if St. Teresa had done what the bishop of her diocese had told her to do she would have stayed in the Convent of the Incarnation and the Carmelite Order would never have been reformed and incidentally, Thérèse Martin would not have had a convent of Carmelites in Lisieux to enter in the first place unless Teresa of Avila had reformed the order three hundred years before. A woman called Madam Acarie brought the reformed Carmelites of St. Teresa of Avila from Spain to France at the beginning of the seventeenth century."*

*"It's always dangerous to disobey one's superiors. St. Teresa of Avila only disobeyed her bishop after much prayer and taking careful advice and she had been a nun for thirty years and had a lot of experience behind her."*

Anthony felt the implied slight: that he was an inexperienced bounder and that when he had been a priest for thirty years and prayed as hard as Fr. Smithes then perhaps he could consider disobeying his bishop. For all his zeal and apparent robust spirituality yet Anthony was intensely sensitive to any implication that he was a novice, a child or inexperienced. The fact that it was true never crossed his mind.

*"Look, even St. Thérèse of Lisieux was quite hot-headed. When she wanted to go into the convent at the age of fifteen and was not allowed to because she was under age she made a special journey to Rome to see the Pope to ask him for permission which, as you know, she got. I think this idea that all the saints were obedient to authority is nonsense. Most of them were very hot-headed and passionate individuals."*

Fr. Smithes looked at his new firebrand curate and nodded his head knowingly and Anthony noticed it and felt furious. He knew he was being patted on the head by Fr. Smithes, the wise and holy one, but Fr. Smithes also felt under attack though he was not so aware of it as Anthony and was only dimly aware that he was withdrawing from argument because he knew that Anthony would always believe he was right and that he was not going to get anywhere with this zealot. He did not feel comfortable with a priest such as Anthony. He took it as an unquestioned assumption that all priests believed that the central sacerdotal desire was to be obedient to the Church. George loved the Church but as the weeks and months went by he began to feel that Anthony did not love the Church and to feel he was harbouring a traitor. George had loved the Church ever since he was a tiny boy when his mother took him along to the Church and sat him beside her. He adored his mother. He loved the Church and all her teachings. This was the guiding principle of his life. All the time that he had been at the seminary in Lisbon and listened to the various wranglings of theologians over such matters as predestination, grace, God's creativity and man's free-will they had really flowed into one ear and out of his pen for examinations but they had nothing to do with the work he was going to do on the parish. They were a sort of trial, a penance sent by God, to test the would-be priest. He loved the Church as it was and he never expected it to change except in minor details until the end of time.

It was particularly difficult for him then that, at the precise time that this reforming zealot zoomed into his orbit, the Vatican Council was announcing radical reforms that were beginning to affect the central foci of parish life. It was the greatest surprise to George that the Council had decided that the Mass should be said in English. It had been in Latin for sixteen hundred years and George had always believed that it was a sacred language and that it evoked a mysteriousness that put people in touch with the mystery of God himself. When he read of the first deliberations of the Council on the liturgy he thought that perhaps some little bits here and there of the Mass might be put into English. He had secretly thought from time to time that it would be more sensible if the Epistle and Gospel were in English and he always felt rather annoyed that at Mass on Sunday it had to be read first in Latin and then read again in English for the benefit of the people but that the whole Mass, including the sacred words of consecration, should be put into English was horrifying to him. It was the words of consecration – the actual words *'Hoc est Corpus Meum'* that turned the wafer of bread into the Body and Blood of Our Lord. He had been taught that even if one word was not said or that if the priest said 'Hoc est Corpus Suum' by mistake then transubstantiation did not take place. And now here there were bishops in Rome, bishops of his beloved Church, suggesting that the whole Mass including the words of consecration should be put into English. If he had heard such a suggestion from anyone other than a bishop he would have thought it was heretical and secretly he did wonder once or twice whether some great heresy was not scooping up a great segment of the hierarchy against the Church as had happened at the time of the Arian heresy in the early days of the Church. He felt uneasy and troubled about what was happening and even more so, as it seemed to have come onto his own doorstep in the person of Anthony Stonewell. He prayed for Fr. Stonewell every day after Mass. He so hoped to help a new priest find his way into his priesthood and the thought that this priest under his care seemed to be so opposed to him and the way he did things was a great disappointment to him. He had never had someone whom he could not in the end win over. He deliberately let Anthony teach him about the new liturgy and gave him scope to teach the parishioners about the new Mass. When Anthony started a course of lectures on the meaning of the liturgical changes he supported him wholeheartedly. He supported him also in some Bible study groups which he ran among the more active members of his parish. He did not like though the tendency that there seemed to be in all this new pastoral activity to hand over to the laity matters that belonged to the priest. The priest was the interpreter of the Scriptures and also of the Liturgy and he did not like the way Anthony allowed the laity the role of interpreting for themselves the New and Old Testaments. Surely this was exactly what the Protestants had done at the time of the Reformation and many of the things which he heard Anthony saying reminded him of what Luther and the reformers had said in the sixteenth century. George Smithes distrusted Father Darrell, that theologian from Newman College whom Anthony and many other young priests admired so much. They seemed to believe Fr. Darrell more fervently than the Pope himself. Yet he had to admit that Anthony Stonewell had great energy and enthusiasm and he found him a great help in inaugurating the liturgical changes in the parish. He had to admit that without the knowledge of one of these young priests he would have found it difficult to implement the new instructions from the Vatican. But he disliked the time that Anthony spent in Ecumenical activity. Anthony joined a Bible Study group with two Anglican priests and a Methodist Minister and they were even joined sometimes by the Jewish Rabbi when they were discussing the Old Testament. If only Anthony would get on with the Catholics of the parish instead of rushing about apparently doing missionary work among those outside the flock. The truth was that George felt rather threatened by some of the questions that were now being put to Catholic priests by the clergy of other denominations especially when the latter were much better read in the Scriptures and Biblical Criticism. However, on the whole George managed with his curate for the first two years and it was during that time that the main changes instituted by the Vatican Council were implemented at parish level. While Anthony was engaged in that, then some sort of equilibrium was maintained but as soon as that had been established Anthony began to take things further and it was precisely at that moment that George got hepatitis and went into hospital. While he was in hospital George was visited by one or two of his parishioners and a couple of them had told him of what was happening in the parish and in particular the circumstances surrounding Mrs. O'Shaughnessy's death were reported to him. He decided that it was his duty as the parish priest to bring Anthony to heel but he would not do it by confrontation. He would slowly assert his authority not in an autocratic way but no less determinedly. To his surprise Anthony found that the George who returned from hospital was a significantly different person from the priest who had departed ill some four months earlier. He thought that George would accept all his changes even though he did not like them but in that he was mistaken.

* * *

The first thing George did was to tell Anthony that on Saturday nights after they had heard confessions he wanted to have a meeting with him to discuss what was happening in the parish and for him to report on his different activities. George explained that he knew they saw each other frequently during the week but that often they were in a rush and they did not have the time and leisure to discuss things fully. George thought that by talking to Anthony gently and over a whisky or two he would be able to calm him down but here it was George who was mistaken. He did not know that to the person of violent passions the 'calm down' and 'take it easy' tactics is anathema and in fact experienced by Anthony as patronizing and only inflamed him all the more. He felt that George was trying to corrupt him, to undermine his ideals and bring him down to the level of 'being practical' In all George's quiet talk Anthony detected a pervading atmosphere of cynicism that he found more and more throttling. In one way this was what George wanted: for Anthony to give up his more iconoclastic enthusiasm and to leave the parishioners content with the Church in which they had been reared since childhood and always trusted but it also had another effect which he had not calculated for. As slowly Anthony had to give up one activity after another under George's gentle but unrelenting pressure he became dispirited and disillusionment took hold of him. He decided that he could not do anything on a grand scale in the parish so instead he would concentrate on what was personal and, more quickly than one would expect, his inner system of values began to alter.

When he had been at Newman College the spiritual director of the College had discouraged him and the other 'divines' from forming 'personal relationships'. Personal relationships were dangerous unless they were between priests. When Evelyn Waugh's biography of Ronald Knox was read publicly in the refectory and it was mentioned in that book that Ronnie Knox was supported in his priesthood through the close friendships which he made, the president of the College had gone out of his way to give a special discourse to the 'divines' telling them that this was a very wicked allegation of Waugh's because to say of a priest that he was dependent upon friendship was a terrible calumny. And when a friend of Anthony's who had been ordained two years before him became involved with a woman on account of whom the priest had left the Church in order to marry her, his bishop said to him that to have sinned sexually with her was pardonable but to have made a personal relationship with her was unforgivable. For the first two and a half years Anthony did not have any friendships except the one with Clarence and the other members of the Doktor Klub. He was too dedicated to his missionary work to have time for making friends but as disillusion set in, the desire for friendship and personal relationships began to arise in him. This was the result which George had not foreseen although he had been worried by it, half unawares. The other reason why George had insisted that they have this meeting on a Saturday night was he had noticed that Anthony had begun to go out on Saturday nights to socialize with one or two of the parishioners and he was determined to put a stop to this. Fr. Smithes knew that there was nothing more harmful in a parish than a priest favouring a particular clique. George's endeavours made Anthony even more obstinately determined to seek comfort and friendship within the parish so he went out almost every Friday night to the houses of one or two friends. In particular he began to spend evenings with Tony and Andrea. George was shocked that Anthony was friendly with Andrea and Tony, neither of whom came to Church and, as far as he could see, Anthony had made no progress in bringing these erring sheep back into the fold. George could not believe that Anthony had no wish to do so. He could not understand a priest who would think in that way but in fact Anthony believed he was following in the footsteps of Jesus, eating and drinking with the publicans. He even *dissuaded* Andrea from coming to Church. He told her that her salvation did not depend on coming within the four walls of that stone building every Sunday and that her own relationship with God was much more important. Andrea and Tony liked Anthony and they had fun together mocking conventional parishioners and this included Fr. Smithes and some of his faithful followers. Each time he came back from Andrea and Tony's he felt the psychological distance between himself and George widening until he began to feel that they belonged to different religions altogether. He read one day in a spiritual book by Caryll Houselander who was a contemporary mystic, the statement that there was nothing more untrue than the idea that we all worship the same God. Anthony felt that his God and George's God were totally different.

Anthony was in rebellion against George's mental outlook. He also slowly became convinced that George was not holy but in a state of complacent self-satisfaction and he hated him for it. His developing friendship with Tony and Andrea was fuelled by an exasperated rage towards George. Anthony had in himself an antenna that was sensitive to the slightest hint of self-congratulation and the idea that George was building and cementing a community of people who believed they were, in some way, superior to others was anathema to him. He hated it in a deep level of his being and his basis for selecting friends slowly became determined by whether or not they displayed this character trait. Why he hated this character trait so much was a question that he did not ask himself. He felt more and more suffocated by Fr. Smithes's desiccated conservatism.

When Anthony refused to baptize a baby or to perform a marriage in the Church, Fr. Smithes did so instead. He did not directly undermine his curate but he would go and talk to the couple who wanted to get married or to the couple who wanted to have their baby baptized. He would then explain that it was the policy of the Church not to administer the sacraments to those who had no intention of practising and that Fr. Stonewell had been right in refusing them. But then after a quiet talk they would tell Fr. Smithes that though they did not practise they would come back to Church again. That assurance was sufficient reason for Fr. Smithes to offer the couple the sacrament of baptism or matrimony. He would tell Anthony quietly on a Saturday night of his talk with the couple and how he had reason to believe that they had the sincere intention of returning to Church so that he would administer the sacrament to them. When Anthony, smarting within, said that he doubted the sincerity of the couple Fr. Smithes just said that even if that were so there was more chance of the couple coming back to Church if the priest had not been rejecting towards them. Whenever Anthony tried to say that he was more concerned with the individual's relationship with God he was met by a glazed look. One of the difficulties between these two men was that they were both fanatics in their different ways. Anthony was manifestly so and was perceived as such by many people but George was also. Perhaps it would be truer to say that George was mesmerized by the fixed idea of getting as many Catholics into his Church on Sunday as possible and then to get as many of those to the sacraments as possible. No amount of debate or argument could dislodge the idea. He knew logically that the act of charity was the goal of the Christian endeavour but it did not have any influence on his pastoral practice. Fr. Smithes had no concern or interest in those who were not Catholics and Fr. Stonewell had no interest in those who were not dedicated to forming the Christian community of love on earth. What caused such friction between the two men was that each thought the other should be imbued with his own idea and could not tolerate the other's contrary goal. The other reason for conflict was that neither were 'their own man'. They were each followers of particular saints, like St. Teresa of Avila and St. Thérèse of Lisieux. Now the probability is that if these two saints had been able to leapfrog time and place and meet each other they would have got on well together and respected each other because they had each found themselves and been true to an inner call but both Fr. Smithes and Fr. Stonewell had their eyes on the dazzling attire of their heroines and heroes which they had tried to don themselves. This produced bitter antagonism between the two men because each believed the other should follow his hero or his heroine. The person who has taken the path of not being himself is secretly unsure of himself and guilty about not being who he is and compensates by trying desperately to convert the other. In this case neither man converted the other but slowly Anthony began to give up his missionary endeavour but George did not.

Now Anthony slumped into hopeless disillusion which one day became sealed into a brittle concrete. Within the parish was a huge rambling building which housed people who were in what was called 'Part Four Accommodation.' Here lived families who could not pay rent, who had just arrived over from Ireland or Greece and had not found accommodation yet and those who had been chucked out of their flats by the council for their anti-social behaviour. Whole families lived in one room. There was urine running down the corridors as children ran undisciplined shouting and screaming both within the building and also in the large yard outside. Anthony had been there from time to time, usually when asked to come and try to bring some peace when some fearful row had broken out between two Catholic marriage partners.

It was about six months after Fr. Smithes had returned from hospital and as disillusion was seeping further and further into Anthony's inner world that the telephone rang one day and the director of this latter-day Victorian slum rang to say that one of the children, who was a Catholic, had been killed in an accident so Anthony went straight away on his bicycle to the scene of the disaster. A little boy of five, Tommy Sweeney, had been playing round the back wheel of a milk float, the driver had not seen him and backed and gone straight over his neck and the boy had died instantly. Anthony did what he could to comfort both the mother and the other four children of the family and he stayed with her until her husband returned from work. Soon after the woman's husband returned Anthony, having prayed with the family for their dead son, went off but not before he had arranged the funeral. He was touched by the generosity of all the other families who quickly collected a sizeable sum of money which they gave to the Sweeney family.

When Anthony returned to the presbytery he told George about it. He was upset and the sight of the dead child and the aching distress of the mother brought tears to his eyes as he told George. George felt kindly towards Anthony at this moment and tried to comfort him by saying,

*"You know, Anthony, it is probably just as well that poor Tommy Sweeney died because if he had grown up into manhood he probably would never have come to Church or gone to Holy Communion."*

George was trying to offer comfort but Anthony did not appreciate his intentions. The words he had spoken sent a chill of horror through him. There was nothing he could say and what is more he did not want to say anything. He just knew that he wanted to get out of the presence of a being who could say such a thing. He got up from the armchair in George's office and walked to the door quite silently but as he passed to the other side of the door he got it by the handle and slammed it with all his might. Fr. Smithes looked at the quivering door-frame utterly bemused. He knew something terrible had happened and that it came from what he had just said but he did not know what it was. He was confused and upset. For the first time in his life as a priest he just did not know what was happening. He had always prided himself on knowingly understanding the talk and actions of those around him but he now felt utterly dumbfounded. He waited a minute and when he was sure that Anthony was not going to return he knelt down on the pre-dieu in his room and faced the statue of Our Lady of Lourdes which he had had since his ordination. It had been his mother's present to him on that great day. He knelt and implored Our Lady to help him. He could not even say the Rosary, his favourite prayer. He just said again and again,

"Oh Mother of God, please help me ..."
and he sobbed just like the mother of Tommy Sweeney.

\*   \*   \*

It was early December and although it was only half-past four the leaden sky cast the world into darkness. Anthony clumped heavily down the stairs and went into the housekeeper's sitting-room and told her that he would not be in for supper. Then he went to the top of the house to his bedroom and put on some leather boots and fastened a raincoat around himself. Then he crept downstairs, slipping past Fr. Smithes's room and down more stairs and stepped out into the foggy grey of London's coming night. He did what he always did when he was upset: he walked. This time he headed towards Wapping – it was always to the river. As he walked along Bow Road he looked up at the Council flats and saw lights coming on in each of them. Young lads and girls working in the City were just getting home, glad to get out of their suits or blouses and skirts and get into jeans. Others, returning from the docks, were clambering out of their filthy boots and trousers and tumbling into a bath before getting into shirts and trousers that were fresh and clean.

It was a Friday evening. Normally Anthony, on the other week-day nights, would be with the Young Christian Workers (YCW) or a family group but Fridays were evening out for the young and for married couples. It was the priest's time to read, prepare Sunday's sermon and to be ready for a full-on week-end. As Anthony walked on he thought of the warm family gatherings in the houses and flats. He felt alone, cast out by humanity, like a leper banished beyond the city walls. He could not go visiting at this hour and the thought of sitting through supper in an atmosphere of high tension was impossible. He had thought of ringing Clarence, Joe, Jamie, Stephen or Rudolph but he was in such an electric state of tension that he wanted no other company but his own. So he walked on, leaving the cinema at Mile End on his right and turned down Burdett Road which brought him south to the junction of Commercial Road, East India Dock Road and Poplar High Street. In twenty minutes he had turned right into Commercial Road. A few people hurried past him in tightly buttoned coats. They all had a definite destination and were hurrying towards it. Only Anthony was wandering not aimlessly but in no hurry. His next duty was on Saturday morning at nine o'clock when he had to offer Mass for the nuns at the local convent. He looked at his watch; it was just a few minutes past six. He was free for fifteen hours. He suddenly remembered his office. He had not said Vespers or Compline. He thought of Fr. Conan's severe face declaring that it was a mortal sin to miss praying any of the hours of Holy Office. He raised his mind to God and said the Our Father slowly and carefully. Then he noticed a bench facing a small square and park; he moved to it and sat upon it. He said the Our Father again taking each phrase slowly. 'Our Father' and his mind went to the length and breadth of the universe that had lain in the mind of God for all eternity until some mysterious moment in the heart of God, a big bang burst forth and unrolled its contents down thirteen billion years. The planet earth was the merest speck and England, let alone the parish of Bow and his own small life, were microviruses. Then he noticed a tramp shambling towards him. The man put his hand out towards him and Anthony pulled out a half-crown from his pocket and handed it to him. Then he felt an impulse to talk to him,

"Do you know why I gave you that half-crown?"

"Because you're a man of God, Reverend," replied the tramp looking surprised. He was dressed in a huge loose-fitting overcoat that was heavy through the dirt which it had accumulated in it and become impregnated within the fabric every time he had got wet. His hair was thin and grey and his face was weather-beaten, lined and brown, like discarded shoe leather.

"No, that's not the reason," said Anthony, " it's because I think you have a good life. I don't feel sorry for you at all."

"It's true, Reverend, me life's not nearly as bad as some 'ave it. I am me own master. I have no bills to worry about – just live from day ter day, free from worry."

"Have you been a wanderer all your life?"

"Oh yes, Reverend, ever since I was sixteen when I left 'ome and started on the road."

"So how long have you been going?"

"It'd be thirty-five years."

"Do you ever miss having a wife and family?"

"Well sometimes I do, Reverend, like on Christmas Day I sometimes wish I 'ad a family around me like other folk."

"You know I feel like that on Christmas Day too."

"Do you really, Reverend ? Ain't you married then?"

"No, I'm a Catholic priest you see and we don't marry."

"Oh I see, Reverend, I know what you mean."

"Have you ever seen any of your family since you left at the age of sixteen?"

"No, never. Not wanted to either really."

"Weren't they upset when you left?"

"Well, I wouldn't know, Reverend, how would I know, like. Me father 'ad no work and there was nine of us, there was. I think me Dad was pleased to 'ave one less of us."

"Do you find your life worthwhile?" asked Anthony.

"Well, that's a funny sort of a question if ever there was one. Well I can't really say if it's worthwhile. What do you mean 'worthwhile', Reverend? I 'ad no choice about being born."

"But are you glad that you were born?"

"Well I 'ave been and that's all there is to it."

"You've never thought of taking your own life?"

"Oh good God no; what would I want to do that for, Reverend? You ask queer questions and no mistake."

*"Well I think you are lucky, you seem to be content with your lot."*

*"I am Reverend I suppose, never thought about it really."*

*"Are you afraid of dying?"*

*"Not really, Reverend. When the end comes then that's it. There's nothin' more to be said is there? It's like being born. It just 'appens."*

*"You don't seem at all ruffled by anything?"*

*"Ruffled, that's a funny sort'er word. You does use funny sort'er language, Reverend. It's not me own type 'er language, if you know what I mean. Don't mean no offence, Reverend. During the war when everyone was worried about Hitler's bombs it didn't trouble me. I said to me 'self, 'If one of 'em gets me then that's it. I could ni'ver understand what everyone was so worried about.'"*

*"Well, sorry for troubling you,"* said Anthony, *"but I must be getting along."*

*"Oh it's been nice talkin' to you, Reverend,"* and the tramp shambled off. He did not know why but that conversation with the tramp raised his spirits ever so slightly. It was a contact that was distant but somehow close; it was a sympathetic human contact; it gave him sacramental nourishment.

The emotional storm that had blown up between himself and Fr. Smithes seemed to dwarf the universe. He sat utterly still and repeated slowly several times *'Our Father'*. As he said 'Our' he tried to include Fr. Smithes within it but he saw before him an amoeba-like cell with a thick gelatine wall and a small pointed structure trying to penetrate it, like the semen trying to burst the walls of an ovum but it would not yield. The amoeba-*Our* could not embrace the vocal tones of Fr. Smithes. Anthony stood and strode around, exasperated and then turned and sat again. *'Who art in Heaven'* and now he felt angry with the prayer. God is not up there, he said to himself, but all mankind and the whole world is contained in him. That's the trouble, he thought, God is not in a place up there; God is not in a place like the Catholic Church; he was in Tommy Sweeney's heart as much as Fr. Smithes's or his own. Then anger surged up in him again. He tried to calm himself but it would not work. The storm had swamped the peace. He sat for a few more moments then he stood and tramped on. He had wanted to say the Our Father peacefully for half an hour and that would replace Vespers and Compline. Then a dark mood descended upon him. If he could not say the Our Father he could not say Vespers and Compline either. He gritted his teeth as anger welled up in him. The mentality that had generated the remark of Fr. Smithes's about Tommy Sweeney was abhorrent to him. He could not, would not give it living space in his inner home. He walked on rapidly until he turned south down Hardinge Street until he reached The Highway and crossed it into Glamis Road walking past the Prospect of Whitby. Posh people from the West End were arriving to dine there. He walked on along Wapping Wall and High Street by the river. He had reached his objective. There was a little landing stage between two warehouses. He walked down it and sat on one of the bollards. The black river was seeping past him. Suddenly he wanted to be in it. The early Christians, he thought, were baptized by plunging into the river. The Baptists kept up the tradition. He felt strongly that he was crossing a threshold into a new current of living. He would dive into the river. It was past seven o'clock and it was now December but he did not care. He had no towel; he stripped off all his clothes and in a moment he was in. It was very cold. He did a rapid crawl out into the middle of the river but as he felt the current beginning to pull him downstream he headed back to the landing stage and had a moment of panic as he thought he might not get back to it but he lunged with all his might against the current and swam upstream back to where he had left his clothes. He clambered out shivering. He jumped up and down to shake the water off him. Looking up to the street and seeing no one he dried himself on his underpants then donned his trousers and the rest of his clothes. The soaking underpants he chucked into the river and started a rapid walk back. He was pleased to find that in twenty minutes he was warm, warmer than he had been before. He kept up a steady trot for another twenty minutes. He snaked his way through Poplar and into Bow Common Lane. As he looked up at the flats again his loneliness hit him and quite unexpectedly he was overcome with self-pity. That's my life, he thought, alone in the presbytery, alone in his thoughts, isolated from the rest of mankind. He did not want to return yet to the presbytery. The thought of bumping into Fr. Smithes sickened him. He found a pub and ordered steak and chips and drank some red wine. His face coloured pink and his cheeks tingled. Now he was tired; he spoke to the barman for a while. He knew he would sleep when he got back. He drank some tea and walked rapidly on his way. He let himself in very quietly through the front door, passed Fr. Smithes's sitting-room and he could see the flicker of television under the door and he passed on up to his bedroom. He slipped into bed very quickly and was soon sound asleep.

When he woke something had happened to him. This final act in this clash with Fr. Smithes had broken the spirit of his pastoral mission, like an eggshell which had cracked irreparably and from within came a presence he had not met before: a person in search of another but this time it was not God that was calling him but a human soul mate. A soul-hunger rose up in him. He rose, celebrated Mass for the nuns at the convent down the road. He knelt for no longer than two minutes and then went into the convent parlour. There in the centre of the room was a square table embroidered with a large doily in the middle of which was a vase with miniature gladioli. Anthony wondered whether they were imitation or real. He felt them with his right hand. They were real. Sister Josephine entered in her white Dominican habit and asked him in a quiet sweet voice:

*"Would you like a cooked breakfast, Father?"* Anthony knew that the nuns had some hens in their backyard so that the eggs were always marvellously fresh.

*"Yes, I'd love two boiled eggs."*

*"To be sure you shall have them, Father,"* and she smiled sweetly at him under her white veil. He looked at her pretty blue eyes and soft pale skin. At that moment he thought it a pity that she had given herself to Christ. She rustled out of the parlour and Anthony sat there. He looked around the small neat room. There was a print of Bellini's painting of St. Dominic above a side table on which stood two candlesticks with cream-coloured candles in them. There was a blue bowl between them with a pomanda surrounded by dried rose petals. Opposite was another side table with an electric hotplate upon it. Through the laced curtains he could see a concrete path leading to a wooden hut. There was a hushed silence as Anthony waited patiently for his breakfast to arrive.

Sister Josephine returned. She brushed past him, put a tea-pot on the table in front of him and then lowered the tray that was in her arms onto the edge of the table and placed two boiled eggs that were brown in colour. Then she put down a little jug of milk and a toast rack with toast. Anthony could sense a slight burntness from the toast. Then the unobtrusive nun put down a little glass boat with marmalade with a small silver spoon and beside it a round white container an inch in diameter with a pat of butter in it.

*"Will that be alright for you, Father ?"* she asked.

*"Yes, it's perfect,"* said Anthony. She looked down at him and smiled coyly and turned and slipped out of the room almost as quietly as she

had entered it, almost as if she had never been there. She was as noiseless as an apparition. Anthony ate the eggs as if executing a solemn ritual. The ordered surrounding seemed in such contrast to this man who had been a few hours before swimming naked in the Thames that he felt like a wolf in the clothing of a soft downy sheep. He knew the ritual well. When he was finished he rang the little bell sitting on the table. He waited no more than twenty seconds. Sister Josephine was standing beside him,

*"Thank you, Sister."*

*"Say a prayer for me, Father."*

*"I will,"* said Anthony. In case he forgot he said an Our Father for her as he walked down the road back to the presbytery. Again he thought what a pity it was she was betrothed to Christ rather than to a man of flesh and blood.

He walked into the presbytery gingerly and, stepping into the kitchen, saw Ethel, the sturdy housekeeper, and asked her whether Fr. Smithes was in. She stood there placidly in her green overall and with her head which looked as if it had been screwed with iron bolts into her wide shoulders onto which God had forgotten to mould a neck.

*"No,"* she said in her Yorkshire accent, *"he asked me to tell you he's out and will only be back in the the afternoon."*

*"Oh, thank you,"* said Anthony, *"I'll be going upstairs now."*

*"You've 'ad breakfast I 'ope?"* she asked.

*"Yes, I had it at the convent."*

With that he went to his room, looked through his books, took down a book on Creation by Sertillanges and sat down to read. After a while his head nodded and he dozed. He had a lectern in his room precisely to avoid falling asleep when reading so he put his book on it and stood up to read. He read on for a while until his feet were sagging. He sat down again, lay down on his hessian covered sofa and was soon dozing like a cat in the sun.

# CHAPTER FIVE

A bell was clanging and he saw Italian peasants streaming towards a village Church. His head started and in a misty slur as he stirred forwards on the hessian settee he heard the front door-bell. He cursed the housekeeper as the bell went on ringing and he heard no footsteps in answer to it. He pulled himself out of his reverie and as the bell continued to ring insistently he tumbled downstairs and opened the front door. A smart young woman was standing there, square-faced, black hair and dressed in a black skirt and jacket surrounding a grey blouse. She looked at Anthony hesitantly. She did not speak, but she stood waiting for the priest in front of her to beckon her in.

*"Oh, please come in,"* said Anthony.

The self-possessed lady stepped purposively across the threshold, still not speaking. Anthony walked ahead of her and into the interview room. He pointed to a chair and she gathered the skirt from under her and sat silent with measured deliberation. She sat still, staring at him silently with gazing eyes that never blinked.

*"Can I help you?"* asked Anthony feeling awkward.

She still did not speak but just stared at him with vacant intensity.

*"If there is anything I can do ...?"*

then a voice came out of the plaster figure:

*"Peter was always the quintessence of refinement ..."*

and said no more. Anthony looked at her immobile features and felt turned to stone. Her eyes were black, her hair was black, her shoes were black and she just stared. As he looked at her with increasing embarrassment an image of the Gorgon Medusa with snakes hissing passed visually across his inner television screen. He sat and looked at her. She was still staring at him. Finally as though shaken out of a spell he said,

*"Are you a Catholic?"*

*"Yes, Father?"* He felt a tremor of relief pass through him. She had spoken at last.

*"And Peter too?"* he said trying to enlarge the circumference of knowledge.

*"Yes, Peter's a Catholic too ..."*
and the two dropped again into a chasm of silence. They sat and a low-flying plane broke the silence and Anthony felt its presence overhead as a relief. He looked up at the ceiling and let his eyes follow across in the direction of its flight path. Suddenly she said,
*"He died, Father."*
*"You mean Peter?"*
*"Yes, he died"* and she took out a handkerchief and dabbed her eyes. Then she looked at him,
*"That's the first time I've cried; I did not cry at the funeral."*
*"When was that?"* asked Anthony but she did not reply but just stared at him intently.
*"I'll go now,"* she said.
*"Do you want to come back?"* asked Anthony.
*"Yes, I'll come to Mass to-morrow."*
Anthony walked in front of her and held the front door open. She stepped into the street and then turned back,
*"When will you be saying Mass, Father?"*
*"I am saying the ten o'clock Mass in the morning."*
As she turned to go Anthony said,
*"By the way what is your name?"*
but she looked at him with that vacant stare and did not answer; she gave a slight nod that had in it a hint of reprimand and then turned round sharply and walked off with slow purposeful paces, like a surveyor measuring out the distance between two points.

Anthony turned back into the presbytery; there was a puzzled frown on his face. Shortly after he had to go to the hospital but as he went round the wards and spoke to the sick people the face of his mysterious visitor kept returning to him. Her face had such a mesmerizing effect on him that only as he was returning to the presbytery at lunchtime did he realize that he would now have to face Fr. Smithes for the first time since the high tension wires had jangled into each other the day before.

\*   \*   \*

When George unwrapped himself from his pre-dieu he had made a decision. After weeping profusely for some minutes he then asked Our Lady to help him. When he had done this he knew at once where his duty lay. *'I must go and see Cardinal Molony,'* he said to himself. At the last parish priests' meeting the Cardinal had instructed all parish priests to report to him immediately if they had any worries concerning their curates. Anthony was George's first curate as he had only been appointed recently as parish priest. He had always been so loved and admired by priests, old and young, that it wounded him deeply that he was not loved and admired by Anthony. He had done everything he could to be kind and helpful to Anthony but each time he took a kind fatherly interest in him, it seemed to make him more and more enraged. He went over again and again his last comment to Anthony about Tommy Sweeney. Why on earth did Anthony get so enraged? He was only trying to help him feel better. He could see that Anthony was upset so surely it would be a comfort to him to know that when the boy grew up he would not have gone to Church or the sacraments? At that young age of five Tommy would certainly go to heaven, but if he grew to manhood and did not receive the sacraments he would lose his soul and go to hell. He remembered the old conundrum put to him when he was studying over twenty years ago in Lisbon: if after baptism the baby will go straight to heaven why not kill it there and then to ensure its salvation? Of course the answer was that to kill would be breaking the sixth commandment. So, it would be wrong if someone had killed Tommy but if his life was taken by accident then it could only be a blessing. He had tried talking to Anthony on many occasions in this vein but every time he did so it inflamed his curate to boiling point. He had a moment of hatred against Fr. Darrell who was brainwashing all his students with Lutheran propaganda, then he felt guilty and returned to his pre-dieu and said a prayer for Fr. Darrell and another prayer for Anthony also. But then, having said these two prayers, he stood up with resolution. He would ring the Cardinal and ask for an interview.

So he picked up the telephone and rang Archbishop's House and said he wanted an interview with the Cardinal. To his surprise he was asked to come and see him at half-past eleven in the morning. A great tide of relief swept over him. He had heard Anthony creeping out of the presbytery while he was praying to Our Lady of Lourdes so he went downstairs and old Ethel, his housekeeper, brought him his favourite dish: toad in the hole. He pretended he did not know that Anthony had gone out.

*"Is Fr. Stonewell coming to supper?"*

*"Oh, didn't he tell you, Father? He's not in."*

*"Where did he go?"*

*"Oh, I don't know, Father, 'e just came in and tole me he would'na be in for supper. I thought he'd 'er told you."*

*"Oh well, thank you, Ethel. He's probably just popped out to do some parish visiting. Often parishioners give us something to eat when we are visiting, as you know, so he probably thought if he ate before he went out then parishioners would be offended if they offered him food and he refused it."*

*"Well I 'ope it's that,"* said Ethel.

*"What do you mean?"* asked George.

*"Well I think Father's been a bit off colour recently …"*

*"What have you noticed?"*

*"Well, e's been out late and been keepin' strange hours of late. 'e don't seem very 'appy to me. It's not for me to say but I wondered if anything is wrong like."*

*"Perhaps he needs a holiday,"* said Fr. Smithes.

*"Well I suppose a good 'oliday helps a lot 'er people but I don't think it will help Fr. Stonewell,"* said Ethel.

*"Why, what on earth makes you say a thing like that, Ethel? What do you think is wrong?"* asked Fr. Smithes.

*"Well, I think he's been doin' too much – all them married groups and youth groups an' the rest of it. He just needs to settle down to ordinary parish work. He's for ever runnin' Bible classes and all that."*

*"He's doing it because the Pope recommended it."*

*"Well I 'ope the Pope knows what 'e's doing. All them changes – they may be alright for them Italian countries but it's no good for us 'ere in London."*

*"Yes, well it's difficult for us older ones, Ethel, to take on all these new ideas but we've got to get used to it. The Mass is in English now you know."*

*"Well all I know is that all was much more peaceful when the Mass was in Latin and everyone knew what they was doin'."*

*"OK Ethel – thank you very much for the toad-in-the-hole,"* and with that Ethel waddled out and Fr. Smithes ate his meal thoughtfully then went upstairs to watch television. He soon slumped asleep. While dozing he heard Anthony come in and slip upstairs to his bedroom. He switched off the television, picked up his breviary and said Vespers and Compline. He was relieved that he was still allowed to recite them in Latin. He knew so much of it by heart that he hardly had to look at the words. When he finished he looked at his watch. It was half-past eleven. He wondered where Anthony had been. It never crossed his mind that he had been swimming in the Thames. When he was sure that Anthony was in his bed asleep he crept upstairs to his own bedroom and, after kneeling by his bed and saying a decade of the rosary, he got into bed and was soon sound asleep.

The next morning he continued to avoid Anthony. He said Mass at eight in the morning and by the time he had finished and made his thanksgiving Anthony was at the convent saying Mass for the nuns. Knowing that Anthony would be back shortly after ten o'clock he left at quarter to the hour and walked nonchalantly down to the tube station and an hour later, after having got out at Victoria Station, he went along to Burns and Oates bookshop. He had half an hour before he was due to see the Cardinal. He looked through the books. He saw a new biography of the Curé d'Ars. He looked through it but then the thought of all those ascetic exercises depressed him. Then he saw a new biography of Pope Pius X. Fr. Smithes sighed with nostalgic love for that saintly Pope and only wished his holy influence was more present today. He looked at the price. It was 18/6. He took out a pound note and paid for it and wandered off slowly down Ambrosden Avenue along the southern wall of Westminster Cathedral until he reached Archbishop's House. He rang the door-bell and was answered by a middle-aged janitor who looked as if he had been born there.

"I have an appointment to see the Cardinal at half-past eleven," said Fr. Smithes meekly.

"Come on in, Father, I'll show you up."

"Your name's Gerry isn't it?" asked Fr. Smithes.

"Yes, that's right. That's how everyone knows me."

"You've been here a long time, eh?"

"Yes, I've seen four Cardinals since I've been here."

They had reached the Cardinal's waiting-room. Gerry showed him in and said that the Cardinal would not be long.

Fr. Smithes sat down and looked with pleasure at a photograph of St. Thérèse of Lisieux and then a statue of the Sacred Heart on a little table against the wall and a photograph of Cardinal Molony with a group of Catholic pilgrims at the shrine of Lourdes. George felt at home in these familiar Catholic surroundings. George had known the Cardinal for many years; in fact longer than most of the clergy. Thirty-five years earlier in 1930 he had been Fr. Molony's altar boy in Barking and it was he who had encouraged George in his vocation to become a priest. Fr. Molony had then been made a bishop in the north of England and then finally two years before had been made Archbishop of Westminster and with that was given the Red Hat by Pope Paul VI in Rome. As George looked round and remembered his parish priest of long ago and the familiar objects of Catholic devotion in the waiting-room he felt sure that Cardinal Molony, for all his public exuberance about the Vatican Council, was still at heart a devout parish priest like himself. They spoke the same language. He would understand his consternation over his young curate.

The door swung open.

*"Hello, George"* and his erstwhile altar boy moved forward obediently and, as the Cardinal proffered the ring on the third finger of his right hand Fr. Smithes bent down and kissed it.

*"Remember George, it's not my ring but the Church's ring you are kissing. I always remind myself of this. It's very easy for someone in my position to become proud."*

*"I pray for you every day, your Eminence ..."*

*"Oh thank you, George, you know you can call me Fr. Molony if it makes you more comfortable."*

*"Thank you but Oh No you are the Cardinal of all England and I don't want to forget that and I have come to you as my bishop."*

*"Well, what's wrong, George? I know you wouldn't have troubled me for an appointment unless something was wrong. Sit down."*

Cardinal Molony gestured to a seat at the side of his desk and sat down himself behind it. He looked penetratingly at George through his bi-focal lenses. George squirmed awkwardly. The Cardinal had not changed. Ever since George had known him he was practical and got down to business. He had no time for doubt and hesitancy. George stammered.

*"Come on George, you haven't changed. Come out with it. What's wrong?"*

*"Well it's about my curate, Fr. Stonewell."*

*"I've heard many good things about him ..."* said the Cardinal.

*"Well yes, he's very energetic and has put all the new liturgy into effect ..."*

*"Yes, that's one of the reasons why I sent him to you. I know he's very up with all the new liturgy and we have to institute it in all the parishes and I thought a young one from the seminary who knows all about it would be just what you needed."*

*"Yes, he's been very good in that regard and I couldn't have done it all on my own. We've got the altar facing the people and we say the whole Mass in English and it has all gone down very well, largely thanks to Fr. Stonewell, it's true."*

Cardinal Molony looked at him. George was a faithful priest but a bit slow. He began to feel impatient. He remembered him as an altar boy thirty-five years before. He would often forget to ring the bell at the Sanctus because he was still fumbling with the card to follow the Canon of the Mass. The Cardinal waited.

*"Look the trouble is Fr. Stonewell is proud; he does not love the Church."*

*"How do you mean, George?"*

Then George told him about how Mrs. O'Shaughnessy had died without the last rites. As George recounted it the Cardinal frowned in an ever darker manner. By the time George had finished his recital something was boiling inside of Cardinal Molony.

*"Do you mean to tell me he refused that poor old lady the sacraments because Joe Murphy was coming to pray with her the next day with her papal medal?"*

*"Yes, I'm afraid so."*

*"He must be a fanatic,"* said the Cardinal.

*"He is,"* said George,*"that's exactly what he is."*

The Cardinal stroked his chin pensively.

*"Is that all he has done of that nature?"* asked the Cardinal.

*"Well he tells parishioners that it's alright to practise contraception."*

*"I am afraid he's not the only one."*

*"I didn't want to trouble you. I know you must have a lot of difficulties at this time with young priests."*

*"I am less worried about the contraception matter. Quite frankly the Church has got herself into a difficult situation over it but that refusal of last rites to Mrs. O'Shaughnessy is another matter."*

*"Is he a humble man?"* asked the Cardinal.

*"I don't like to say it, your Eminence, but I think he is proud. He always thinks he knows best and he is most contemptuous to the good faithful Catholics of the parish. Recently in a sermon he said it was not a mortal sin to miss Mass on a Sunday and it upset several of my most devout parishioners."*

*"Oh dear,"* exclaimed the Cardinal, *"several young priests are scorning our ancient Catholic customs. They forget those who risked death to get to Mass on Sunday only two hundred and fifty years ago."*

*"Do you want me to move him for you?"* asked the Cardinal.

*"What I need now is just a good faithful priest who will visit the parishioners ..."*

The Cardinal looked at him doubtfully. A memory of George as an altar boy floated again before his eyes. He remembered George mumbling to him that one of the people coming up to Communion was a lapsed Catholic and how he had had to reprimand George for making a judgment he was not entitled to.

*"You know, George, we have to move with the times. We have to be engaged in Ecumenism and making links with our Separated Bretheren. It's not like it was when we were both in Barking back in the 1930s."*

*"Oh yes, I know,"* said George nervously. The Cardinal looked at his old altar boy. He was always something of a goody-goody without much spirit of adventure. He had some sympathy for Anthony Stonewell. He began to think it had been a mistake to put these two men together.

*"Does he have devotion to Our Lady?"* asked the Cardinal. He knew that Fr. Darrell had been telling his students at Newman College that the Church was guilty of Mariolatry. The Cardinal knew that love of Our Lady lay at the heart of a priest's devotional life. Our Lady was the guarantor of his chastity.

*"I have never see him say the rosary,"* said George, *"and the other day I heard him telling a parishioner that the time spent saying the rosary would be better spent reading the Gospel."*

*"Is he faithful to his vows?"*

George hesitated. He had no evidence to suggest that he had broken them but he thought of the conversation he had had with his house-keeper the previous night. Nothing had been said but there was a hint that something untoward might be going on with these late nights Anthony was keeping.

*"I think so,"* said George hesitantly.

*"Why do you hesitate?"* asked the Cardinal sharply.

*"Well I have no evidence …"*

*"But you think he's become involved with a woman?"*

*"Well I'm not saying that …"*

*"Oh George, don't be so cagey."*

*"Well he's getting into dangerous habits. He stays up late. Often he only gets back into the presbytery after mid-night …"*

Realizing that the Cardinal did not seem concerned about his archaic suspicions he returned to the point that had really inflamed him.

*"Look, my worry is his attitude to the good faithful parishioners. That incident with Mrs. O'Shaughnessy has travelled round the parish. If we lose our faithful parishioners we'll be in a sorry state."*

*"Would it help if I saw him?"*

George looked nervous. He knew that Anthony would be incensed if he knew he had made a special visit to speak to the Cardinal about him. The Cardinal saw him hesitate.

*"Look George is there something else? Does he know you're worried about him?"*

*"Yes, I think so,"* said George. George realized that he was failing to impress the Cardinal and then he said,

*"Look – another thing. After he had heard about Joe Murphy's papal medal and it had been given to her specially by Fr. Fitzpatrick – you remember him?"*

*"Old Fitzpatrick from Hendon you mean?"*

*"Yes, that's him."*

*"Now there was a truly holy priest."*

*"Well,"* said George gaining confidence, *"Fr. Fitzpatrick gave her that medal after her only son had died. He went to Rome and had this medal blessed by the Pope and brought it back and gave it to her. He knew how devastated she had been by the loss of her son. That was the medal she used to take with her when people were sick. She would put the medal on some part of the person's body and then pray with them. Well, when Fr. Stonewell learned that she was doing this he went and told her that she was engaging in superstition and that it was contrary to the Church's teaching and he demanded that she give the medal to him which she did."*

This infuriated Cardinal Molony. He treasured the faithful love and devotion of the good ordinary Catholics and the thought that one of his priests was behaving with such insensitive cruelty enraged him. He thought for a moment and then said,

*"Very well, George, I will move him but I shall wait a couple of months, see him and then move him soon after."*

*"Need I tell him that I have seen you?"*

*"No, this has been a confidential talk,"* answered the Cardinal and the two men looked at each other knowingly for a moment; George genuflected and kissed the ring on his finger again. George walked out feeling good that he was in favour with the Cardinal once more. What he did not know was that, as he walked out, Rudolph Novak, was just been shown into the waiting room and saw Fr. Smithes leaving. He guessed immediately that he had been talking about Anthony.

*       *       *

Anthony got back to the presbytery, saw that Fr. Smithes was out, and went up to his room. There was about twenty minutes before lunch. He had just got to his room when the telephone rang. It was Rudolph Novak.

*"I've got some news for you,"* said Rudolph, *"I went to see the Cardinal to-day. He had asked me to come and see him. He is sending me to Rome to study Philosophy at the Angelicum."*

*"Are you pleased?"*

*"Yes, very,"* said Rudolph, *"but I've got some other news for you. Your p.p. had just been in to see the Cardinal before me."* Anthony whistled and knew instantly that he would have been the subject of their conversation.

*"Did he see you?"* asked Anthony.

*"No, he definitely didn't but he was walking off looking very pleased with himself."* At that moment Anthony heard the front door open and close and knew that George was back. As they shared a phone line Anthony decided to ring off,

*"Very glad about the Angelicum,"* he said, *"but I must go now. Will ring you soon."*

Anthony sat down and looked at his watch. It was ten minutes before lunch. Anthony tried to think out what he would do. He was sure that George would have been asking the Cardinal to move him elsewhere. He sat quietly wishing that George would vanish and this difficult problem dissolve. Then he got up with resolution and walked down into the dining-room where George was sitting beaming a smile at him.

*"Had a good morning Anthony?"* asked George in the softest tones. *'His speech is smoother than butter'* said Anthony to himself.

*"Yes, not bad. I said Mass for the nuns and then came back and then spoke with a young woman whose husband had died recently; and yourself?"*

*"Yes, I went down to Burns and Oates and bought a new book"* and George handed him the biography of Pope Pius X and Anthony looked at it. George looked at him quizzically.

*"What do you think of it?"*

*"The Church has taken a step away from the attitudes of Pius X,"* said Anthony, *"most of the changes that have been introduced by the Council are undoing the knots of conservatism that had been tied by Pius X."*

*"He was a very holy man,"* said George, *"and he's been made a saint, as you know."*

*"He has been declared a saint but he paralysed the Church with all his fear-ridden attitudes to modern scripture scholarship and antiquated views on evolution."* Anthony's anatomy was firing up as he said this.

*"I think you'll find that when all the excitement of the Council has blown over good Catholics will recognize the saintliness and wisdom of Saint Pius X and return to his good example."* George put down his cutlery for a

moment, looked at Anthony with patronizing eyes, speaking with complacent certainty.

*"Well I hope you enjoy reading it,"* said Anthony with bitter irony. He wondered whether George was going to reveal anything more than his visit to Burns and Oates bookshop. There was a silence as the two men ate their sausages and cabbage. A turmoil was churning around within the two of them. Eventually Anthony asked,

*"When you were so near Archbishop's House it would have been an opportunity to visit your old parish priest, the Cardinal. Did you pop in to see him?"*

George hesitated. Anthony looked at him. George took off his glasses and wiped them:

*"No, it's a busy time of year for Cardinal Molony so I did not want to bother him."*

Anthony wanted to shout out *'You bloody liar, you pious hypocrite; you and all your good Catholics ...'* but he could feel the heavy oppressive hand of good manners, taught to him by his mother and father and reinforced at boarding school; social etiquette crushed a surging clamour within. There he was with sword and shield wielding both in the heat of battle and now suddenly an enemy had struck him a fatal blow and he was on the ground, defeated and helpless.

Atmospheres are stronger and more powerful than any words can be. Anthony remembered the words *'his speech is smoother than butter but war was in his heart'.* It was the disjunction between what was spoken and what was in the heart which fashioned the atmosphere. The war in the heart rose up and overwhelmed the words and poured out through the pores in the two men's skin until the whole room was flooded with fog issuing from the inner passion of the two of them. Here in this sombre presbytery a nuclear bomb was exploding.

While Anthony was raging at George's complacent hypocrisy George was overwhelmed with guilt at the lie he had just told. But it was not only guilt; he was worried lest Anthony should somehow find out that he had been to Archbishop's House. Apart from Gerry there were a few cassocks swishing about and he might have been seen. To be caught in a lie by Anthony was an unbearable thought for George. Then he was desperately trying to pacify his protesting conscience. He had definitely told a lie. He knew from his moral theology that equivocation or evasion could be permitted but a lie? Could a lie ever be justified? He twisted and turned, and blushed within. He thought of martyrs who had died rather than tell an untruth. He squirmed. *'Perhaps it was not really a lie?'* he pleaded out-law wise with himself but, try as he might, that just would not work. Then he had a sudden inspiration: after all St. Peter had told a lie. He lied three times to the servant girl until the cock crew. There St. Peter had told three lies whereas he had only told one and Jesus had founded his Church upon him. So Jesus founded his Church upon a liar. With this thought he could feel some relieving balm cooling his brow. He imagined Jesus turning and forgiving him.

George could not however, in good conscience, offer Mass the next morning and go to communion with this sin on his soul. He knew he would need to go to confession. So when the agonizing meal had finished he rang Fr. Brickwell who was the parish priest at Finsbury Park. As soon as he was in his room and out of Anthony's earshot he rang Ian Brickwell and shortly after set off on the tube to see him. He rang at the presbytery door beside the huge Church in Tollington Park which had once belonged to the Methodists but had been bought by the Catholic Church shortly after the war. As Irish immigration swelled in that part of London the small Church could no longer accommodate the huge numbers coming to Church on Sundays and, in an opposite way, the Methodist congregation had shrunk so the two Churches swapped. Ian Brickwell had been appointed shortly after this business transaction had occurred. He was a quiet well-groomed priest. He never failed to do his meditation each morning; to do his spiritual reading and say the rosary. He spoke quietly and cultivated a softened presence. It was difficult to laugh or joke in his presence. On his annual holiday he always went with his sister to Lourdes. George Smithes had been to confession to him faithfully for twenty years. Ian Brickwell was older than George by fifteen years. So George went into his study, knelt at his pre-dieu:

*"Sorry, Father, for I have sinned."*

*"It is one week since my last confession and since then I have told a lie, been distracted in my prayers and had impure thoughts."*

*"Well, Father, for your penance say a decade of the rosary."*

*"Ego te absolvo a peccatis tuis in nomine Patris et Filii et Spiritui Sancti. Amen."*

The confession was over and the two men looked kindly at each other. George had a moment of embarrassment. He had not confessed a lie before and Ian guessed that some excruciating circumstance had forced George to tell a lie but, now that the confession was over, no reference could be made to what had just been said. The seal of the confession was kept absolutely faithfully by all Catholic priests, so much, so that George knew he could make no reference to the lie in their ordinary discourse and that Ian would have to act as if he had no knowledge of what had just been communicated to him under the seal of confession. This forced impossibility of making any reference to what had just been said steered the subsequent conversation into an empty-sounding pathway, it was not only that they started talking on a completely different subject matter but also that the tone was drained of all life. It was like two puppets speaking to each other. Each man wanted to talk about the circumstances that had led to George having to tell a lie but this was forbidden so the difficulties he was having with his curate remained also sealed off from any intercourse between them. So they spoke instead about Ian's forthcoming pilgrimage to Lourdes. As Ian was talking about it, he suddenly had the thought of asking George to come with him but something stopped him. He imagined being with George for three weeks in France and he realized his company would be difficult to bear for so long a time. George listened kindly to his confessor and, after a cup of tea, he thanked Ian and left the presbytery.

After confessions that evening George said that he had some parish work to attend to so they could not have their accustomed meeting. Anthony was relieved. He was due to go to a re-union of the Doktor Klub at Clarence's room in the catechetical college of Christ the King at Notting Hill Gate. There was a tube strike so he had to get there by bus which took at least half an hour longer. When he arrived all the others were there. Stephen Warrior was entertaining the others with an account of his fellow curate who had dropped a consecrated host on the carpet of the atrium in the Church. Although he had picked it up instantly the whole carpet had had to be washed by the nuns in holy water and the water which had been used was then poured into a rose garden by the presbytery and then a fence put round the rose garden lest anyone should enter and tread upon it. The others were laughing and gasping as Stephen was recounting this. Anthony, though, could not laugh about it. He was emotionally constipated by what had happened at lunchtime with George. Anthony said,

"It's ridiculous. It's treating the host not with reverence but with superstition. Thomas Aquinas said that if a mouse ate the host it would not be eating Christ – that it takes a human being to place a constructive meaning upon it and only then does it become the Body and Blood of Christ." Clarence's room was not unlike his room at Newman College. He had the same Taizé counterpane over his bed but the bed was in an alcove off his office but the two rooms displayed the same Protestant severity. The window looked out upon Ladbroke Road. The square window starkly framed the road with its plane trees planted into the pavement. Clarence had constructed a bench under the window so that four of them – Stephen, Jamie, Rudolph and Sean were sitting with their backs to the view and hemmed in by a neat pine oblong table. Clarence was sitting at the end and, as Anthony came in, he sat opposite those four and next to Joe Feeney. Anthony had heard what Stephen was saying and made his reply as he was sitting down.

*"That's not the way that our parish priests or fellow curates think about it,"* said Clarence crisply.

*"Then they are all superstitious; they are not worshipping God but idols,"* said Anthony solemnly. Then Rudolph Novak looked at him and said,

*"Did George tell you that he had been to see the Cardinal?"*

*"No, in fact he lied and said he hadn't."*

*"What you asked him?"*

*"No, well yes, he told me that he had been to Burns and Oates so I asked him if he had popped in to see the Cardinal and he said 'No'. It was quite a natural question for me to ask because George used to be the Cardinal's altar boy when he still a parish priest down in Barking."*

*"When who was a parish priest?"*

*"Cardinal Molony used to be a parish priest down in Barking and George Smithes came from there and was his altar boy."*

*"So what did you say?"* asked Rudolph lighting a cigarette which muffled his speech.

*"Nothing but I was seething inside?"*

*"Why didn't you say that you knew what he said was not true?"* asked Rudolph taking a puff and blowing the smoke deliberately up to the ceiling with his head in the air but this was a question that Anthony was unable to answer. He bit his lip, looked down at his shoes.

*"It's impossible to convey the atmosphere,"* replied Anthony, *"he's so overflowing with niceness that to tell him he was lying would be like assaulting an unprotected child."*

*"Oh what nonsense,"* said Rudolph impatiently, *"you should have just told him he was a bloody liar because he had been seen coming out of the Cardinal's office."*

*"You could have cut the atmosphere with a carving knife,"* said Anthony but as he looked up he saw Rudolph raising his eyes to the ceiling and turning to Clarence and fashioning on his face a sardonic smile.

Anthony felt hopeless but forced out the words, *"Atmospheres that are so powerful that they can prevent the challenge of words,"* said Anthony.

*"There is no atmosphere that can't be challenged,"* said Rudolph, *"at the time of Dunkirk the War Cabinet tried to persuade Churchill to seek some peace terms with Hitler via Mussolini or Roosevelt. There was an atmosphere like a London smog but Churchill withstood it. When he said 'We stood alone' he meant that he stood alone in the War Cabinet."*

*"Well that's hardly a fair example, Rudolph,"* said Joe in his mellifluous Irish accent.

*"Why not?"* demanded Rudolph abruptly. At that moment he stood up and took off his black coat and returned sat down again, putting the coat on his lap.

*"Well Churchill was somethin' of an exception, altogether 'e was. We are not all Churchills, you know, even if we wanted to be, for God's sake. And anyway he wasn't all that good towards us in Ireland,"* said Joe with an ironic grin.

*"Yes, you are asking a bit much of Anthony,"* piped in Stephen.

*"Look here we all are,"* gritted Rudolph, *"pretending that we are going to bring a new message to our grubby parishes and Anthony falls at the first fence. In the face of an 'atmosphere' he capitulates: **Veni, Vidi, Tradidi.**"*[1] Rudolph's face became pinched and his eyes looked bitter.

*"Yes, that's true,"* said Clarence.

There was a glum silence. Anthony knew what had been said was true and yet he felt that Clarence and Rudolph did not know the sort of atmosphere he was talking about. It was like trying to explain a London smog to a foreigner. He could not even explain to himself why it had felt impossible to challenge George. He just knew that it was like trying to scale the Berlin wall. For an instant the image of Fr. Salter flashed before his eyes. He believed that Fr. Salter would grasp his predicament, that there would be an emotional current between them that would cement something deeper than intellect, that would illuminate his understanding. For a moment he regretted being Sid Darrell's disciple, being a devotee of the Doktor Klub. Then he remembered Peter Cradle and his two mates, Joseph Gorce and Raymond Cluedo. He did not want to be with them and with Nanny Conan. He despised all of them but at this moment he did not want to be part of the Doktor Klub either. He looked up, Clarence was waiting for an answer from him,

---

[1] I came, I saw, I surrendered.

"*It would have been the end of me at the parish,*" said Anthony weakly.

"*Well, so be it, there we are complaining that the Church is always compromising its witness to the truth for fear of damaging its reputation or its institutions and there you are doing exactly the same,*" said Rudolph with icy coldness. He fished into the coat on his lap, flicked out his packet of cigarettes and took out another, tapped one end on the table and took a lighter which was on the table and lit it with geometrical precision so that the tip of the flame just singed the end of the cigarette. As soon as this had happened he snapped the cover of the lighter and inhaled, held the smoke within for at least half a minute and then opened his mouth and blew it out across the table like a dragon breathing fire on his foe. A silence fell on the group. Joe broke it by saying,

"*Well talking of atmospheres ...*" as he brushed away the smoke with his right hand. Everyone laughed.

This turned the conversation to less challenging subjects but Anthony felt defeated. His dilemma was not understood. He stayed for the rest of the evening but when he left, self-pity crept over him. He walked most of the way back to the East End in a state of dejection. He could have caught a bus but he walked as far as Aldgate before catching a bus that took him back to his dismal presbytery. All his lectures and learning had done nothing to prepare him for this. He put his key softly into the door and stepped gingerly across the threshold and closed the door with a quiet click. He took off his shoes, crept up the stairs and past George's room and up to his bedroom. He felt relieved that he had already prepared the sermon for the next day. His first Mass was at ten o'clock. He looked at his watch and decided to go back to his office and have a whisky so he crept down the stairs again. He had made a private vow with himself not to drink on his own once he became a priest but now he was breaking it. So he returned to bed half an hour later even more dejected than before. There was a chair beside his bed. He sat in it. He tried to reach down to those currents within him that had been awakened by the personal integrity of Fr. Salter but he felt hopeless.

"*I am just like a bit of chaff before the wind,*" he said to himself, *I hear Peter Cradle and his cronies hissing with cynicism and I fling myself into the arms of Clarence and his mates. Then I let myself be burnt up by their apostolic zeal but I don't believe what they are saying either. I just lack the courage to believe what I know. I am a hopeless specimen.*"

Then Anthony sank into a silent melancholy. An image arose of a speed-boat ploughing through the water and an abundance of flotsam and jetsam being carried in its wake. He was just one of those bits, carried on by the violent enthusiasm of the Doktor Klub. Then he stopped thinking, he stopped feeling, he just bathed in self-pity. Half an hour must have passed before he threw off his clothes, left them lying on the floor, donned his pyjamas and slipped into bed. His dismal thoughts or pure exhaustion acted like a potent sleeping draught. He was asleep within four minutes.

* * *

The Church was full and Anthony was sitting down while old Mr. Diplock read the Epistle in English. It was the famous passage where St. Paul praises love or charity above all other virtues. As it was being read Anthony looked at the packed Church and quickly saw the mysterious widow in the second row, dressed in black and he found his eyes drawn to her in hypnotized fascination. Who was she and why had she not told him her name? For a second, as he looked at her, he caught her eye and he looked away quickly in embarrassment. He turned his attention to the words of St. Paul's letter. It was read out in the new translation from the Jerusalem Bible:

> "...if I have faith in all its fulness, to move mountains, but without love, then I am nothing at all. If I give away all that I possess, piece by piece, and if I even let them take my body to burn it, but am without love, it will do me no good whatever..."[2]

Anthony started to think of his sermon and pulled out a card and looked at the few headings he had written upon it. He was sitting in golden Gothic vestments with his hands placed politely on each knee. In a moment the reading was finished and he and the congregation were standing up to hear the Gospel recited and Mrs. Twomey came forward to read the short passage where Jesus is in the house of Mary and Martha and tells Martha that Mary has chosen the better part. When this reading was finished Fr. Stonewell moved from his place at the side of the altar and came into the pulpit. He walked up into it slowly and when he was firmly established in the centre of it he looked around searchingly at the congregation and again, for a moment,

---

[2] I Corinthians Ch. 13, vv. 2–3.

though he had consciously not wanted to, he found his eyes resting on that woman in black once more and, to his chagrin, their eyes met yet again. Then he looked down to the back of the Church and was pleased to see that all the pews were full.

> *"It is a happy chance,"* he began, *"that this great passage from St. Paul is placed alongside that domestic incident from the life of Jesus. When we hear that passage from St. Paul we nod our heads and marvel at its beauty but I wonder if we ever ask ourselves what did Paul really mean? In Greek the word Paul uses is* **'agape'** *and let us all pretend for a moment that we do not know what it means and that no one anywhere knows what it means so we will just substitute the word* 'blank' ' *if you give all you have to the poor but you have not* blank *then it profits you nothing, if you give your body to be burned but have not blank it profits you nothing.' What on earth did Paul mean? What is this quality without which every-thing you do is dross? We could extend his words to include ourselves to-day: 'If you go to Mass every Sunday but have not blank it profits you nothing, if you go to communion regularly and confession every week and you have not blank it profits you nothing, if you put your money into the collection plate and have not blank it profits you nothing, if you dedicate your life to the service of your neighbour but have not blank it profits you nothing. If you pray every day and have not blank it profits you nothing, if you keep all the commandments of the church and have not blank it profits you nothing. If you bring up your children well and are faithful to your spouse but have not blank it profits you nothing. Now it is clear that Paul was saying that we can do all these things but if we lack this special quality it is all just sounding brass; he says, in other words it's all quite useless. What on earth did he mean then? What quality was he talking about? It is certainly worth us trying to comprehend it because he said that if we do not have it then all that we do is useless. It is no good just saying that what we need is charity because Paul says that if we do the things which we would normally designate 'charity' but have not got this other quality then it is useless. I wonder if any of you have any ideas?"*

At this moment Fr. Stonewell looked around and peered searchingly into the eyes of various members of the congregation. Again to his acute embarrassment he found himself looking at the same darkly dressed stranger and her own eyes instantly glued to his and although it was only for a moment yet a tide of feeling, like milk in a saucepan expanding at boiling point, arose in his breast. The widow herself looked at Anthony with unashamed determination. She also did not know what was hap-pening but she saw Peter in front of her dressed in priestly robes. He was living; when she had seen his coffin lowered into the ground she had not believed that this was death. Now she was certain that Peter was living in the person of this priest in front of her. It was not a fantastical image but sure conviction. She believed this as surely as Anthony believed that the bread and wine were shortly to be converted into the Body and Blood of Christ. Sermons were things which droned in the ears but which were never heard with the inner ear. They were things which the priest had to perform, sincerely no doubt, and which the congregation had piously to listen to but in all her years of Mass going both as a child and as an adolescent she could not remember one single thing which had ever been said. What the priest had said was dead but the words of this priest in front of her were alive. Peter had risen from the dead. She had never had a sense that a priest in a sermon was addressing anyone, only that he was performing a required part of the ritual and thereby sparing his congregation from the import of his words. What she was experiencing now was totally different. First she knew that Fr. Stonewell was talking to her because he **was** Peter, her loved one. In a mystical miracle he had come alive in a new incarnation. She knew that it was <u>he</u> speaking to her. She looked up at his stirring figure and knew there was a special intercourse between her and him and when his eyes fell upon hers she had then total conviction. She knew he was saving her from a tragic death. On the Third Day Jesus rose from the dead. The mystery of the Resurrection had now become real to her. It was no longer just a doctrine buried away in a catechism. The fact that Anthony was talking in a very personal way out of his own experience made this fantastic resurrection into certain reality. And Anthony was speaking out of his own experience. That moment of freedom that he had experienced when reading his office and the slow disillusion culminating in the incidents surrounding the death of Tommy Sweeney was now being translated into the medium of his sermon and reaching from him straight into the breast of the widow where it was being instantly translated into a personal doctrine of resurrection. She looked up at her priest and he was still talking.

*"Well, I ask myself what on earth can Paul of Tarsus have meant? And for a good while I find that my mind is a* <u>blank</u> *too. I just don't know exactly what he was talking about but I do know that he was talking about something that he had experienced very personally. I think we can take it that he had been someone who did all these things but in the absence of this special quality. Then that makes me wonder what really was that experience of his, on the way to Damascus? He had clearly been chasing after Christians*

*but without <u>blank</u>, he had been preaching the message of the Judaic law but without <u>blank</u> or else he would not have written to the community at Corinth with such vigour about it. So what was it? There is a hint in the Acts of the Apostles when in his vision Jesus says to him '**Why go on kicking against the goad?**' In other words he was engaged in an activity which was against himself. It did not issue forth from his own personal centre. It was a pseudo activity. If we pursue this line of thinking then it would follow that what occurred on the road to Damascus was a striking change where a thunderbolt broke through this outer shell of meaninglessness and the real Paul, the true Paul came alive. Christ was not just a meaningless dead word but suddenly was alive and living.*

At that moment something rose into the widow's head. As he said 'Paul' she heard 'Peter'. Peter was alive. She went on listening. Peter had risen from the dead.

*"I think we can take it a step further and say that the Paul before Damascus was a proud Paul, a tyrannical one that was trying to impose his own ideas upon those around him. We all know that pride and tyranny go together but if what I have been saying is right then pride is not located at the personal centre of the human being. Rather it is in that part of the personality that does things because it is told to do so. It is the robot personality. So pride and robotic behaviour go together. That very great Englishman, Saint Aelred of Rievaulx, said in one of this treatises: If the person who is chaste is also proud then this chastity is not a virtue because pride is a vice. I may be very proud that I go to Mass often, that I say my prayers, that I come to Communion every Sunday, always put money into the collection plate but if I do it because I feel I ought to, then it is a robot that is doing it and not me. Pride, the robot, the tyrant are in possession of my soul. In all these cases then there is an absence of 'blank' but if we are to search positively then what does he mean by this 'blank'? I think it means this: that an action is no good unless it comes from the personal centre of yourself, unless it is living, throbbing with life in fact. That it is something that you really want to do, that you feel you want to do. Most of us, as soon as we pass through the portals of a Church, get a sinking feeling that now we shall have to do what is good, do what goes against own inner nature, sacrifice ourselves. I think St. Paul was saying that all this is empty ritual. The kernel of all virtue lies in our wish to do something because it seems to be co-natural to our own living nature. The best way for a musician to please God is to play good music not to put money in the collection plate. You probably have all heard the story of the boy who was a juggler and he did this better than anything else so when*

*he went into a church he did a juggling act with four balls. A priest rushed out to stop him but Jesus spoke from the crucifix behind the altar and said, 'Let him be; his juggling pleases me'.*

"*Many of us are so overlaid with rules and regulations that we find it extremely difficult to reach down to this area of life and energy within ourselves from which our personal action emanates. In certain areas it remains undisturbed – in the field of taste for instance. One of you likes tea, another likes coffee, another strawberries. One person likes margarine and another doesn't. Now with such tastes as these it is usually our own true selves talking but when we get higher up the scale of aesthetic appreciation and moral values then we have been so overladen with what we should do and what we shouldn't then our own personal sense of things and choices are completely buried beneath a heap of rubble. This is what Paul was talking about. And if this is so then it means that our first task is to reach this personal core of ourselves? But how?*

"*Now I think we can get some hint about it if we think about the Gospel passage that has been read to us today. Martha was rushing around, cleaning the house, attending to this thing and that and no doubt if any person had visited her they would have praised her for the nice and tidy state of her house. She felt annoyed that her sister, Mary, was just sitting at the feet of Jesus and listening to him – perhaps not even listening but just being there in his presence and deriving something from that. Martha complained to Jesus about her sister who was not helping but Jesus rebuked Martha and said that Mary had chosen the better part. Mary had found the centre of things, she had discovered what was important. Now I think it is a mistake to interpret it in such a way that you think that Mary had found the better part only because she was with Jesus, the Son of God. I don't think it is meant this way. I think that Jesus would have said the same if Mary had been sitting with Lazarus or some friend of hers, man or woman. If any man and woman are together in that special way they are doing what St. Paul said lay at the heart of Christian living. Two people can be together in a living intercourse or they can be together like two stones next to each other but with no life passing from one to the other. St. Paul was making a comment about life and its meaning and its purpose, irrespective of whether Mary was sitting at his feet or that of another. The same applies to all of us here. You can be a Martha rushing around doing very praiseworthy things but you will have missed the essential. You may come to Mass every Sunday, perhaps every day of the week or even twice a day, visit the sick, look after your sick mother or father, be dedicated to some charitable work, or even to a good cause like famine relief but you may have missed the essential.*

*"What is it that is so recommended in the behaviour of Mary – just sitting and being with someone. It is here I think that this Gospel passage links up with what St Paul said in his letter to the Christians at Corinth. That quality of soul, that deep sense of personal being is fed by the quiet living presence of one person to another. In this case it is a woman to a man. It is not that the other person <u>does</u> anything. It is just his or her presence and that you allow that presence to permeate into you. Your own soul becomes fertilized through being open to the soul of another. We are each of us food to each other's souls. This is why that same St. Aelred whom I have referred to already a few minutes ago said that it is in a living friendship that love finds its root. He believed that in that passage of St. Paul's you could substitute the word 'friendship' for 'love' on each occasion. It is in friendship of the sort where it is the presence of one person to another that is essential and that this special personal quality of the soul is born, fertilized and grows. That I think is the message God is trying to teach us to-day."*

With that he looked around for a moment at the congregation and then stood there silently for a few seconds as if he wanted some element of the Jesus–Mary experience to permeate the atmosphere. And again, despite himself, he found his eyes magnetized to the eyes of the widow in black. Her own heart was beating. As she listened to this mystical priest she knew with total certainty that Peter had risen from the dead. He was no longer in the grave; he was in the priest in front of her. Then Anthony turned back down the four steps leading to the sanctuary and continued with the celebration of the Mass.

The widow saw Peter at the altar. His living vibrating presence ran through her. He had announced to her his living presence. She knew for certain that now she was re-united with him. Her eyes remained fastened upon this young curate for the rest of the Mass. She never looked to right or left. The other members of the congregation had been obliterated from her field of vision. From the moment when she caught Anthony's eye he remained fastened to the retina of her mind and body so forcefully, with such power, that she was no longer in a parish Church with children crying and people sneezing around her. She was with Peter just as Mary had been with Jesus. Martha was bustling around, like the members of the congregation, but she was with Peter. The priest and her were now together in bodily ecstasy. Her eyes glued themselves to the priest, the risen Christ, the risen Peter who had now come to her. The Christian mystery had been accomplished for her in all its glory. When she heard the words of consecration 'THIS IS MY BODY' she knew it was Peter's, it was Christ's, it was the priest in front of her. When she went to receive it between her lips, put on her tongue by her own priest she knew a mystical union had been accomplished. She had seen Peter's coffin buried but she now knew he had risen from the dead. Peter was the priest in front of her. From now on she would allow nothing that could interfere with her own celebration of her mystical union. It was a union she would consummate in spirit and in body. She would do it; nothing would stop her.

When she walked out of the Church at the end of the Mass she saw Fr. Stonewell chatting to some people around her but, as she walked towards him with purposeful strides his eyes turned to her and their hearts met through the agency of their eyes and by miraculous intervention the people standing around him disappeared. Just Mary and Jesus were together now; Martha had been banished to the kitchen. There was not another soul in the universe. She continued towards him with unperturbed pace:

*"Hello, Father, your sermon was* **so** *beautiful. It gave me great comfort. It brought Jesus to my soul. All my grief is over."*

*"Oh good. I'm so glad,"* said Anthony, *"I am so glad when a sermon brings new life. That is what it is supposed to do. It is supposed to bring the Risen Christ to each one of us."*

*"Would it be alright if I came and saw you again, Father?"* she said smiling triumphantly.

*"Yes, of course."* Then he looked at his watch and turned towards her:

*"When would you like to come?"*

*"Could I come this evening, Father?"* she asked unashamedly.

Anthony thought for a moment; he remembered with glee that George was celebrating the evening Mass and then going out straight away to celebrate his brother's twenty-fifth wedding anniversary down in Barking.

*"Would half-past seven be alright?"*

*"Yes, that would be just fine, Father."*

The widow had gone and Anthony spoke to several parishioners but he was in a daze. He was speaking to them but his voice was detached from his heart. His heart had been glued to the widow's soul through a bondage, sealed through an ecstatic current passing through the terminals of their eyes. He confirmed a meeting with one of his couples groups the following Wednesday, he confirmed his meeting with his Young Christian Workers (YCW) group. Eventually the rest of the parishioners melted away and he was left on his own looking at some clouds scudding high in the sky southwards way above the Church. He walked slowly on autopilot back to the presbytery and lunch with George. The two men had not seen each other since that heavy-laden lunchtime of the previous day. As Anthony walked into the dining-room George was already sitting at the head of the long table. Ethel had put cabbage and boiled potatoes and four lamb chops on a tray in front of him. George looked up, his lips and cheeks moving into a smile but his eyes, half hidden behind his glasses remained unaffected by these activities of the lower part of his face.

"*Come and eat,*" said George, "*you need a square meal after labouring in the vineyard all morning,*" and grinned.

"Yes," said Anthony, "*I put my heart into the sermon.*"

"*Oh good,*" said George, "*well have some lamb chops and vegetables. You have to keep the body nourished as well as the soul, you know.*"
As Anthony sat down an awkward silence descended. For a couple of minutes nothing was said and the only sound was of the cutlery of the two men clanging upon their plates. Eventually, summoning some false effort, Anthony said,

"*There were a lot of people at the Mass to-day, more than usual.*"

"*That's good,*" said George, "*I think it shows that slow faithful visiting of all the Catholics in the parish is reaping its rewards.*"

"*The Church is certainly fuller on Sundays than it was a year ago,*" said Anthony reluctantly and the two men lapsed into silence again. It was a relief when Ethel came in and told George that someone wanted him on the telephone. As soon as he had gone Anthony ate as quickly as possible. There was some apple pie on the side table. Anthony helped himself to some with custard. By the time George returned Anthony had finished.

"*I hope you don't mind I'll go up now to my room. I would like to say some Office while I am still fresh.*"

"*Oh yes, of course, Anthony. How sensible of you,*" and George beamed at him through his spectacles which were large and enframed in light horn. Anthony walked out and went upstairs to his room.

\* \* \*

Even his tone of voice had been a large component in the effect which the whole experience had had on her. She was determined to see Fr. Stonewell on her own. She would not allow her resolution to be thwarted. He was her saviour; she knew it for a certainty. "My saviour" she said to herself and then smiled. She had never known what salvation meant but now it all seemed clear to her. Her saviour had broken the bonds of death. Jesus is Risen. Peter is Risen, she said to herself. She knew that Peter was the priest who had celebrated the Mass. She walked on until she reached her sister's flat. She had a key and let herself in. To her horror, as she let herself in there was only one person there – her father. She turned to get back to the door but he was too quick for her. He ran to the door and stood with his back to it so she could not get out.

"*I won't speak to you,*" she screamed and ran to her bedroom.

"*Well I'll speak to you,*" he said through the bedroom door. There was silence on the other side of it.

"*Andrea has told me that Peter died. She told me he killed himself.*" When there was no answer he turned the handle and pushed the door open. She was standing holding a glass with her hand up. As he came through the door she threw it at him. It hit the wall just beside him and smashed. She collapsed on the bed and screamed:

"*It's all your fault.*"

He moved over as silently as a cat and sat on the bed. She cowered away from him.

"*Look 'ere, Stephanie, yer might say it's the wrong moment to speak te yer but I wants to bring yer to yer senses. Ye've done enuf damage and it's time yer bloody well stopped. Yer broke yer mother's 'eart an' now ye've broken yer 'usband's. It's time …*"

Stephanie screamed, threw herself on the floor. At that moment the door of the flat opened and shut, and the next moment Andrea had come in the room.

"*So you told him I was here?*" yelled Stephanie.

"*Yes …*"

"*You traitor …*"

"*He's your father.*"

"*He's yours not mine.*"

"*Calm down.*"

"*Get him out immediately.*"

Andrea turned to her father,

"*You'd better go, Dad.*"

Frank stood up, looked at Stephanie, kissed Andrea on the cheek,

"*OK, it's probably for the best if I do,*" Frank turned his face and had a last look at Stephanie and walked out.

\* \* \*

It was exactly half-past seven when the door-bell went. Anthony ran gingerly down the stairs and there was Stephanie on the door-step.

"Come in," said Anthony and he led her upstairs to his office-cum-sitting-room. One of George's house rules was that no women were to come up the stairs into either of their sitting-rooms, only men. Anthony had never broken this rule before and he hoped Ethel would not hear him take her up the stairs so he led the way to his room in silence. He opened the door and, as he opened it, he gestured to a sofa and he took the armchair. He looked leftwards to the large island book-case, the one which had been made for him by, Andy, the West Indian parishioner.

"A **charming** room," she said, looking around as she put special emphasis on the word 'charming', the word echoing round the room.

"I'm not really supposed to bring parishioners up here into my sitting-room but I thought you would be more comfortable here."

"Well, that's **extremely** kind of you," she said, this time stressing the adverb. The way she spoke was as if she was under direction from a theatre producer who was teaching her how best to cast her lines for the audience. "I wanted to see you, Father. You see it was such a beautiful sermon, the most beautiful I have ever heard."

"Thank you ..."

"You see, Father, Peter died just ten days ago and he disappeared into a void. When I saw the coffin ..." she buried her head in her hands and then fifteen seconds later with equal suddenness she raised her head sharply and continued, "He ceased to exist but when I heard your sermon I knew he had come alive again; that he was living."

"Yes, he has risen with Christ, our Saviour and Redeemer," said Anthony slipping back momentarily to Newman College and Sid Darrell's lectures. He thought passingly of Clarence.

"Yes, Father, it all became real to me as I looked at you giving your sermon. I knew Peter was living again. You see, Father, he was such a **wonderful** man," the same emphasis this time once more on the adjective, "You know Peter was a saint, Father; he would go and see the sick people in his practice at any time of day or night and if they were ill and poor he did not ask them for any money. He loved all the people who came to see him. He was such a wonderful man, Father. He was the quintessence of refinement and courtesy. You know, Father," and at this moment her eyes glazed with excitement, "I believe he will be canonized?"

"Oh, I think that would be a bit difficult. Canonization is a huge process. You have to have two miracles and then a devil's advocate."

*"What's that, Father?"* she said in a combative tone and sitting up even more erectly.

*"Well the Church sets up someone who acts as a barrister, as it were, for the prosecution. He brings all the arguments **against** the person's sanctity."*

*"Oh, what a horrible idea. I know that the barrister would not find anything wrong with Peter. Peter was just a saint in every way. The devil's …what do you call him …"*

*"Advocate."*

*"He wouldn't find anything against Peter."*

*"Well everyone has some sins …"*

*"Not Peter, Father,"* she said and she looked away from Anthony. She would allow no contradiction on the point. Her manner would brook no further argument.

*"How did he die?"* asked Anthony.

At that moment Stephanie burst into tears. She took out a handkerchief and dabbed her eyes.

*"Please don't ask me, Father."*

Anthony looked down with embarrassment. He was not sure what to say. Then she sat up again like a rabbit sitting up at the sound of an intruder approaching.

*"Please don't mention the word 'death'. I know he is living now so I needn't think about that any more. I know from this morning that he is really alive. Oh, your sermon was so moving, Father. I know now Peter is alive …"* and she wandered into a silence that must have lasted a minute. Anthony broke it:

*"I'm sorry but I don't know your name."*

*"I'm Mrs. Terrain. Terrain, that's the name."*

*"Well Mrs. Terrain I am glad that you know Peter's living."*

*"Yes, he's truly alive but in a real way. I am not like Saint Thomas who did not see Jesus, Father. I have really seen him,"* she thrust her head up and looked at Anthony with her magnetizing eyes, *"I really have,"* she said hitting the adverb like a strum on a ukalele and then hesitating she looked up, *"you know, Father, it's just like Pentecost, the apostles in the Upper Room. Saint Peter …yes …Peter. I've seen him. He's completely real."*

*"Yes, Jesus rose from the dead and that is the guarantee that all of us will too,"* her words stimulated Anthony into another theological statement. He was not talking to Mrs. Terrain but to an audience come to hear a theological exposition. They were like two people passing each other in the street but not meeting.

"*Oh, it's **so** wonderful, Father…*" and tears flowed slowly onto her cheek and she took out a handkerchief again, wiping her eyes and dabbing her face. She had dark brown hair that was almost black but not quite; there was a hint of brownness as the light caught the top of her head. She had a square-ish head. She was no longer dressed in black but had a light grey jacket, light blue blouse and light grey skirt. Yesterday when she came she looked stolid and matronly whereas to-day a summer breeze had blown through her and she looked alive. God bent down and breathed the breath of life into Adam; he had breathed the breath of life into Mrs. Terrain. Anthony could no longer think of her as a Mrs. She had for a moment the aspect of a frolicking girl at a party. Anthony did not think of himself as a priest interviewing a recently widowed parishioner but as a young man in the company of a cheerful young girl. In this brief instant the professional veil was lifted both from him and from her. Here was a young man and a young woman enjoying each other's company. In that moment he suddenly wondered where she came from and how she came to be in his parish.

"*Where are you staying?*" asked Anthony.
Suddenly she re-assumed her role as the distressed widow and that fleeting moment had gone,

"*Please don't ask me, Father. I find all questions like that so upsetting. I so want while I am here with you to think of Peter and your sermon and his Living Presence…*"
and she gestured an imploring smile at him. He was flattened back into his priesthood.

"*I'll pray for you,*" he said, "*I'll offer Mass for you to-morrow.*"

"*Oh thank you **so** much, Father…*" her voice again hitting the guitar string on the word 'so' and her eyes switched swiftly towards the window. A small flock of sparrows had just landed on the branch of a plane tree. They were twittering and she looked at them very intently. This made Anthony turn completely round and watch them for a moment.

"*Oh Father I've suddenly thought of something…*" and she looked bashful and did not want to continue.

"*Yes,*" he prompted.

"*I want to ask you a very special favour?*"
Anthony was a bit nervous; he wondered what was coming,

"*No, well…please tell me.*"

"*Would you come and bless Peter's grave? Sprinkle holy water on it and give it your special blessing?*"

*"Where is it?"*

She bit her lip.

*"It's at Wadhurst in Sussex, Father. You see Peter's practice was there. It's near Tunbridge Wells."* As she said the words 'Tunbridge Wells' it rang a bell in his mind but he was not sure why. His eyes lifted up to the ceiling in a moment of attempted recollection but she interrupted him,

*"If you could come soon, Father ..."* she said pressingly, *"you see then he would be truly risen from the dead."*

*"Yes, alright,"* said Anthony nervously but then added, *"you know the holy water is not what brings him to life."*

*"Oh yes, I know, Father, but it's your presence there that would make such a difference. I keep thinking of that sermon. I know you would understand in a special way, in a way that Fr. Hamilton did not. I can tell you're in touch with the spiritual world. I have got psychic powers. I just know that, Father. This is the astral plane. You do believe in the astral plane, don't you, Father?"* but she did not allow time for an answer, *"Peter and I believe in the astral plane. We both always lived in it."*

*"Yes'ss,"* he hovered on the word doubtfully,

*"Oh please,"* she said imploringly, leaning forward and fixing him with her stare.

*"Alright I could come on Tuesday. Tuesday is my day off."*

*"Oh dear on Tuesday I have to go to visit Peter's mother. Could you please come to-morrow, Father?"* and she looked at him pleadingly. Monday was George's day off and he always took Tuesday. On Monday he had his YCW meeting. This Monday they were having a special yearly review of their year's action pattern. She could see the doubts surging in his mind,

*"Please Father. It would mean **so** much to me,"* strumming the word 'so' again. *"I think the work of your sermon would be truly fulfilled then."*

*"Alright I'll come."*

She smiled radiantly at him, raising her eyebrows.

*"I could leave mid-morning. Where shall I pick you up?"*

*"Oh no, Father,"* she said in a second of panic, *"I'll come round here."*

*"OK,"* he said hesitantly, *"I do not have a car but I could borrow one from a priest friend. It will be a grey Mini Traveller. I'll be in it just opposite the Church at eleven."*

*"Oh, **thank** you, Father,"* she said hastily getting to her feet, looking at her watch. She was now hurrying to get out as quickly as possible. She wanted to avoid any further awkward questions. Her mission had achieved its purpose. She wanted to allow no time for any back-sliding.

*"I must go now but thank you so much, Father,"* and now her voice was a bit different. She was no longer in the theatre but a business-woman with her interview concluded. Anthony led her gently downstairs, past Ethel's little sitting-room next to the kitchen and out to the front door. She put her hand out in a stiff gesture. He shook it firmly, opened the door and in another moment she was gone.

When he got back upstairs, Anthony was in the dumps. He knew he would have to ring Terry Hughes who was group leader for to-morrow's YCW meeting. And where was she? He did not even know; she had just vanished. He wondered for a split second whether she was an apparition. Then he got a grip of himself and went to the telephone and rang Terry Hughes' number:

*"Is that Terry?"*

*"Yes, Fa'ver."*

*"Look Terry, I've run into a problem for to-morrow. Is there any chance of us meeting on Tuesday instead?"*

*"No, 'fraid not, Fa'ver."*

*"It's going to be difficult, impossible in fact for me to make it."*

*"Oh dear, Farv, I 'ope it's nothin' serious."*

*"Well,"* said Anthony guiltily, *"it's just something I have to do. Something that's suddenly come up."*

*"Well that's that then, Fa'ver, ain't it?"*

Anthony could tell he was deeply disappointed. Anthony had gathered this group, trained them in their Gospel Enquiry and inspired in them a passion for the message of the Gospel and now here he was cancelling. He knew how crucial it was to be faithful to their commitment.

*"Could you meet without me?"* asked Anthony weakly.

*"No, wouldn't work, Fa'ver. You know 'ow it is. Look I'll ring round the others and just tell 'em we'll 'ave to cancel, Fa'ver."*

*"OK, I'm sorry Terry."*

*"It's alright, Fa'ver,"* but Anthony knew it was not alright.

Then he rang Stephen Warrior to ask if he could borrow his car for the next day. It was no problem. Then for the second time, he drank a glass of whisky, sat down and watched television until feeling sleepy he went off to bed and tossed and turned many times. He felt he was made of a glass casing with just a few bits of straw rattling around inside. He had become a weak vessel. He heard George returning, going to his bedroom. It was at least two hours before he drifted off to sleep.

# CHAPTER SIX

Her hatred of her father was so intense that she dared not go back to her sister's flat. Her sister had betrayed her. She imagined taking a knife and stabbing her father, and, at this moment, her sister too. After her father had left she had screamed at Andrea. Andrea had managed to calm her down; she explained that she thought just when Peter had died it might be a moment for reconciliation but Andrea knew it had misfired and regretted her action. Stephanie walked on past, the turning to Tredegar Square and on to Mile End. She looked at her watch and then at the Odeon Cinema and saw that *The Sound of Music* had just started. She would go in and see it. She was relieved when she got in, that the main film had not started and she watched a trailer of a Walt Disney *True Life* film of Alaska. Then she sat back and was soon enveloped in the film and was entranced by the story of the nun who left the convent. Something surged in her as the reverend mother of the convent told Maria she was to go out to face God in the world. Her mind at that moment was transported away from her father and her sister to her saviour, Fr. Stonewell. She knew that Peter lived in him. Death and killing had been transformed into the bright light of Resurrection. When she saw Maria leaving the convent something leapt inside of her. Her mood had lifted when the film was finished and Maria was now married to Count de Trapp.

It was a long film and it was past eleven o'clock when it was finished. She had not told Andrea of her interviews with Fr. Stonewell or even that she had been to the Church. When she got in Andrea was in a night-dress and going to bed. Stephanie told her that she was going down to visit Peter's grave and that she had to discuss the design of the tombstone with the undertaker. Andrea asked her how she was going and she lied and said she was going by train to Tunbridge Wells and that a friend was taking her from there. Andrea was relieved that she would be out all day and that two days later she would be leaving altogether. Stephanie had always been trouble and she had not changed. Andrea had taken pity on her when Peter had died but she realized now that it was misplaced sympathy. So, after a brief interchange, the two sisters went to their respective bedrooms.

\* \* \*

So she was in the car with her new-found priest driving past Bromley out towards Sevenoaks and Tunbridge Wells. She had deftly parried questions that threatened to reveal her identity and concentrated all her attention upon him:

*"Are you on your own in the presbytery, Father?"* she asked. Anthony felt it ridiculous that she continued to address him by his formal title. He had undone his clerical collar as soon as the car was nosing its way out of the Rotherhithe Tunnel and thrown it onto the back seat revealing just an open shirt and jumper with the only sign of priesthood remaining in his black trousers and shoes. There was an emptiness inside him and the memory of his conversation the previous evening with Terry Hughes drained all priestly life out of him. He was ashamed.

*"Call me Anthony."* Stephanie started when he said this. She had not expected it. She wanted him as her priest and she wanted to remain Mrs. Terrain. The living presence of Peter was in the priest not in an Anthony. She hesitated:

*"Oh no, it's alright. I think I prefer to call you 'Father'…"* but as she said the word "Father" she felt a surging of hot flush from the back of her head to her forehead so, after hesitating, she said, *"… well perhaps I could call you Anthony. What is your surname?"*

*"Stonewell."*

She laughed,

*"Stonewell; perhaps I could call you Stoney?"* and she laughed again. His face tightened into a forced smile,

*"Alright."*

*"Has anyone called you that before?"*

*"Yes, at school they used to call me 'Stoney'"*

*"I'd love to call you that,"* and she giggled and threw her head back and passed her hand through her near-black hair.

*"So, are you all on your own in the presbytery?"*

*"No, I'm only the curate. There is a parish priest. He's called Fr. George Smithes."*

*"Oh, it must make it nicer to be two of you – less lonely."*

*"Oscar Wilde said, 'I never felt less alone than when by myself,'"* he answered in a grim tone.

She felt a strange sensation going through her breast. A few moments before he had become a schoolboy called "Stoney" and now a fierce grimness came into his tone. The sensation in her breast was a uniting one. It was as if she and he were joined like twin brother and sister in a grisly thundercloud.

*"Tell me,"* she asked.

Anthony hesitated. The story of his conflict with George was complex; even his friends of the Doktor Klub did not understand it. There was something essentially unspeakable about it. So he tried to explain with a piece of short-hand,

*"There is a failed connexion between us ..."* he turned and looked at her and she raised her eyebrows in uncomprehension.

*"It's two different mentalities."*

When he said that, it alarmed her. That's what Peter used to say to her about herself and him. She had completely forgotten anything disparate between them. When he died, it sealed off all rows and disagreements and there remained just a luminous ecstasy. Anthony's words brought back a glimpse which remained with her only for a split second. It was of Peter screaming "bitch" at her. It was a subliminal flash across her mind's television screen.

*"Oh, I **so** understand,"* she said and he turned half towards her, puzzled at the intensity of her tone. He sensed that something had changed but he did not know what and she went on,

*"I know so **exactly** what you mean,"* and again there was this special emphasis. She was trying to cancel out what had in that unwelcome moment passed through the eye of her mind.

*"It's so wonderful when two people have a total union of souls. Peter and I were so united in all that we thought and did. It was a unique oneness. From the first moment we met, our souls fused into a unity. It was deep down, far below all surface things."*

There was silence for a couple of minutes while he negotiated the car around the green at Westerham and headed towards the motorway that would take them to Tonbridge and then Tunbridge Wells. Then she said to him,

*"You don't have to tell me about you and your parish priest. I know so well what perfect union of understanding is, that **anything** that clashes or destroys harmony must come from the devil."*

At that moment Anthony tottered on the edge of two totalities: utter disagreement versus sublime accord. He thought for a moment of all his theology and his own hard-nosed disparagement of attributing motives to the devil which clearly belonged to the person himself. In a similar way he despised attributing motives to God which belonged to the person's own good impulses. The theologian fought with a mad one inside him. The mad one was being driven hard by a violent force emanating from this bizarre widow beside him. Here he was about to sprinkle holy water on a grave; did it come from her or from some depths which had not been penetrated by all Sid Darrell's theology at Newman College? Even more he thought that on the day when he suddenly experienced God as a friend and him in free relation that a superstitious madness had been banished from his soul forever but a sensation running through his head and chest spoke of a violent tussle and as this wrestling match was beginning to be fought within him she spoke again,

"I *do* so understand what it must be like for you," and the sound of her words gave the mad one inside him a triumphant victory. The image of Terry Hughes and his Young Christian Worker (YCW) group flashed in front of him. He was defeated. The mad one had won. She had that subtle ability to stimulate the mad one in him into existence. He found himself pouring out all his exasperation with George.

"Oh, how terrible it must be. I know *exactly* what it must be like," she said with that same emphasis which had come into prominence in everything she said especially in the last few minutes. From the moment that scene of Peter yelling "bitch" flashed before her, she was driven like a wild animal fleeing a forest fire into the arms of her saviour and, at the same time, Anthony escaping the shaming image of Terry flung himself in his inner being into Stephanie's arms. The road to disaster had become a one-way autobahn with no turning back. So he told her all about Tommy Sweeney, the way George had lied to him after having been to see the Cardinal and his exasperation with his superstitious practices. By the time he had finished they had arrived at the Catholic Church at Wadhurst. Now, Anthony was totally in the grip of the mad one. He took out the holy water which he carried in a little plastic bottle and a small brass sprinkler. He was now utterly in the power of this spider woman beside him. They walked past the little modern presbytery on the right and the primary school on the left, and then past the Church itself.

"Let us go in for a moment," she said and she pranced like a horse doing dressage towards the door of the Church.

*"Alright,"* he said unwillingly. He wanted to get this whole procedure over as quickly as possible but they went in and knelt in the back pew of an empty Church. He had never felt further from God than at this moment. He looked at the plaster statue of St. Thérèse of Lisieux holding a bunch of roses on the left of the altar. A bitter poison came into his head which he wanted to spit out but he couldn't. As they walked out she said,

*"It's such a lovely little Church. Peter loved coming here."* In that inner wrestling match the hard headed theologian had been utterly smothered but something more than the theologian or the Doktor Klub member. His own deepest self which had flushed out of his soul's undergrowth when he had been with Fr. Salter had been suddenly smothered like the Princes in the Tower. He had been reduced to a straw scare-crow coming apart in a gale.

*"Yes,"* he said with meek violence. They walked down a little incline and came to the graveyard and she led him to a big mound of earth. As she looked ahead her eyes became bright and full of excitement. She tapped Anthony on the shoulder and said in a loud whisper:

*"Please sprinkle."* He took out the little bottle and the brass sprinkler and did as he was told. At the moment when the little drops of water showered upon the muddy earth she gripped his left arm, looked into his eyes in a transport of devotion. Peter had gone from the grave. His phantasm had passed into Anthony the day before during his sermon but now, what had been mere foreplay, had become consummated, or nearly so. Peter had disappeared totally into Anthony. He had become Anthony. Her eyes gleamed with passion. In that ritual moment as the water sprinkled from the brass hyssop in Anthony's hand the magic circle had been completed. Peter now was Anthony.

*"Oh Stoney, we can go now,"* and her eyes radiated into him an irresistible cannonade of subatomic particles that rendered him helpless. He had become like one of those toy boats that children play with on the Round Pond in Kensington Gardens. They travel this way and that across the small patch of water depending on the child's directing hand upon a small power panel. There was no spring of life within Anthony's own heart. It had been totally given over to a strange hypnotic power that resided in Stephanie's breast and that was transmitted, like an electric current, through her dark brown eyes.

*"Oh Stoney,"* she said, *"I want to show you where we **live**".* As she said the word **live** it again had that special absolute tone and she gripped his left arm and steered him back towards the car.

*"Yes, down this road ... turn left ... then first on the right"* and Anthony pulled the car up at a small terraced house in a little side street leading off the main road. She jumped out and travelled in mechanical steps over the ground and stopped in front of the door. She waited until he had locked the car and was at her side. She pulled out the key and handed it to Anthony who protested weakly,

*"Oh Stoney,"* she implored, *"**you** open it. It 'll mean **so much to me** – **please** do."* So the obedient robot took the yale key, inserted it in the lock and turned it to the right. She saw Peter in front of her.

*"Oh no,"* she said, *"you have to turn it to the left."* He reversed the movement and he could hear the bolt move back and he pushed the door which opened easily. He stepped back for her,

*"Oh, please go in first,"* so he stepped forward and found himself in a small old-fashioned hall with a hat-stand on the left and a small oblong table carrying on it a jumble of inconsequential bits and pieces – a bar of soap, two opened letters, an old brass paper-knife and lying over the back of it and dangling towards the floor, a stethoscope. She then led him through a door on the right into a long sitting-room which was packed with furniture. **Please** sit here and she indicated an armchair with its back to the window and facing the fireplace. As he sat down he found himself looking at a brown monochrome portrait of an elderly man's head sideways on. Anthony looked at it and she said suddenly in hot panic,

*"Oh no, don't look at that,"* in a voice that had suddenly become harsh. Anthony looked at her in surprise and she quickly altered her tone,

*"Oh I **am** sorry. That was ... Oh, I can't bear it"* and she buried her head in her hands for an instant.

*"Tell me, who was it."*

*"Oh don't, Stoney, don't. He is an evil man."*

*"Is it Peter's father?"*

*"Oh don't, don't,"* and she again buried her head in her hands, *"I didn't want it there but ...Oh don't, Oh no. If it hadn't been for him ..."* and she threw herself on the sofa and sobbed. Anthony sat woodenly on his chair.

*"Oh please comfort me, Stoney."* Anthony got up awkwardly and laid his hand on her head for a moment and, as he did so, he felt a rush of revulsion swell into his chest. He removed his hand.

*"Oh please, **please**, put your hand there again. I felt healing the moment you did that."* He put his hand there; he had been told to do it and he did it. He was a lifeless automaton. He returned to his chair and sat

down heavily. She continued to sob. Then, as if suddenly awakened out of sleep, she leapt up.

*"Would you like a drink of water?"*

*"Yes, thanks."*

*"Oh, would you like a whisky?"* He was about to say "No" when he remembered the whisky he had drunk the night before. Perhaps it would bring him relief, he thought.

*"Yes, I would, thank you."*

She got up and walked in measured paces out through the door. He continued to sit impassively in the chair. He could hear glasses clink and the gurgle of liquid. In a couple of minutes she was back with a Waterford tumbler with whisky and ice in it. She handed it to him. He stood to receive it and stayed standing.

*"Are you going to have one?"* he asked awkwardly.

*"No, I **always** drink pink gin"* and she giggled and turned with a flourish, went out of the room and in a few moments was back again with a twin Waterford tumbler filled with clear liquid. The two of them, both standing, drank in uncomfortable silence.

*"I'd like to take you upstairs,"* she said. She noticed him hesitate.

*"Oh **please** come, Stoney,"* and she smiled her eyes at him but her mouth was fixed in a hard stone-like mould.

*"Alright,"* he said, his voice processed through an invisible synthesizer. He waited for her to step onto the stairs.

*"Oh please go first,"* she said, so he did as he was bid. He walked up the narrow stairs and the bannister turned back on itself at the landing.

*"Turn round to the right and go straight ahead. Just open the door."* He walked diffidently forward and turned the round handle and pushed the door open. The room was surprisingly large for a small house. He walked in, past the large double bed and to the window. As he did so he looked across at a dressing table and at a framed photograph of a young man in his thirties,

*"Oh, don't,"* she cried and rushed in and grabbed it and quickly put it away into the top drawer of a chest of drawers and she sat down on the dressing table chair. He looked around awkwardly for somewhere to sit and then unwillingly sat on the bed. As he did so he noticed that she had closed the door. She was sitting with her back very straight, a priestess about to perform a pre-ordained rite.

*"Oh, now you're here it is all different. I **feel** I'm in a new astral plane. That's a different dimension ..."* her voice trailed off.

*"Oh **please** would you lie right back on the bed."*

*"No, it's OK, I'll just stay as I am."*

*"Oh **please, please** do,"* she begged imploringly, *"it would change everything – just like when you sprinkled the grave"* and her eyes gleamed brightly.

He was under a spell. He lay back with his head propped up against the headboard. He put a pillow between him and the headboard and swung his legs onto the bed. He was in a sitting posture, using the bed like the resting chair of someone in an old people's home. The priestess, having performed the first stage of her rite, sat back on her chair satisfied.

*"Is that ..."*

*"Hush, please don't speak. I can feel transmutation. The silence of mutation ..."*

Anthony sat silent as commanded. Then she stood up, strode with deliberate steps towards the window and back. Then she suddenly rushed from the room and Anthony remained sitting upright looking at the door through which she had disappeared and then his eyes wandered back slowly across the room to the window. A flicker of sunlight was cutting its way into the carpet and as far as the edge of the bed. He heard a rustling in the room next door. Suddenly the door burst open and she ran in, a changed creature. The crysalis had burst open and a butterfly had flown out. A young girl in a light blue dress had burst forth from the widow in mourning, dressed in a stiff dark skirt and matching jacket. This stiff dark crysalis had broken open and a light blue butterfly had flown into the room. She no longer walked stiffly as if she were an ambassadress in ceremonial attire but a young girl playing the flirt at a coming out dance. Before she had been androgynous and now she was a sexual young girl; before she had been middle aged or ageless but now she was a young woman; before she had been dead, now she was living.

The change took Anthony entirely by surprise. Although he was dressed in mufti or semi-mufti yet until that moment his life and manhood had been imprisoned within a skin as hard as a lobster shell. When suddenly those ten years ago the Hound of Heaven, after chasing him down the labyrinthine arches of a mind in terror, had caught him in its inexorable net, sexual desire had been paralysed in him. He was like a caterpillar stung by a mason wasp numbing his genital organs as effectively as the most powerful anaesthetic. There was one moment when at Newman College he had been woken up from the anaesthetic momentarily but through an act of grim determination it had re-asserted itself. Women, as objects exercising emotional attraction and sexual desire, had hardly entered into Anthony's orbit since going to Newman College. One holiday he had gone skiing with three other "divines" and in the small inn at Gréolières-les-Neiges, a skiing resort in the Alpes Maritimes, he had been captivated by a girl in another skiing party. Instead of skiing one day he went on a trip to Nice with her, at her suggestion, and he felt massively attracted to her sexually but he managed through determination to resist sexual contact. He had felt "thrown" by it and, when he returned to Newman College, felt in confusion but he and the girl, whose name was Joanna Pimble, inhabited different universes. She was extremely attractive, had been a debutante three years before and her interests and ambitions were so different from Anthony's that no emotional bond of any strength could have been possible. After he had discussed the incident with his confessor it evaporated; the anaesthetic had been re-injected. Apart from this one damp squib Anthony had hardly been troubled by temptations from women at all. They had hardly come across his path because personal friendship had been so restricted that it had prevented it happening. He had in this way been obedient to the Church's counsels for priests. He had avoided friendship except with priests, had devoted himself wholeheartedly to this priestly work and had a devotion to Mary, the Mother of God, who was the protectress *par excellence* of the priest's chastity. But his devotion to Mary had waned under the influence of his ecumenical enthusiasm. This process had started in the seminary when the central place of Jesus Christ in man's redemption became his guiding dogma and then Mary moved more into the sidelines than was customary in traditional Catholic piety. He saw Mary as a personal symbol of the Church, the first of the redeemed in the hierarchy of saints but he no longer said the Rosary every day and he despised those priests whose devotional lives centred around Mary. He felt it was not manly or worthy of a healthy robust spiritual life. He thought that the Church needed to present a different image to the world. But now suddenly in this Upper Room his paralysed sexuality in a morgue-like house was changed in a twinkling from robotic deadness into a womb wriggling with new life.

The change in Stephanie was so dramatic that he wondered if he was dreaming. Here was no stiff, wooden widow but a young girl in a sexual passion. The dead Peter had risen in glorious splendour and her Stoney radiated rays of brightness. Darkness had been transfigured into brilliant sunlight. Mount Tabor was no brighter than this. Anthony was Peter transfigured. Her eyes beamed into him in intense penetration. He found his eyes glued to hers – first to her eyes and then his eyes lowered to her breasts which had become enlarged and fulsome but then his eyes were magnetized back to her eyes and he felt a sensation in his chest pulling a hollow within towards those breasts. His eyes stuck to hers and his chest inwardly closing the distance between them. His mind began to swim with a hot flush passing through his forehead. Was she physically closer? He did not know. His chest was drawn into her and his loins rose up in violent revolution. The anaesthetic was suddenly lifting. He was *in* her. His eyes went back to hers. Before they had been brown but now as he looked they were dark black taking him into a powerful inferno. A furnace was roaring inside him. She moved a foot towards him. He heard the movement but it was like an echo in a dream.

For six years in the seminary he had been a mind. He had discussed matrimony, contraception and the sexual imagery so prominent in the Bible but anything bodily was dissolved in mind. Now suddenly it was totally reversed; he *was* body and those dark eyes looking at him from a subterranean canyon were hot plates stirring his head, his chest and his genitals into a fermenting cauldron. His mind, his hard head, his spine, his solid chest had all melted down into a bubbling rubber liquid. His self-determination, his fanatical control had passed into her eyes which had now become huge black revolving discs like black spots in the sun. There was a bright flash in his head and he passed out of consciousness. It did not last long but when he woke it was to a savage beast that was upon him ripping his fly-buttons open and grabbing his phallus in an act of righteous possession. It was not his; it was hers. It belonged to her, it had been taken from her. She was reclaiming her rights. What had been taken from her she would make her own. No one would stop her. She had taken what was hers into her and thrusted with insensate vigour until her whole being surging from below swamped her anatomy in orgasmic ecstasy. She screamed the high pitched yell of an alto soprano until at the highest pitch she fell back across the bed, her mission accomplished. He, like a towel soaked in a thunderstorm, slopped onto the floor and in a daze found the bathroom where he attempted to recover some semblance of his former self.

He locked the door, was glad to see a towel and some soap; he stripped himself and stepped into the shower. He turned the taps until the water reached a temperate climate and he washed himself, applying it like a baptismal rite to wash away his sin. He had soaped himself and was washing his body clean when she rapped on the door:

*"What are you doing?"* she yelled, *"How dare you use my bathroom – it's not yours."*

She rapped even harder on the door:

*"Come out, how dare you."*

A hot rage surged within him. He wanted to finish washing and drying himself in his own time but against his own will he was anxiously hurrying to the tone of what sounded like the tempestuous snapping of castanets as she rapped louder and louder upon the door. He was trembling inside as he threw open the door and yelled:

*"You savage bitch."*

*"How dare you."*

She ran down the corridor and picked up a tennis racket and came rushing at him. He grabbed it, tore it out of her hands, threw it on the ground, pushed her back into the bedroom, slammed the door and ran downstairs, opened the front door and the moment he was through it, he whammed it shut and ran for his car. He sang with relief as the engine clattered into life. As he drove off she was rushing towards him and she shouted,

*"I'll report you, I'll report you,"* but the roar of the engine drowned her words.

# CHAPTER SEVEN

Anthony had no idea how he got back to the presbytery. He remembered vividly the engine kicking into life and driving furiously away from that crazed woman shouting from the pavement outside a terraced house in a small side street in Tunbridge Wells but how he had driven back through Sevenoaks, Westerham, Bromley and then back through south London, through the Blackwall Tunnel to his presbytery he had no idea. He could not even remember it though he knew he had left the car outside Stephen Warrior's presbytery and put the key back through the letter-box, as arranged. He knew he must have cycled back to his parish but he had no memory of that ride. When he walked into his room and slumped into his armchair, dazed and overcome, he realized that he could not remember how he had got there. He had obviously driven the whole way from Wadhurst to Poplar and he was conscious that there had been a passage of time but could recall no bit of the journey. For some reason he knew he had come through the Blackwall Tunnel; he could remember the entry arch above him as the car descended into those dark depths beneath the Thames. He looked at his watch. It was just half-past eight and it would soon be dark. He got up and went to the cupboard beneath the window and drew out the bottle of whisky. He filled a glass and took a great gulp. It burned its way down his throat and into his chest; the chest that had been burning with turbulent passion a few hours earlier. He brought it back into his mind but then quickly took another gulp and drowned it. Then to his relief he began to feel tired. He went upstairs to his bedroom, ripped off this besmirched clothes and donned his pyjamas and jumped into bed. He pulled the bedclothes over him right up to his chin. He laid his head on the pillow which felt like a soothing lullaby. In a few moments he was sound asleep.

He eased out of sleep at three in the morning and, as he did so, the words 'Tunbridge Wells' were echoing in his mind. He saw the words floating unattached like an advertisement slogan being carried in the sky by a plane from which it had come adrift. Then suddenly he saw the words coming out of Frank Jenkins' honest mouth. 'My God', he said to himself and sat up in bed like a rabbit all alert at the sound of a trespasser, 'Stephanie is Frank's daughter, the bad daughter and married to a doctor in Tunbridge Wells and Andrea's sister.' In a flash he realized why Stephanie had not wanted him to know where she was staying; that Andrea and her father would reveal to him her true nature. Something like relief came over him. It was the relief that comes when disorganized events that confuse the mind suddenly fall into a meaningful pattern. As he realized, he gasped. He knew that he would go and visit Frank Jenkins and Andrea and that in some form or other he would tell them what had occurred. It would mean a confession, perhaps the first real confession of his life. As soon as the word 'confession' came into his mind he thought of the fact that he was due to say Mass at nine in the morning and that meant receiving Holy Communion. A layperson could attend Mass and not receive Communion but the priest had to eat and drink the Body and Blood of Christ in the sacrificial meal known as the Mass to Catholics. He broke into a sweat when he thought of it. What was he to do? One thing he knew was that he would not make a confession to George Smithes. He had performed a sexual act; he had broken his vow of chastity and committed a mortal sin. To receive Holy Communion in the state of mortal sin was the supreme sacrilege, like driving one of the nails through the palms of Jesus' hands and pinning him onto the cruel wood. He would be a Judas and a vision of that traitor's end flashed terrifyingly into his mind. Then he thought of Frank Jenkins and this calmed him.

'Now Anthony,' he said to himself, 'apply the principles you apply to others to yourself.' Had he committed a mortal sin? He had certainly had sexual intercourse with a woman which was a mortal sin. Certainly it was a mortal sin according to the book but was it for him? What if he heard exactly what he had done from someone else? Was there true internal consent? He remembered the discussions at Newman College about what constituted consent? There could neither be a sinful act nor a virtuous one without true internal consent. Well he had certainly not consented to the sexual act. He had been raped and the very essence of rape was that there was no consent to the act. A tide of warm light stroked his brow. What he had done was not a sin. He had no need therefore to go to confession. He would say Mass and take Communion. He lay back in relief and soon he had gone to sleep again.

\* \* \*

He was bending over the large round white wafer intoning in English the words of consecration that changed the paper-thin substance into the Body of Christ and a few moments later he was speaking the solemn sentences that changed the wine into the Blood of Christ. His theological studies had taught him that the full presence of Christ was living glorious and triumphant in each and both species. He broke off the little piece of the host and dropped it into the chalice and after he had said the Our Father and then the Agnus Dei he bent over and ate the sacred host and drank the Blood of Christ. He turned round and saw just four people kneeling in the Church: Mrs. O'Brien, Joe Murphy and George Smithes, his parish priest and nine-year-old Tony Rifle, his altar boy. George, he knew, was making a thanksgiving after having celebrated Mass himself just shortly before. He was looking pitifully towards Anthony who knew that he was praying for him but this annoyed rather than comforted him. He did not like being pitied. Only Joe Murphy came forward to the Communion rail and Anthony placed a consecrated host upon her outstretched tongue, like a mother bird feeding her nestling. He returned to the altar and finished his ablutions and five minutes later he was back unvesting in the sacristy. Tony Rifle solemnly put away the vestments and Anthony went back into the church and sat in one of the pews. Joe Murphy was still there but Mrs. O'Brien and George had gone. He sat quietly and thought of what he had just done. Had he committed a sacrilege? If he died now would he go to hell for all eternity? All eternity – not just a human life sentence but unending punishment? It was more than he could contemplate. It was like the holocaust; it was so immense a disaster that it could not be comprehended. Was God going to banish him forever? for all eternity? He said 'No' that it could not be, but a sneaking doubt, a dark uncertainty troubled the lower reaches of his mind. He could not throw it off. He felt alienated and out of fellowship with George, with Mrs. O'Brien, with Joe Murphy and with Tony Rifle who had looked at him so innocently, so trustingly when the Mass was over. St. Teresa's image of the devils tugging at the priest who was celebrating Mass in mortal sin returned uncomfortingly to him. He tried to banish it by saying a 'Hail Mary' but it would not depart. He thought of Jesus casting out devils and only wished He would cast this one out of his heart. Then his mind went back to Stephanie. Was what had happened yesterday real? It seemed like a hallucination. Had he really gone with her all the way down to Wadhurst in Sussex? Had he really gone and sprinkled holy water on her late husband's grave? And then … had she really ensnared him into a sexual act? Was that really him that had acted thus or was it just a phantom? Thoughts began to race through his brain. 'Am I going mad?' he asked himself. He shook himself, stood up and walked resolutely out of the church and into the presbytery. He knew it was true however because he remembered and knew he had dropped the car back at Stephen Warrior's presbytery in the next door parish and then cycled home.

Ethel had left a thermos of coffee for him. He made himself some toast and ate and drank in silence. He sat at the end of the table in the room lined with dark brocade wall-paper. He looked momentarily the two framed pictures of the Sacred Heart of Jesus and the Immaculate Heart of Mary. He pondered on what he should do. He knew he had to go and visit Frank Jenkins and then Andrea but he was not sure what he was going to say to them. It was a Tuesday morning and Frank would be at his picture framing shop while Andrea, he thought, would be studying at home. Where would he go first? He would go and see Andrea. Nervous within but resolute without, he finished off the coffee and toast and then, without even going upstairs to brush his teeth, he strode off down Bow Road heading for Tredegar Square.

He had reached No. 46. He rang the door-bell. There was no answer. He rang it again and the door buzzed; Anthony opened it and walked up to the top flat. He reached the door and rang the bell. It was longer than usual before the door opened and Andrea's face peered at him, looking hesitant.

"*Can I come in?*" asked Anthony nervously.

"*Yes,*" said Andrea unsmilingly. She was not her usual self. She led Anthony into the sitting-room and, as he entered through the door, he saw Stephanie sitting upright as if poised for a fashion photograph upon an upright chair. She gave him a disdainful sidelong glance. He looked at Andrea who bustled out of the room and into the kitchen. Anthony stood rigid, stuck to the floor as though with super-glue. An instinct told him not to speak until Andrea had returned. The silence screamed at him. Stephanie looked away. She had the carriage of a deposed empress. She was dressed in a black jacket and skirt, the model widow. He waited; she waited. After an age Andrea returned with a tray which had upon it a tea-pot, mugs and a plate of biscuits.

"*Would you like a cup of tea, Stephanie?*" asked Andrea.

"*No, thank you,*" she replied putting extra stress on the word 'No'.

"*Would you, Anthony?*" she asked fearfully.

*"Yes, thank you, I would,"* he answered stolidly.

*"Shall I pour it for you?"*

*"Yes, thank you."*

Andrea held the tea-pot high over the blue and yellow mug so the sound of the liquid splashing into the mug broke into the atmosphere like the curtain going up at the opening of a play. Speech could be delayed no longer.

*"Have you told Andrea what happened yesterday?"* asked Anthony looking at Stephanie.

*"Yes, she is **extremely** shocked,"* Anthony looked at Andrea for confirmation.

*"What you've done is disgraceful,"* said Andrea, *"to have done it to any woman but to someone who has just been widowed ... and you, a priest, whom she trusted and we trusted is scandalous and after all the kindness and hospitality we have given you."*

Anthony could not believe his ears. This was so unlike Andrea. He did not know what had been said but some malign power had taken her over just as he had been taken over yesterday. He was in a law court; the judge had just passed sentence, condemned him to death, the guards had taken him down below into a black maria and he had no voice of protest. All had been decided. He was paralysed. He sat down, stroked the hot side of the mug. Then an inspired thought came to his mind; turning to Andrea he said,

*"Do you believe what you have been told?"*

Andrea bit her lip. She knew Stephanie was a terrible liar. She had told Peter's father and mother that her parents lived in Kensington and Andrea's own father had always told her that Stephanie had been a lying trouble-maker since her earliest years. *"Stephanie 'as a devil in 'er'"* he'd often said. Anthony had asked just the right question to shake Andrea out of her trance. He could see that a battle was going on in her mind. Stephanie could also see it and she knew that she had to strike and strike soon if the edifice she had fashioned were not to fall down into a heap of rubble.

*"I don't know why you are hesitating, Andrea. You **told** me that you knew that Anthony, as you call him, was very frustrated with his parish priest and that you could imagine that he would attack and rape me in the way I told you,"* Stephanie looked hard and coldly at her sister. Anthony turned towards Andrea who immediately looked down. Stephanie dressed as she was in a black jacket and tight black skirt was the self-righteous victim of an

assault. She sat erect and imperious. It was impossible to imagine her surging with sexual desire. The excited girl in a light blue dress had vanished. The most fertile imagination could never have conjured that fresh excited girl in a blue dress out of this black empress. It was not difficult though for Andrea to imagine Anthony overcome with passion. She had felt some stirrings in herself towards him which reinforced her feeling that what Stephanie said might be true. Andrea looked up, took courage and asked Anthony,

"*Did you seduce my sister?*" Anthony hesitated and in that microsecond he had lost his case. Andrea looked at him and was then certain that Anthony had done what Stephanie had asserted.

"*It, it was … well, the other way round,*" said Anthony fumblingly and blushing scarlet.

"*At **least**,*" said Stephanie emphasizing again the word *least*, "*you've had to good grace to admit that something sexual occurred even if you are not gentleman enough to take responsibility for having done it.*"

Anthony had been bowled middle stump. The gorgon Medusa had turned him to stone. He sat in violent confusion. Blood was rushing from his cheekbones up into his head.

"*It wasn't like that; it wasn't, it wasn't,*" he said slumping his head into his hands. Stephanie stood up and looked down upon him with supreme disdain. She took a packet of Gaulloise and removed from it a cigarette with cool deliberation, lighting it from a giant box of matches on the table next to her. She took three puffs and turned, looking for an ash-tray, and stamped it out.

"*I don't think we need to continue these proceedings any further. Andrea could you do me the favour of asking your priest to leave.*"

"*I think it would be better if you would,*" said Andrea with some gentleness. Anthony, defeated and nonplussed rose slowly and moving like a scarecrow with a robot engine inside of it, left the room and let himself out of the flat door.

He looked at his watch. It was just twenty-past eleven and up above a thin blanket of grey stratus cloud stretched out across the heavens to block out any direct sunlight. There was total concordance between the inner and outer ambient. However, the inner emptiness had not robbed him of his sense of purpose. He knew that he would go directly to the picture-framing shop and speak with Frank Jenkins. He put his faith in his down to earth common sense. After all, he it was who had told Anthony that Stephanie was "a bad 'un'" The framing shop was on the corner of Roman Road and Lyal Road so he crossed diagonally Tredegar Square and into Coburn Road and headed northwards. This side of Bow Road had been spared the depredations of council development and the small cottage homes had been allowed to stand in peace. Children were already at school so as he walked up Coburn Road he only passed a couple of elderly women returning from the shops both with heavy shopping bags. As he walked under the railway a train lumbered noisily overhead. The buildings were all two-storey. He looked at his watch. It was twenty-seven minutes past eleven. It had taken him only seven minutes from Andrea and Tony's flat. He turned left into Stanfield Street which was lined also on each side with the same two-storeyed terraced houses made of ageing brick. A minute more and he was in Lyal Road and at the end of it on the corner was the picture-framing shop. It was surfaced outside in wooden veneer which was painted bright yellow and over the doorway in large red lettering: ANDREA'S PICTURE FRAMING. He pushed open the yellow swing door and walked in with confidence.

*"Oh, hell, Fa'ver. Didn't expect to see you ... Oh, I sees yer not lookin' any too bloody good."*

*"No I'm not and it's all because of that bad daughter of yours, Stephanie ..."*

*"What you've met 'er, 'ave yer. I told yer she was a bad 'un and yer would not listen to me."*

*"But I didn't know she was your daughter."*

Frank looked at Anthony with furrowed brows.

*"What yer mean – yer didn't know?"*

*"Well,"* said Anthony rubbing the thumb of his right hand on his clerical collar, *"she didn't tell me her name."*

*"Didn't tell yer. Well, cor blimey, why didn't yer bloody well ask. Ye've got a tongue in yer head."*

*"Well, well ... she didn't want to tell me ..."*

*"Well I'm sure she bloody didn't but ... do yer mean to say that yer just lay down and accepted that? Anyway what's she done that's upset yer?"*

*"Well, you know her husband, Peter, has just died ..."*

At that moment the telephone rang.

*"Wait a minute, Fa'ver,"* and he picked up the telephone. Anthony could hear that it was a woman's voice on the other end of the line. He guessed instantly that it was Andrea.

*"Yes, well, go on,"* Frank was saying. Anthony could only hear a muttering on the other end of the telephone but he could see Frank's

brows contracting into a frown. At one moment he glanced up at Anthony and then he continued listening. Anthony knew that Andrea was relating what had happened or rather Stephanie's account of what had happened yesterday. Then he whistled, looked at Anthony again and then said peremptorily,

*"Well, e's 'ere wi' me now. I'll speak to 'im. OK Andy dear. I'll 'andle it."*
He put the telephone down with sombre deliberation and came over to Anthony and sat down on a stool opposite him,

*"Well, I'm old enuf ter be yer fa'ver so I'm goin' ter speak to yer, like ye was me son. So I'll calls yer Anthony. Now I wants to know, no muckin', did yer seduce me daughter, Stephanie, yesterday?"*

*"Let me explain,"* protested Anthony, *"you see ..."*

*"Look, as yer knows, Anthony, I'm a plain speakin' fellow. Don't go now beatin' about the bush. Did yer or didn't yer?"*

*"Well Frank ..."*

*"Look Anthony it's no good pretendin'. It's either one or t'other. Either yer did or yer didn't. Yous even speakin' like Stephanie. She's always hesitatin' like that and, what's they say, dissimulatin' or what's they call it. Ye've been with 'er that's for sure."*

*"Well I was with 'er; that's true."*

*"What's was yer doin' wi' 'er then?"* Frank was sitting on the stool opposite him with his grey trousers and shirt covered with a white apron that was heavily stained and had bits of wood shaving stuck to it.

*"She wanted me to go with her to her husband's grave in Sussex and bless it for her."*

*"An' was 'at yesterday?"*

*"Yes, that's right,"* and Frank looked up at the ceiling, thinking for a moment.

*"So ter-day's Tuesday, so it was Monday. Didn't yer tell me that Monday was when you 'ad your YCW group you's was tellin' me about?"*
Anthony blushed and put his head down,

*"Yes, you see Stephanie ..."*

*"Yer means to tell me that you cancelled your YCW meeting, letting down all 'em yung 'uns cos ye wanted to go off and 'ave it off wi' me daughter?"*
Anthony started stammering.

*"Yer a disgrace. I'm not wastin' me time wi' yer,"* and he pointed to the door. Anthony could not find what to say. He got up like a wettened rag-doll and walked to the door. Just before going through it he looked back and Frank had already turned his back on him and was starting to

measure a piece of wood for a frame that he was making. Anthony was just about to go out when he turned back:

*"You told me, Frank, that she was a bad one so why do you believe her?"*

*"Look, 'ere, you ain't been in the East End long enough, me lad, sure enough you ain't. Blood is thicker than water for us East Enders. Yer needs ter remember that before you goes muckin' wi' one of me daughters."*

Frank turned back to the piece of wood he was measuring. He gestured to the door. Anthony could see that there was no way forward. He slumped out of the door.

\* \* \*

Early in the afternoon he was in his in the presbytery reading a passage from St. Paul's letter to the Philippians:

*"... though he was in the form of God, he did not count equality with God a thing to be grasped, but emptied himself, taking the form of a servant, being born in the likeness of men. And being found in human form he humbled himself and became obedient unto death, even death on a cross."*[1]

He knelt down on the floor and looked up at the picture on his wall of The Crucifixion by Velazquez and prayed passionately,

*"Now I am totally with you, Lord; I am in you and you in me. Let this chalice pass from me. Not my will but thine be done."*

His eyes were riveted upon the dejected figure. Even his most faithful disciples Peter, James and John could not watch one hour with him. Even Andrea and Frank had deserted him. He had become Jesus.

*"I am now living the true Gospel,"*
he said to himself.

*"I have become you, O Jesus."*
He swayed on his knees while his eyes gazed at his Crucified Lord. He knew he was one with him; one with him in his greatest suffering. He felt suffused with a warm inner light. He read on to the next verse of St. Paul:

*"Therefore God has highly exalted him and bestowed on him the name which is above every name."*[2]

---

[1] Philippians Ch. 2. vv. 6–8.
[2] Philippians Ch. 2. v. 9.

He knew now he was with God; that he would live forever. At last he was joined with Jesus for eternity. He got up and rushed to his desk and grabbed off the wall above his desk a wooden baroque crucifix and held it tightly in his hands:

*"O Jesus, O Jesus – now I am truly with you in your Agony. I am awake with you."*

A jump of excitement leapt through his breast. Still clutching the crucifix he turned back to the picture of Jesus crucified in the Velazquez painting:

*"I am with you now, Lord, in your agony. I know I will be raised with you on high, the first fruits of salvation."*

He was still clutching the crucifix. The cornered edge of the wood was digging into his right hand. He unclasped the hand and looked at the raw red mark across his fingers,

*"Your nails are in my hands. My hands are your hands. I am on the Cross with you. I know Your dejection. You were misunderstood and rejected. I am joined now in my inner heart with You ..."*

He was just about to pick up the Bible to read Psalm 22 when the telephone rang. He moved back to his desk and picked up the receiver.

"Hello, you've forgotten," he recognized Clarence's voice. He remembered instantly that there was a meeting this Tuesday of the Doktor Klub.

*"Heavens ..."*
*"Well it's not too late. As you know we are at Stephen Warrior's. We are all here and you can get here in ten minutes ..."*
*"OK. I'll come straightaway."*

Anthony put down the telephone and rushed downstairs to the shed at the back of the presbytery and pulled out his old faithful police bicycle which had got him home the night before. As he pushed it out across Bow Road and then clambered onto it to steer himself southwards down Devons Road he glanced up Bow Road. He thought he glimpsed Stephanie with her head down walking westwards towards his point of departure but he then thought it was his imagination. He thrust the image out of his mind and rode, back upright, down past St. Andrew's Hospital and in five minutes' time the spire of St. Stephen's church in Poplar came into view between the serried ranks of council flats.

When he burst into Stephen's sitting-room they all looked at him. Clarence looked forbidding sitting at the head of a long oval table. Stephen was sitting on his left with a large writing pad in front of him and opposite him was Joe Feeney and then Sean Casey and Jamie McCleod were next to Stephen and Joe, respectively. Then at the end of the table was Rudolph looking severely at his right hand in which was clasped a cigarette between his thumb and index finger. Stephen was obviously in the middle of an impassioned declaration. Anthony did not feel part of them. The *camaraderie* was outside of him. He was living in an alien land. There was an empty seat at the end of the table next to Rudolph. He shyly slipped into it.

*"It's alright,"* he said, *"carry on from where you were."*

*"Stephen is just explaining his view of the Real Presence of Christ,"* said Clarence,

*"So, carry on Stephen,"* said Clarence. Stephen glanced at Anthony and carried on,

*"The Presence of Christ to-day is in our actions,"* said Stephen, *"if we receive the Sacrament but do not live with Christ in our actions then there is no presence of Christ. Christ only lives in the Sacrament if what we receive in our mouths is translated into actions that are Christ-like. The Sacrament has the power to transform us into Him but only if we are receptive to Him. If we receive the Sacrament but then block ourselves to his inviting presence then we have not received the Presence of Christ at all. St. Thomas Aquinas said that if a mouse eats a consecrated host it has not taken in Jesus but only a wafer of bread. It is the same with all of us. If we take the consecrated host with our mouths while our hearts are full of fear and superstition we are mouse-like. We have not received the Presence of Christ ..."*

*"Do you mean to say,"* asked Sean in an alarmed voice and his accent was even more Irish than usual, *"that many Catholics who come and take Communion on Sundays are really as far from the Presence of Christ as that there mouse that Aquinas spoke about?"*

*"Yes, that's exactly what I mean,"* said Stephen.

*"But I thought,"* said Sean, *"that the Presence of Christ was there whether or not people were receptive ..."*

*"That's just sheer magic,"* said Stephen.

*"But if Christ is in our actions,"* asked Sean mystified, *"then what is the point of the the sacrament of the Eucharist at all?"*

*"When we priests pray over the bread and wine in remembrance of the Last Supper we invite those present to enter into a transformation of themselves*

into the life of Christ. If they do, through an act of faith and trust, then the presence of Christ is there. It is the faith in the priest and in the congregation which transforms the bread and wine into the Presence of Christ."

"You mean," asked Sean, "that if there were no believers there would be no transubstantiation?"

"If a parrot said the words," said Stephen, "it would remain bread and wine. It is the faith in the heart that transforms, not the words in themselves. If a priest said the words under hypnosis there would be no transubstantiation." As Stephen said this he thumped the table and looked round. The table they were sitting round was made of light pine covered with a high varnish. The chairs were all in matching pine and on the wall was a large batik of the Risen Christ. It was a copy of one of the mosaics in Ravenna that Stephen had bought when visiting the city. The pine table stood upon rush matting. The walls were whitewashed in the brightest white. Opposite the batik was a large oblong window that looked onto the front entrance of the Church which was approached by a line of cherry trees.

"If you hold anything different, Sean," said Rudolph, "then you believe in magic."

"But all Catholics I know believe that the bread and wine turn into the Body and Blood of Christ through the pronouncement of the words alone, to be sure they do," said Sean.

"Then they believe in magic," said Rudolph with hurried sharpness.

"Then that's the majority," said Sean, "and it can't be that they are all wrong. You would be saying that every Catholic in Ireland believes in magic and that their faith is distorted."

"And right you are there," said Joe Feeney, "we from Ireland all know that it's a lot of superstition. Three years ago I was down in Killarney at the Lake Hotel at Christmas and the New Year and we all sat up in the bar one night and once everyone had a few whiskies inside them they all started talking and suddenly an old man said that he did not believe that the bread and wine really turned into the Body and Blood of Christ. At first, to be sure, they all looked shocked but then one after another everyone in that room agreed with him. Not one of them believed it. But the next day we all met at a party and they were all guilty and whispering to each other and making promises that they would not repeat what had been said to anyone else, especially the children."

"That's why there's so much drunkenness in Ireland," piped in Jamie McCleod, "there's no inner faith. It's all superstitious addiction to ritual bits of magic. The drunkenness is to drown the inner emptiness. It's why so many Irish abandon their religion once they reach England and many of the

*famous Trade Union leaders were Irishmen turned Communist. They hadn't
rejected a true Catholicism; they had put Communism into an empty space."*

"All this sounds like heresy to me" said Sean, "it's surely not possible to
have so many deceived?"

"Look Sean," said Stephen, rousing himself to another impassioned
speech, *"huge masses of people can be wrong. Have you read that book
'France Pagan?'"* and he looked at Sean challengingly.

"Well, sort of ..." said Sean.

*"Well it deserves more than a 'sort of',"* said Stephen, *"what that book
shows is that although almost everyone in France, except a few Huguenots and
sophisticated intellectuals, are baptized Catholics but that they are pagan in
their religious practice and outlook. They go to Midnight Mass at Christmas
and about twenty per cent go to Holy Communion at Easter but that about
eighty per cent do not know that Jesus was a Jew from Palestine, they do not
know that there are three persons in God, that everyone who is baptized enters
into the personal life of God, that our changed nature spontaneously generates
in us a love that transcends selfishness and self-interest. What Godin found
was that the majority of the people were pagan although they called themselves
Catholic. There you have a whole country which calls itself Catholic but is in
fact pagan and that is exactly what Joseph Cardijn found among the working-
class in Belgium. The truth is not in the majority. In the fourth century it was
the few who retained belief in the Christian doctrine of the Incarnation. The
whole Church was swept into Arianism, the hierarchy included and it was only
a few lay people who kept the candle of true Christian faith aflame. We are in
exactly that position now.* Stephen stopped for two seconds to draw a deep
breath but then charged on, *"And we Catholics pride ourselves against the
Anglicans pointing to the numbers of people that we have coming to Mass in
our churches on Sunday but most of the people who herd into our churches
come out of superstition and fear – fear that if they don't go to church on Sunday they will go to Hell for all eternity. If someone comes out of fear rather than
love that is a perversion of the Christian gospel. It is anti-Christ rather than
Christian because it prevents the act of love, it blocks it and, at the same
time, all those who fill our churches on that basis go swaggering around self-
righteously believing that they are better than others because of this external
act that they have performed. It is pure superstition: that by entering that stone
building on a Sunday and muttering incantations they have, by this stroke of
magic, saved themselves from Hell and believing that God is now smiling upon
them but they are like the Pharisee in the parable of the Pharisee and the Publican. The Publican to-day is the person who never comes inside a church but*

*humbly acknowledges before God that he is not so bloody marvellous. Whether someone is a follower of Jesus or not depends upon his inner state not whether he kisses a statue or takes Communion, believing superstitiously that it will pacify an angry God. The pagans believed that if they offered an animal in sacrifice they would appease the local God who would then give the tribe a good harvest. If the God is pacified he will be satisfied. If I go to Church on Sunday God will give me good health. One of my parishioners went to Mass on the first Friday of every month believing that he would have a happy death. He had heard a priest preaching that and guaranteeing that if people did that they would have a happy death. So this old man loyally went to Mass on the first Friday of every month for nine months and then, can you believe it, he fell and broke his leg shortly afterwards and then he got a thrombosis and he was in incredible pain. I went and visited him in hospital. He was bitter, that he had done what God wanted but God had now deceived him and let him down. I listened while he cursed God and he did not want any sacraments or for me to pray with him. He died bitter and cursing God."* Stephen was speaking extremely rapidly with the words tumbling out of his mouth like coins out of a jackpot. He stopped and expelled a great breath of exhaustion.

Anthony was listening to him and when he reached the part where he was saying who were to-day's publicans he thought of Frank Jenkins. Two days before he would have embraced what Stephen was saying wholeheartedly but now he was in a paralysed state. He could hear Stephen's enthusiasm but it passed over his head like a high-flying flock of birds. He was not hearing the words but looking at them. As Stephen sat and smiled something made him say,

*"I agree that Christ lives in our actions. We are in him, in his suffering, in his martyrdom."* He spoke slowly and deliberately. Stephen said emphatically,

*"Exactly,"* but Clarence looked at Anthony and was a bit perturbed. There seemed to be something odd about him. No one else noticed and Joe Feeney took up the point in theological accuracy.

*"We are in Christ,"* said Joe Feeney. *"Jesus was put to death by the High Priests of the Temple but, to be sure to-day, we to-day are persecuted by the Establishment, the pagan Church."*

*"Well,"* said Anthony, *"we suffer from the Church but also all those who misunderstand us."*

*"Yes, of course,"* said Jamie quickly but without conviction.

*"Yes,"* agreed Rudolph, *"my Cistercian abbot was hated and misunderstood by all his monks."*

*"Like Jesus who was misunderstood and hated by the Scribes and Pharisees,"* said Anthony, *"and we are living in Christ when we are misunderstood."*

After this, the conversation wandered off into a discussion about contraception and the morality of males having a vasectomy. Anthony's attention was still lingering upon being misunderstood and living Christ's martyrdom. Until two days ago he would have entered keenly into the conversation but his heart was not in it. He thought of Velazquez' painting of the Crucifixion. Clarence was speaking but his words carried no meaning for Anthony. Suddenly he felt he could bear to be there no longer. He felt not understood by the members of the Doktor Klub, his closest friends. He thought of trying to explain to them what had occurred but he thought he could explain it no better to these zealots than he could to either Andrea or her father. He decided to leave. Clarence had just started to speak. Anthony interrupted and said he was not feeling very well and was going to return to his presbytery.

*"Oh stay and have a drink,"* said Joe Feeny, *"then you'll feel better, to be sure you will."*

*"No, I think I will be better if I go home and lie down."*

They could all see that this was what he intended so they stayed silent until he had got up and walked out of the room. They all looked at the door through which he had departed.

*"Things are not right with him,"* said Clarence.

*"What do you mean now, Clarence? "*asked Sean puzzled.

*"There is something troubling him. I think he is in some trouble but can't speak about it,"* said Clarence.

*"Oh I shouldn't worry,"* said Stephen, *"he's probably just had a row with George Smithes. He'll get over it."*

*"Trouble with him,"* said Rudolph, *"is that he keeps everything up inside him like champagne in a bottle. One of these days he'll explode. You know George Smithes went and complained to Cardinal Molony about him and then lied to Anthony and said he had not been to see him but Anthony could not challenge him. He just sat and listened to the lying prat without saying anything. There is nothing anyone can do to help Anthony with that,"* said Rudolph severely.

*"Surely we should help him then,"* said Sean.

*"You can't help anyone with that. You can't make someone speak. It's like an addiction that a person can't resist. The force silencing him is too strong. You saw him here a few moments ago. Something was bloody well troubling him. If he can't tell us what it is then there is no hope for him,"* said Rudolph savagely.

"*He'll lie down and have sleep,*" said Joe "*and then he'll feel better. It'll blow over.*"

"*I think there is something deeper than that,*" said Clarence, "*I'll ring him tomorrow and go over and see him. I hope he'll be alright until then.*" Clarence's forehead contracted and he looked at them all with glazed eyes. A sombre mood descended on the group and unusually they soon broke up and each scattered across London to their disparate presbyteries.

\* \* \*

Fr. Smithes had just turned on the television in his room. He heard Anthony go out. He looked at his watch. It was just time for the football match between West Ham and Millwall. He had just settled into his chair when he heard the front door-bell go. He guessed that Ethel had gone out shopping. He wiped a tired hand across his brow and went downstairs and opened the door. A smart young woman dressed in black was standing there.

"*Are you Fr. Smithes?*" she asked.

"*Yes, I am,*" said George slightly confused. This stylish woman who knew his name unnerved him. She did not look like an East Ender.

"*Could I speak to you?*" she asked.

"*Yes, please come in,*" and he led the way through into the reception room.

"*I have a serious matter to discuss with you, Father,*" she said, looking at him challengingly with the elbow of her right hand resting on the table.

"*Don't worry. You can speak to me about anything.*"

"*What I have to tell you will be a shock to you,*" she said and stared at him piercingly.

"*We priests hear a lot of things that may sound shocking but we get used to it, so don't worry,*" and he smiled at her benignly but he felt ill at ease within.

"*It's about your curate, Fr. Stonewell,*" and she looked at him again with her dark brown eyes.

When George heard this he felt in conflict. There was something about this woman that was troubling to him. She spoke in a deliberate and sophisticated voice. She did not sound like an ordinary parishioner. He felt a loyalty to Anthony because he was a priest but, at the same time, to hear another misdemeanour like he had committed with Joe Murphy would be a relief. He could then be certain that he had done the right thing in speaking to Cardinal Molony.

*"You can speak to me in confidence,"* he said *"but could you tell me your name please?"*

*"Mrs. Terrain,"* she said, emphasizing the second syllable of her name. There was a silence. Then George said,

*"Please go on Mrs. Terrain. Don't worry about it shocking me. We priests are not easily shocked. You know we hear distressing things every day."*

*"My husband died ten days ago."* As she said this, tears welled up and she reached for her bag, took out a small red handkerchief and dabbed her eyes. George murmured a sound of sympathy.

*"I came here to Mass on Sunday and afterwards I decided to speak to the priest and ask him to say a Mass for my late husband."* Again she dabbed her eyes.

*"I saw the young priest who had said the Mass standing on the pavement outside the Church so I approached him and asked him if he would say a Mass for ..."* she faltered in her speech, *"for my husband, Father. I gave him a pound note to offer the Mass and he said he could see I was upset and would I like to come and see him that evening at half-past seven. He seemed so sympathetic and understanding that I thought it would be a good idea to have help from a priest. So I came round at half-past seven as he had suggested. I came to the door and he took me upstairs to his sitting-room."*

As she said this she watched George carefully and she noted with satisfaction that a shocked flicker crossed his eyes. So she went on choosing her words carefully and deliberately,

*"You see, Father, my husband died just ten days ago. He was a GP with a practice near Tunbridge Wells. He was buried in the little cemetery behind the Catholic Church in Wadhurst. Well, I was telling Fr. Stonewell this ..."*

She paused for a moment.

*"... well, Father. He asked me if I would like him to come and pray with me at the grave."*

*"What all the way down in Wadhurst you mean?"*

*"Yes, precisely,"* she said with strong deliberation and theatrical stress on the word 'precisely'.

*"So what did you say?"*

*"Well, Father, I thought Peter would like a priest to say prayers over his grave. You see, Father, Peter and I are both very devout Catholics."*

She watched George carefully. He nodded approvingly as she said this.

*"... and I thought Peter would like it very much if a priest were to say some special prayers over the grave. But I said to Fr. Stonewell that it was a long*

*way to come and that I could ask the parish priest in Wadhurst to come and say some prayers. I said to him that I was sure he had a lot of parish duties to attend to and that I did not want him to come all the way to Wadhurst just for my sake. But, Father, he was absolutely **insistent** on coming."* She put weight on the word 'insistent'. There was a somewhat false ring to her voice as though a ventriloquist were speaking through her.

*"Yes, I know Fr. Stonewell can be a bit headstrong when he gets an idea into his head."*

*"Exactly, Father,"* she said accenting the word 'exactly'.

*"So, although I felt uneasy he persuaded me that it would be a very good thing if he came and prayed over the grave. I tried, Father, to dissuade him. I did not want to take him from his parish duties but in the end I gave in."* There was a long silence.

*"There is no hurry,"* said George, *"would you like me to fetch you a cup of tea?"*

She dabbed her eyes again and then sat even more erect than before,

*"That would be splendid, Father,"* and radiant sunlight beamed out of her. For a moment the mournful widow disappeared and a flash of that triumphant young girl crossed the stage.

George went out and she could hear him rattling about in the kitchen next door. He came back about seven minutes later with two mugs and a pot of tea,

*"Do you take milk and sugar?"*

*"Milk please, Father, no sugar."*

She picked up the mug as if she were raising a rifle to take aim at a very small target in the distance which it was essential not to miss. As if the mug were the sights she looked steadily at Fr. Smithes.

*"So he told me that he could come down on Monday. It was not a very convenient day for me but he was **very** insistent, Father. I told him I was planning to go back this week-end and that it would be better if he came one day once I was there but he said that he could take me down this Monday in a car he could borrow. He asked me to come to a point just down the road from the church at eleven o'clock in the morning. So I came as he asked me. Well, when I arrived he was in his car parked about fifty yards down the road on the other side. When I got in I was shocked to find that he was dressed in an open shirt. I know the Church is letting up on its regulations but Peter and I always liked all the Church's traditional customs and rituals and it made me extremely uneasy to see him dressed without his clerical collar."*

*"Did he pray at the grave just dressed as a layman?"* asked George.

Her eyes flickered for an instant but George did not notice.

*"When we arrived at the Church, Father, he put on that black covering and his dog-collar. Oh sorry, Father, I mean clerical collar,"* she half giggled for a moment and George smiled at her,

*"So when we were at the grave he was dressed as a priest. So, Father, he knelt and prayed at the grave and asked me to pray with him. Then, Father,"* and she bent her head and cried. George waited quietly looking at her through his light yellow-rimmed spectacles,

*"... then, Father,"*
she said, raising her head and speaking with confidence,

*"as soon as we were in his car again he took off his clerical collar. I asked him to keep it on as it seemed right but he said it was the inner attitude that made the priest and not the outer clothing."*
She watched George who sighed noticeably and she knew she had hit the right mark.

*"So, Father, he drove me back to my house in Tunbridge Wells. When we arrived I thanked him and asked him if he would like a cup of tea. Perhaps I shouldn't have done that, Father, but ..."*

*"Oh well why not, that was quite reasonable."*
George had already guessed what was coming. He had heard priests' confessions for many years and knew how often their vows of chastity were broken. He looked sympathetically at her. She went on completely confident now that she had played her part just right,

*"then, Father,"*
and she cried once more,

*"he said he would bless the house for me and asked me to take him to all the rooms of the house. When I got to the bedroom ..."*
she buried her head in her hands,

*"... and to think it's the room where Peter and I ..."*
she wept again,

*"Don't feel you have to say anymore, Mrs. Terrain. I think I know what you are wanting to tell me."*
Then she sat up again erect and confident,

*"He raped me, Father, and then just left me and I heard his car driving off and to think dear Peter had just died ..."*
and she collapsed in tears and cried but then again raised herself and spoke with decision,

*"I plan to go to the police but I thought I should tell you first, Father."*
George said to her,

*"Look Mrs. Terrain I know how you feel and you have been badly sinned against but I would prefer that you did not go to the police. It will cause great upset and scandal here in the parish."*

*"But he must be punished,"* she said savagely.

*"Can you leave it to me?"* asked George.

*"What will you do?"*

*"I will speak to the Cardinal and he will discipline Fr. Stonewell."*

*"What will he do?"* she asked.

*"He will send him away from the parish and demand that he makes a long retreat at a monastery."*

*"I will only agree not to go to the police if you assure me that you will do as you say."*

*"You can trust me, Mrs. Terrain."*

George stood up and Stephanie rose, shook him firmly by the hand and moved towards the door. George said,

*"I will offer my Mass for you tomorrow morning, Mrs. Terrain."*

*"Thank you, Father."*

George took her to the door:

*"Good-bye, Father."*

*"Good-bye, Mrs. Terrain."* She moved off with a decided walk. George watched her until the wall of the church hid her from sight.

*"Oh, dear,"* George said to himself, *"I never asked her how she came to be in this parish or where she is staying."*

As soon as she had gone George went straight into his office and picked up the telephone. He looked up his Catholic Directory to find the number of Archbishop's House. It took two minutes of fumbling before he found it. He dialled the number:

*"Can I speak to Cardinal Molony please?"*

*"Who is that speaking?"*

*"It is Fr. George Smithes."*

*"I am not sure if he is available."*

*"Could you tell him that it's Fr. George Smithes on the telephone and that it is very urgent. I think he will take my call if you tell him that."*

*"Please wait a moment, Father."*

George held the receiver and his hand was trembling.

*"Hello George, what's up?"* George heard the Cardinal's familiar voice.

*"Look, Father, a very serious thing has happened. You know what I was telling you about my curate."*

*"Yes, come to the point, George."*

*"Father, I've just had a woman come to see me who was sexually assaulted by Fr. Stonewell and I promised her that you would discipline him and that if you don't she said she would go to the police."*

George went on to say that it was a young woman whose husband had just died and that Fr. Stonewell had gone down to bless her husband's grave at Wadhurst near Tunbridge Wells.

*"She was genuinely terribly distressed, Father. She was assaulted unexpectedly. She said she would go to the police but I promised her I would send Fr. Stonewell to you instead …"*

*"Send him to see me at once."*

*"When?"*

*"Straightaway, George."*

*"He's not in at the moment."*

*"As soon as he comes in tell him that I rang and want to see him."*

*"I am not sure when he will be coming in."*

*"I am in all evening."*

"OK," said George, *"thank you"* and he gave more detail to the cardinal of his interview with Mrs. Terrain and then he rang off.

As soon as he had rung off George collapsed into his armchair and buried his head in his hands.

\* \* \*

Anthony cycled back from Poplar along Bow Common Lane and into Burdett Road and northwards until he reached Mile End. It was a long way back but he liked cycling along Bow Common Lane which still had the character of a country lane winding its way among timber yards and he liked to feel the rush of air on his face as the bicycle pushed its way through a buffeting head wind. At Mile End he turned into Bow Road and headed eastwards back to the presbytery. As he cycled slowly along with the tyres rhythmically attuned to his mood of melancholy towards the turning that led into Tredegar Square he saw Stephanie coming from the East and turn sharply but decisively into the square. His heart sank. Where had she been? An instinct told him that she had been to the church to call on George. He pedalled slowly and passed the Bow Road tube station on his right. In another three minutes he turned into the presbytery on the left-hand side of the road. He wheeled his bicycle and put it into a little wooden shed at the back of the building. He took off his bicycle clips and pulled out the door key and entered apprehensively into the presbytery.

He looked up and saw George coming towards him. He could see that his lips were quivering and his face was blushing livid.

"*Oh Anthony,*" he said with pretended casualness, "*a telephone call has come in from Archbishop's House asking you to ring Cardinal Molony.*"

Anthony clenched his teeth. He knew that it was George who had rung and not the other way round. He now knew that George would lie to protect himself from the possibility of accusation.

"*Oh I wonder what he wants?*" asked Anthony in a semi-rhetorical tone but looking at George for an answer.

"*I think you'd better ring. The Cardinal seemed anxious to get hold of you.*"

"OK," said Anthony and went upstairs to his room to telephone.

"*Yes, it's Fr. Stonewell.*"

"*Oh yes, just wait a moment, I'm putting you through.*"

So the person answering the telephone had been told to expect a call from him.

"*Is that Fr. Stonewell?*"

"*Yes, Your Eminence.*"

"*I want to see you, Fr. Stonewell.*"

"*When?*"

"*Straightaway.*"

"*What now?*"

"*Yes, I want you to come and see me straightaway.*"

"*Alright, Your Eminence, I'll come now.*"

Anthony put the receiver down. He looked at his watch. It was just after half-past five. He paced up and down his room. He looked at his print of Velazquez' Crucifixion. As he looked at it he had a strange sensation of being sucked right into it. He felt his whole soul disappearing into the dignified body of the crucified Jesus. As he disappeared into the image on his wall he felt all his life-blood drain out of him. He turned and looked out the window. The plane trees were blowing and one poplar tree was rattling but their sound and the outside world was unreal.

Fr. Stonewell travelled to Archbishop's House as in a dream. He left the presbytery without saying a word to George who had gone into the Church to avoid an awkward meeting with Anthony. Anthony bought the ticket at Bow Road tube station, sat like a plaster dummy in the train and got out at Victoria and walked the short distance to Archbishop's House and rang the door-bell. An elderly janitor in a grey blazer and black trousers opened the door to him.

*"I have an appointment with Cardinal Molony."*

*"Please wait in there,"* said the man in a quiet voice, gesturing to a small room with three upright chairs and a square wood table. Anthony sat bolt upright and waited. His body was tense but his mind was in a dream. He had only been there a couple of minutes when the janitor re-appeared,

*"The Cardinal is ready to see you."*

*"Which way do I go?"* asked Anthony.

*"Just go up the stairs and the Cardinal will meet you at the top."*

Anthony moved obediently towards the broad stone staircase. For almost the entire width of it there was a purple carpet kept in place with brass rods. He climbed mechanically right up the centre looking down at his shoes. He saw they were muddy and unpolished. Then he heard a noise of footsteps and, looking up, he saw the Cardinal standing there looking down at him. He looked upwards and hurried the last few stairs. When he reached the silent figure in black cassock with wide scarlet sash and scarlet kippa on his head he genuflected and kissed the ring on the Cardinal's extended hand.

*"Follow me,"* said the Cardinal curtly.

*"Thank you, Your Eminence."*

Anthony followed at heel like a well-trained gun dog. The Cardinal reached a large polished walnut door and flung it open. Anthony saw a large oblong desk on the left-hand side of the room. There were books and papers upon it. The Cardinal closed the door behind him.

*"Sit down here,"* said the Cardinal motioning Anthony into a low seat beside the desk while he himself sat in a higher chair and looked down on the young priest through his bi-focal spectacles. The little boy was unprotected in the headmaster's study.

*"You know why I have sent for you?"*

*"I, um, I am not sure."*

*"Well I'll tell you. Your parish priest, Fr. Smithes, rang me this afternoon. He had just been visited by a young widow who had lost her husband ten days ago and in the guise of going down to bless the grave of her husband near Tunbridge Wells you took advantage of her sexually."*

The Cardinal looked down at Anthony piercingly through his bi-focal spectacles. Anthony glanced up at him and looked into cold light blue eyes. They swam in front of him like great saucers of light. As he looked at them he felt drawn in like he had been so shortly before into the figure of Christ in Velazquez' painting that was on the wall of his room in the presbytery. The glance at those staring eyes could only have lasted a second but it was a moment in time that seemed to last an age. They were the eyes of Pontius Pilate. He was about to be condemned to death. He could hear the rabble and mob shouting *'No, not this man but Barabbas'*. The traffic down Victoria Street had become a crazed mob that he could hear crying out. In the sound of acceleration at the lights he heard even more insistently the mob crying out *'We have no King but Caesar.'* His own eyes travelled back for an instant to those of his condemner. He looked away and the desk had become a Cross. A voice called him back to the presence of the Church's supreme prelate,

*"You should be ashamed of yourself. You are a wicked priest; a Judas."*
Anthony hung his head. Anger surged up in Cardinal Molony. How could a priest and a priest he had ordained with his own hands have committed such an outrage? As he looked down at this distracted figure in front of him, he spoke with metallic severity.

*"You have disgraced your priesthood. To have fallen into temptation – that would have been bad enough but to take advantage of a young woman who had just suffered a bereavement. You are no better than Judas."*
Anthony was mute. He tried to open his mouth to speak but a powerful force gagged him. The Cardinal looked at him with scorn.

*"Well, have you got nothing to say?"*
Anthony lowered his head. In his mind he tried to explain but what could he say? The facts as the Cardinal had spoken them were so close to the truth and yet so distant. An essential element had been transposed but under those piercing eyes and scorn-filled voice he was confused. Was it as the Cardinal was saying it? Perhaps that memory of Stephanie rushing into the bedroom in a light blue dress was a hallucination? Had he suddenly turned on her, ripped off her black widow's clothes and raped her against her will? After all were not the words of the archbishop in front of him the register of the truth? Was not what he was saying far more likely than his own fantastic memory? Suddenly an illuminating flash of understanding passed through him.

*"It's like, I mean, it's like Potiphar's wife,"* stammered Anthony.
*"What **do** you mean?"* shouted the Cardinal.
*"Potiphar's wife said Joseph…"*
*"You've caused enough harm, Fr. Stonewell. I am not going to listen to such vile calumnies. Fr. Smithes said the widow was in a distraught condition,"* the Cardinal's eyes retreated inwards as he understood Anthony's reference to Potiphar's wife, *"I have known Fr. Smithes for over thirty years*

*and he is a very experienced priest and knows true distress from any histri-onic displays. The best thing you can do is to ask God for forgiveness and repent for what you have done. I am going to send you to a monastery and you are to stay there for six months. I am going to remove you instantly from the parish. You have also put Fr. Smithes through a great ordeal and he has not been well. You owe him an apology."*

Anthony was utterly beaten. The voice of the Cardinal had become that of Pilate. He was in the Velazquez crucifix; the eyes of Jesus covered with forlorn hair swam in front of his eyes. He bowed his head. Then he stood up abjectly and genuflected to kiss the ring. For a moment Cardinal Molony felt sorry for him. For an instant he wondered whether he had made a mistake. The priest in front of him did not look as if he had committed the crime he had been accusing him of. It was only an instant flash but it troubled him for a moment when Fr. Stonewell said,

*"Good-bye, Your Eminence, I cannot explain but it is not as you believe it to be,"* but it was said in a tone that denoted he did not expect the Cardinal to make any further inquiry. In a softer tone the Cardinal said,

*"What do you mean? Explain yourself."* He sat staring at Anthony.

*"I did go down to Wadhurst to bless the grave of her husband and that is why I went. I did not go to rape her. That is a calumny."* Anthony stopped. There was a silence.

*"Well, yes, go on,"* said the Cardinal.

*"It was only after I had done that ... well, she insisted I went back to her home."*

*"What do you mean she insisted?"*

*"She implored me to come back to her home."*

*"And you just obeyed?"*

*"Well, yes,"* said Anthony awkwardly, *"her distress was enormous and she implored me, she pleaded with me."*

*"Well where was your priestly decorum? Sense of propriety? You learned in the seminary the dangers of being alone with a woman in distress."* Anthony felt fleetingly that the Cardinal saw Stephanie as Potiphar's wife but that instant hope evaporated,

*"Yes, it was a mistake,"* but Anthony spoke the word 'mistake' in a forlorn manner which angered the Cardinal.

*"So then I suppose it was a **mistake** when you raped her."*

*"But I didn't ..."*

*"So nothing sexual occurred?"*

*"Well ... something."*

*"I've had enough of this."* said the Cardinal, *"there's no point in beating about the bush. Did you take advantage of her sexually?"*

*"Well, yes, I mean no ..."*

*"What do you mean 'Yes–No'. Either you did or you didn't,"* the Cardinal stopped and looked at him and waited.

*"Well she took me into the bedroom ..."*

*"What you just went into the bedroom, into a single woman's bedroom?"*

*"She asked me to ..."*

*"So a woman asks you to her bed and you just go like a dog being pulled on a lead."* The cardinal's cheeks became flushed with a bright red, *"I've had enough of this, trying to blame her, a Catholic woman who came to you in distress and you take sexual advantage of her. It would be a shocking thing for any man, even an atheist, a communist. It would be even more shocking if that man were a Catholic but ..."* Here the cardinal stopped for a moment and looked at the ring on his finger, *"... for a priest whom that poor woman utterly trusted. The priest is the one person that a good Catholic can trust when in distress. For a priest to have done what you have done is a sacrilege."* The cardinal's chest swelled up and he looked straight into Anthony's eyes, *"And this is not the first thing I have heard about you, Fr. Stonewell. I heard of the cruel way you refused the Last Sacraments to a woman who was dying because she was going to pray with a devout Catholic woman who was coming to visit her with a medal blessed by the Pope. I've had enough of you young priests who despise the old and wise priests who have laboured for years in the vineyard faithfully and what you have done now is just the climax to all your sickening behaviour."* He looked at his watch. He reached for a notepad,

*"I am sending you to Magdalen Abbey in Devonshire. It is a Benedictine monastery and you will find the abbot there is a man who will instruct you and lead you to God if there is even the smallest streak of humility in you. It is your chance to reform your life, apologise to God for your disgusting behaviour. The abbot's name is Fr. Joseph Reid. He is a very holy man. He knows what prayer really is, he has been faithful to God down the years, he is a humble man. He will teach you what holiness is if you can open your ears and listen to him. I will write him a note right away."*

Anthony waited while the Cardinal took some headed notepaper and wrote upon it. He wrote quickly and Anthony could see that he covered nearly two sides of large writing paper. He knew by reputation that the Cardinal always dealt with things straightaway. He got things done. He did not wait or deliberate. When he had finished his letter he folded it and put it in an envelope and wrote upon it 'Fr. Stonewell.' He handed it to Anthony.

*"I will inform Fr. Reid that you are coming but you give him this letter when you arrive at the monastery."*

*"Thank you, Your Eminence,"* and Anthony genuflected and kissed his ring. As he got up to leave the room the Cardinal walked with him and shook hands at the top of the stairs. Anthony was just about to turn to the staircase when the Cardinal tapped him on the shoulder,

*"Kneel down, I will give you my blessing."* Anthony obediently knelt. The Cardinal raised his right hand high above his head and said loudly,

*"Benedictio Dei omnipotentis, Patris et Filii et Spiritui Sancti descendat super vos et maneat semper. Amen"* and as he pronounced the last word he placed his hands firmly on Anthony's head.

*"Thank you, Father,"* said Anthony and he turned and walked down the staircase but before passing through some swing doors he looked back up and the Cardinal was looking at him with a sad expression on his face. For a moment the Cardinal wondered again whether things were as Fr. Smithes had told him and how the widow had told things to him. He remembered a priest who had been untruthfully denounced when he had himself been a parish priest. He entertained the thought for a moment but then quickly dismissed it. He had to prepare a sermon that he was due to give the next day at the consecration of a new church at London Airport and he turned back to his office, settled at his desk and addressed himself to the task.

As Anthony passed out of the heavy wooden door that propelled him back into the secular world, the world of London's bustling humanity, he felt doom-laden. He looked at his watch. It was half-past six in the evening. As it was summer it was still light and would be for another two hours. He walked back to Victoria Road just as a bus to Ludgate Hill was about to draw away from the lights. He hopped on it, paid his fare to a conductor who patted him on the shoulder and then sat down. He felt he was in a dream as the bus swung into Parliament Square and round into Whitehall and through Trafalgar Square. As the bus stopped outside the National Gallery Anthony thought of Frank Jenkins who came here every Sunday afternoon. He would be coming there this coming Sunday, thought Anthony. Then, as he thought of his last parting from Frank, something caught in his throat; he could feel tears welling up but he dammed them just before they reached his eyes. He looked forwards as the bus swayed on into the Strand. It seemed no time before the bus was climbing up from Ludgate Circus towards St. Paul's. As it stopped before the Cathedral, Anthony got out. He went into St. Paul's and knelt and said a prayer. Then he got up and walked around the side aisles gazing vacantly at Kitchener's tomb and then at Wellington's. He could derive no comfort or inspiration from looking at the tombs of these military giants. Was this the way to God? he asked himself and if not why were they given such prominence in a Christian Church? He could not think of a Catholic Church that lionized soldiers in such a way. Perhaps all his enthusiasm for ecumenism had been wrong? Perhaps George Smithes was right to enfold all his flock within the walls of his protective church? Was Sidney Darrell wrong all along? Had he torn off Stephanie's black widow's clothes and raped her? Was the image of her in a blue dress a figment of his imagination? Was George right about Tommy Sweeney? As the thought of George came to mind he looked at his watch. It was now just after seven o'clock. George would be starting the evening Mass this Tuesday at half-past seven. To-morrow he knew was the Feast of St. Peter and Paul and a Holiday of Obligation for Catholics. George would be celebrating a Mass shortly so that Catholics could fulfil their obligatory duty the evening before. He himself was due to celebrate Mass tomorrow evening, he reminded himself. He thought of Frank Jenkins and the Michaelangelo carving of the Pieta in the right hand side chapel of St. Peter's in Rome. He wanted to be there rather than in St. Paul's. 'The Dead Body' – the dead body was glory, he said to himself. He looked at his watch again and decided he would go and attend George's Mass. He walked decisively out of St. Paul's, looked at the statue of Queen Anne facing away from the Cathedral, Christopher Wren's snub to his insensitive monarch. He stood on the kerb and two minutes later hailed a taxi which carried him back smoothly to Bow Road. As he arrived at the church the last of the parishioners had gone in. It was just twenty-five minutes to eight. George Smithes was always punctual with the celebration of his Mass. Anthony went into the church, knelt down in the back pew and bowed his head into his hands. There was George with his sandy hair and flushed face at the altar, facing the congregation. He looked awkward and ungainly. Tony Rifle was serving his Mass. There were about twenty people in the church. Anthony's mind was still riveted to the recent memory of Cardinal Molony looking at him severely through his bi-focal spectacles. He was wakened back to the altar as George was reading a passage from St. John's Gospel:

*"I am the Vine and you are the branches you ... live in me and I in you."*

*'O Jesus I am with you now in Your sacrifice to your Father.'* Anthony knew now that there was no boundary between him and Jesus. He was Jesus. He saw dancing before his eyes the cold eyes of Pontius Pilate. At the moment of consecration when the bread and the wine were turned into the Body and Blood of Christ he heard Tony Rifle ring the bell and he saw the meagre congregation bow their heads. Anthony looked straight ahead and watched the white wafer being held high. At that moment he heard clearly the words:

> *"Greater love than this has no man than he who lays down his life for his friends,"*

he looked round. He had definitely heard the words. Jesus was speaking to him. He would obey; he would lay down his life. God the Father had spoken to him, His beloved Son. Then he looked at George at the altar. He was speaking the transforming words over the chalice of wine and then he said very clearly,

*"Do this in memory of me,"*

and Anthony suddenly felt gripped by passionate adoration for his Lord and God.

*"I will offer the supreme sacrifice together with you O Jesus,"* he looked at the Crucifix. There was his saviour dying in lonely agony on the Cross,

*"It's really true O Jesus you did it for me. I will be crucified with you. I am in you and you are in me. You laid down your life, O Jesus, for all of us sinners. I will lay mine down with you. I will offer the supreme sacrifice together with you for the sake of your beloved bride, the holy Church,"* he looked at Fr. Smithes and he saw shining light around his forehead.

*"Oh he's a holy man! Have mercy upon me a sinner,"* Anthony cried out within himself.

*"I came from you O God and to you I will return. Accept the supreme sacrifice. I will offer you my all, my life. Dear Jesus let me be together with you for all eternity. Help me to bear this cup. Do not let this chalice pass from me."*

Fr. Stonewell was in a transport of religious ecstasy. His eyes were staring at the crucifix on the altar, his lips were quivering prayers. He was still kneeling there with a transfixed stare as the Mass ended and George walked, hands joined, back to the sacristy with Tony Rifle walking solemnly in front of him. The few people who had been attending this Mass came out from the church and they all, without exception, looked at their curate wrapt in ecstatic prayer. Mrs. O'Brien looked at him and offered a little prayer to God. She knew that priests enjoyed a special intimacy with God and that they enjoyed states of prayer not granted to poor layfolk. She blessed herself and went on her way.

\* \* \*

An hour later Anthony was sitting with George. George had wanted to avoid speaking to Anthony but when he saw his curate coming through out of the church and into the presbytery he felt moved by his downcast dejection. He came up to him and put a hand on his shoulder.

*"You have heard from Cardinal Molony, have you?"* asked Anthony. George nodded and Anthony said,

*"He has ordered me to leave the parish and go to Magdalen Abbey in Devonshire for six months."*

*"Yes, I know,"* said George, *"you are to leave this Saturday".*

Anthony was shocked by the suddenness. He had listened to the Cardinal's directive but had not expected it to be acted on so suddenly. They were sitting now at the end of the long refectory table in the sombre dining-room.

*"Have you got another priest to come on Sunday then?"*

*"Yes, I've got Fr. Conan from Newman College. He is a good reliable priest and has promised me he will come every Sunday for the next few weeks until we've got a more permanent arrangement."*

George had not been looking at Anthony as he spoke but then he turned and saw that his curate was upset.

*"I know it's a big sacrifice for you to have to offer up,"* said George.

*"Not greater than Our Lord's sacrifice. I want to join with Jesus and offer up the supreme sacrifice. To-morrow at the evening Mass I am going to offer up in sacrifice my whole soul and my whole body to God."*

*"That's the spirit Anthony. The life of a priest is one of total sacrifice to God."*

*"Father, I have never done that before but I am going to offer my life in sacrifice. I have chosen to-morrow evening as the moment of my supreme dedication."* George looked at his curate warily for an instant. There was something about his tone of voice that sounded unreal but it was only a momentary impression,

*"Then it's a lifelong sacrifice,"* said George.

*"It lasts for all eternity,"*

*"Yes,"* said George still slightly puzzled but went on, *"You find solace at Magdalen Abbey. Fr. Joseph Reid is a very holy man and you will have no cares but the care of your own soul."*

*"Jesus was both Priest and Victim, wasn't He?"*

*"Yes, that's right Anthony. He was both the one offering the sacrifice and the victim that was offered. We all learned that in our training."*

*"That's what I'll be doing to-morrow night. I'll offer myself totally. I will pass with Jesus to the Father. Jesus bid us repeat His Sacrifice."*

*"That's right, Anthony. I offer myself with Jesus at every Mass."*

*"To-morrow will be the supreme Mass, the perfect sacrifice."*

*"I know what you mean Anthony. One offers Mass every day but sometimes a particular Mass seems to consume the whole of one and you feel in a loving union with Jesus."*

*"Yes, I will be totally consumed,"* spoke Anthony in a mechanical voice.

*"I am so glad that you are going to accept with obedience the Cardinal's wishes. I thought things might be going to go badly for you but now I can see you have bowed your head in obedience to your bishop. Obedience is the highest virtue for a priest,"* said George.

*"Yes, I am going to offer myself in total surrender to God. This will be the meaning of my life forever."*

*"I have never heard you speak like this before, Anthony,"* said George hesitatingly.

*"I was kicking against the goad like St. Paul. Then on the road to Damascus Jesus struck him down. I was kicking against the goad. Now I have turned to Jesus."*

*"So, you don't mind that the Cardinal has ordered you to leave the parish?"*

*"No, I will pray for the Cardinal and for you George,"*

*"Oh thank you, Anthony. I so much need prayer."*

*"People often think I'm good and that I don't need prayer but I do very much. I have found the priesthood very hard and a great sacrifice. Sometimes I have felt I just cannot go on but Jesus always helps when he sees that you cannot manage anymore on your own. I need your prayers, Anthony."*

*"Jesus can help because he knows the path of Calvary."*

*"That's right,"* said George, *"Jesus and his Blessed Mother are the only ones who really understand the soul of a priest."*

*"Please pray for me that I will be able to offer my life in union with Christ to-morrow evening. It will need courage."*

*"I will Anthony. I cannot tell you how often I have prayed for you. I pray for you every day. Every day I have prayed that you would turn with love to the Church."*

*"The Church is the Bride of Christ."*

*"Yes,"* said George.

*"And Jesus offered Himself up on Calvary and that is what I am going to do."*

*"I will always pray for you, Anthony. There will be rejoicing in heaven to-day."*

There was a pause in the conversation. George looked at Anthony. He looked exhausted,

*"Why don't you go to bed now Anthony. You look so tired."*

As he said that, Anthony felt a stiffness throughout his whole body. He nodded and in a dead tone agreed. He got up from the table and put out his hand. The two men shook hands and George saw that there was a tear trickling down Anthony's cheek. George trembled and then Anthony turned and went out the door. George heard him going slowly up the stairs and finally into his own room and the door close. George sat there musing. He felt happy but worried. He knew that dramatic conversions did take place. He had often read about them in the lives of the saints but he had an English pragmatism that made him distrust such epiphanies. George was not a man of extremes. One of his favourite quotes was from St. Thomas Aquinas who said that the truth lies in the *via media*. George sat for a further few minutes and then went upstairs to watch television. There he stayed for two hours until he pressed the 'OFF' button. The screen flickered as if reluctant to disappear and then there was just a black patch in front of him.

*   *   *

There was a large congregation in the church for the eight o'clock evening Mass on this feast of St. Peter and Paul. Fr. Stonewell walked out on the dot of eight o'clock. As he faced the people he looked out over them and with his eyes on the Missal he raised his hand towards God in Heaven and started to recite the prayer of Jesus Christ to His Father, the prayer where Jesus offers himself in sacrifice to God the Father on behalf of sinful humanity. Anthony knew he was united with Jesus as he said the prayers loudly and carefully. Then the moment came and he bent over the large wafer lying on the corporal and he said the words *'This is My Body'* and Anthony paused. He looked heavenwards. He felt a tingling sweetness in his chest and tummy. *"Yes, I am with Jesus now. My body is His Body. Now starts my supreme sacrifice. I will go to the Father."* He turned back to the altar and bent over the chalice of wine and spoke the sacred words:

> *This is the Chalice of my Blood, of the New and Eternal Testament, given for you and for many unto the remission of sins.*

He paused. *"Yes,"* he said, *"it's new and it's eternal. My sacrifice is new, it's once and for all like Jesus on Calvary. Once done, it becomes eternal. My sacrifice will be once and for all. I am totally with Jesus now."* He felt a blissful radiance. He went on with the prayers of the Mass, the Our Father, the Agnus Dei and then he took up the host in his fingers broke it and said the words:

> *'this is My Body broken for you'.*

He muttered a quick prayer, *"Let my Body be broken with you, O Jesus. Dear Lord give me courage."* Michaelangelo's *Pieta* flashed across his inner television screen. He ate the host and then he took the chalice and drank the Blood of God and again stopped, *"Oh Jesus let my blood be united with yours in this supreme sacrifice,"* for a moment he was in a trance. He shuddered out of it and took the ciborium of hosts and went down the steps to the Communion rail and gave Christ to his Bride. He placed sacred host after sacred host upon the tongues of the faithful. Each one had head bowed until the moment when he stood directly opposite and then the tongue begged humbly for the Bread of God and Anthony did not fail to oblige. He returned and cleaned the chalice and turned back to the missal and said the Communion prayer followed by the Postcommunion. Then he opened his arms wide to the people and said,

> *"Go, the Mass is ended."*

Then he looked at the congregation and put in words usually spoken only by a bishop:

> *"Peace be with you"*

and the people resoundingly replied,

> *"And also with you"*

and Anthony said quietly,

> *"Eternal peace, O Lord."*

Then the Mass was ended. As he walked back to the sacristy his lips murmuring:

> *"Unto you, O Lord, I surrender my spirit."*

The altar boy, Tony Rife again, looked at him and thought he'd better not say anything. Usually he waited for the priest's blessing but because Fr. Stonewell was deep in prayer he slipped quietly away. Anthony did not want anything to interfere with this final and perfect sacrifice. He picked up his breviary from the sacristy and bending his head over it he walked solemnly and with a certain majesty into the presbytery. Ethel came running out and asked him if he wanted tea and biscuits. He did not talk to her. He turned and just waved his hand from left to right. She saw that the curate was engrossed in prayer. She watched him climb prayerfully up the stairs, past Fr. Smithes's room and further on up to his own bedroom.

Fr. Stonewell had it all prepared. He knelt down for this last time and looked adoringly at the crucifix, *"Now all is consummated,"* he said aloud. He opened the bottle of aspirins and put fifty on the palm of his hands. He took five at a time and swallowed them down with whisky. He muttered with each mouthful *"Dear Jesus I am with you now. This is the one and perfect sacrifice."* He repeated it ten times. His movements were mechanical. Then he took another large mouthful of whisky.

*"Dear Jesus I am with you now in your one and perfect sacrifice."*

Then he went to his bed. He reached for the Cardinal's letter. He took it out of its envelope and his eyes went over it then he held it to himself. This was the baptism by fire that Clarence had first told him about all those years ago at Newman College. He began to feel drowsy. A flashing thought came through his head, *"Have I made a mistake? Is it all a dreadful confusion."* but then he pulled his teeth together: *"Begone Satan,"* and his head flopped back on his pillow.

\* \* \*

When Fr. Smithes woke in the morning he was glad that he was not saying the seven o'clock Mass. He felt tired and he wanted to say Matins and Lauds peacefully while Anthony was saying Mass and he liked offering the evening Mass on the day following a Holiday of Obligation. The nuns from the convent always came to that Mass on a Friday morning and answered all the prayers very clearly and with such obvious devotion. So he got up slowly and as he was dressing he looked at his watch and saw it was ten minutes to seven. He buttoned his clerical collar and put on his jacket. He came out of his room and it was just five to seven. He knew Anthony was due to start the Mass in five minutes time but he heard no sounds downstairs in the sacristy.

He ran down. The lights were not on. He turned then and went into the church. He rushed to the back of the church and opened the front door to a waiting group of people, including the nuns.

*"Come in. The Mass will be five minutes late; I am sorry."* Then he rushed upstairs. He knew that Anthony must have overslept. He knocked at Anthony's door but there was no reply so her turned the handle and went in. His curate was lying still in his cassock on top of his bed,

*"My God, he's ill,"* said George trembling. He turned and saw the crucifix on top of the chest of drawers and then he noticed the aspirin bottle on its side and a bottle of whisky beside it, almost empty. He turned and gasped as he looked back at the figure on the bed. He saw the letter from the Cardinal clutched in Anthony's left hand.

*"Wake up Anthony,"* he cried. He lifted his curate's right hand and felt that it was quite stiff. He could hear no breathing. He rushed out of the room, down the stairs to the telephone. He was quivering and trembling as he dialled the doctor's number because he knew, even before he picked up the receiver, that his curate, Fr. Stonewell, was dead.

\*　\*　\*

Printed in Great Britain
by Amazon.co.uk, Ltd.,
Marston Gate.